WINGS O[F]

by

ROBERT MENASSE

translated by

DAVID BRYER

CALDER PUBLICATIONS · RIVERRUN PRESS
Paris London New York

First published in English as Wings of Stone by
Calder Publications Ltd Great Britain and Riverrun Press in the USA 2000

Originally published by Residenz Verlag, Salzburg and Wien 1991 and subsequently by
Suhrkamp Taschenbuch Verlag 1994 under the original title Selige Zeiten, brüchige Welt.

©Robert Menasse 1991, 2000
©This translation David Bryer 2000

ALL RIGHTS RESERVED
ISBN 07145 42954

British Library Cataloguing in Publication Data is available.
Library of Congress Cataloging in Publication Data is available.

Printed by MPG Books Ltd, Bodmin, Cornwall

TRANSLATOR'S NOTE

I am grateful for the assistance of several people in the often quite complex task of translating this novel.

Daniel Steuer of the University of Sussex was kind enough to look through all those passages where there was some doubt as to the author's exact meaning. His painstaking work illuminated many a dark corner.

Andrew Chitty, also of Sussex, kindly checked all those areas relating to Hegel, making sure that readers familiar with this philosopher's work would not be confused by unfamiliar English renderings.

Phillip Warnett, a former teaching colleague and friend, read the penultimate draft, suggesting many improvements to style, syntax and word order so as to enhance the flow and clarity of the English.

Last, and of course very far from least, the author himself gave me three solid days in Vienna, during which we were able to go through the entire novel to make sure his intentions were honoured and to find solutions to a number of translation problems. Some of these solutions involved liberties with the original that I could only have brought myself to take with the author's active encouragement and spurred on by his own suggestions.

DAVID BRYER
Brighton, February 1999.

On 26th February 1959 in Munich's Alter Pinakothek gallery Kurt Walmen, then 52 years old, threw a mug of 'All-Purpose Paint Remover' over Rubens' 'The Fall of the Damned into Hell'. The corrosive solvent disfigured the painting permanently. The perpetrator was able to walk away scot-free from the scene of the crime but, before entering the Bavarian State Picture Collection, he had sent off letters to news agencies and newspaper editors in which he confessed to the action and gave his reasons for it. He had to "sacrifice" this work of art, so he said, in order to save all the other artistic achievements of mankind and, indeed, mankind itself. For the world was heading for another war. But he—Walmen—had developed a philosophical system to end all philosophies, one which, if mankind were to learn of it, would fundamentally change the world and bring about lasting peace. Being a complete nobody, he had no possibility of drawing attention to himself other than through this action, by means of which his philosophical ideas, vital to the future survival of the world, might find a hearing. The atom bombs, wrote Walmen, would remove things somewhat differently from a little bit of acid. It was his intention to make the court proceedings the stage from which he would present his findings.

The next day Walmen gave himself up to the police. At the hearing, however, the presiding judge gave short shrift to the accused's presentation of himself. The Rubens attacker, described by the media as a 'madman' and 'crank', being found legally fully culpable, was sentenced to an unconditional term of imprisonment and soon afterwards sank back into his former obscurity.

When, however, in the early part of 1965, Leo Singer and Judith Katz were getting to know each other, it was precisely this same Kurt Walmen who became the subject of the first of one of their longer conversations. Singer spoke at great length of this self-declared, unrecognised genius who had failed to change the world, and with an emphasis that he himself found surprising in view of the almost numbing physical attraction that Judith Katz was exerting over him, and which, as he thought, made him so brainless and inarticulate that he didn't quite know where all his many words came from. But in fact this

1

overture was so in tune with their relationship—which from this day on was to last (with interruptions) for eighteen years—that Singer might have thought it up consciously, as if, having foreknowledge of what he was to do in the end, he had sought at some later point to be able to excuse his action by showing it to be a logical consequence of something whose foundations had been laid down at the very beginning.

It's really come to this, said Singer, now expecting agreement and an immediate pact with this woman against all the rest of the absurd world, you're said to be mad nowadays simply if you aspire to change the world or if you say you've found the philosophy to end all philosophies. But what, for example, did Wittgenstein say after he had written his Tractatus? Exactly the same!

I don't know about that. But this, what's his name, this Walden, they didn't call him a madman because of that, but because he destroyed a Rubens painting.

No, he was a madman way before that, I tell you, long before he destroyed the painting. That's how Löwinger described him always: the madman!

Yes, it was in discussing this thwarted world saviour that Leo Singer came to speak of Löwinger. Leo Singer had seen Judith Katz at the university, in the canteen next to the main lecture hall, had been immediately captivated by the sight of her, so much so that he had gone up to her table as if in a trance in order to speak to her. This had seemed to him for one decisive second more natural than, say, eating because you're hungry, or than your heart hammering because you're frightened, and by the time he had woken up once more in the grip of that kind of mental paralysis that entails weighing up the possibility of being in some way humiliated or rejected, he had already said his: "Do you mind? Can I sit here?" and had already seen, as through clouded glass, Judith nodding. After only a half an hour they had left the university together in order to continue their conversation somewhere else in peace, to tell each other everything, already almost a devoted couple, indisputably meant for each other.

Such a wonderful coincidence that we met.

It was unavoidable, said Judith, either way we were bound to sooner or later.

Yes, perhaps it's true that every chance meeting is really an arranged one!

They were both children of Viennese Jews who had fled National Socialism in 1938 and landed up in Brazil. Singer, born while still in

Vienna, grew up in São Paulo, while Judith came into the world in Porto Alegre and she finally moved with her parents to São Paulo. Now they were both studying in Vienna, Leo Singer because 'unfortunately', as he said, he had come with his parents in 1959 when they had decided to return home 'since everything was back to normal'. While Judith, on the other hand, had wanted to study in Vienna, the home town she'd never known, but had had to go against the wishes of her parents who, although they had always, oddly enough, spoken German at home, would not hear of returning to Austria under any circumstances.

On the way to the *Café Sport* they checked to see whether they had any mutual acquaintances in São Paulo. Leo asked if she knew Löwinger. Josef Löwinger, also a Jewish immigrant, best friend of Leo Singer's parents and like a second father to Leo, had risen to the post of director of a large bank and, with the same degree of application and responsibility that had driven his professional career along, had built up one of the largest private art collections of his time. In his spacious house in São Paulo he conducted a *salon* where not only São Paulo's German-speaking colony but also Brazil's, if not Latin America's, most important artists and intellectuals came and went. Judith said that, as far as she could remember, her parents had been to Löwinger's a couple of times but they had never taken her along with them probably because she had been too little at the time. Leo described how he, by contrast, had spent a great deal of time at Löwinger's place as a child, and not only when there was open house. The house and large garden were far more interesting than his parents' appartment and Löwinger— Uncle Zé—loved him in a restrained and patient way, bestowing in the end more attention on him than Leo's real father did. He showed him the works of art from his collection and, as if addressing an adult, inquired after his opinion with serious interest. They sat together in deep leather armchairs in Löwinger's library, which was so extensive that it needed a full-time librarian. Leo would sit over a volume of pictures with the earnestness which he had learned from watching the figure of Löwinger himself bent over a book, blind to the illustrations in the heavy tome on his knees, sensing in himself a diffuse feeling of reverence and a momentous, beautiful awe. Then finally Uncle Zé sat Leo on his lap and told him a little story, asking him questions all the while to excite his imagination, and to provoke answers in him, which gave Leo the feeling in the end of having partly thought up the story himself. He romped about all alone in the huge garden, Leo recounted, because Löwinger was none too enamoured of what he called 'the beastly domains'—for him the garden was solely a peaceful view from the window and a protection from a directly adjoining neighbour. During the course of two or three walks in the expansive grounds, embarked on together in the beginning, Leo had profoundly irritated Löwinger with constant questions as to what this plant or that tree was called, so that, after initially giving absurd or tautological answers ('Those are azaleas except they're bigger than azaleas but at least something similar!', or: 'That bush there? Well, that's actually a bush!'), Löwinger had clammed up and ceased to accompany Leo into the garden. But Löwinger's stories, which he had heard in the house, sitting there so transfixed, these he took outside with him and lived out in his imagination. He related how he marched through the garden as a *bandeirante* forging a path into the interior, subduing it and founding São Paulo. Then again the garden was the whole of Europe and he was Napoleon and on the tips of his fingers he could still feel the book that he'd been holding in his hands earlier and he imagined that this book was the *Code Civil*, which he was bringing to the peoples of Europe. And then there were the crowds of guests there all the time, whenever it was open house, or the individual visitors, important figures who, when they came to São Paulo, would have considered it unthinkable not to have visited Löwinger, such as Otto Maria Carpeaux, who always gave Leo chocolate, or Jorge Amado, Carlos Drummond, Guimarães Rosa, de Cavalcanti, Cândido Portinari, Villa-Lobos—even Jorge Luis Borges supposedly appeared on one occasion. He, Borges that is, gave Leo the impression, so he said, even more than with uncle Zé, of a man who had come into the world already an old gentleman.

He took me onto his lap and whispered something in German in my ear, yes, in German. His voice sounded as if it came from far away and from round many corners, as if, Singer lied, from a labyrinth! And afterwards someone said to me: Do you know who that was, young fellow? That was Borges! And another asked: What did Borges whisper in your ear back there?—I'll never forget it!

And this Kurt Walmen character also turned up at Löwinger's at one point—someone from the German colony had probably brought him along. The story went that he had fled to Latin America from the Nazis, struggled by on casual work in a whole variety of places and was now wanting to stay in São Paulo. Walmen let it be known he was a philosopher and Leo could remember him particularly clearly, not just because he claimed to have come to Latin America as a stowaway, which naturally must have excited the child's imagination, but chiefly because of the way Walmen performed: whereas with Löwinger's other guests Leo was always simply told how important they were, Walmen cultivated his own particular manner, one that emerged from out of himself and which any child could see marked him out as an important and brilliant individual. Leo didn't understand a single word of the heated discussions in the *salon* unlike the stories which Löwinger told him, but the flamboyant gestures of Walmen imprinted themselves lastingly on his memory, Walmen's impatient and conclusive way of speaking, of disposing of objections, jumping up from his chair and resorting to an evangelical style, tirades from which he only caught words like 'unquestionable', 'unfathomable', 'absolute', and again and again 'the world' or 'mankind' uttered with a degree of strength that suggested he himself had coined them.

When Leo told this to Judith, he noticed how intoxicated he was, in a state of verbal intoxication. He made alterations and embellishments, described Walmen's 'flashing eyes' and the mood of 'cold astonishment' that had reigned among those others present, something that he had in truth only learned about later when, on some occasion afterwards, Walmen had once again been the subject of conversation. But at this moment he was getting so much pleasure from his story-telling that the question as to whether everything had in fact been precisely and in every detail the way he described it was of no importance.

Nevertheless, Leo had soon run off into the garden, as he obviously hadn't been able to understand the discussion in the *salon*. Some time later he slipped back into the house through the servants' door: now he was *lampião* in the fight against the *coroneis da terra*. He crept down the corridor of the country house and was going past the kitchen door, which was ajar, when he heard strange noises. He peeped in. There he saw stockinged feet, a dress pulled up, the back of a man, hands which were tugging at a shirt—Walmen was the man, and he and the maid were rolling about on the stone floor of the kitchen like two wrestlers.

I then ran into the drawing-room and, standing in front of Löwinger and imitating Walmen's mannerisms and way of speaking, announced: Mankind is locked unfathomably in a life-or-death struggle in the kitchen! Everyone laughed, except Löwinger who looked at me thoughtfully and went to the kitchen, having understood what I'd seen.

You're making this up! said Judith.

Of course he was. It wasn't like that. It's true that Leo had peeped through the kitchen door and seen Walmen lying on the floor with the maid, and it might also be true that he thought they were having a

5

wrestling match. However, at the same time it had seemed awkwardly puzzling to him and shocking, too. He had known straightaway that it was something he ought not to have seen. But as for his then imitating Walmen in the drawing-room, that idea had come to him in the telling. And if Leo had been honest, he wouldn't even have been in a position to say whether it was Walmen's manner in the *salon*, or his adventure with the maid, or whether it was something quite different that had so blotted the man's copybook that from then on he was never seen at Löwinger's again, even though he continued to be present, so to speak, occasionally, as the subject of heated discussion—for years afterwards, in fact. For example, according to Leo, he'd heard in one of these discussions that after the war Walmen had set up an organisation in Rio to help Germans migrate to Brazil, but that this, so Leo had somehow learned, involved some highly shady dealings.

Leo now remembered how he had got onto this subject. They had been checking to see whether they had any mutual acquaintances in São Paulo and Leo had asked Judith if she knew Löwinger. And this reminded him that in 1959, when Leo had visited him for the last time before leaving for Vienna, Löwinger had shown him a newspaper cutting with a photograph of Walmen—the newspaper contained a report of the attack on the Rubens in Munich—and had said: Do you still remember the madman? Look what he's done now!

You have to bear in mind, said Leo, I really love Löwinger a lot— I love him like a father. And yet there is this sensitive art collector, one of the most important art collectors of our time, reading in the paper about a man who destroyed what was probably Rubens' most important painting, and this man had some time before been a guest in his house. The fact that he doesn't understand him is only too clear. But perhaps Walmen is right. I mean perhaps he really does have a philosophical system that could change the world. Not one person ever heard him out. Not one person ever discussed it. It must be terrible—no, wait a moment! Just imagine! It must be terrible to have knowledge of the ultimate and to see that no-one wants to hear about it. Such a predicament may well call for some striking sign. After all what's a Rubens painting set against the whole world, I mean if it had worked. But it was only then that they were justified in branding him a lunatic, that's the problem, they drove him to it so that they would be proved right as regards what they had earlier assumed him to be: a lunatic. Seen like this, though, it's all the others who should take the blame for the destruction of the painting, not Walmen!

6

Leo looked at Judith in a way which thrust all the noises in the bar against the wall where, if possible, they would then stick like pictures and he knew he had to continue talking for hours, to intrigue her for hours, so as then to be able to seduce her perhaps. Everything about him was so tense and yet lacking any power, and there was nothing but this knowing smile all the time that makes it so easy to ingratiate yourself with everyone, yet which is so naive when looking into a face like Judith's.

But really, it's totally absurd, said Judith, for someone to think they can change the world all by themselves and just through their ideas.

Why? That's the way it's always been! Despite his twenty-nine years Singer was unusually innocent and naive. Napoleon, for example, changed the world and the hubbub he made in the process was heard by Hegel sitting in his study, who was inspired to write his philosophy which again was supposed to change the world, and so on. What we learn about in history is nothing other than changes in the world effected by individuals. That's what Singer had learnt. Judith laughed; and her laughter seemed, through the breadth of her mouth, to take on a metaphorical breadth as well and thus to be a privilege granted only to a blessed few. He was a small, scrawny man with a sharp-edged, one might almost say abrasive, ugliness—everything about him had sharp edges: the curving nose which dominated his face, the narrow mouth with a bottom lip that protruded to a point when he talked and was yet somehow obscenely fleshy as it curved up, the thick lenses of his black-rimmed spectacles which, when they pressed down on the wart on his nostril, he would sometimes push back up into his hair, greasy hair it seemed, combed back with military strictness. Yet Judith liked him; in his sharp features she saw a sensibility and goodness tapered to their fullest extent and at the same time the gleam of an as yet untested readiness to engage with the world. And she was touched as she watched him gesticulate with his small, delicate hands and heard the intonation of his speech, the almost imperceptible accent that no-one else could have identified, but which for her was instantly familiar, being compounded of a Brazilian childhood and Viennese parents. Leo would so much have liked to know everything about Judith, learn everything about her, every second of her life till now, but she never got a chance to speak because his curiosity about her was so extreme that he himself talked uninterruptedly. The subject of Walmen, albeit now much more generalised, would not let go of him: he spoke about his aspiration to change the world and the reasons why the world today felt that such an aspiration was an expression of madness. The Nazis had wiped out everything, he said, including the most basic understanding of history. And because they had wiped the slate so completely clean, the generation who had suffered this and then been party to the reconstruction period saw everything that went *beyond* simple reconstruction as mad. He just came out with this, like he just came out with everything, excited at all the things that spontaneously entered his head, only because it was Judith's presence that inspired him and because it sounded as if he were revealing to her alone the results of long hours of reflection. His ideas sounded odd in a city so particularly and stolidly ignorant of any notion that things could be different from what they were, a city that seemed so set in its ways that the expression 'Vienna will always be Vienna' came across as a lie only because it sounded too much like a euphemism: the verb 'be' was far too dynamic. They had driven to the *Café Sport* because at that time this bar seemed more liberal than the city and was the only relatively cosmopolitan place in Vienna. But he no longer noticed time or place, neither the café's scruffiness, which provided ample opportunities for meditation for those romantics who could make use of red wine stains on marble table tops, nor the urbanity, unusual for Vienna, of the other guests, dice-throwing Arabs, Persians or Greeks for the most part. Yes, the *Sport* was more urbane than Vienna was, even though some of the guests were Viennese, a few who had been out there in the world and who were now sitting there looking defiantly worldly in their Canadian fur-coats or Peruvian ponchos. The majority by far, however, were artists, who grouped themselves together and practised issuing bans on other guests, something which they would become past masters at later when they themselves had risen to the rank of café proprietors. But Leo was deaf to the Greek or French recordings coming out of the juke-box, blind to the people playing backgammon or deep in discussion and shouting, and to those others who because of the volumes of Villon's poems and editions of Kerouac lying around were apparently preoccupied with the thought of giving up reading altogether, and were drinking themselves stupid. Blind as well to the wood panelling of the walls and the mirrors hanging there, all clouded with age and therefore blind themselves. Judith, however, took all this in, absorbing the details which then evaporated immediately before her into a pleasant mood; and all without once taking her eyes off Leo, whom she looked at concentratedly, contentedly. She found it agreeable, the mood of this place which

8

she had only just come to know through Leo. Its tatty, colourful and loud simplicity reminded her of the *Sarado Bar* in the Rua Dona Veridiana in São Paulo where she had so liked to sit before the military putsch, the haunt of students from the nearby Mackenzie University, the place to which Judith owed her very first hangover, the result of too much *Brahma* beer and endless conversations about God and the world.

Leo watched hungrily, ready to pounce on the smallest sign of amused interest shown by Judith, who leant towards him, smiled, with her chin resting on her hand, then threw back her head, laughing out loud. What a lot of cigarettes she smoked—Leo had never known anyone to smoke as much as she did. The wine was awful but it had its effect, it inflamed him and loosened his tongue, but he knew that if he didn't get something to eat soon, he would get ill. Judith was hungry too but she didn't want the Boer sausage nor any of the speciality sandwiches on offer here, so they both decided to switch to another café. They drove in Leo's old VW beetle to a pizzeria in the seventh district that Leo knew because he lived close by in Schottenfeldgasse. Judith immediately wound down the window, even though it was still pretty chilly, and said: It feels just like being back home, back in Brazil, in such a *fusca*!

Do you get very homesick?

Occasionally. Isn't it funny: it's like we were two *namorados*, how do you put it? you know: *namorados* in São Paulo, going to the *Bexiga* for a pizza in the *fusca*!

Leo peered with obvious ardour through the windscreen, flushed, despite the open window, by this offer, as he saw it, to establish an already long-assumed togetherness that could be summoned up at any time in very few words, words which only had a meaning for the two of them, here in this place.

Tudo bem, he said, off to the *Bexiga*!

The *Pizzeria da Roberto* was a small establishment: only a few tables with those red, rough-woven, ubiquitous tablecloths which in Vienna were to be found in Italian, Yugoslav or Chinese restaurants as well as in those serving Styrian or Viennese food. On every table a candle was stuck in a raffia-wrapped Chianti bottle. When Leo himself wasn't talking, he had to concentrate so hard on not playing with the wax that had trickled down the side of the bottle, on not fiddling with it, not kneading it, that he occasionally had difficulty in understanding what Judith was saying.

9

After the putsch, she said, she couldn't wait to get out of Brazil. Her parents hadn't understood this. As her luck would have it—luck in inverted commas—the universities were no longer running then. The day-to-day business of teaching had simply folded. Leftist professors had been arrested, others had fled and emigrated, the military had had the university libraries ransacked for Marxist literature, and then the students and professors had gone on strike. Her parents, said Judith, had always wanted her to study. There was never any question of anything else. That's why she said 'luck', for now she could tell them: if you really want me to study, then pay for me to study in Vienna! Those were terrible times, said Judith, bizarre and terrible—maybe you don't know about that, you'd been away from Brazil for nearly six years, but after the putsch there were people who disappeared, simply disappeared, and a close girlfriend of mine also suddenly disappeared—no-one knows where she is.

A pizza Cardinale, a pizza Quattro Stagione, a half litre of Chianti, said Singer, continuing to radiate heat like a large pizza oven in the middle of the restaurant.

They said she was a member of a Trotskyite organisation, said Judith—it could well be true. The parents, who had lodged a missing person notification at the police station, were just kept dangling—there were only some dubious statements from the *delegado*—you knew they knew it was a political matter, so there was nothing they could do except do nothing, but they could never say so in so many words. She simply remained missing.

And Judith's parents finally agreed, all right then, we'll pay for you to study abroad—what's wrong with Paris? Because I can't speak French, Judith had said, I speak German, because of you—we've always only ever spoken German at home but I don't want to go to Germany (still an occupied country, an American colony) but this she only thought, she didn't say it. And haven't you always told me about Vienna—I want to get to know it now, for your sakes, since you're no longer there—it's where you come from, your primeval mud, stuck in my head—she didn't say that either but her parents realised finally, no, not Germany, all right, Vienna then.

My parents weren't at all happy about the strikes at the University and with my girlfriend disappearing and all those strange goings-on, just imagine—you didn't know about that, did you—the staff of the Philosophy Faculty of the University of Rio Preto drove through the streets in their cars, cars fitted with sort of *alto-falantes*, how do you call them, yes, sort of loudspeaker vans, giving out propaganda in support of free love. And? What do you mean, and? Some of them were arrested, some went underground. That's what it was like. Touch-and-go, dangerous and childish all at the same time. And then I arrive here, from a place like that—I imagined Vienna to be very different. In what way? Just different, fascism defeated, socialism with the upper hand, I don't know, but whenever I tell anyone here about it, about my girlfriend, for example, they have no idea, no idea what a Trotskyite organisation is, for example, here in Vienna it's as cold and dark as on the other side of the moon. They don't even know that Marx is spelt with an "x"—the military putsch must have been announced under a 'News in Brief' column, because if you mention Brazil here, people just think of football and carnivals.

I didn't understand what you said, said Leo, about the staff of the *faculdade* of Rio Preto—what do you mean, they gave out propaganda in loudspeaker vans in support of free love?

Well, they drove through the streets in these cars making announcements about the need, what's the word, about the merits of free love.

Leo leant forward with interest. Then the pizzas came. Cardinale? That's me! said Leo. He hadn't read a single line of Trotsky either—nor, by the way, had Judith—but that free love thing was certainly something worth exploring. They were getting to the point.

Leo now looked Judith resolutely in the eye, a long, possessing look, hot and almost coarse, a look that, so to speak, laid a glowing question mark on the anvil and hammered it properly into shape: an exclamation mark. And then, hacking into his pizza, Leo began to poke fun at the promotion of free love via loudspeaker vans—it was, he said, without doubt an unconsidered reaction against the intolerable bigotry of Brazilian Catholicism, the underbelly of social conditions, neither of which were understood, rather like the carnival perhaps, which is quite plainly there as a mediaeval safety valve to make bearable the dull impotence and stupid Catholic chastity during all the rest of the days of the year. But if you think instead how Walmen, he said, when he entered the kitchen, must have made everything clear not with loudspeakers but just with one look, before he pulled the maid down onto the floor, absolutely certain of what he was doing because his look must have told her what he wanted and he could plainly read from her eyes that she understood and shared his desire—then you can see that only the philosopher, in a moment of total clarity, can liberate carnal craving as well.

11

Judith's grin, so Leo believed, was not just a reaction to what he'd said but seemed to him to be much more the desired answer to his desire, an anticipation of the smile that, as he imagined, she would have when they were later embracing and caressing each other in bed. He saw Judith's bright eyes sparkling in such a way as if they mirrored back a gleam of what he was now feeling and thinking, as if she shared his feelings and thoughts. The eyes are the windows of the soul only for those in the know, he said, and by that he meant that they were keyholes which could open the door to the body. Accordingly he made a big effort to produce a look like Walmen's. He was now absolutely certain that the points had switched, that the engine was pulling hard in its race towards its destination and that one could lean back comfortably with crossed legs in the train compartment, chat a bit or eat or look out of the window, it didn't matter which, for sooner or later you would arrive. He chose to eat.

Leo had just noticed and found it rather odd—and this was an impression that could be put down to the wine or the flickering candle—how Judith had a way of not mulling things over. She stubbed out her cigarette in the ash-tray and, giving Leo a smile, also began to eat.

The silence, however, made Leo suddenly nervous. Perhaps it would be better not to allow any room for quiet and boredom, otherwise the mood in the compartment could so easily become oppressive and tiring. While he was still considering what he could still say on the same subject, Judith began to talk again, to Leo's relief at first, but relief soon gave way to a wooden and numb bewilderment. Judith was once again describing everyday life after the military putsch—she was so happy to be able to unburden herself finally of all that, and with someone for whom it meant something and who didn't think of Brazil only in terms of beaches, samba and coffee. She talked chiefly about the reactions of those she knew to the sudden disappearance of people, people who emigrated or who were arrested, the ignorance, fearfulness or anger expressed, depending on whom you spoke to, and how friend-ships broke up because of a fear that a particular friendship could compromise you, or the other way round, because you so despised the sudden, stupid and ignorant opportunism of former friends; and she spoke about censorship, how it spread into people's heads and how at the same time it debarred, from every thinking person, all those pleasures that you had up to then been able to enjoy without thinking, because they could only be experienced now as a substitute and means of pacification. There were street festivals, she related, hundreds of thousands of people on the streets to celebrate the putsch, the "victory of the revolution", as it was called, and in the newspapers it said: the people were grateful that Brazil had been rescued from Communism! It was unbelievable, Judith said, you should have seen it, those *imbecils*, what's the word, those morons, suddenly they were everywhere, among your friends, your acquaintances...

Leo was confused by Judith's stories, which made something that was familiar to him—familiar indeed to them both—so strange. He listened to her in amazement as if her voice were coming from a great distance. He recognised her all right, could see her clearly as from a window which had a good view but, because he hadn't been outside for a long time now, everything he could see from his window dissolved into unimaginable and unknown shapes. The Brazil he had left over five years earlier was quite another country from the one Judith was describing—his was a lost paradise, a land of happy childhood and youth, the land of his first and, at the same time, last romantic experiences. One long, eternally blue day, holidays in Guarujá, the gentle lapping of the sea on the beach of Pernambuco, the daring 'Mustang' cigarette smoked with a girl on whose brown skin drops of seawater glittered in the sun like so many diamonds. A kitsch picture, admittedly, but that was exactly how Leo remembered it: not a damp film on her skin but lots of little droplets and each one glittered and each one of those glittering droplets was a metaphor for each single occasion of feeling that came from the big world of feeling. And, like Judith, the girl had blue-black hair, wet and combed back so that you could see the lines that the comb had drawn, and there's still enough money for two chilled coconut juices each with a shot of pinga, and talking about what you're going to study—do you want to be an engineer? No, I want to study philosophy! And then this dark peal of laughter like an urubu flying up from the beach, laughter that he'd never heard again in Vienna, not once and not even from people who thought it absurd to be studying philosophy. Pale yellow and blue shimmering heat and then the touch of a hand still cool from the water, so different from that of hot damp hands, just pulled out of a pair of gloves, on skin that is forever numb with cold in the Viennese winter. And then again the rain in São Paulo, the *garoa*, like fountain shafts of green, red and yellow in Löwinger's garden, and inside in the house the warm yellow-ochre light of the library where you sit in a leather armchair like a violin in its case and listen to stories as if to the music of the spheres with a happiness couched in the velvet certainty that you too will be able to play that one day.

Censorship! What's a word like 'censorship' doing in such a story? Can you see it from where you're standing? Firmly Leo closed the curtain, so to speak, in front of his window. Now he could see nothing, and he clearly attributed the difficulty in seeing Judith to the wine, which, though no doubt better here than in the *Café Sport*, he had clearly partaken too much of, so he imagined. The second half litre had already gone, and in a very short time, and the exalted stage of his animatedness had evaporated—he was staggered how quickly it had gone. Leo interrupted Judith in order to answer her—'Regarding that I'd have to say that,' 'It's quite clear to see that,' 'We both know that,' he said with artificial emphasis in order to rekindle in himself the emphasis he had mislaid, and he held forth, talking, as he himself knew, the most outrageous ethnopsychological nonsense about 'the Brazilian mentality', nonsense in which he became ever more entangled the more energetically he tried to talk his way out of it again.

Judith didn't understand a word of what Leo was now saying. She was having trouble following him. She opened her eyes wide and stared at him in concentration. She waited—in just the same way as she had for the wine they'd ordered—for a little chink between the serried ranks of Leo's sentences, for anything which she could seize hold of again and which would carry her along to the rhythm of his words, easily and naturally as before, but instead she sank leadenly down into nothingness. By the time she had once more bobbed up to the surface with blurred vision, and had adjusted her sight and given Leo a sharply focussed look, she had again missed so many of his sentences that she now understood even less what he was saying. Why didn't he talk about himself again—what he had told her about his childhood in Brazil, about Löwinger was so fascinating—or why doesn't he talk about how he coped with life here in Vienna after moving back, or what it was like when he heard about the putsch in Brazil, what kind of information he had received, whether he had telephoned Brazil. What was the point of all this general pontification about the political situation, about Catholicism in Brazil, the Brazilian mentality and such-like nonsense? She should have interrupted him but now it was too late, she'd missed the chance. Maybe it really *was* interesting, what he was theorising about, she was simply no longer able to judge. She didn't want to either—she felt good with Leo, this strange man who already seemed so familiar to her, and if only he'd been quiet, it would have been wonderful. Then the wine came and she drank, sipping continuously from the glass, which she now kept in her hands. With her elbows on the table, holding her glass in both hands in front of her mouth, she observed Leo's mouth over the top of the glass. Again and again, as it opened, his mouth pushed out and forwards up to a point and then spread back out again between the corners of the mouth, which were were struggling animatedly to move apart from one another, and seemed to be clamped together only by his bottom lip. And she watched his small, agile hands, which opened and closed rhythmically, and again and again his index finger would jump forward to stab at imaginary points. Leo's mouth and hands seemed to Judith like small exotic animals which were performing some mating ritual with each other to the musical intonation of his words. What Leo was saying, though, was really hard to understand—he was making heavy weather of his words, but it wasn't just because of the wine or because it really was difficult to sustain the arguments he was making—but because he, too, was in quite another place in his thoughts, far away from what he was actually saying. He was astonished how little it mattered what he was saying, whether it made any sense or sounded stupid, for this didn't in the least change the fact that everything was on track and heading indeed towards its goal. He looked at Judith sitting opposite him with face bowed forward and almost thrusting towards him—they would soon be in bed together, he thought—if *she* wasn't ready for it, then no-one was. Somehow, though, he felt the situation had gone totally wrong now. He was talking rubbish and knew he was talking rubbish. Judith already meant so much to him, so much more than anyone else had ever done before, and yet it was precisely with her that not a single straightforward sentence would work properly for him any more, that all natural gaiety, all easiness, all lightness somehow eluded his efforts, that everything was going wrong—and yet still going towards the goal for which he yearned. Leo didn't understand why, and he didn't understand himself—hadn't he always been, until now, the master of the beautifully highfaluting blind alley? How often had he shone and scintillated, only to be left standing there at the end with just a 'Thank you for the lovely evening!' He had always distributed his sexual favours among women in a highly democratic, if not to say voracious, way, for he had no ideal type when it came to beauty, and didn't have any particular expectations of intellectual or possible emotional rapport but felt himself rather impelled to greater efforts by the least of allurements, whether these might be the particular or unparticular way in which a woman smiled

15

or gesticulated or walked, sometimes simply because of the way a woman was dressed and how the contour of her body through the clothing made her stand out—it was an attitude beyond his control like that of a gambler. His great yearning, for the jackpot, for the chance 'deliverance', stemmed certainly from the loneliness he felt after nearly six years of living in Vienna without ever really having come to feel at home there. At all events, this lust of his had always been like a magnet which arranged all the words that can be exchanged when getting to know someone, like iron filaments put into beautiful, harmonious patterns, despite the fact that these, whenever bodily matters had their way, would be brusquely jumbled up and destroyed. For this reason Leo had far less experience than he otherwise might possibly have had. For his age he was indeed unusually innocent in such matters, though the guilt for this lay entirely with him. He had never behaved in any other way than that of a gambler who, even though he was very serious about what he wanted, always looked to blind, ruling chance for the big jackpot, an attitude that made active curiosity and a realistic appraisal of a situation fundamentally obsolete. For this reason, in the same moment of thinking that he had now at last got his jackpot in the person of Judith, Leo became aware of not only a tense and joyful excitement, in himself, but also—and this confused him no end—of a certain disappointment. What disappointed him was that a woman like Judith would immediately go to bed with him, whereas more insignificant acquaintances had been so hard, or often even impossible, to seduce, and this despite the fact that, unlike today, he had succeeded in giving non-stop firework displays of wit, intelligence and charm which had so enthused him that he had been regularly bowled over by it, he himself, that is. Just now he would have so much liked to have remained scintillating right up to the last second and then, without further thought, have transformed this verbal success into the pure elation of his bodily functions. And after everything had been successfully concluded, this being in any case on the cards, he would have liked to feel—and with none of this muddying of the waters and turbulence that he sensed working somewhere behind his forehead, and which he was now silently fighting—he would have liked to feel: yes, I am in love!

Leo didn't understand why Judith of all women didn't care whether he 'shone' or not. This reduced what he was now expecting to happen to merely a forlorn and solipsistic act. Surely Judith couldn't be that type. On the other hand, he wouldn't for one moment have been able to cope, if he'd felt he had no chance at all with her. Leo wondered whether he shouldn't lecture Judith further on his theory regarding the teleology of Latin-American development, a theory which he had once elaborated spontaneously in a moment of playful exuberance during a conversation with a female fellow-student whom he had wanted to impress; out of his blending of native Latin-American stories with the historical dialectic of Hegel's phenomenology he had conjured up the most bewildering prognoses, which had almost given him the appearance of being a prime mover behind the scenes of history. Owing to the success this theory had had with the said female fellow-student, he had recited it so often later that he could now deliver it in truly spellbinding fashion. Meditatively he broke off a lump of wax from the bottle with the candle, kneaded it between his fingers and looked foggily at Judith over the rim of his spectacles, which had slipped down over his nose. Not a word had been spoken now for one or two minutes. Judith was smoking and looking at Leo. She was now brimming over with a romantic feeling which soothed her inner tension, as it were, and then came this strange, ever-recurring desire, flying in the face of all reason, to drink so much that she would slither under the table, a gnawing hunger for an excess, a hunger that she experienced again and again, either to deaden an unbearable feeling or, as she began to feel more content, to lose all self-control for once and to immortalise the moment in an induced stupor. It was a compulsive condition which she experienced in better moments—maybe because she wasn't so sure they were in fact so good—and certainly in the worse moments. She noted gratefully that she wasn't feeling it right now—only a little, or anyway not enough to prevent her from being able to say: Come on, Leo, let's settle up!

Bill! Leo barked, so startlingly that Judith had to laugh, to which Leo responded with a sickly smile. They left the restaurant. Judith took Leo's arm and clung closely to him, so that their steps harmonised perfectly but not in such a way that might have led to them stopping suddenly and embracing. Can you take me home? she asked. Yes, Leo said softly. He wanted to add that he lived just around the corner from there but Judith then gave her address. She lived in the third district in a side street off Landstraße Hauptstraße. During the journey Leo barely spoke a word. He was confused—very happy and very unhappy at one and the same time. And he was freezing cold. Judith had rolled the window down a crack and was humming a Brazilian song. Leo recognised it but he had forgotten the title and the words. As they turned into Petrusgasse, the quiet little backstreet where Judith lived, she cried Stop! that's

17

the house, I can jump out here. They sat side by side in the car and looked at each other. Leo's hands, which were stuffed inside thick-lined gloves, held firmly and rigidly onto the steering wheel, even though the car was stationary. Couldn't I, said Leo, and he cleared his throat, it seemed to him, absurdly loudly, couldn't I come up for a moment? No, said Judith, I'm really very tired, I want to get some sleep. She opened her handbag, took out a little notebook and pencil, wrote her telephone number on a sheet which she tore out and gave Leo, then asked for his number, which he recited as if it were the combination of a strong box, oh, if only Judith would open it now, perhaps she'd find it contained countless treasures. Judith made a note of the number, kissed Leo on either cheek while he meanwhile continued to keep a tight hold on the steering wheel.

That was a lovely evening!

Yes, said Leo, but tell me, can't I come in for just a minute? He almost croaked the words. He was beside himself, deaf, dumb and blind.

We'll talk on the phone tomorrow, alright? Sleep well! said Judith with a smile and climbed out. He would liked to have screamed, but there was only his numb, raw throat and the noise of the slammed door.

Far rather than love her, he would now have liked to be her. He no longer wanted to hold her in his arms now but to be her. How dearly would he have been able to love himself then, and with such under-standing and such tenderness towards himself; he would have happily driven home then and gone to bed.

He started the engine, grabbed at the wheel in order to turn round, accelerated and at the same time tried to watch Judith in the rear mirror opening her front door. He saw Judith look back again at him, then her image disappeared from the mirror as if it had been wiped away. Leo swivelled his head back, then there was a crunch and a jolt that threw him forward—while turning, Leo had driven into a tree on the opposite side of the street.

He stared speechlessly at this tree that he could see so close up against his windscreen that it looked as if it were growing out of the front boot. Then he got out and looked at the damage. He had hit the tree head on. The bumper and boot of his beetle had a v-shaped dent. The headlights of the car were angled sharply inwards like someone cross-eyed. The glass of one headlight was broken. Suddenly Judith was standing next to him. If that was a ploy, it won't do you any good—you must go back to your place.

Leo climbed into his car again and backed off a few yards. Then he checked whether there was enough play in the front wheels despite the dented wings; the car was in fact driveable enough for him to get back home if he had to. He turned to Judith, conscious now for the first time of what she had said. He was completely speechless. But she had gone. He saw only his breath hanging in the cold air like a thick arrow of smoke pointing in the direction of Judith's closed front door. Slowly he drove home to the seventh district, through the godforsaken nocturnal streets of Vienna, and what occupied him during the journey, what he thought about, was one thing and one thing only, like a person stamping ceaselessly on one spot: Judith. Love, which almost hurt, and hate, a deep, dull hate. When with a loud bang he hurled the front door behind him, shut, it sounded like an angry door slam but it was simply a drunken lack of control. He omitted to turn on the timed light in the corridor and it wasn't long before he was stumbling and would nearly have fallen over. He then came into the inner courtyard of the building. He lived up two flights of stairs. The courtyard with its cobbled pavement was full of angels: praying angels, singing angels, angels kneeling and in flight, angels holding candles and angels bearing lanterns, guardian angels and intertwining groups of angels, stones with angel reliefs: a wasteland made up of stone angels who in the blue-grey moonlight offered up a flaking picture of craftsmanlike salvation. The angels were the creations and display pieces of Zahradnik, the monumental stonemason who had his workshop here at one end of the courtyard. Bugger Zahradnik, thought Leo as he climbed the steps to his flat.

The grey-blue light also fell through Leo's window and into his damp, cool bedroom. As he was falling asleep, the melody Judith had hummed in the car was in his head again.

At home, after she had poured herself a vodka and lit a cigarette, Judith now put on one of her favourite records: it was an old samba. Even when she was exhausted she couldn't go straight to bed without some transition. She always had to let her last impressions and thoughts drift away or clear, and to wait until her mind had become completely empty and unconcerned once more, like a cinema screen after the end of a film when the very last credit had rolled and the projector was switched off. Only then could she close her eyes. Bedtime didn't come easily to Judith. Sleeping gave her no pleasure. It was not something she looked forward to or sought to prolong. When she woke up in the early hours, even when she'd only slept a short while and had no engagement that might have forced her to get up immediately, she felt her heart beating as strongly as if she'd just drunk some coffee and she would jump out of bed. As a child and even as a schoolgirl she had been forced to sleep regularly for an hour after lunch and Judith had always experienced this habit of her mother's, who herself loved to take an afternoon nap, as a torment, a senseless interruption to a game or a book she would have preferred to have continued with.

When she heard her father talking once about so-and-so being lucky because he had died in his sleep, had gone to sleep peacefully and simply not woken up anymore, she hadn't understood then what was so lucky about that. But the fact that one could die in one's sleep developed into a proper phobia, into the firm conviction that she was destined to die in this manner and that every time she slept longer than was absolutely necessary, she was putting herself in mortal danger. For this reason she had always lain awake during these compulsory afternoon naps, concentrating solely on staying awake and listening out to hear whether or not her mother was coming at last to wake her again. It was this that had doubtless given rise to her sleeping difficulties. But it had also given her an exaggerated sense of the duration of time: one hour, for example, was an eternity, or one night—that could last a lifetime. No wonder then that it ended in death.

The feeling that 'something wasn't worth starting' if time was short was foreign to Judith. Even if in an hour's time she had some engagement, she would, until then, nevertheless set about doing tasks in that little eternity as if she had the whole day ahead of her, filling this hour in fact so productively as if it were indeed a whole day. And she always enjoyed the hours that she stole from sleep, just like now, putting off going to bed without as a result sleeping longer the next day—this she felt to be a little triumph, even if at the same time she longed for nothing more than to be so dead on her feet that she would feel not just shattered but also certain, certain of being able—with no fuss, no further thought or fear—to fall asleep. She walked up and down in the room with her glass of vodka and cigarette listening to the music; sometimes the needle jumped because the record player was on the floor which shook under her steps. She made a face and took a drink from the glass. The samba came now, 'Se você jurar', the one she had suddenly hummed in the car during that strange and silent journey home. And now Ataulfo Alves sang the words which Leo hadn't been able to remember when she'd given him the melody, the words which, as she listened to them, she now realised for the first time Leo should have sung, realised too that it was out of a feeling for Leo that she had begun to hum this particular samba. 'Woman is a game / that's hard to win / And man is a fool / who can't stop playing / What I can do / if you swear you love me / bet everything on one card and lose again / Or this time win the lot.' She remembered Leo's hands, his small hands which had moved continually in front of her eyes in such a graceful and yet authoritarian way, until, that is, they disappeared inside those ridiculous thick gloves which seemed to belong much more to the steering wheel than to him. And then that childish bumping into the tree, 'Ele é um bobo,' he is a fool, she thought but with an undeniably pleasant, warm feeling in her stomach which could of course be a result of the vodka. She poured herself a drop more and paced again up and down in her room. The needle jumped again and she switched the record player off. Judith had such a smooth skin that it looked almost unnatural. As if her skin had no pores, no veins underneath. The skin of her face, which was without the slightest flaw and had no lines, seemed like an enamel mask. But when Judith was very, very tired—she didn't use the expression 'dead tired'—then her eyes swelled up and around them black shadows and rings formed like a second small mask on her face. Judith looked at the rings round her swollen eyes in the mirror which hung on the wall in her room; another mirror stood on her desk, a third hung at eye-level in her bookcase, in a gap between the books. She looked fixedly and emotionlessly at her reflection as if she were examining under a microscope a piece of cellular tissue with which she was conducting an experiment. When the picture began to swim before her eyes, as if it would dissolve and disappear into the silvery surface of the mirror, she knew then, without any shadow of doubt, that she would be able to sleep. She knocked back her vodka in one gulp and went to bed.

For one week Leo Singer managed to stick rigidly to his resolve not to ring Judith immediately but to wait first and see if she would ring him— rigidly, that is, with one sole exception: but Judith hadn't been at home. He had found this one attempt extremely humiliating: with his ear pressed to the receiver and nervously sweating, listening to the ever-lasting monotonous drone, clearing his throat several times while he waited, with the strain of thinking that at any moment she might in fact pick it up. After this he did not waver one jot in his resolution, not least because immediately afterwards he had fallen ill. He was first given a forewarning of the illness when he was at his parents', the day after meeting Judith—'on the day after the accident,' he would have said. His parents had invited him because of his birthday, which was actually not till April, but his father would be away on business then and he wanted to see Leo again before the trip.

Leo planned to ask his father for the money to pay for the car repair, maybe as a birthday present, although he was sure his parents already had a present for him. With a monotony that was nothing short of religious he had always received the same thing, ever since they had returned to Vienna, without ever being asked what he perhaps might like. Regularly for Christmas and for his birthday he received 'something warm', a thick vest or a pullover, thermal underwear, sometimes a blue suit made of thick winter material—he would go about in these suits even in summer, since they were the only ones he had. He had always received a pair of gloves too—and had in the process amassed the largest private glove collection in Vienna. Doubtless this had to do with the fact that his father had built up a wholesale textile business in Vienna, and every time Leo was due for a present his mother would look out something for him from his father's 'wares', as she said, and would wrap it up in used paper that she got from department stores where she asked for everything she bought to be 'gift-wrapped, please.' (The paper thus acquired she kept in an ugly cupboard which also contained sweets and spirits that she'd been given on some occasion or other, and which she kept there unopened, so that she had, when needed, something to take as a present to their hosts when they were invited somewhere.) His mother would then put this parcel on a chest of drawers with a mirror that she called 'the commode', and when he came she would always say in a thin and detached voice, as if she were frightened to touch this junk herself and so become infected with the tastelessness to which she was happy to expose her son: Your present is on the commode, Leo!

Leo hated his mother so much that he could have cheerfully killed her, but only if by so doing he could have committed the perfect crime, for if he had had to suffer a penalty because of her—because of her!— then this would have meant that she alone had triumphed once again. On the way to his parents Leo was already shaking with hatred. On not one single occasion, as far as he could remember, had his mother ever been able to spare a tender gesture, a kindly word, not even what might have been interpreted as a loving look for his father, this gentle and, in

22

every sense, soft man, who, as correct as he was weak, as capable as he was fruitlessly ebullient and craving of affection, was as full, almost to bursting, with a vague geniality and an irrepressible, cock-eyed optimism, as a balloon filled with water, and for this fact alone Leo could never forgive his mother. Although in fact, just because of this softness, and because of his pathologically accommodating manner, he despised his father, too. As Leo was changing from the number 58 to the J-line tram in the Ringstraße, he pictured to himself Judith's parents, and concluded that he admired them for their refusal to return to Vienna— 'we were persecuted in Vienna but we can live and work here in peace!'—such a position seemed perfectly sensible to Leo, self-evident and thoroughgoing. And didn't his parents have to leave Vienna, too, to escape by the skin of their teeth? And since things had gone well for them in Brazil, very well in fact, and he had grown up there, that surely should have led them to conclude: Vienna is the name of your birthplace but nothing more. Why go back? Why give the Zahradniks of this world further opportunity to chisel out that deadly programme of events: born and died in Vienna!? But as if that weren't enough— returning to Vienna even though they had established themselves meanwhile in Brazil—Leo's parents on top of that didn't return in triumph, self-aware and as the victors, no, on the contrary they grovelled, all the time anxiously concerned about their stupid reputation, and his father, bowing and scraping, called on officials who had served under the Nazi regime in order to obtain a ridiculous so-called 'reparation'. But if that, which would have been a trifle, weren't enough, his father then began to celebrate Christmas in Vienna, because everyone does. While on the one hand every month he made over a certain sum to the Jewish Religious Community, he began on the other hand to celebrate Christmas—that's what one does here, it has nothing to do with religion, it's a social, a cultural, basically a commercial imperative. He received Christmas presents from customers or from business colleagues, mainly those sweets and spirits that Leo's mother collected in that frightful cupboard, and consequently believed that he too was obliged to give presents and hold a Christmas party at work. Whereas at home? At home in the flat where there was no-one to check up on his conformity, his uniformity, his servility, a tree was erected, and his flabby, greasy father had the nerve to chant Christmas carols before the presents were exchanged: for Leo, gloves in used wrapping paper from the Gerngroß department store. And while his mother, at least only coldly, and standing there stiffly stock-still, saw to it that the ceremony was carried out correctly, that everything went as she thought it should, his father got himself worked up into such a state as if all the card-carrying Catholics of Vienna were watching to see how he sang 'Silent Night'.

When the tram turned from the Ringstraße into the Landstraße Hauptstraße, it came off the rails 'for no explicable reason', as the newspaper reported the next day, but Leo immediately had a bad conscience. He believed, though this was not really conscious, that it was his shaking hatred, the trembling fury towards his parents that had escaped from him and triggered the accident. All the passengers had to get out but, while the majority of them stood huddled together in groups studying and commenting on the accident, Leo sloped off at the double like a criminal on the run. As all tramcars coming on from behind were now blocked because of the tram fittings lying next to the track, Leo had to walk as far as Rudolf-von-Alt Platz, and, feeling the cold wind on his sweating skin, he knew he wouldn't survive this madness in one piece. His father opened the door. His face shone as if it had been oiled. As always happened whenever he greeted his son, it seemed at first as if he wanted to give him a hug, only to bring his open arms suddenly forwards as you do in order to keep someone at arms' length, and at the same time lowering his left arm again and with his right giving Leo two short pats on his upper arm and saying 'Hallo, my boy.' As on previous occasions Leo was again taken in by first appearances and automatically opened his arms—more vigorously and animatedly than usual owing to his inner turmoil and bad con-science—in order to hug his father, at exactly the same moment of course as his father's gesture changed seamlessly into one of self-defence since his fear of physical contact really was too great and had once more prevailed. As always, Leo stood there again in a stupidly contorted gesture that was so awkward that his father abruptly turned on his heel, said, 'Come on in, Leo' and hurried on ahead into the sitting room. There stood his mother, rigidly and with one hand on the back of a chair next to the dining table, which was already laid for tea. He gave her a quick peck on the cheek she stiffly offered him, and, while he was feeling a mixture of disgust and pity at the luxuriant beard that his mother had recently started growing, she said, after looking him over critically: 'Don't you ever get a haircut, Leo? It's not done to go around like that, you know!'

Leo said that it was very windy outside and... In which case one should take something to cover one's head! his mother said. 'Have a chair,' Leo, said his father, rubbing his hands continuously as if they were about to partake of the rarest delicacies, sit down. So, what's new?

On a small plate there lay four thin slices of cake which his mother served first to his father, then to Leo and then to herself, pouring out tea in the same sequence.

One doesn't speak with one's mouth full. That offered good enough reason at least not to begin talking immediately and Leo swallowed his cake with a relief bordering on panic, noticing far too late his mother's reproving look because he was eating with his hand instead of using the fork. The sound of the forks on his parents' dessert plates felt to him like a skinny finger prodding him reproachfully again and again in the chest. But it was too late, his plate was empty and he stared longingly at the last piece of cake that was still lying on the plate in the middle of the table. Help yourself, Leo, said his father, there's enough. There's more outside, isn't there? he asked Leo's mother. So help yourself, Leo.

Leo looked at his mother and said no thank you, he couldn't manage any more. The waves in her hair looked as though they had been made with curling tongs.

Leo noticed that he was becoming helplessly tensed up. He pushed his chair back a little and crossed his legs, and in so doing his foot knocked so hard against the table-leg that the teacups rattled on their saucers and the tea almost spilled over. He felt a hot flood boil up in him, followed immediately by a shiver of cold.

Why did Leo recount all this in such detail when he met Judith in the *Café Landtmann* eight days later after having only just recovered from his cold? Judith seemed lacking in concentration and impatient; they were sitting at a window seat, and Judith kept looking out through the pane of glass into the street outside, the Ringstraße, or past Leo into the room as if she wanted to catch the waiter's eye in order to pay and leave immediately. Leo was also intensely on edge. After having spent a whole feverish and lonely week at home, he found the general murmur in the room deafening, as if he were exposed to the pulsing rhythms of so many speech choruses. He therefore thought he understood Judith's nerviness only too well—didn't he feel exactly the same—though of course his own edginess was made worse as a result. Judith's impatience and lack of concentration made him feel he had only a very short measure of time at his disposal to say what he wanted, but everything he said awoke so many associations and memories in him that he felt he had to describe every detail even more exactly and go further and further back in his story, so that he could get everything across to her.

But the faster he spoke, in order to say what was most important in the shortest possible time, the more quickly he found one reason after another to elaborate, never-endingly, on what he was saying.

If you could only imagine, said Leo, all the things that rose up in me again when I knocked against the table leg with my foot.

Leo leant forward as if he wanted to whisper something in Judith's ear over the coffee table. Judith dragged nervously on her cigarette, and the smoke she blew out formed itself into a finely wrought grille in front of Leo's face, billowing like a thin curtain, behind which Judith inclined an ear—no, she didn't, she gave another quick look out of the window—what did Leo want, to confess and be absolved? To convert to Christianity out of sheer despair at the prospect of this father and his celebration of Christmas? Leo pressed his face between his palms and, as if it had happened only the day before, excitedly began to relate how, as a small child, he had once been taken along by his parents to an afternoon of bridge at the house of other Austrian emigrés in São Paulo. For hours he had sat there on an armchair to one side of the table where they were playing cards—it was hours according to his memory—and there he had kept quiet, as was expected of him. Then at a certain moment he'd no longer known what he should do, that is, he couldn't do anything other than sit there and look at everything around him in that room. And he'd looked at everything now, had let his eye wander across the room so many times by now. And suddenly—Leo related—his mother, who hadn't paid any attention to him whatsoever since their arrival, turned to him and said: It's not done to fidget like that with one's legs! She then picked up the cards which had just been dealt and continued playing.

And it was this that came into my mind at that moment, said Leo, this brutal contempt of my mother for everything uncontrolled; and everything she *can't* at all times rigidly control, as she does herself; this lack of control is immediately bestial, carnal and therefore contemptible; she has always given me the feeling that I was the very embodiment of dumb carnality, and it's this that always brings out the murderess in her, and—and! he repeated, for Judith was looking out of the window again, her head bent right up against the window—what was that noise—Leo raised his voice a little, but really only a little, for he still had a slight sore throat and besides he didn't want to shout out the private, innermost things that he was publicly unveiling in feverish nervousness in front of Judith. And—he murmured, now a little louder —that wasn't all, far from it. It was in fact only very rarely that his

26

parents took him along with them, the regular exception being the visits to Löwinger, because the latter insisted on seeing Leo. As a rule, however, he was left at home in the care of the housemaid. Leo remembered this *empregada* as a girl with a coarse, shapeless body, an off-putting, unhealthy complexion the colour of ashes, and an extreme servility towards and fear of his mother. His mother, you see, had the habit of putting on a pair of white gloves when she came home, walking through the house with the nervously cringing *empregada* skulking behind her and running her gloved fingers over the furniture as she went along. And woe betide the girl if the finger-tips of the snow-white gloves became discoloured with dirt or dust. Imagine that, said Leo, massaging his temples, but now comes the best bit: Maria, this *empregada*, was so frightened of my mother that she would tie me, a small child, with a washing line to the leg of the dining-room table when my parents were out. She tied me to the table leg while she was cleaning and tidying up just to stop me from untidying the place or making something dirty again when she wasn't looking, for which she would of course be punished by my mother. Only when she saw my parents coming home would she untie me quickly and then do this tour of inspection with my mother.

You're not serious, said Judith,

It's perfectly true, said Leo, and that came back to me, too, when I kicked the table-leg and my mother, of all people, gave me such a reproachful look again. Instead of my—I don't know. To this day I can't for the life of me understand why Maria didn't hand in her notice and also why I never told my mother about it. I expect I thought she knew about it anyway and wanted it that way, for that was precisely what she always wanted, that I should keep quiet, that is.

The noise in the café grew louder and for one second Leo had the impression that the people on the neighbouring tables were discussing in horrified tones Leo's stories about his mother—someone shouted behind him: that's criminal—Leo was suddenly very hot, perhaps he really had got up too soon and was now having a relapse and beginning a fever again.

And did you get the money to have your car repaired? Judith asked.

Leo said that he had then told them about the accident, although the atmosphere at home had been so soured from the start, but on the other hand it had always been like that anyway, so he had told them briefly and in general terms of a driving accident, such as can happen to anyone, he explained, and that if, in view of his approaching birthday, he might be permitted to put in a particular request, then he would ask just this once for financial support to be able to pay for the repair, for the monthly sum he received for his studies naturally did not take into account such an exceptional outlay.

Money for your birthday? his mother had said. One doesn't give money for birthdays. Your present is on the commode, Leo.

I should also add, said Leo—but he didn't get to continue because a few people from the middle tables or the cubicles at the back of the café jumped up abruptly and surrounded the window tables in order to look out into the street. All of a sudden one of the waiters was standing next to Leo, also looking curiously out of the window into the Ringstraße and saying something about the savages on the march again. Leo turned his gaze from the waiter's black dinner jacket to the window, behind which on the whole he could see nothing but a tremendous amount of running about, just people rushing up and down the Ring-straße, running in the gathering dusk like herds of black shadows past the café windows. You could hear car horns sounding and—were they shots? Some kind of detonations, anyway, a banging which, in the interior of the café with its jumble of voices, sounded strangely unreal, as if it were wrapped in cotton wool.

The anti-Borodajkewicz demonstration, said Judith.

The anti-what? asked Leo.

Borodajkewicz. The old Nazi who teaches International Commerce at the university. Come off it, Leo, you surely know about that. The anti-fascists are demonstrating because he's been giving extreme right-wing, anti-semitic lectures all the time. There was a rally the day before yesterday which was set on by the neo-Nazis and—

How should I know about that? said Leo. I was ill.

And today another demonstration was organised, said Judith, this one. And again the Nazis are attacking it. Come, Leo, we must get out there.

They should have their noses in their books, that lot, said the waiter.

Come on, Leo, we're going, said Judith, and paid for her coffee without giving a tip. Leo gave a bigger one, since he felt most uncomfortable.

What a prat, said Judith, putting on her coat.

What's the point of us going out there, then, said Leo, I mean—

Come off it, Leo, you're not just going to sit there while outside those neo-Nazis beat up the anti-fascists.

What I mean is, said Leo, laboriously buttoning up his coat, what purpose does it serve getting ourselves beaten up as well. Judith, listen—

She was already on her way to the café exit. He ran after her—her stern, upright gait, her ascetically slim body, no, she didn't remind him of his mother, whom he saw as if she were there. He was like a sleepwalker and full of fear, not so much because of the danger reigning outside, but because of the danger that he might lose the love of this woman he so much wanted before he had succeeded in even winning it. In front of the café Leo seized Judith's hand, in fear, a woollen little fist in a clumsy, fur-lined glove, a lumpy sensation lacking the clear feeling of touch. The square between the café, the Burgtheater and the Ringstraße was full of people, thousands of people, an unheard of agitation, running and pushing and shoving. The fist slipped out of the furry grasp of the glove—Over there! cried Judith. Leo ran after her. Then he saw directly in front of him three youths in leather jackets swinging chains. Averting his face, Leo ran off at an angle, then detonators and mortars exploded—he wanted to dodge into the road leading off the Ringstraße, but a tight phalanx was bearing down on him shouting 'Yids—to—Au-schwitz!' He flattened himself against the side of a house—a deafening noise filled the air: Free speech! Free speech!— where was Judith? Leo rushed off again in the direction Judith had taken—what was that? Knives! Knives were flying through the air and burning torches—like will-o'-the-wisps they whirled in great arcs over the jostling crowds. Nazis out! Nazis out! It all seemed to unfold according to a choreography of which Leo was ignorant—he felt dull blows on his back and side—now he hit out around him—all he wanted was to get out and away from there. Suddenly he found himself on the steps of the Burgtheater—he ran up and half hid behind a pillar and from this elevated position looked out over the whole teeming rabble. Eggs, oranges, tomatoes flew through the air. Smoke rose up suddenly from the middle of a group of students who were carrying anti-Borodajkewicz banners—the banners crumpled up and shrivelled and the group scattered in all directions, their arms shielding their faces—The bastards are throwing tear-gas, someone suddenly standing next to him shouted breathlessly—tear-gas, the bastards. All the time he saw people running away but amazingly the square never became empty—again and again it came back to life. Once more there were people pressing forward, trying to regroup. That was particularly amazing, even admirable, Leo caught himself thinking. Then he saw young people trying to keep others at bay with flag-poles, fighting the ones with the iron chains, rubber tubing or steel rods and he got scared again. Nazis out! Nazis out! Jew-ish pigs! Jew-ish pigs! And stewards with armbands shouted: Up the Republic! To the Monument! To the Monument! They were trying to restore order to the demonstration, to give the march a direction. Leo stood there bemused and from his elevated position gazed down on the scene as if through the wrong end of misted-over opera glasses. Hovering in a darkness criss-crossed by street lamps, the smoke from the tear-gas canisters and torches hung before his eyes like an aura of dirty milk. His vision of it all, however vivid, was dismal. Now, as they passed excitedly along, the march stewards could be heard giving the order 'To the Parliament!' Suddenly he saw the police there, too. They were forming a cordon between the anti-fascist demonstrators and the neo-Nazis. The demonstrators once more formed themselves into a procession which then set off to the accompaniment of chants, while the neo-Nazis roared back counter slogans. Communist pigs! he heard. The part of the Ringstrasse in front of the Burgtheater began to clear— Funny, thought Leo, the anti-fascists were wearing anoraks, the neo-Nazis leather jackets. Where was Judith? He looked for her half-heart-edly in the thinning crowd but he did not find her, of course. Two or three times he wanted to shout 'Judith!' just because he had seen a girl among the demonstrators, and it was then that it struck him for the first time how few women there were taking part in this demonstration. They're all sitting in a café with their boyfriends, he thought, or lying in bed with them. Judith. He carried on simply standing there for a good quarter of an hour like a blind man by the side of a busy road waiting for someone to take him by the arm and lead him across. Then he noticed how cold he was. He was shivering despite his thick suit and warm coat. Even his hands were icy-cold in spite of the fur-lined gloves; he had received a new pair for his birthday and a woollen vest. One has to keep oneself warm: 'He who keeps warm keeps in good form,' his mother had said, as if she owed her survival, her narrow escape from the Nazis, to her clothes. You do know, don't you, his father had said when Leo's mother had cleared the table and was in the kitchen for a moment, you do know your mother means well by you. She wants you to be warm, but you must get your car repaired too of course, that's quite clear—at which point he had slipped Leo two banknotes out of his wallet. Thank you, Papa, said Leo, just at the very moment, of course, when his mother was coming back into the room. And how are your studies coming on? said his father in an unnaturally loud voice. Fine, thank you, Papa.

Fine. Was he writing his dissertation? He was standing in front of the entrance to the Burgtheater and watching the performance of a play on the street. A walk-on who would like to play a role in the life of a female walk-on. He was so cold. He set off back to his car, which he had parked between the Burgtheater and the Volksgarten. He walked very slowly to see if Judith could be looking for him somewhere around there. Suddenly he turned round and ran back to the café. Perhaps she was waiting for him again in the café—that was where they had arranged to meet after all. But she wasn't there. It was warmer in the café but that was all. So back to his car and then home.

At his car, which he had collected from the garage only that morning, he found the bonnet stoved in and the front bumper bent down on one side. Demonstrators had probably climbed onto his car and jumped about on it. Leo wept. Days later he would read in the newspaper that someone had died during this demonstration.

With a scream Leo jumped backwards onto the bonnet of the car parked next to his. But he didn't do it any damage. Obviously denting a car wasn't nearly so simple a matter. The bone at the base of his spine hurt him for two days after that.

Leo looked really ill when Judith visited him the next day. She had rung and he'd told her he was ill, a relapse, and so he couldn't leave the house. But he'd be very happy if she came to his place. Not only did he clearly have a cold, but he also bore such an expression of suffering that Judith, in a rush of motherly warmth, almost felt like putting him to bed, administering to him a hot infusion, getting him to sweat and keeping watch over his sleep and feverish dreams. This feeling was still resonating when Judith, in order to scotch it, said: You'll soon be better. Look what I've brought you. And she opened her wicker basket even before taking off her coat and took out a bottle of Brazilian rum—The last bottle of *pinga* I still had at home but which I didn't want to drink by myself.

Judith couldn't help smiling to see how smartly Leo had got himself up for her visit. He was wearing a grey flannel suit with a waistcoat and looked like an old professor who had fallen into the fountain of youth but hadn't quite been able to rid himself of all the infirmities of age. As elegant as ever even at home, said Judith, running her hand over the lapel of the lounge jacket—what, said Leo, oh I see, no, I always get these suits from my parents, from my father's store—I told you before, I don't have anything else to wear.

And, said Judith, while, like a magician pulling a rabbit out of a hat, she drew a pineapple out of her bag, a real pineapple, *abacaxi*, she said, *fruta bem típica brasileira*, I had such *saudades*, what's the word, she said, you'll see, Leo, it'll do you good.

Leo seemed touched.

I saw it in the market and simply couldn't resist it.

Come on in, come on in, he said, making an incredible number of polite gestures, helping her out of her coat, walking on ahead, walking back, continual lively gestures, please have a chair, make yourself at home. Oh, I'm sorry, he said, taking the books away that were lying on the armchair, putting them down on the floor next to the armchair, then changing his mind and picking them up again from the floor and putting them on the writing desk, bending down hectically to pick up more books, magazines and papers which were lying around, picking up his briefcase, too, which was sitting in the middle of the room, and taking everything over to the writing desk. He seemed to be forever bowing and scraping and bending over.

Leave it, Leo, my place always looks exactly the same when I'm working, I don't mind it in the least. Sit down, he said, wait, I'll fetch some glasses and plates, and he went out.

A small, low sofa upholstered in a stained, plain, brown material—on top a crumpled-up brown blanket, like a hospital blanket—it looked as if Leo always slept there in his clothes and boots, ready at any moment to make a dash for it. He would then only have to throw his books and folders into the suitcase which was lying on the floor to the right of the desk. To the left of the desk the old armchair which, being now free of the books that had been lying on it earlier, somehow gave an impression of having been abandoned in haste. Next to it was a small side-table—on this a telephone and teacup, empty—inside it on the bottom the brown stain of dried-out tea dregs. To one side by the wall a cupboard. Perhaps it had clothes in it or books or perhaps nothing at all. Perhaps the clothes were in the suitcase. In the corner of the room a small iron coal-stove. It was still warm. Whoever lived there can't have been gone long. Nowhere was there any personal object to be seen that might have allowed one to infer anything regarding the identity of the occupant, his preferences, his tastes, his history. Nothing that betrayed any desire to arrange the space in such a way as to make it pleasant to live in. As if someone had lived there for just a short time, read a few books and made some notes with a pencil perhaps. A pencil on the desk was the only writing implement she could see. If it were left behind, it could easily be replaced. There were no plants—they would need regular looking after and would then die when you moved on. There were no pictures—yes there was, just one, standing on the desk behind the stack of books in a beautiful frame made out of Brazil wood. Judith picked the photo up—it showed a middle-aged man sitting outside a café, surely that was—yes, it was, no doubt about it—it was the Copacabana in Rio. The man looked the same as the bohemians always did in the Brazilian films of the forties and fifties: straw hat, a light suit with a large silk handkerchief sticking out of his top pocket, black and white shoes. Judith had the impression that the man, especially around the nose and mouth, bore a certain resemblance to Leo but she wasn't sure.

Where was Leo? Suddenly she had the feeling that he really had run off and left her behind here all by herself. She put the photo back on the desk and listened. She was relieved to hear noises coming from the kitchen. She was looking out of the window when Leo came back into the room. Outside she saw several lighted windows opposite and, down in the courtyard, the tarnished silver glimmer of the cobblestones and stone sculptures, and at the same time, in the reflection of the window pane, she saw Leo putting a tray down on the desk. On the tray were two glasses, a plate on which the pineapple lay with the rind already cut off and a large knife which Leo now picked up. She saw Leo standing behind her with the knife and looking towards her—she saw him standing there with the knife about four paces behind her, but at the same time she saw him in front of her like a ghost hovering outside in the darkness of the courtyard—it was if she had eyes in the back of her head, but simultaneously she also saw him face to face—he hovered motionlessly in front of her, looking at her, and she looked at him—the Leo behind her back put the knife down, the Leo hovering outside in the darkness put the knife down, too, and from both sides, from in front and from behind, he came towards her—she didn't move—he now put his arms round her, kissed her on the neck and throat. Judith stood there stiffly, letting it happen and stiffening more as she did so—he kissed her with such ardour and naturalness that she kept still, neither warding him off nor coming to him—he kissed her like a statue, his damp lips were like moss on a stone sculpture. For one second she thought that all the angels down in the courtyard were Leo's victims, women he had kissed exactly in this way, at which point they had sprouted wings in order to fly away, but too late, they had already turned to stone. He had then put them down there.

Judith threw her head back and laughed—Leo floated out over the courtyard, while behind her Leo drew back—she turned round—he was standing by the desk and avoiding her eyes—he had the knife in his hands again and was hacking off slices of pineapple. That was a wonderful idea of yours, he said, I haven't had any pineapple for ages—once from a tin but that's not the same of course—fresh pineapple is so expensive here in Vienna—wasn't it very expensive? You shouldn't have. Now I've gone and forgotten the cutlery—hang on a moment, I'll fetch some quickly—

Don't, Leo, we'll eat it in our hands.

Leo licked his fingers clean, picked up the bottle of rum, held it helplessly in his hands. Unfortunately I don't have any lemons in the house, he said, otherwise we could have made *caipirinhas*, but we could—

—drink it neat, said Judith, *prefiro emoções puras*.

They ate the pineapple and drank rum standing by the desk like at a small, chaotic bar on some street corner in São Paulo—Judith savoured her rum by first taking small sips, then emptied her glass in one draught—Leo watched her with feverishly shining eyes and followed suit—another glass—while eating the pineapple both of them thrust their heads forward and held one hand palm upwards under their chins to catch the juice which oozed out of the pineapple—they looked at each other and giggled, Leo as if with an effort, although it was from relief, too. Judith poured out more rum, licked her fingers, then Leo again gave her that serious look—he took her hand and raising it to his mouth kissed it, licking off the pineapple juice on the inside at the same time. Judith pulled her hand away and stuck the last piece of cut pineapple into his mouth. Doesn't it taste good, he said with his mouth full, but what are we doing standing around like this—please, do have a seat—don't you want to sit down?

Who is that in the photo there? Your father?

No, said Leo, that's Uncle Zé, Löwinger, I told you about him.

So that's what he looks like. I imagined him older.

It's an old photo. He looked like that when I was a child, a really small child, that is—my first clear memories of him are as he looks in that photo.

And why do you have it standing there?

Because. I like it. I like him. I told you, remember. My parents have never given me the feeling they love me. But he does. Besides, he is a model of universality. The success he has had with his career might

34

have enabled him to remain as stupid and limited as my parents, for instance. But he is a man of fine sensibilities, well-read and highly educated in both literature and art, the best art critic I know. You should hear him when he stands in front of a painting and gives his interpretation of it. Suddenly the world assumes an order. The whole chaos of so-called creation is a chaos because all it amounts to is just so much material for the real creation of art. Only with art does necessity appear. You can—

So you really think it's only through art that the world acquires order? Or is that one of Löwinger's ingenious interpretations?

Leo gave Judith a glassy stare, took a swig of his drink and shook his head. When my mother, he said, when my mother was here once and saw the photo there, she kept on asking questions like that. Why do you have that photo there? Yes, yes, and I suppose that nonsense is meant to be interesting, is it? One should not seek to emulate madmen and rogues, Leo! And so on. I got the distinct feeling she was somehow affronted that I had put Uncle Zé's picture up here. It was funny, I've no idea why. It doesn't matter either, but if it's true, then there it's going to stay.

That was taken at Copacabana, wasn't it.

Yes.

Are you feeling better now, Leo?

Yes, he said, and emptied his glass, then looked at Judith for a few seconds, during which Judith thought she could hear his heart beating, but perhaps it was her own. Then he added: I'd be feeling better still if we were at Copacabana now, lying in the sun on the warm sand far away from the cold of Vienna—are you cold, you're not too cold, I hope, are you? Leo went over to the stove and put on more coal.

What a fuss Leo made, fussing over everything, so—worrisome, is that the word? Judith lit a cigarette while she watched Leo fiddling about by the stove, a stoker in a smart suit in crude, temporary lodgings. Whether it was sympathy, whether it was partiality, the rum or the hot stove, she felt a strong feeling of warmth, an inner glowing, in which her fear burnt up like a piece of white paper in a fireplace, so quickly and so casually—in a trice the white paper turns completely black and then it's gone. A sudden fear of loneliness had seized her that afternoon when she'd been at home, fear of time moving sluggishly towards the night when she would then be lying under a cool sheet unable to sleep, fear of death that doesn't come and which she cranes to see with open eyes in the darkness of her bedroom. And she'd had a longing for rum, a longing for the stupor and stimulation it gives, and fear of drinking alone. Her cold bed, unconsciousness.

Oh yes, an ashtray, said Leo, after he had straightened up again. I'll go and get one.

No, stay here, Leo, I'll use that teacup there—can I?

They drank more rum, still standing, though silent now. Judith could see that Leo wanted to say something but clearly didn't know how to begin, but perhaps it was only his cold that made him breathe through his mouth all the time, something which then made it look as though he was about to say something which he didn't in fact then say. Judith found this funny and laughed—Leo smiled back. Yes, you're much better, I can see, she said. You've taken your medicine like a good boy. I now prescribe for your convalescence a holiday by the sea. Copacabana, for example. We're leaving immediately. Come.

Judith took Leo by the hand—he looked at her helplessly and long-ingly—she took another swig of rum and then walked out of the room, leading Leo by the hand. There was the kitchen—Judith could see that through the open kitchen door, but what's behind that door there? The bedroom, said Leo, and took two steps, but Judith stood still, pulled him back and asked: Where is the bathroom?

There, said Leo, this door.

Aha, said Judith, ladies and gentlemen we will shortly be landing in Rio de Janeiro.

She turned on the light, a simple bathroom, white-tiled walls with an old enamel bath-tub resting on small ornamental feet. Is there a heater?

Yes, said Leo, here.

Above the door there hung an electric heater which he switched on.

The temperature is hot, being summer, and the humidity is ninety percent. We wish you a pleasant stay, said Judith and turned on the taps of the bath. Shall we take a little dip in the sea?

While the water was running into the bath, they undressed—Judith fetched the rum and glasses from the room, and the chair, too, which was by the desk. She used the chair as a side-table next to the bath-tub, put the bottle and glasses on it and slipped with a sigh into the hot water. She raised her glass to Leo, who now climbed into the tub as well—she liked his body, it was slim and firm but not stupidly muscular like with those body fanatics who play at sports all day long and then strut about on the beaches like roosters. His chest was hairy, his sex hesitantly aroused—*gostoso*, said Judith.

36

Again Leo gave her one of those lofty, serious looks and made to put his arms round her, rub soap into her, wrap himself around her.

Wait, said Judith, relax.

Leaning back, they sat opposite each other, snuggled down into the hot water, drank rum.

Is the water too hot for you? asked Leo, and began to fiddle with the taps—a jet of cold water poured out into the bath—Judith gave a shriek and pulled up her knees—water slopped over the edge of the bathtub. Don't, it was great like that, said Judith. Frantically Leo turned off the tap.

Such a beautiful day, *Rio é uma maravilha*, said Judith. *Está melhor*, are you feeling better, she asked.

Yes, said Leo, I'm fine again now. And he told her how awful he had felt all day, actually since the evening before, when Judith had disappeared during the demonstration. That was really stupid, going out there into it all, like we did, he said, we should have—

Why stupid—do you want to let the fascists have the streets to themselves? Judith asked. Anyway, even if you do get separated for a moment, you always meet up again if you let the demonstration carry you along—you must have seen how we were being drawn in the direction of the parliament.

Yes, of course I did but then those characters with their iron chains and cudgels kept on appearing and I got shoved to one side. What's the point in getting myself hurt by them. What's more, there were thousands of people there, police, too—it's crazy to say that if we hadn't gone out we'd have been letting the fascists have the streets to themselves.

Leo, don't talk such nonsense—if everyone had said that, then there wouldn't have been thousands of people on the streets and then we really would have given in to the fascists without a fight.

No, said Leo, the fascists were on the streets because of the demonstrators—they wanted to harass the demonstrators—

No, my friend, the demonstrators were on the streets because the fascists had crawled out of their holes a long while ago, in the form of Nazis, for instance, who give anti-semitic lectures at the university and students who enthusiastically applaud him.

Yes, well, it doesn't matter how it began, said Leo, but what has it got to do with me? With you? What has it got to do with us? We are Brazilians—

Our parents are Viennese and they were humiliated by this mob and driven out, had to flee to Brazil—

Luckily for them, said Leo, they were better off there, and we would rather be there now, too,

Leo, you're crazy and—

And anyway, said Leo, times have changed—there were thousands of people on the streets, weren't there, in protest against a few Nazis—our parents would never have been driven out, if things in their day had been like they are now.

No-one said that today is like it was then, but that's what it's all about: seeing that it *doesn't* become like it was then.

It won't, regardless of whether I run out now from the café onto the streets or not, and even if it were to, that would in no way depend on whether I let myself be beaten up outside the café or not. Don't you understand?

You clearly don't understand what you're talking about.

Yes, I do, said Leo, hitting the water with his hand—you really do have a totally abstruse conception of history. Can't you see that these things, precisely because they are finished, over and done with, may be permitted to twitch a bit—it is of no significance whatsoever. You can sit in the corner seats of the café and watch it all through the window—the police protect those taking part, and then once more the press have the opportunity to solemnly dissociate themselves from the fascists. But if it'd really had any significance it would have affected the people in the café quite differently, but we were the only ones to go running out. It's like with the hair or finger-nails of a corpse, they go on growing even though the person's dead—it doesn't mean a thing—the corpse won't ever rise up from the dead again because of it. All right, all right, yes, it's good that people demonstrate when the Nazis dare to show themselves again, fair enough, but what I'm saying is that these things happen whether we take part in it or not, whether we get ourselves beaten to a pulp in so doing or not, whether we get a cold as a result or not, whether we get our car smashed up or not—my car!

Leo told her what had happened to his car and Judith asked sarcastically whether perhaps he was now going to blame her, too, for the fact that someone had jumped about on his car.

No, said Leo and laboriously went into how humiliating it had been asking his parents for money to get his car repaired and that he couldn't ask them for help again, if only because of what his mother would say, if within the space of one week he were to go to them twice with a request for money.

What is this problem you have with your mother, Judith asked. Don't you feel humiliated when the Nazis bellow out 'Yids to Auschwitz!?' Besides, your car would have got damaged even if we'd stayed in the café, so please take your complaints to the Nazis, not to me.

That's true, said Leo, but why did we have to meet in that particular café—you had already planned to join the demonstration and I was there to kill time for you until the demonstration reached the Burgtheater.

I suggested that café because I had a lecture beforehand and the *Landtmann* is the café closest to the university. And if perhaps I also planned to join the demo, then I assumed, too, that we'd go together, since with your history and awareness it directly relates to you just as much—

The only thing of which I am aware, interrupted Leo, is how contemptible I find it, this total giving of oneself to a thing that'll happen anyway. People should do only what they specifically can do—

And what might that be, asked Judith, wait! I know what. Single-handedly make the world a better place, is that right? Like that, that, what was his name, the one you were raving to me about, the one who ruined the Rubens painting—

Walmen.

Yes, that's the one. Like him, yes? The philosophy to end all philosophies. That was what only Mr Walmen could do. And destroy a Rubens painting. Only Mr Walmen could do that. He, too, of course, had no time for demonstrations. And that's why the world is such a fine place now, all thanks to our dearly beloved Mr Walmen.

Leo hit the water with both hands and shouted that it was absurd to make him out to be a lunatic simply because he didn't regard it as necessary to go trotting along to every demonstration—that would mean all philosophers were lunatics, Hegel and—

Are you comparing yourself with Hegel now just because you're scared of three Nazis and therefore don't want to go out onto the streets, shouted Judith—

You're the one doing the comparing—comparing me with Walmen!—and it's you who are scared of three Nazis! Because you immediately need a mass demonstration when three Nazis turn up somewhere.

Calm down, please.

You calm down.

Judith tried very calmly to explain her point of view again to Leo. He retreated scornfully to the frigid position of the thinking man, standing perforce alone, who, at the most, observed demonstrations cursorily from the window of his study. Oh right, said Judith, what sort of demonstrations have you got outside your window then: demonstrating cemetery statues, the angel of death, the fallen angel or what? And when you've observed them, you then sit down at your desk and think again about your philosophy to end all philosophies, do you?

Leo leapt up—Go on, run off and join them then, he shouted, those morons of yours who fancy they're so strong and important in their herd, but—but, was Leo weeping? Or were they only streaks of bath-water running down his face, like the water running down his body—Judith poured herself a rum up to the brim and emptied it in three large draughts—she looked at him icily, as through a filter—she narrowed her eyes—there was a filter—it filtered away every illusion that one person can have with regard to another—she saw him very clearly suddenly in his slippery pitifulness and with this pretentious behaviour of his. He trembled with agitation whenever the way he behaved was not appreciated—but who would anyway, hence this craving to slither away, like a snail, his shrivelled up sex in front of her eyes, like a snail without its shell that would like to be held carefully between two cupped hands and there be protected from the stupid world which had no understanding of snails—this craving for an accomplice to whom he could present his slithering away as a heroic act and furthermore to have it confused with love. He stood in front of her wet and shivering—stepped out of the bath—then Judith noticed for the first time Leo's blueish goose pimples, noticed that the bathwater had in the meantime become ice cold and that she was wretchedly cold. They had been quarrelling so long that they'd ended up sitting in cold water—now she couldn't help laughing.

Judith, said Leo.

They rubbed themselves down quickly and ran into the bedroom to warm up in bed but all feelings of intimacy and tenderness had been banished for good.

You have to smoke even in bed, said Leo, sipping his glass of rum. Everything he said sounded like a reproach—they were both drunk, their thinking erratic, their speech slurred.

And then that bleak look, a clear look actually, a look through a filter, in fact. A ridiculous bedroom, a little closet almost completely taken up with the two huge beds that had been pushed together to make a double. Old German-style beds with high wooden headboards like cathedral walls. To the right and left of this double bed were matching bedside tables, or more like bedside chests each with a top surface made of black stone—marble? Granite? Like the lid of a tomb. A small lamp on top with a glass shade in the shape of a Victorian bonnet. Turning her head away in despair, Judith saw another huge Old German-style cupboard which projected so far into the narrow closet that it half blocked the view to the window. No-one surely could buy such furniture for themselves, Judith thought—where would you go anyway to find it? It must have been already here when Leo moved in—he had moved into a furnished flat, left everything as it was, hasn't changed anything around, hasn't thrown anything out, hasn't added anything of his own, something he liked. Not even one picture hanging on the wall—the art lover! Art is his speciality, aesthetics. And he lives like this. Here he thinks about aesthetics. And about the world, like he just said: tato, toti, totality, Judith scoffed, please, Leo, that's harder to understand than to pronounce.

Judith thought she was dreaming, no, seeing clearly. Leo. Another swig. Talks now about insisting on social totality and can't even manage to sort out his own little world—twenty-nine and still tortured by his mother's coldness. Can talk for hours on end in an Old German-style bed. On the desk the photo of an uncle figure, this because of the fact that this man loved him more than his own parents. As if all those people who *were* loved by their parents had photographic displays of them on their desks. The main thing was: it had annoyed his mother—that confirms it for Leo. Totality, Leo repeated. He reminded her of Laurence Sterne's Tristram Shandy. Tristram was also unable to realise his plans because he couldn't cope with what his mother had said during his conception. And because his father gave him that Christian name. Never got over it, never got beyond it, but what an enormous challenge: to narrate your whole life? And Uncle Toby, no, Uncle Zé. Why on earth should Leo's mother be so annoyed by the photo? Perhaps something happened at conception there, too. The main thing, the unloved son was pleased—yes, yes, revenge is sweet.

Did Judith say all this? If she had said something, she wasn't saying anything now at least. Leo's domineering manner smothered all conversation, like this huge pillow, like this bed, like this room really.

41

The next day Judith could only remember the following words that Leo spoke:

Let me finish.

That's irrelevant.

You're avoiding the point.

You have to understand that—

It's indisputable that—

You're changing the subject again.

You're off the point.

That's got nothing to do with it.

I've already made it clear that—

Those are just stories that don't help to clarify a thing.

That may seem to be the case but the fact of the matter is that—

You have to clearly understand that—

Judith got up, went to the bathroom, gathered up her clothes and got dressed. She fetched a brush from her bag and brushed her hair long and hard in front of the mirror with her eyes fixed on her reflection— her face looked like a white mask, behind which quite possibly she may not have been hiding at all. Suddenly in the mirror she saw Leo standing behind her and looking at her.

Without turning round she said: Leo, go to bed, you're ill.

Then she went.

Leo in his room. How late was it? Midday perhaps. Even the dull light of this grey day hurt his eyes. He rolled down the blinds. Now in the half-light of the room there was nothing that might have ensured that a thin ray of reality could flow into his consciousness. After this ordeal of a night, thrown across the bed now as if he had to display his pain to someone, after a sleep in which everything he'd dreamt had tormented him, Leo now felt dead. He wished he really were. Just this headache alone. Just that alone. He was incapable of any orderly thought but, what was worse, incapable of no thought. Why did he love Judith? He didn't know.

After a while he suddenly remembered how the day before she had been standing naked in front of him in the bathroom. How beautiful he had thought her. But beauty. Hadn't what he longed for always been a much greater concern: symbiosis with a woman with whom he also mentally...? Like-mindedness. By that he meant.... Not something banal, pleasurable, a vacant, cosy submergence, but—Judith shaved even under her arms as well as her legs. A congenial woman. By that he meant that union of beauty and intelligence which...—How natural Judith's movements were when she was undressing. So harmonious. No timidity. Beauty. And intelligence—the intelligence, he meant, that excites the senses and also the mind.

Also intellectually stimulating. The mind is—Mind you, this darkness is depressing. Leo yanked the blinds up with a whirr and looked out of the window. There were some pigeons sitting on the angels. Judith's movements were harmonious like the beat of a bird's wing, a homing pigeon flying in from the future with the good tidings that love, liberated sexuality and meaning exist. Like-mindedness. The meaning is meaningful life—no tautology!—united in an order that can also be of use to others as a code for living. This order is called—Cold. Leo was freezing. The stove had gone out of course. He managed to light it again with difficulty. Soot. Ashes. Leo wiped his hands on the seat of his trousers. Judith's bottom. If only he could see it. In his memory. Man's ability to recall pictures is enormously overrated. Memory is when we observe formulations and sentences which we have made with regard to something while believing we merely see it. Make a note of that straightaway. What for. Why did he love Judith. He didn't know. Why Judith was obvious. Why love. To—Better to ask why Judith. In order to hang around her neck. As a message. In order to be carried by her into the future. The message ran: Someone thought order. That is the meaning. The meaning is the task.

The task. Leo stepped back a few steps. Away from the window. Did he hate Judith or did he hate himself because of the events of yesterday? Leaving the question unanswered, he continued walking. After a moment he thought—nothing. But—yesterday he had come close to grasping hold of her—Judith—the question—yesterday it might have been possible to grasp—Judith, no question. The right answers always precede the questions. Questions are nothing but—This headache. I'm racking my brains. How beautiful the question was—her body, perfectly formed—no question. The questions were wrong. What are questions. Nothing but pointers which lead back to the point being made. They didn't lead back. Why? Exactly. Perfectly formed question. Close to being grasped. Innocent as long as innocence still prevailed. In a flash everything was clear. Form and desire. Flash in the pan. All one: desire and form. And yet no fusion. Why? That's the question. Exactly. They didn't lead back, they led astray. To the wrong life, wrong! to life. Life means: Two people are two people, not one. Action and love: not one. In neither one had he succeeded so far. Desire notwithstanding. It went like this: if the task succeeds, love will succeed. If love is pure chance, then the task is not preordained. Wrong! Completely wrong. Leo crawled into bed. Of course he hated Judith. The things she said. If he could remember them. Nothing that was relevant now. That was all relative. That—and this. This and that. All made up from lots of beginnings. No meaning. No purpose. The purpose is—The redoubling of strength so as to get there more quickly. Happiness. The task. No question of that. Instead of which, nothing but questions. Why did she say that. Why this gulf. This gulf had opened up by chance—bridging it still didn't lead him to his task. Gulfs like that could always open up again by chance. These gulfs disappear if you do away with the craving for fulfilled love. That's what's needed. Do away with Judith. These thoughts, this resolve, they came and went in his head, came and went. A prayer wheel. He loved her. Didn't. He hated her. Didn't. Came and went. These thoughts were not painful. It was pure chance that he had a headache. The rum. His craving for Judith. Craving is so banal. Judith's craving for alcohol and nicotine. Banal. And leads to pain. That's life all over. Pure chance. Life is nothing, the task is everything, life is all chance, and the task is fate itself. Yes. Make a note of that now. Tomorrow. This headache. Judith's fault. Life's.

Leo felt a lot better the next day—he almost felt well. His hope that he would get flu and would therefore be justifiably unable to work for a week was not fulfilled. It was clear that the physical pain of the previous day really had been due only to the excess of rum. Leo required the whole day to get used to this state of affairs. In the evening while sitting in his armchair drinking peppermint tea it came as a shock to him to realise that he really didn't know what he should do, apart from what he should do. The task. But what sort of task? He hadn't worked on his dissertation for months on the pretext that he was working on his dissertation. But a doctoral dissertation is not a task in the sense he meant. Completing it is as meaningless as the noise of a door clicking shut. On completing it you're aware that you've left an open space behind you and now the door has closed and the way back is barred.

Then what? If you're lucky you might be invited to contribute to the annual philosophical publication. But other than that? What do you live on? Life is pure chance. He'd wanted to make a note of that. He sat down at his desk, wrote some things down—oh yes, and that thought about longing and form, too. But those were arbitrary notes drawn from the chance circumstances of an albeit present but trivial life experience. No. Perhaps his thoughts regarding this complex—cross out complex— no, keep it in, were exemplary, perhaps his life struggle was exemplary. His life exemplary? He wondered for a moment who he could ring up, who he could tempt into tempting him into killing some time. He couldn't think of anyone. He didn't have any friends, at least none that he could ring and meet up with immediately. And to ring Judith, to not get hold of her, to wait and see if she rang him, no, that was precisely what he had to stop—that's what he had resolved—waiting would make him depressed, he'd get ill from drinking so much tea and if she then did ring, he'd have a headache the next day, that's all. That was the terrible thing: that's all. No. He was completely alone. Was that exemplary? This banal, uninteresting life, so rudimentary and yet so beyond his control, was this exemplary? That couldn't be the sum of things for him or for others. So! No. But that's why it was in fact exemplary. In an exemplary way it showed the contradiction between living and doing. That's how he saw it and—make a note of that straightaway!—the meaning is in the doing. He skimmed through what he'd noted down, chewing his pencil—no, these words were so random—he ought to make an essay, he ought to make some essays out of them—out of the stalactite cave of his frozen thinking he ought to break off essays and carry them out into the light of day, into the world, and publish them. If his life was typically average, could it then be raised above the average, given form, be preserved? No. Life is pure chance, action is born of necessity. Exactly. His life was uninteresting and that was good. These notes had arisen by chance from his life— uninteresting—he would have to give these words a new exemplary direction. He wrote: Idea for an essay: Longing and Form. Next line: Idea for an essay: The Concept of the Exemplary vs. the Typical. Next line: Idea for an essay: suddenly he faltered. Judith. He jumped up and paced up and down in the room. He made himself a fresh pot of tea. He set the pot down on the very same sheet on which he had earlier been making his notes. He paced up and down the room. How beautiful Judith was. Her naked body was. When she undressed in the bathroom she was—Her face. How mask-like it was in the end. All those things she said. If only he could remember. If only he could forget. Leo worked feverishly for the whole week on the essay which was meant to be his exemplary renunciation of life, his renunciation of Judith.

It was a week of suffering, and the exorcism of his suffering served to make matters worse since he thought about nothing else besides his suffering. All the time there were pictures of Judith in his head—luckily they weren't pictures. Judith was in his head continually but not as a picture, rather as a fog through which his thoughts trekked, feeling their way systematically, making sure of what was solid and safe, on which his thinking could then take a hold and orientate itself, and the more the fog lifted, the more euphorically he worked, writing as never before, writing in support of her and against her, that he didn't need anyone—didn't need her either—when he was working, since a little bit of productivity was enough and he didn't need anyone. Of course it would be nice if there were to be someone—but who? Someone strong enough to be able to be a mirror. He made a note: Idea for an essay: The Mirror (poss. imit. of Simmel's *The Handle*). Mirror image, reflection and the orderly life.

He set things in order. He wrote. He needed Judith to make it clear he didn't need anyone. He needed the fog in order to clear it. The essay on which he worked a whole week in order to exorcise his false longing for Judith was not really an essay, it was a dialogue. His plan—and what kept him at it—was that, after he had finished the work, he would send it to Judith as a farewell present, as a statement, as a door leading into a vital way of living.

What he wrote was a dialogue between two students about Laurence Sterne. The basic idea was two students discussing his novel, *Tristram Shandy*. The first—and Leo spent a long time looking for a stupid, unfashionable name, finally settling on Vincent—is a run-of-the-mill student, a simple enthusiast for literature and life accustomed to reaching out and grabbing with both hands immediately any pleasure that offers itself. An opportunistic hedonist. An epicurean predator. If pleasure beckoned, he didn't quibble about differences of attitude but instantly lunged at the pleasure. Vincent argued, of course, in support of *Tristram Shandy*, defended him. The other student (he was called Joachim, which was Leo's second name but Judith didn't know that, which Leo found entertaining to reflect on) was a man of the highest principles, driven by a stringent moral sense, a man who exacted an ideal standard both from himself and his undertakings. Joachim, who is painted as intellectually the superior of the two, is critical of *Tristram Shandy*.

This verbal combat takes place in the presence of a girl to whom both are paying court.

Joachim is critical essentially of Sterne's inability to live and to think a thing through to the end. What he finds lacking in Sterne's life and work is that both have neither consistency nor aim. And this was what his life consisted of, Joachim argues, and goes on: beginnings that were never allowed to continue, which came and then disappeared without trace, bringing him not one step further on his road. What Sterne is missing is a basic yardstick which would allow him to distinguish between what was important and what was not, an ethic that would allow him to determine 'fixed points for life'.

Leo knew that this was tough, that Judith would probably not be able to take this. She would interrupt him if he said this to her, but he wasn't going to tolerate any disagreement from her any more. He forced her to listen, to follow Joachim's argument—that was his statement, his last word on a false, unproductive and trivial life that would lose itself in the pleasures of the senses. In Leo's text the girl present during the two students' discussion was a quiet listener who, however—and this was Leo's tribute to Judith's intelligence—is finally persuaded by Joachim's superior arguments. And what does Joachim do? What is the punch-line of Leo's dialogue? As victor in the debate, it is when, on the point of winning the girl's affection, he sacrifices this affection in the finale of the discussion, on the altar of his ice-cold, mental inflexibility, his intellectual arrogance.

When he was writing this passage, Leo thought for a brief moment that he might be having a relapse, back to the flu, but it was only a surge of mental excitement, a feeling of triumph that had welled up hotly into his head. With the burden of life removed, he wanted in future, so he observed, always to feel this way in life: this was his resolve. He spent two more days putting the finishing touches to this essay in a mood of blessed euphoria. When he took his portable typewriter out of its case and typed out the text, he knew: This piece of work is flawless. The line of argument was impressive but not one-dimensional. The conversation could be interpreted as a dispute between his id and his super-ego, or just as easily as a settling of accounts with his former life, with its reliance on moods and cravings for banal releases; then as a sermon of importance to world history preaching a monumental, ethical demeanour, or equally as a private miniature work of art, rich in allusion, in which nevertheless the immanent, compelling logic of the argumentation is not forced into the background.

When Leo had written Judith's address on the envelope, had inserted the text and taken it to the post, he felt—the first rays of Spring sunshine! On the way to the post office he blinked into the sunlight in melancholy euphoria—like a plant which has just begun to sprout. My life is completely plant-like, he thought—this is not an estimation, it is a statement. This is what I am and in this way I must live. He was seized with disquiet when he thought of the asexual implications of this image.

He was sitting at home in his armchair drinking tea. Judith's naked arm, beautiful like carved marble, lying on the counterpane—what did he say? You have to smoke even in bed. Her hard face, not beautiful, so lovely. It wasn't a picture but a knowing that this had happened, and that he hadn't snuggled up to her. What had she said? You remind me of Tristram Shandy. Well, now he had made things clear. It was out. Out without a hitch. This headache. A pain that begins diffusely in the diaphragm and, like a gas whose molecules have sharp barbs, spreads into the gut, climbs somehow up the spine and into the head where it materialises, a glowing leaden current—it flows to behind the forehead and runs, wonder of wonders, out of the nose in the form of stupid snot . . . Perhaps he really should have taken something to cover his head on the way to the post office. After days of apathy, days of leafing listlessly through his dissertation material, days of staring in total incomprehension at his idea sheet, as he called it (Idea for essay: . . .), of tea-drinking, dozing, sleeping, he realised that the week of great suffering and of the pain of separation had been the happiest week of his life. The rift with Judith, the literal rift, had made him happy and meaningfully productive, but now that everything was out he threatened to sink back down into the old lethargy, out of which earlier only some kind of erotic revelry had briefly released him; however, this he had now forsworn when he had made his majestic choice of The Opus. He had been able to write a brilliant essay because he had recognised the necessity for a renunciation of Judith and of that life which she, as the object of his longing, represented; because he had recognised the necessity for an absolute purity of thinking, for an uncompromising dedication to his Opus, which would only be able to unfold in total concentration.

Now, since the separation was complete and he found himself alone with himself in total concentration, an almost unbearable nervousness seized him. For whom or rather against whom should he now continue to work? He needed Judith more urgently, more unconditionally than he had previously believed he had—that is, he needed her still. He needed her in order to renounce her, a renunciation which each and every day he had to make the effort to renew. He needed her as his polar opposite: by keeping her at arm's length he would maintain his position in the realm of thought. He needed her as the recipient of his Opus, in which he has to explain why he doesn't need her as the 'recipient' of his life. He needed her as the constant object of a longing which he forbade himself. One has to get rid of the longing for consummated love, but not of the longing itself. Now that it was all over, all impetus had deserted him. To fulfil the purpose of the essay, he should never have sent it off.

Perhaps she hadn't received it yet—he could ring up and ask her to destroy it unopened, and—Of course she'd received it, she must have received it a long time ago. He rang her. She didn't answer. Half an hour later he rang again. From now on he redoubled his efforts to regain her as an object of unconsummated longing. And if it so happened, if desire should, like a spanner, so to speak, jam up the works and he should win her completely, fuse with her, just once, who would say no, who wouldn't understand? But then the effect would be to thrust him back all the more deeply into the happy pain of concentration. For that was all that he required: a condition of constant longing.

He courted her with persistence but always as if from a great distance, which he stuck to with equal persistence. He continually built bridges between them which he never set foot on, spanning the gulf which separated him from the life of the senses. This gulf existed only in his fantasy, but his fantasy required this gulf in order, when he looked down, to get a sensation of depth and the pleasant shiver of gentle vertigo. And the bridges, which were as much a part of his fantasy as was the gulf—would they bear his weight if he were to step onto them? No, they bore his weight because he didn't step onto them, creations carved out of air, put together with self-imaginings. On days when he didn't see Judith he wrote her letters as if he were sending them from another country. He ended these letters with the words: 'As ever, your sincere friend, Leo' or 'With warmest greetings from your true friend, Leo.'

When strolling with Judith in the Vienna Prater, he adopted the habit of walking like an old man, reflectively and bent forward slightly, with his hands held behind him. To touch Judith, hold her by the arm or put his arm round her shoulders, could well have entered his head, but the one hand held the other firmly behind his back. He repeatedly replied to the thoughts Judith expressed, even if he was hearing them for the first time, with a sharp 'Wrong!' under his breath, so that he could arrive systematically by such rejection at more wide-ranging and radical thoughts that he would then make a note of later when he got home.

In moments of exuberance Judith would tug him by the arm or skittishly shove him from behind in order to get him to walk faster, but he stuck to his old-man's gait, let her run on a little and observed how finally she would wait for him to catch up with her. Confronted thus with this craving of youth for movement and life, Leo was able consciously to stir up in himself a strange feeling: serenity, as he thought. For he only needed to think the word serenity and the feeling came to him.

The spectacles, which before he had worn only very sporadically, he now wore all the time. He was convinced that these gave him a more intellectual air, even when, more often than not, he would push them up into his hair because they pressed against the wart on his nose.

He sought every opportunity to be near Judith, in order to cultivate in her company the outward signs of a remoteness and distance from life which then of course rooted themselves deeply inside him. Soon he could no longer cross the road with Judith without, after looking right and left, having to reckon with some profound thought.

The more often he met together with Judith, the greater became his longing and his melancholy, because a real and lasting union with her was supposed to be prohibited to him. The greater the longing, the more often he met up with her, or wrote to her. Sometimes there were kisses. But at the end of the day the warmth was like that between siblings, even if his feelings were somewhat more inflated. Leo suffered because of this. But the suffering paid off. 'Longing and Form' came out of it.

Once he spent a whole night at Judith's place. Over tea and whisky Dostoyevsky was discussed, of course with Leo drinking more tea, Judith more whisky. Suddenly they noticed that it had grown light outside and through the window they could hear the birds twittering. That was their first night together. From this arose a piece of work on Dostoyevsky that Leo wanted to turn into the starting point of a comprehensive theory of the novel. However, nothing came of this.

Judith's flat astonished Leo—more than astonished him: it made him envious. It was so lovingly and cosily arranged. No comparison to his flat. How much better he could work, if he were to live here at Judith's place. How comfortable everything was here—you wouldn't ever have to leave the house. You could stay at home all day, you could read for hours on end with no difficulty on the soft sofa with all its cushions, write at the large desk with its comfortable office chair—and the oil stove was also far more practical than his coal stove: you wouldn't have to think about putting on more coal and so interrupt important thoughts all the time. The idea was absurd. He would have to make his own flat more liveable in, he thought, create pleasanter and more appropriate living and working conditions. Then he would feel more at home at his place, wouldn't have to escape so often, would be able to increase his productivity. This thought was equally absurd. Just as absurd as the thought of buying other things to wear simply because he suffered so much from wearing those suits he always had on. This was out of the question. Not just because Leo didn't have much money. The expense, though. You'd have to walk around town looking for what you had in mind, comparing prices in the various shops—you'd have to make as much as possible yourself to bring the cost down and even then probably have to take on some kind of other work to earn yourself something on top—no, only someone with no other purpose in life other than seeing to the external arrangements of his life could contemplate such a thing. From now on he knew, though soon afterwards he forgot it again, that precisely because he had a flat which didn't offer pleasant living conditions, this would increase his productivity. He wore his suits because he had them. Didn't they keep him warm? Of course they did. He lived in his flat because he'd been able to rent it as it stood for a very low price. It even had a desk, didn't it? He could sit and write at this as well as at a more beautiful one, as well as in a cosier sort of room. Leo walked around Judith's flat as if it were the exhibition room in a social history museum. So this was how people lived.

He was flabbergasted by how many mirrors Judith had. There was a mirror even on the desk, there, roughly, where on his desk he had the photo of Löwinger. Was that a place for a mirror? On the wall there hung a series of pictures, all the same size and with the same slim, black wooden frames. They were portraits of Sterne, Kleist, Hegel, Marx, Dostoyevsky. Then a mirror, the same size and with the same frame. In this way, when Leo made an inspection of the row of poets and thinkers, he beheld his own image at the end. He was thrilled. Brilliant, he thought, so ingenious—something like this at least he would like to put up in his flat. He did another inspection of the row of portraits. Sterne, Kleist, Hegel, Marx, Dostoyevsky, Singer. A hot flood of excitement came over him, a feeling of importance, of fascination for the great riddle of the future, the answer to which was so fleetingly revealed in the mirror. Such a portrait gallery, if he had one in his place—how it would spur him on in times of crisis in his work. But maybe not. A sudden feeling of oppression. What if every effort he made, no matter what, were to turn out in the end like a mirror picture of a story written down by others? A mirror doesn't give a damn who steps in front of it, does it? Think of Sterne. Hadn't he thoroughly and irrefutably disposed of Sterne? Leo stepped to one side and now saw Judith in the mirror, sitting on the sofa and watching him motionlessly.

The hard face of his mother. The pedantically rigid bearing. Not once did she ever brook contradiction. She never for one moment expected there to be any. Once she had had her say, there was nothing more to be said. His father wasn't looking at all good. Was he ill? Perhaps it was only that this situation was particularly unpleasant for him, too. We have had the patience of Job, said his mother, and all the understanding in the world. On our return to Vienna one had to find one's feet, one had to get accustomed to things. We understood that. But one can't study for ever, though. One can't study for ever, Leo. The Ungars' son is the same age as Leo, she said to his father—he has his doctorate and works in a lawyers' office. The Pongers—their son is two years younger. He teaches in a school. People have said: why is young Singer studying philosophy. What will he do with that. We have been understanding. We said: he will know. But, she said, giving Leo a stern look, all understanding, all patience must come to an end at some point. It might cost us dear and one wouldn't be doing you a favour. One cannot study for ever.

My mother, Leo explained, always says 'one' or 'we' when she speaks. I have sat there and done nothing but try to remember whether I have ever heard her say 'I'. I can't recall a single occasion. She says patience must come to an end as if that were an objective matter, as if it were quite impossible for her in person to have any more patience, as if patience or understanding or love were not something individual that she could feel. No, patience must come to an end, that is an objective fact about which she can do nothing. All she can do is state the facts of the matter. Full stop, finished, money supply cut off.

Now I know where you get it from, said Judith.

What?

Your tendency to formulate every one of your thoughts as an object-ive fact, said Judith—every idea you have is straightaway a general piece of data. You never say: 'I think that—,' but always: 'There is no doubt that—.' Well, that's the impression I get.

There are no two people on earth more unalike than my mother and I, said Leo—then almost shouting: My mother, you're crazy—she's got no idea, sits at home or in the café with her bridge cronies—beyond that she knows nothing and yet she has her notions about life. How to write a dissertation—she hasn't the first idea.

And you, you've got some idea about life, said Judith—she ran on a few steps, turned round and then continued walking, but backwards, in front of Leo, laughing the while. You don't even play bridge.

It was a beautiful Spring day. The chestnut trees in the Prater were in full bloom. Leo had no eyes for them.

That's mad. It's impossible talking to you, he said. Panic seized him. He was to receive money from his parents for one more year—that was the compromise. This time he had really expected some understanding from Judith—he really needed some. But what she had said was outrageous.

His anger with Judith had its effect, however. One chapter of his dissertation resulted from it. An interpretation of the Hegelian concept *Subjective Spirit*. This piece of work was meant to be an illuminating analysis of the beginning of Hegel's Phenomenology but what really excited Leo was that this text, in the minds of Hegel scholars so to speak, though without their noticing, constituted an argument with Judith and could be read by her as a message addressed to her personally.

In this private subtext to the academic one Leo held up a mirror before Judith in which she was forced to see herself as *Natural Consciousness*, full of aporia and capable only of false objectivisations of reality. Leo wrote this part with some tenderness but unsparingly, filling it with allusions to things that Judith had said to him. Then Leo himself made his entrance as *Philosophical Consciousness*, with a second mirror which he held opposite the first. Unending reflection could now be seen in the mirrors which mirrored each other back and forth ad infinitum, this making Judith/*Natural Consciousness* dizzy but which Leo/*Philosophical Consciousness* fully controlled. He, of course, had the matter in hand. The mirrors. Was that the truth, then? No. With relish, Leo led Judith to the truth. Where before she had seen only the singular, now she was able to see an awful, endless multiplicity. Now Leo took Judith by the hand so to speak—he loved her hands—and said: So now plunge your hands into the fullness of life, plunge down into the depths which open up before you in all their wealth. Leo revelled in the fact that Judith didn't catch hold of anything or, as he wrote: grasped nothing. He loved

53

puns, something he got from Hegel. Her hands knocked against the smooth surface of the mirror—the glass—her beautiful slim long fingers. What is that? Illusion only. The depth—illusion only. Infinity—illusion only. This is the work of mirrors. Do you see: What is simply reflected is not the truth. Only knowledge of the mirror, that is, reflected reflection is the truth. Look—and he pulled Judith close to him. Have we fused together? Formed a unity. Or are we distinct? For the mirror it's all one—it makes no distinction. On the other hand we are many. Just look at the number of duplications of ourselves the mirror makes. With Judith snuggled up to him he twisted and turned around between the two mirrors. And now pay attention. He turned one of the mirrors round. The duplications had disappeared. It was a conceptual dance, a ballet of the mind, a festival of reflection. He spun around with Judith, hip to hip, leg against leg, another turn—then he turned the second mirror round—and now? Have we disappeared? Yes, it seems as if we have, and yet we are here—your word and mine assure us of that; he turned one mirror back and asked: what do you see now? Something quite different. And I can mirror that, too, into infinity. He showed her this with the help of the other mirror. And now I'll show you the truth! He smashed both the mirrors—do you see: only glass, only illusion. The truth does not lie in what is mirrored. The truth lies in the knowledge of the nature of the mirror. What is simply reflected is arbitrariness. Only the reflection of what is reflected makes true objectivity possible, not the knowledge of this or that but of the objective arrangements of visible reality.

He let Judith go but she was immediately impelled back towards him. Individual consciousness, once it realises its contradictions, is impelled towards philosophical consciousness. How harmoniously they moved together now. That was the choreography of the mind.

Before Leo put the text in the envelope to send it to Judith, he read it through once more with satisfaction. Flawless, he thought. The interpretation was sound, the language coruscating, its sleight of hand audacious. Leo's eyes roamed across the typed lines as if through a familiar childhood landscape—this is the only thing, he thought, which in my heart of hearts is important and meaningful to me.

In an accompanying letter he wrote amongst other things: 'When you have read this, when you have really read it, then you will know everything about me: then you will know the best part of my life; more and better than I could otherwise say. Then you will also know—you know this, don't you?—to whose mind I am indebted for this piece of work, whose image stood so graphically before my eyes all the time during its composition, thus enabling me to have these perceptions.'

Leo was euphoric. Maintaining this tempo, he would even be able to complete his dissertation on time. Whatever might come later, what he would live on after this year, this he would leave undecided for the time being. Live. Undecided.

The euphoria, however, didn't do him any good. His work faltered. His letters to Judith were not answered. His chapter on Hegel and the accompanying letter: no answer. Every time he rang Judith, he couldn't get through. And she didn't ring him. His work came to a standstill. It lacked opposition. Who should he turn to in order to prove something to. The world? However broad were the terms in which he thought, they were too abstract to motivate him. Furthermore, 'the world' was where life took place and he felt himself to be cut off from life. He wanted something from life—but obviously not to lose himself in it. He knew that he could only be productive by renouncing life. But for that he had to have that minimum of life at least that would enable him to say: this I renounce. Absolute nothingness. No incentive. Even a visit to his mother did nothing to improve the situation. He had undertaken it consciously for this reason: to have something again to push against, as he thought. Hatred, any kind of incentive. But there was nothing there. He thought of suicide. But suicide without having at least one manuscript tucked away in a drawer? With no evidence of how much genius had gone to so early a grave—no, without some opus, that would be as if he had never existed. And suicide without an *Early Life*, without a *Last Years*—that was unthinkable. He would have to have completed at least the main features of a brilliant piece of work. Enough for a posthumous publication taken from off his desk where it would need to be found. For one second Leo, sitting listlessly in his armchair and gazing at his wall of books, believed that the incentive to work was beginning to stir in him again. But unfortunately this was not so. He couldn't work for death, only against life.

In town he walked from one coffee house to another, and read all the newspapers, just to kill time. 'Negro Demonstration in Washington. Thousands of blacks held a demonstration in front of the White House.' If Judith had been there, this newspaper announcement would have provoked him to a virtuoso performance, a pointed display of linguistic criticism. 'Salzburg. Students held a noisy demonstration with wind instruments against the Beatles'—that would have stirred him into making a nice little sneering observation to Judith, at the very least. But Leo read just 'demonstration' and thought of Judith—he was a seasoned veteran, wistfully recalling past battles: the demonstration in front of the Burgtheater, the discussion with Judith in the bathtub.

On these walks he overestimated the warmth of the Spring sunshine. However, the resulting pharyngitis enabled him to get a lot of sleep for two weeks. When he was feeling physically better again, he finally received a letter from Judith.

'Dear Leo,' she wrote, 'I expect you'll be thinking that I can only receive and post letters but not thank people for them and reply to them—well, now you can see that's not true. First and foremost I must say that your last letter, along with your piece on Hegel, was a real joy to read—it showed me (even if you don't believe it perhaps) a very fine side of you which is a pleasure to see. For it's possible to sense, despite the rather melancholy self-analysis,'—Leo was sweating with excitement as he read. He wiped his forehead with his handkerchief but he had forgotten his spectacles which he had pushed up into his hair and which now clattered down in front of him on the desk top—he started violently. Self-analysis. He shook his head—'the genuine hunger and healthy appetite with which you are now working. They say a man loves a woman properly when he recognises and loves everything that is hidden in her: he has to devour her down to the last morsel and lick the plate clean. That's how it is now with you and philosophy—this comes across in your letter.' The rest of the letter couldn't further increase Leo's emotional confusion. Well, well, that can be cleared up. Everything can be cleared up. In the letter Judith suggested they meet at the *Café Sport*.

Leo planned such a lot in advance of this meeting. He wanted to ask Judith what she meant in certain places in her letter. Where had she been hiding for so long that he'd never been able to get hold of her? Was the fact that she hadn't got in touch with him for weeks a sign that he meant nothing to her? But Judith's praise put paid to all this. Not Judith's praise, of course, but Leo's reaction to it. Judith said that she had found his work on Hegel extremely interesting—extremely interesting, she said, but unfortunately she knew far too little about Hegel—she hadn't yet read anything of his. She wanted to have some things that Leo had referred to in his essay explained to her in more detail. She asked for this. Leo gave her a lecture. This lecturing made him happy. It gave him faith again in his intellectual powers. Assertions which fell as a matter of course from his lips, bold and creative theses which he never arrived at otherwise unless he was working at home. My thesis is, Leo said repeatedly.

On this evening at the *Café Sport*—Leo would otherwise have almost been completely happy again—they made the acquaintance of Lukas Trojan.

Leo had many reasons for being defensive and mistrustful. For a start Trojan was drunk. Secondly—and this was probably attributable to the well-known relaxing effects of alcohol, though not in the case of Judith unfortunately, but somehow with her, too—Trojan was making advances to Judith. It was clearly for this reason that he had come over to their table. Thirdly, Trojan was fat. He wasn't markedly so but the overall impression he gave was anything but ascetic. In intellectual conversation—which Lukas Trojan did his level best to join in with— Leo trusted only thin, lanky people. Only such people showed that they were fully committed to an aversion to outer life and dedicated to a life of reflection. Reflection does not put fat on your thighs. But the soft rotundity of Lukas, that had to be the result of sensual pleasures to which he was clearly far from being averse. And lastly Trojan's trendy style irritated him: his hair half covered his ears and, at the back of his neck, came down over his collar. He must have bought the shirt he was wearing that same day—it looked as if it had never been in the wash— what's more, shirts that you've had for some time don't have such large collars, thought Leo. And his jacket, too—that had definitely not been a present from his parents, even though he was noticeably younger than Leo. It turned out that Lukas Trojan was twenty-one, exactly the same age as Judith. A good year, said Trojan, beaming at Judith. Leo gave a tortured smile. He felt himself being sidelined by this bloated, softly-leaking barrel of a man. Why was he making the effort to smile? Angrily he made a solemn pledge on the spot to adopt an unfriendly expression—it was as if he had ripped off his smile with a quick jerk like a piece of sticking plaster. Trojan's breezy manner of joking with Judith, grinning ingenuously at Leo or looking on with curious interest, smarted like salt in a wound. Aggressive looks simply bounced harmlessly off his smooth, well-padded face. How could he get rid of him? Leo experienced Trojan as a force of nature which the mind confronts helplessly like a coming storm. The invasion of life into his life. So that's what people are like. They do what they want. Chaos ensues. There is no longer any distance, no respect, no form. Judith was laughing as if amused. And the way she held herself: she was attracted to Trojan. Leo pushed his chair back a little and crossed his legs. His foot made a loud knock as it hit against the table-leg. In my experience, said Trojan. Experience, of course, what else could he have to talk about. Everything he said was so spongy. Leo didn't believe a word of it. Trojan was one of these fat fellows who, when they are young, look a lot older, but then, when they are older, give the impression of being young again, which is a way of avoiding being who you really are.

The noise in the café was getting on his nerves. Judith's soft smiles were getting on his nerves. Look at the way Trojan was eating his savoury snack—those amorous, delicate gestures with his hands that fat people make when they're eating. Leo would have liked to have punched Trojan in the face. Leo felt the table-leg against the calf of his right leg which he had crossed over his left. He had the feeling that he was roped to the table-leg. He had a bad attack of wind. He pushed his spectacles up into his hair—Trojan now leaked out of himself completely. It's very important to see clearly that, Leo said shrilly—he meant that Trojan should see that he was not wanted there. But Leo was speaking about Hegel. The second chapter of the Phenomenology: *Perception, or The Thing and Deception.* Leo was forced to fall back on his subject: the illusions that an individual consciousness can fall prey to regarding objective reality. Such insincerity. Leo knew that he wasn't being serious and he began to sweat. But what was he to do? It was the only thing he knew to do. We were just saying when you came over here and sat down that . . . said Leo, by which he meant it was now time Trojan left them in peace again. Leo began to lecture. Would it be possible to bore Trojan? That might take quite a while perhaps. In the relation that ensues, said Hegel, said Leo, looking at Judith longingly, every moment is not just an *Also*, that is, an indifferent unity, but also *One*, that is, an exclusive unity. Leo stressed the word 'exclusive'. Trojan couldn't understand that but he would have to in the end. Can you drive someone away with intelligence? Leo drank more wine than usual. He talked and talked, suddenly fascinated by all the things that came into his mind, as if a lock-gate had opened. It's important to understand first that . . . said Leo and Trojan nodded. At this moment an earthquake couldn't have given Leo a bigger shock than that slight movement of Trojan's head. Trojan's face was, of course, expressionless and smooth but his eyes—they were actually intelligent in some way. Trojan was an intelligent boy. Leo felt uplifted by this nod and by the concentrated look of the listener whom he saw in front of him now strongly magnified and at the same time hazily, like a sea of people, a numberless spellbound crowd. Leo had in actual fact now doubled his

audience. That inspired him. The words poured out of him of themselves. He had the feeling he could now lean back comfortably and
listen with the others to a brilliant speech coming out of the radio, to
then ask afterwards: how was I?

An interesting thought! said Trojan. Do you mean by that, that . . . ? By
that I mean that . . . ! said Leo enthusiastically. He wasn't yet completely
clear as to what was happening to him but intuitively he understood—and
so deeply that he nearly lost himself in this feeling—that what he had been
missing up till now in his mental life was a pupil. He needed not just
opposition, he needed a pupil, too. Only then would the reflections that
came to life as a result of opposition be conveyed back into life. He polished
off his wine in one draught and energetically ordered some more, as if
wishing to demonstrate publicly that all those attributes ascribed to prominent intellectuals applied to him as well, even alcoholism.

His pupil was not concentrating. He was leaning across to Judith, was
whispering something to her. Leo bent forward and raised his voice. He
bent even further forward over the table towards Trojan. Trojan leant
even closer to Judith. Judith threw her head back and laughed—it was
as if a storm were blowing through the café and everyone was bending
in one direction like blades of grass.

Now what had she said? Trojan was looking at Judith and laughing.
How noisy it was in this café. An unbelievable racket—in Leo's head.

Lukas! said Leo sharply. Judith! said Lukas Trojan. Leo kept on at
Lukas, who then said something to Judith. It irritated Leo when Judith in
one of his pauses for breath said something that distracted Trojan again.
What was she talking about there? Why doesn't she let Trojan listen? Why
doesn't she leave now? He stopped, horrified. Quickly he turned to Judith
with a helpless, appealing tenderness of the sort a husband employs to
make up for an infidelity before it is discovered. But this only served to
draw Judith back into the centre of interest, that is, of Trojan's interest,
too, so that Leo immediately began to speak again to Trojan, whose head
was only a few inches from Judith's shoulder, bending far over the table, as
if he wanted to grab him by the collar and pull him towards him. The
aporia of false consciousness is, said Leo, is, he repeated, savouring
Trojan's alarmed expression, and then ending the sentence slowly as if
he were dictating it. Nothing would have pleased him more than if Lukas
had pulled out a notebook and noted down his words. He now even
accepted a cigarette from Trojan, placing his hand in a confidential
manner on Trojan's as the latter gave him a light. Now he was The
Teacher, lecturing with cigarette in hand and eye resting on the bowed

back of the disciple. He took no notice when Judith said something. Her job was to be impressed by the brilliance of his argumentation and its salutary effect on the talented pupil.

Lukas Trojan did in fact find it interesting, what Leo was lecturing him on. The difference in their ages inspired likewise a certain respect in him, and his present drunken state had the further effect that he experienced the situation as if through a fog swirling about some deep archaic secret. He had indeed sat down at this table because he had felt instantaneously attracted to Judith and also because this man she was sitting with didn't seem to belong to her. But now the intellectual favours that Leo was bestowing on him with such intensity were proving irresistibly alluring. He had a weakness for a demonstrative preoccupation with the mind, if it was idiosyncratic enough to come across as daring and convinced. Convincing, convinced: Lukas didn't distinguish between the two. That was just a question of presentation. He was studying Art History and Philosophy, which meant that he was cultivating, with relish but with no ambition, vague, aesthetic interests. As the son of a well-known Viennese university professor he had never lacked for anything in his life except for the intellectual prominence his father had attained. Leo fascinated him because he couldn't decide whether he was a genius or a loophead. However, he had none of this suffocating, bourgeois narrow-mindedness with which his father graced the family after he had finished his daily stint on his new standard work. On the other hand there was Judith. His trousers were pinching him round the waist—he adjusted them with a swift movement like a shrug of the shoulders. Should he order something else to eat? He pressed his leg up against Judith's as he listened to Leo.

An intelligent boy, said Leo later as he was driving Judith back home. Judith didn't reply—there were deep shadows around her eyes like a small black mask on her face. She remained hidden behind this mask.

And so in the summer Leo, Judith and Lukas drove together to Venice.

What was Leo doing in Venice? Vienna was alien enough to him. If he had come to Venice at the invitation of some annual conference where he was to give a lecture, he would have been only too happy to have looked around the city. If he had come to Venice because he had written something on Giorgione and for this reason had wanted to study the originals which were currently on exhibition at the Academy, then, once back in Vienna, he might perhaps have sung the praises, not only of these, but also of the Piazza di San Marco, of the *tortellini* in the *trattorie*, the *tramezzini* in the bars and even the *vaporetto*. However, he was in Venice for no rhyme or reason, but simply because the mood, as they say, had taken him, and he asked himself while wandering around, lost between vaporetto stops and hotels, sweating in his hot suit and with the handle of his travel bag cutting painfully into his fingers—asked himself immediately after his arrival, therefore—how he could have allowed himself to be 'taken' by such an impulse—the above mood, that is. The search for hotels in this heat totally exasperated Judith and Lukas, making them aggressive towards Leo, as if he could do anything about the fact that the first hotel, the second and the third where they had inquired as to the price for a night, were each so expensive that Leo had had to give the order for an immediate resumption of the search.

This trip had to turn out a disaster. Every trip was, that was Leo's firm conviction. Everything is unfamiliar and costs you money that you don't have. You can't have a decent thought in your head because all the time you're taken up with things which at home were all sorted out long ago— like where you live, for instance. And in return for this you receive impressions that you immediately forget, or which at the very best become jumbled up, because you have no connection with what you see—it has nothing to do with you and because of this you never really understand any of it anyway. Leo resolved to say when later they were sitting together bored over a coffee: Everything that you see abroad can be summed up as follows: I have never seen this before. In this respect this is no different from other things that one has never seen and will never see, either.

That would annoy Judith who had been so keen to make this trip, and it would give Lukas something to note down.

When they found a *pensione* that was as cheap as it looked, it turned out that it had only two single rooms which were only marginally cheaper than a double. Leo, for whom, with the modest monthly allowance he received from his parents, the smallest economy was important, suggested that Judith took a single room, while he and Lukas could share a double. That would work out even cheaper for him, he may have thought, than a single, and anyway there weren't enough singles to go round. Judith laughed and said she didn't need a single, she could lie down in front of the door of the double room so that no-one would disturb the two gentlemen. Lukas put his arm round Judith's shoulders and said that, as a true knight, he could never allow that and that Judith should share a double with him, of course, and that Leo could occupy the single. No, never, said Leo, shocked. He didn't put it past Lukas being serious about this suggestion. I only thought that it costs nearly the same and that one could—

Well, whatever the case I'm taking the double, said Judith. There's virtually no saving to be made with a single and I'd prefer to have more room.

In the end they moved into three doubles. They decided that, after the rail journey and the hunt for rooms, they would first have a short rest and freshen up. At two o'clock they would meet up at reception and go on their first walk about town.

Leo was totally confused: now he was lying down in a double room and, when he looked at the completely superfluous second bed next to the one he was lying on but separated by a night-table, he fumed with rage. He worked out roughly how much three nights was going to cost him for a useless bed on which his travel bag was lying—what on earth was he doing here, he asked himself. His bed sagged like a hammock. The cupboard was made of plastic and was opened by means of a zip. When you opened it, it stank of vomit. The wall had cracks which looked like some script he couldn't understand. Hieroglyphs which were warning him of something perhaps, and he didn't understand the warning, or which were mocking him and he didn't understand that either. Through the shutters the sound of loud voices and laughter penetrated. The natives, thought Leo. What wouldn't he give now to be one of those outside there, for whom everything was familiar. But no, he just had to be in a place where he had nothing to do, lying in a room where he had nothing to do. And what was the point? If everyone was as crazy as Judith, then those people shouting down there would now be in Vienna just like he, Judith and Lukas were here in Venice. He fetched Hegel's *Phenomenology* from his bag and began to read.

Leo was down at reception on the dot of two. Lukas came a quarter of an hour later and by the time Judith came it was nearly half-past. Leo meanwhile had sunk into a listless mood and, when Judith finally turned up, he hated her, all jolly and fresh after a shower and with fresh clothes on and so well-organised: she had a travel guide, a map of the city and knew exactly where they had to go, what they had to see and where the mysteries were that were on public display. And—Leo was quite unable to avoid seeing how beautiful she was. The words failed him because wherever possible he forbade himself words that sounded kitsch. No, it was Lukas he hated, not Judith—he hated him because of his mere presence—how beautiful, how uplifting it would have been if he could have been alone with Judith here and with everyone taking them to be a couple. Perhaps without Lukas it might even have been possible to have shared a double room with her.

While they were walking Leo felt a sudden exhilaration which bewildered him. The colours, the smells, the voices, everything seemed to glitter in the sun, quite unlike Vienna—it reminded him of happy days in Brazil, although this did not make Venice any less unfamiliar. But it was precisely this strangeness that suddenly seemed to open up to him, and to him in particular. All at once he felt himself rising to the occasion, to this trip. It was as if had stumbled on a new talent in himself. The world—why not? Paris, Rome, London, Alexandria. A practised and thus effortless cosmopolitan air would suit him, of all people, down to the ground. He forgot to look around him because in his mind's eye he was having visions of himself, describing his travels in other, quite different places.

But that wasn't the reason why Leo fell into one of the canals. Perhaps the alcohol was to blame, or Leo's muddled anger with Lukas, or both. But maybe he really did just happen to lose his footing. For everything seemed perfectly all right at first. In order not to work up too much of a sweat he sauntered slowly between Judith and Lukas, happier than he had been for a long time. The cobblestones, the swinging hem of Judith's dress, her beautiful, delicate feet stepping forward one after the other always parallel to his, a consummation in movement promising something disquieting if the thought was followed through, the legs disappearing up under the dress, future journeys—London, Paris—cobblestones—his imagination ground to a halt and he saw only cobblestones—he felt so happy that he could have flung his arms round Judith and dictated Lukas some notes.

Lukas, though, tended to create harmonies which, as it were, grated on Leo's ear, and to wreck moments of happiness faster than Leo was able to savour them to the full. When Leo noticed that he could only see his own feet in front of him, he looked up and saw that Lukas and Judith were walking a good twenty steps ahead, arm in arm and quite indifferent to his slower pace. Lukas was, moreover, prone to pamper himself at every opportunity with earthly delights: he just had to have a taste of this roll, here—and then that confectionery in the window there that looked so mouth-watering, no question but he simply had to sample some of that, too. In the first bar they found, Leo just drank mineral water while Judith and Lukas drank campari. Leo was annoyed. Why after only ten minutes did they have to stop for a drink—it cost money and meant they weren't seeing anything of the city. When he wanted to pay for his mineral water, Lukas said he could have it on him. Soon afterwards in the next bar Lukas persuaded Leo to join them in a campari. Leo, who was belatedly peeved that he had been drinking only water earlier when Lukas had offered to pay, agreed. He was surprised how good the campari tasted. He drank it far too quickly and ordered a second. After all, if Lukas was feeling so generous. And he could well afford it. When it came to paying, Judith said: Leo will pay this round—I'll pay the next. The two camparis went to Leo's head so much so that in the next bar, although knowing now for sure that someone else would be paying, he could only drink water. Alcohol in broad daylight and in this heat. It was quite crazy. He was helplessly befuddled. And he'd paid for six camparis only to be treated to two mineral waters which he could have anyway done without.

It was definitely the alcohol. The only question remains why Leo went down the steps that led from the pavement to the canal. These steps were probably there to make it easier to climb into the gondolas, which liked to moor alongside. But there weren't any gondolas there— the steps only led down to the water. Leo said later that he had seen a particularly beautiful palazzo hidden because of a bend in the canal and that he had gone down the steps because he had hoped to get a better view of it from the vantage of the bottom step. Because of the water that lapped over them continually, the steps were algae-covered and slippery. He had only got as far as the second step when he lost his footing and slithered into the water. Somehow it looked artistic, Lukas said later, as if Leo had fallen into the water on purpose in order to then jump back out again, using incredible physical control, and to receive with a laugh the applause of the shocked but admiring bystanders. Leo fell in, however, like a stone. There was no time for any conscious physical reaction—and yet the time that elapsed between the sure knowledge that he was going to fall in and the actual impact was long enough for him to ponder almost forever. The black surface of the water looked like the reverse side of a mirror. Reflecting water. No, not reflecting—it is the reverse side of a mirror. I'm going to break through the mirror into a world that really reflects and leave behind me the unreflecting world that only hides behind the mirror. A loud smack, fragments, splinters—no, splashes, and over his head the engulfing water.

Leo rose to the surface again and what he saw was different from the world he had left behind him, but only insofar as he saw it from a distance that he thought he would never be able to bridge again. The dry people stood on the edge of the canal with that look that could mean any number of things, but one of which would certainly include: How on earth could such a thing happen to anyone? Leo swam back to the steps and climbed out of the water. American tourists with large check trousers and tennis shoes took pictures of him and, laughing, went on their way. Come, we'll go back to the hotel. You must change your clothes, said Judith. Leo wanted to put his head on her shoulder but she drew back. What should I wear, I don't have anything to wear, said Leo. I only have this suit. I thought that for three days in Venice one suit would be enough.

I don't believe it, said Lukas. What have you got in the bag you brought with you, then—you've got a bag with a whole lot of things in. Leo looked about him—the giggling, gawping people. He ran his hand through his wet hair, wiped his face with the back of his hand. My glasses, he said. He looked at the surface of the canal water, once again as smooth as a mirror. My glasses.

You must have something to wear with you, to change into, in your bag, said Judith.

A pool of water had already formed around Leo.

What have you got in your bag, then?

In my bag, he said. Yes. Only books. A change of underwear. And books.

Judith and Lukas took Leo—who now walked much faster than before and like a snail left a damp trail behind him—back to the hotel, instructing him to take a shower—how you stink, said Judith—and to wait in his room. They meanwhile would go and buy him something new to wear.

But the expense, said Leo—the suit will dry out.

Forget the suit, said Lukas.

When Leo was finally standing in front of the mirror all decked out in new clothes, he thought he had vanished and that in his place in the mirror a clown had appeared intent on making fun of him with its sad face.

Judith and Lukas had bought him a pair of blue jeans, tennis shoes and a shirt with a large collar and a multicoloured, complex pattern. And since buying a jacket would have blown Leo's budget, Lukas, who had brought a whole suitcase of clothes with him, gave him a chic, green velvet jerkin. You can keep it, said Lukas. It's a little too tight for me anyway.

Judith thought it suited Leo marvellously.

I can't put that on, said Leo. Nobody would take me seriously in that.

He twisted and turned this way and that several times as if he hoped that from the side or from behind he would present a more familar picture in the mirror, but for him the reflection remained both alien and—supposing it really was himself he saw there—frankly ridiculous.

On the other hand, the way he walked, like a model—that was his first thought, like a model, like a doll—there was something surprisingly elating about it, something more rounded, harmonious—not immediately, of course—he noticed this only by degrees when he allowed himself to be carried along by this elated feeling that came when he turned about and moved—there was something about it—but he had no idea what. It was different. He was different. And yet he wasn't: he was a young man. Now he had a colourful shirt on and looked—like a young man. Why not? Judith liked the look of him. She said so. She said it again. He was very quiet. Not thoughtful. Just quiet and not thoughtful. As if on this new body he had also just placed a new head. Thoughts had to first take shape inside. Form and shape. Lukas was laughing so stupidly. Tugging at him now here, now there, talking smarmy nonsense like a clothes shop assistant. What does that mean—he'll feel more comfortable. A plainer shirt, less garish, wouldn't have shocked him nearly as much, so that he wouldn't now have still needed convincing— and it would probably have been cheaper, too. Besides, it's just ex- ternals. Externals had always been a closed book to him, hadn't they? The colour of the shirt, the cut and material of the jacket—externals. Why was he now so amazed that they—these particular externals— were closed books? He was dressed. That was all. No need to think about it. That's how it's always been—him wearing something. Nothing had changed.

At the very most, his walk had. On the way to the restaurant for dinner. Perhaps it was the tennis shoes—his contact with the ground felt completely different in them, the way he walked felt different—it no longer made his old-man gait possible. Somehow things were looser. Now Leo walked much faster—now it was he who hurried on ahead and had to turn round all the time to see Judith and Lukas dawdling behind.

Perhaps it wasn't just the tennis shoes, perhaps it was also the new trousers. Unused to the rougher and more tightly fitting material, Leo experienced a stronger sense of physicality, of sensuality in them. A young man. That meant of course that he wasn't only rediscovering his youth and the plain fact that he was considerably younger than he had felt and appeared, but that he was also a man. Leo gave a sudden start and stopped short. A boutique. He saw himself reflected in the display window—simultaneously he saw the dummies behind the glass, saw himself, saw the dummies and saw himself in the middle of the dummies. Exactly the same way as what he was wearing, the dummies were modelling as ideal images, the promise of happiness in life which Leo, with beating heart, saw that his own body fulfilled. He shared the ideal image with the dummies but was ahead of them as regards its fulfillment: gender and life. In his own body. Passers-by, young people in jeans, like the shadows and phantoms in Plato's cave, passed through the mirror of the display window, but Leo wanted the light, wanted real life—he turned round and looked at the group of young people who were passing along noisily, laughing gaily in the lantern beam. He himself could pass for one of these. His step became more self-assured, more decisive and—he turned round again towards the group— yes, more elated. And he wondered why all these years he hadn't put up more of a fight against the suits his parents had always given him and in which he had always suffered so much. For far too long he had hidden away in a cramped little shell, in the narrowness of parental limitations, like in an egg, and now this shell had cracked open, fallen away from him and allowed him to appear, to emerge out of the egg as the person he now was. As the one he should be. As the one he really was. A qualititative leap. It was no coincidence, he told Judith and Lukas, that I fell into the canal today—or rather, more accurately, jumped in. And he told them of the regime of terror his mother had established over him with the help of the products of his father's factory, and how freeing himself from this, now, had been long overdue.

Subjectively fell in, objectively jumped in, Lukas laughed—Yes, exactly, said Leo, putting an arm round Judith and hugging her to him briefly.

On arriving at the restaurant Leo didn't go directly to a table with the others but went instead straight to the toilets to have another look in the mirror. With different eyes. It must clearly be seen that... With the insights he now had. Yes. That was it. How could he have thought 'clown'? He was a young man on the threshold of a fine future, liberated from a suffocating past. He was another person—that is, he was now really himself, intoxicated with the feeling of being that other person he could see in the mirror. At last he was really and truly on the threshold, free of the chains of the past. The green jacket—he adjusted it lovingly—could well be regarded as an appropriate allusion to this. And the coloured shirt? It was beautiful. He was young. It gave him a certain air, a certain—artistic air. The shockingly bright shirt and over that the green velvet jacket—the whole thing was bolder and more daring than anything he had ever worn till then, but for that very reason it suited him all the more. The boldness of his thinking, the anti-bourgeois nature of the life he imagined for himself. Yes. And the cruel severity and sharpness of his facial features appeared resolved into soft, sensual contours, ready for whatever experiences life had in store for him. On the first rung of the ladder. Less hard-edged—a softer, hazy look—more youthful. No spectacles. Excitedly Leo washed his hands and examined himself again in profile as he dried them. Completely different. Another man. He was wearing magic clothes.

At table Leo was unrecognisable. He joked, he laughed, he told stories, and kept on giving Judith amorous looks. Not like before. No more strained Walmen-like looks but expressions of frank affection and sensuality which Leo became increasingly aware of and to which he gave full rein. Free of theoretical premises. A qualitative leap. Released. How beautifully Judith's skin glowed after just one day of sun, of sun like in Brazil. The fascinating contrast between her dark hair and light-coloured eyes showed up now even more beautifully. Leo was frightened of Judith. He was drawn to her, drawn more strongly than ever before and at the same time he was frightened, frightened of falling—falling into emptiness, nothingness. I love you, he thought fearlessly, and then there was nothing. Yes, there was: a laugh, a voice which had such a special ring to it that, if he had heard it coming from somewhere, anywhere, he would have felt compelled to explore every room, plunging through the chatter and the tittering of hundreds of people, in order to find out whose laugh, whose voice that was.

Sooner or later we were bound to have met. It was something of that sort that Judith had said right at the beginning when they were getting to know each other. Now, thought Leo, now he wanted this to become true. Now they should meet. Recognise each other. How capable she was in daily matters. How intelligently pragmatic. These qualities should become a part of him. Judith knew as little Italian as Leo but she manoeuvred herself adroitly within the system of similarities and differences to Portuguese with the result that she was able to talk with the waiter and even get him to explain the dishes without any difficulty.

She continually had to ward off Lukas who, as an expert fully qualified in culinary matters and in Viennese tourist Italian, undertook several times to explain the menu, with his hands twirling and pirouetting over the table in a manner reminiscent of a fat television chef.

Lukas laughed as he described the effect Leo's fall into the canal had on the onlookers, and Leo joined in the laughter. Jumped in! Lukas laughed so energetically that the wine slopped over the glass he was holding—jumped in! They laughed until they cried.

Then it was mainly Leo who did the talking. The past, which he had sloughed off, now fused with his present happiness and with his even greater expectations for the future. Oh yes, I must tell you this story, too, said Leo, it's really a prime example. The first time he brought a girl home. He had wanted to introduce her to his parents. Leo described how embarrassed he was by the strong accent of his mother in particular; after so many years in Brazil she still had such a dreadful German accent that it must have been really painful for any Brazilian to listen to, and for this girl, too. But the girl had smiled all the time, had been amazingly sweet and friendly. Leo, though, had almost died of shame because of his mother, who hadn't noticed a thing. Then, during the meal, the girl had asked if she could help herself to some more, whereupon his mother had suddenly said in German: Who does she think she is? One doesn't ask if one can have some more—one waits until more is offered. The girl didn't understand this, of course, said Leo, but she wouldn't have understood if my mother had said it in Portuguese either. She smiled and with her arm reached across to the bowl in question—it seemed to me it lasted several minutes, she sitting there smiling, with her arm reaching out over the table. My mother is a stickler for meticulously correct manners: back straight, as you should sit at table, elbows in, as is only proper—in her hands the cutlery was on its best behaviour, and she demanded the same from me: That is a fork, not a shovel. One doesn't cut large pieces—it doesn't look nice when one has to open one's mouth so wide. One doesn't rush—it looks greedy or as if one doesn't normally get enough to eat. She spoke very decorously but only when her mouth wasn't full. And there was Eliane—that was the girl's name—with her arm stretched right across the table. Someone whose way of eating alone entails such a host of do's and don'ts, as is the case with my mother, is bound to feel that an arm stretched across a table is nothing less than a scandal. My mother would have gone on for hours ignoring Eliane and her arm stretched across the table. So I picked up the bowl and set it down in front of her.

At that moment Leo had of course felt really ashamed of his mother in front of Eliane, and had hated her. He goes and brings a girl home for the first time and what does his mother do? Nothing but check up on whether the girl has mastered some set of conventions.

However, on the other hand—and that was the strange thing, said Leo—he had felt ashamed of Eliane, as well, in front of his mother. He goes and brings a girl home and she doesn't know what's what— behaves in the way she is used to and without a second thought.

But that's exactly what it was all about, said Leo—it was about rules of conduct. His mother had rules of conduct, but then so did Eliane, except they were different. The two hadn't understood each other but he had understood them both and this was why he'd been able to feel mutually embarrassed for them both. But this also showed that he himself had no rules of conduct at his disposal, otherwise he would have immediately taken sides with one or the other. That was the lesson I learnt, said Leo—in life I stand somehow apart, I see it from the outside and can't decide one way or the other. Well, that's how it was then but—that's the past, he said and squeezed Judith's knee under the table.

Was it really true that Leo had once believed, in all seriousness, that life and, by logical extension, love—actual and physical—should remain denied to him? A hare-brained idea that could only have arisen from the hair-shirt mentality that his old suffocating suits had forced on him. An idea that was so far removed from him now. He almost capered as he walked up and down in his hotel room, or rolled from side to side like a sailor. He was spurring himself towards a quick decision. By his calcula-tion they had drunk so much at dinner, and then later in a bar, that Judith would surely fall asleep straightaway. He would have to go to her room immediately, for the last thing he wanted was to wake her and possibly give her a fright. But could he do it just like that? Knock on her door, walk in—say what? Am I disturbing you? Take her in his arms immediately? Feverishly, and while covering her with kisses, remove her clothes? Perhaps she has already undressed. What then? An awkward situation. Her naked and him dressed. Her naked. What then? He rubbed his forehead. Why did he have so little imagination just at that very moment when he was finding himself short on experience.

A naked fact. The naked truth. And like a cloak of invisibility his imagination immediately covered it up. Her naked and him in his magic clothes. An intruder. Would-be intruder. Would be, would like to be, made welcome. Should he then get undressed himself as quickly as possible? But one ought to say something or other at the same time. But what? It should not automatically be assumed that—Even though there is no doubt that—No. He had to come to an immediate decision. He had to go across to her not just before she went to sleep but before she had undressed. Go across. He walked up and down. On the other hand wouldn't it make matters easier if she were already naked? Everything would be plain and simple. The 'imperative tendency'. A tension, an excitement so strong that she... He would. So strong it would be bound to overwhelm them both. Would envelop them immediately. So strong. Of course, to avoid any awkwardness, he might have to go to the trouble of first getting undressed himself, go into her room already naked. They would. Look at each other. In the half-light. Light that filtered into the dark room through the window. And would only be visible from the glimmering brightness on her skin. As if the light came from within her. Reflected light, in truth, reflecting bodies, love that shines like the moon. And... but he couldn't run across the corridor of the pensione. Naked. What if someone came. And what if he—naked in Judith's room and she still dressed? No. Better the other way round. But how? And when? In his pacing up and down the room Leo banged into the side of the superfluous bed a second time. He was a little drunk. And what? He'd lost the point. When did he lose it? He'd definitely been on the point of—Now he wanted to—Now he will—He wound his arms about him, kneaded the green velvet of his jacket, stroked it—he was sweating and shivering with cold at the same time. Why all this huffing and puffing over what was finally a perfectly simple desire? he asked himself. Leo would have liked nothing better than to have banged his head against the bedstead which he had bumped into yet again. No, no more scruples. It was no coincidence that during the course of the evening Judith had allowed him many shows of affection. Had even encouraged him in it. Hadn't she encouraged him? Because the time was ripe. She was probably even waiting for him right now. And here he was wavering in indecision. Up and away. He was now the Other. He was on the point of becoming identical with himself. On the point of going across to Judith. No more ifs and buts. He could walk up and down here for hours after all, without getting short of breath. This was not to be solved by means of thinking. Anyway what does 'thinking'

71

mean in this case? And 'solved'? That was the Other, he could feel it. *Hic Rhodus, hic salta.* The words alone—analysis is endless repetition. For only in the deed do we obtain certainty regarding what someone means to us, what 'to love', what 'I love her' and 'she loves me' means. Only the deed leads to destiny. Whoever desires to know, whoever desires to love, whoever desires earthly salvation, he must make the leap, the leap from word to deed. Subjectively: the fall. Objectively: the spring. To spring—a leak—no, a leap. *Hic Rhodus, hic salta.* The unfathomable black surface of the water. That is the reverse side of the mirror. Coming up to the surface, stepping out into the reflected world. Like the dummy in a mirrored life. A risk. For it can transpire that we don't love the person we love, that the destiny of the one we choose is not our destiny, and that what seems to shine when illuminated by symbolic interpretations loses its brilliance and that we don't find what we were looking for. And yet: *Hic Rhodus, hic salta.* Away with thoughts. Those weren't thoughts anyway. That was a text that ought to be written down sometime later. Idea for an essay. Now for the real leap. He dabbed some aftershave on his cheeks and behind his ears. If only this wind would go away. He left his room. In front of Judith's room he took a deep breath and knocked. He knocked very softly, almost inaudibly because he wanted at all costs to avoid Lukas hearing anything in the next room. No 'Come in!' No answer. It was a real nuisance: he had to knock so softly because of Lukas that it was possible Judith couldn't hear. He tapped once again very softly on Judith's door with the tip of his index finger but nothing stirred. He put his ear to the door but could hear nothing. Suddenly a wave of heat rushed to his head. If someone were to see him now, standing here listening at another person's door. Without a moment's thought he turned the handle—the door wasn't locked. He went in. The room was dark. Judith! He whispered her name. He tried to get accustomed to the darkness. The shutters were closed and not one ray of light penetrated in from outside. His skin didn't glow remotely. Judith! He walked cautiously to the first of the two beds. He knocked against the bed, bent over it carefully and gently— her suitcase was lying there. He walked round the bed to the other one, banged into the side of it. The bed was empty. Leo turned on the bedside light. The room was empty. Judith! Her name was only an unspoken question in Leo's head. She wasn't there. Where could she be? In Lukas's room? But why? That can't surely—Leo turned off the light and rushed out of the room. Breathlessly he stood in front of Trojan's door. His first impulse was to fling open the door and storm

72

into Trojan's room. No. Stop. If Judith was with Lukas, it would be awkward—if she wasn't with him, then it really would be awkward if he burst into the room. He just wanted to know either way. He put his ear to the door. He could hear noises. What kind of noises? Noises. So there was someone in the room. Lukas. That didn't necessarily mean anything. How to determine whether Judith was there with him? Creaking bed? The sounds Leo heard were too indistinct, steps perhaps—were they approaching the door? As fast as it took to put this question Leo was back in his room and had thrown himself on the bed.

Lukas, who had already gone to bed, got up again and dressed. He couldn't get to sleep. Most importantly he had felt a touch peckish. He could see through the window that the bar on the other side of the square was still open. Why not? A dessert and a quick drink—that would certainly be preferable to tossing stupidly to and fro in bed. By the time he was closing the door of his room Leo's vapour trail had only just dissipated.

This trip just had to turn out a disaster, Leo had known it. But he wasn't to have known the disaster would have come up on him from behind. It was, to be sure, a coincidence that Lukas met Judith in the bar opposite, and this coincidence had no significance. Judith was pleased when she saw Lukas entering, just as pleased as she would have been if Leo had suddenly come in. She, too, had not been able to get to sleep. It had seemed even more hopeless to her than usual—the journey, the impressions, the unaccustomed room—she knew that lying in bed in the darkness of her room with her head so full of impressions, thoughts, a flood of pictures with a determined life of their own, that this would be like your whole life on film, which you're said to see again in your mind's eye just before death—a feeling of choking apprehension would have set in, heart pounding, a panic-stricken wait for release, for the call from mother: Wake up!—waiting pointlessly for the echo of an old living threat, the obligatory afternoon sleep, but only the threat lives on, not the echo, for death knows no boundaries, nothing is there, not even a wall that echoes can bounce off. Grappa. She wanted to drink nothing but grappa until everything dissolved—memories, fears—until the screen was blank. Not one picture. Least of all a picture of a man. But men, in an Italian bar, at night, a woman on her own, and already approaches are being made. But even if you ward these off, repulse them, they take it as acceptance, as incitement, as part of the game. And all Judith wanted was peace. She was pleased when Lukas suddenly walked in—a bodyguard with body.

And Lukas was highly gratified, too, when he saw Judith by the bar. The irritation at not being able to sleep was instantly replaced by a feeling of relief, a sudden animation—he became aware that, just as he wanted something more to eat, so he was also keen to talk—he had hardly managed to get a word in during the evening. And there was so much to talk about. With Judith, about Leo, whom together they had kitted out in new clothes that day and who had put on an exclusive performance for them that was crying out to be reviewed. What are you drinking there? Grappa? Fine. I'll have the same. Grappa! Leave the bottle here. You can—leave it—the bottle—here. *Si. Grazie.* And cheese. What kind? Do you have some? Some provolone? Great. And gorgonzola? Do you have some? Which—brands? That's important, he said to Judith who was looking at him astonished, I mean, since we're in Italy.—What does 'the usual' mean? Look on the wrapping. What's the name?—Yes. We have two. 'Santi Novara' and 'Arioli Achille'—that's expensive, of course.—Yes, that one. Great. That's a piece of luck. Santi Novara is an industrial cheese, really good compared to what you can get in Vienna. On the other hand an industrial cheese and what we get at home, that's not proper gorgonzola, of course, they're mock gorgonzolas. Santi Novara's easily better by comparison. But Arioli Achille—Lukas kissed the tips of his fingers—that's one of the last firms who still work according to the classic methods. There's also Carlo Gelmini, Santi & Co, of course, who produce, by the way, the famous Fior di Pannerone, then there's also the Franco thingummy, Franco, oh, doesn't matter, Franco whatever, and a few more, very few, everything else is industrial, plain industrial. *Grazie.* Do you want to try some? No? You should. You won't get many second chances with this. So, cheers. He knocked back the grappa and poured Judith and himself another each—Judith's relief that the men in the bar were now leaving her alone—her astonishment as she watched Lukas eating: the amorous way he looked at the cheese, cut it and raised it to his mouth, the expression of delight on his face and at the same time this abandoned indifference when it came to chewing his food—he stuffed it in, talking at the same time, shoved in a piece of cheese followed immediately by some bread without having swallowed, and he talked and stuffed it in, and then this beaming, happy laughter—it seemed obscene to her whenever someone laughed and you could see the remains of food sticking between their teeth.

Help yourself, dig in, said Lukas. Cheese is quite a turn-on, you know. His face was getting progressively rounder, more and more like a hamster with his cheek pouches full of provolone and gorgonzola—Look! he said rapturously. This is really top class—on the rind here, do you see, you can even make out the bore-holes for the pricking, and do you see the shape of the veins? Definitely not machine-pricked, that's clear to see. The pricking? That's done as follows. Cheese is a science—Oh, apropos of science—the professor had me in stitches today.

That was the first time that Leo Singer was referred to simply as 'the professor'. Judith knew immediately that he meant Leo—she even thought the *apelido*, the nickname, was funny, apt—but she didn't like the tone of voice in which Lukas said it.

Now the way he fell into the canal—or more accurately one should say—Lukas raised his index finger—He jumped. A jump, yes. Off his rocker. Lukas tapped his forehead. Cracked. The sad figure of the professor, he said, with his face stuffed full to bursting, as it seemed, bloated. Wise words, ridiculous actions, said Lukas, shaking his head—delicious, simply delicious, he said—look, you can still see the outlines of the kneaded blocks in this cross-section of provalone. The blocks are warmed up in the whey, cut up into pieces, allowed to curdle briefly and then kneaded in hot water and rolled into hanks, then, once warmed up again, fashioned into pear, ball or sausage shapes—the pear shapes are the classic ones. They're then allowed to harden in cold water before being laid in brine. With really top class provolone, if you cut open the pear you can still see the shape of the fulling and kneading—there, for instance, do you see. Looks like a fine crack. Yes, the professor. A sad figure. He, excuse me—Lukas swallowed with difficulty, shaking his head: he had had to belch at the same time—he clearly wants to make me into his Sancho Panza but—Lukas drained his glass of grappa and gave himself a shake. Cheese! Do you really not want any cheese? You'll never get one as good as this at home.

At home, thought Judith—the way he says 'at home'—so matter of fact. Everything for him is so matter of fact: the way that for him where he comes from is home—that he knows what to stuff into himself here, knows where he is now—that he is the way he is—and that he takes it for granted that people will agree when he talks disparagingly about someone else. That was precisely what Leo was talking about over dinner, the blinkeredness of one's own rules of conduct—if Lukas had understood that, he wouldn't be able to speak the way he's doing now. He disgusted her now. He'd tumbled to a thing or two, that was true, but he hadn't grasped the most important thing, which was—

Did you see how he acted on the way to the restaurant—and then in the restaurant? By the way—the portions were small. Expensive—mediocre—and small portions. Looked so nice from the outside—the restaurant. Never mind. Anyway, Leo at dinner. That was an education. A real eye-opener.

Exactly, said Judith. She wanted to remind Lukas of what Leo had said at dinner, tell him what he could have learnt from it, but Lukas was already talking again, spurred on by what he assumed was Judith's agreement. Acted like some young amateur Romeo. New costume, new role. Ridiculous, wasn't it? If we'd bought him a suit of armour, he'd have believed he was a knight. Actually we should have done. He poured himself another glass of grappa and drank it down in one. An amorous look. Almost like Leo's at dinner. A little more uncertain but cockier and more superficial. For the last time and for just one second Lukas came across as Leo's pupil. Should have done. In a suit of armour Leo would have explained to us, explained the objective meaning as to why he could liberate himself and the world only in this armour. If we'd bought him a grass skirt—oh, yes, we should have bought him a grass skirt—he snorted with laughter. Judith was shocked that Lukas was right in one respect and yet was so wrong. Was so unjust. It wasn't true. Leo was not ridiculous. Not, or rather not just ridiculous. She drank her grappa and tried to think of the right words to say—what words? There were words with which she could have defended Leo but these words wouldn't muster themselves and anyway she was drinking, after all, in order to purge everything, the pictures and the words, too. And there were also words that wanted to see Lukas go to the devil but these words were toothless, a faint echo, echo of response to what Lukas was saying all the same; if he didn't hear this echo, if he talked, then he wouldn't hear it either, even if she moved her lips to form it. She simply watched Lukas, wordlessly, no, not wordlessly: quietly. But you can't say anything to him, said Lukas, he talks and talks—I mean, it was really very interesting what he was saying but—

Quite, said Judith, but she gave up—Lukas had already continued talking. That's right, but you can't say anything to him, he won't tolerate any contradiction, not even when he contradicts himself, because he changes suddenly from one day to the next—I've never seen anything like it—he talks and—Lukas stuffed a bit of cheese and a piece of bread into his mouth—talks—did you see: he even let his meal get cold. But if you interrupt him because you want to make some comment perhaps, then he gets really prickly. Ah yes, pricking—a science. I've eaten nearly all of it but look, here you can see, the cheese was pricked here. The cheese is punctured with long hollow needles so that air can get in. That's called pricking. Without that the blue veins wouldn't be able to form. They form alongside the bore-holes. Those are then the veins. So the cheese ripens from the outside to the inside. People always think the ripening begins inside but it begins outside. From outside to inside. Along the little canals that are made by the needles. The canal speeds up, as it were, the inner ripening. That's the pricking. Those are the veins. Do you see? Don't you want any? Really not? All right, then, all good things must come to an end! Lukas polished off the remains of the cheese, washed it down with grappa—cheese is a good stomach plug, I always say—shall we sit down? No? O.K. we'll stay standing—I like standing, no problem. Where were we—ah yes, Leo—Have you seen the way he grabs me grandly by the arm whenever he says something he somehow thinks, thinks at the time, is particularly significant, vital? What's he playing at? Does he want me to say: Yes, professor? Am I supposed to write it all down or what? Let his meal get cold, he did. Pitiful. Really pitiful. The way he pranced about like some dandy suddenly. Don't you think. It's true, isn't it. What do you say?

What sort of an expression was Judith wearing? Motherly, she thought. Only because she suddenly became aware of the age differ-ence. How could the guzzling, twenty-one year-old goof bring himself to speak in such a way about a thirty-year old, without a second thought, but then of course that was the reason for his ignorant—yes, Leo was—but on the other hand—

His mother, said Lukas. Quite by chance he slips, falls in the canal, I give him my green jacket, and he explains everything in terms of his mother. I mean, really. Grappa? They drank—Lukas refilled the glasses. You can't take someone like that seriously—at least I can't anymore—how can you take him seriously? His face was tilted towards Judith, bloated, blurred and shiny; his mouth still insatiable—when he laughed, the yellow remnants of cheese and bread between his teeth. Judith pulled back stiffly a little—he should stop talking—he should take his hand away from there—A head-case, said Lukas, shaking his—he talked non-stop, talked and drank—Judith drank and was silent, as if paralyzed by a weird play she was watching—finally he took his hand away in order to poke about between his teeth with the nail of his little finger.

77

The bar was emptying. Judith would so liked to have been alone once more. One more glass of grappa and then sleep. She could have said: I'm tired, I want to sleep. Some kind of friendly escape formula. But she said: You're getting on my nerves. She said: Leave me alone. She said: I want to drink my grappa and not hear another word.

Lukas made an attempt to clear up what he tried to make out was a misunderstanding—she'd not heard him right, he'll soon clear things up, a nice fat boy—he reached out and took Judith by the arm—she said just one word, impossible to misunderstand, her eyes as hard as enamel, glinting threateningly within their bordering dark shadows.

Leo was dead tired the next day. Imagination. He didn't have any, as he had noticed, which is why it had marked time on one spot throughout the night, leaving him so enervated. Judith's eyes were puffy; she was reticent and irritable. Lukas also seemed hungover, irritable, brusque. He said he wanted to travel on to Florence. He was going to set off straightaway. Judith was drinking coffee and gave a bored nod. Leo was perplexed. The jacket, he said—Keep it, said Lukas.

Lukas was barely gone when Judith said she wanted to be alone a bit, to spend the day alone—we'll meet up at five in the afternoon at reception, Leo. Suddenly Leo found himself sauntering about Venice alone, not knowing who had walked out on whom. Had Judith walked out on him or had Lukas? Or had Lukas walked out on Judith? But most importantly: why?

Leo didn't know where he should go all by himself. He walked down here and down there. By himself. But who was 'himself'? That was the question. The daylight was brilliant—every view was overlit or, whenever Leo stepped into the deep shadows, underlit. Leo could discern light and darkness. Everything else still lay ahead of him. He was now very young. The days of being tied to the table-leg were past. And past were the days when the rich but familiar world of Löwinger's house and garden was his only world. And everything after that time led back to this point where he was stepping out for the first time into the real world. Everything after that time was only an attempt not to make that step, were phantasies that a Löwinger-like art-world must have produced and to which he had tied himself. Who was he? Who was this young man in the green jacket? He could no longer be a phantasy figure like the one that ran out into Löwinger's garden. Absolutely not. No. It must be clearly seen that—No. Leo couldn't see anything clearly—everything in front of him lay in light or darkness and so disappeared. It is not by chance that—No. Everything was chance, so arbitrary. Led back to this point. Why now. Why here. Step out. Why here. Where to. Leo crossed squares in glittering light, plunged into the shadows of narrow alleyways, the sounds of water slapping against stone, voices, smells—nothing was commonplace, everything sought to pass itself off as commonplace. Time didn't pass. What should he do until five. He knew he wouldn't retain any memories of this day, no pictures. All of them overexposed or underexposed.

But time did pass, of course.

What did you do today?

I walked around in the city and then went and had a look at the Giorgione exhibition. And you?

Me too.

They compared the times when they'd both been in the Galeria dell'Accademia. They must have just missed each other.

Leo evaded a conversation about the exhibition. He had in fact really been there but he hadn't seen the pictures of Giorgione. Not seen. He stood in front of them, walked up and down in front of them. The friendly, smiling girl who had sold him his entrance ticket was more clearly printed in his memory than the pictures of the exhibition. Not as a picture. He only knew he had felt himself blush when she had smiled at him. A group of schoolchildren were being led through the exhibition. Few of them listened to the teacher's explanations or obeyed his admonitions to be quiet. It wasn't that he saw the colourful swarm of noisy schoolchildren in front of him—he only knew that was how it had been—he could tell her about that—but he didn't. Tell her how the obvious lack of interest on the part of the schoolchildren had enabled him to identify with them immediately? What would be the point of telling her that? Judith had asked him about his impressions of the paintings. He hadn't seen the paintings though—he had stood opposite them, yes, to kill time—until it was five o'clock. Just like himself, the schoolchildren were also there not from personal interest—like him, they too were filled with diffuse but clearly urgent interests and longings of quite a different sort. Surrounded by pictures like those in a hall of mirrors which reflected back to them their interests and longings in a distorted and incomprehensible manner. That's how Leo had seen it. But he hadn't seen anything at all. If Löwinger had been there.

Löwinger, with one arm round Leo's shoulders, the other stretched out towards the picture and moving so gently and confidently as if he were conducting the form and composition of the painting as you would a living ballet, Löwinger would have opened his eyes with just a few words and he would have seen. But Leo, when he was alone, could read better than he could see. He had studied the captions beneath the paintings more attentively than the paintings themselves. He hadn't seen the 'Reclining Venus' but rather 'Reclining Venus. Canvas 108 × 175 cm. On loan from Dresden Art Gallery'. Obviously he had glanced at the pictures. Each one spoke to him no differently from what all the others stated collectively, no differently from what they had in common with completely different pictures by completely different painters exhibited in other museums, namely that they were old pictures. A sleeping and rather buxom nude, a Mother of God on a throne, a man in armour, another in a monk's habit: subjects whose countless replications in art history indicate but one thing: this is art history.

Not even 'The Three Philosophers' made an impression on him. He read: 'The Three Philosophers. Canvas, 124 × 145 cm. On loan from the Vienna Museum of Art History'. Aha, Vienna. The Three Philosophers. Which ones. Three men of differing ages, each in differing robes, one sitting, two standing, a country scene. It meant nothing to him. Perhaps if Löwinger had been there. He would certainly have known who these three philosophers were or even which philosophical movements they represented. To him the picture meant nothing. What was there to say about it? That three men, variously dressed, give the impression in varying degrees of being old, or should one say historically removed? And, if the picture is supposed to represent three philosophers, what might it mean that the one who looked the youngest and most modern was the only one sitting? What might it mean being next to older philosophers and yet so 'down'? Did the older ones make him feel weak at the knees? Leo didn't see it, didn't give it any thought—what was the point in talking about it? He was a schoolboy at this exhibition. Lots of pictures, but before his eyes hung his appointment with Judith. The Theory of Art, Three Philosophers, Philosophy—Leo didn't want to discuss anything of this nature. How enthusiastic Judith was about Giorgione. All Leo could do was to agree all the time. Yes, really great art. No doubt about it. They enjoyed each other's company. They enjoyed the art. Art is a good basis for enjoyment. No doubt about it. Italian hit-songs were playing in the bar they were standing in, drinking an aperitif, *porto del sole*. Judith couldn't help smiling when she saw Leo swaying happily in time to the music. What was wrong with Lukas? The eyes drop. Seesawing tennis shoe. Judith ducked the question about Lukas. What could she have told him? The truth? I met Lukas last night in the bar opposite our *pensione*—he poked fun at you the whole time and in the end I insulted him? The truth, after all, is only a pretext for making an endless series of interpretations, by means of which you can distance yourself even further from that truth than by keeping quiet. No interpretations. So silence, then—and yet noise not silence reigns, in the midst of which we beat the rhythm, sway back and forth, light a cigarette, raise a glass—cheers. Nuzzled up close almost—prelude to a dance—the substitute for one.

A nice day, said Leo, for now it was a nice day. That's what's needed sometimes, said Judith: a little bit of time on your own.

Yes, that's right, said Leo; he was so pleased to be alone with Judith now. Wasn't this what he had wished for? A double room for the two of them. One bed that was superfluous because two can lie in one. Two more camparis. Yes, two. They'll be taken for a couple.

They became a couple. They avoided each other and drew closer to each other. It all went as smooth as clockwork. The dinner. The journey back home to the *pensione*. The way their footsteps interwove harmoniously. The newly-clad desire which wanted to shed its clothes. Leo's room. After they had undressed, and while still standing, a defenceless embrace full of promise.

When Leo turned out the light there was nothing more for an uninvolved observer to see in the darkness of the room. Judith was the uninvolved observer. Why was Leo so coarse. And at the same time so melodramatic. What exactly Leo's melodramatics consisted in was irritatingly unclear. It just was. It was a put-in, put-out, put-up, put-up-with job. There was nothing to be seen. One person—or two. Judith got up and groped for her dress. Stay there. I want to be alone. One bed is too narrow and if we're going to sleep in two different beds then I might as well go to my own room. And—I can smoke there. She didn't say that. I've got a bottle of grappa in my room. She didn't say that. I didn't understand all that. She didn't say that. Then again there was something hairy, something sinewy. There was something damp. There was something unbearably oppressive. A suddenly anxious enveloping. An enveloping weakness. And in face of this was a squirming endurance, a soft mouth that grew hard beneath a hard kiss, a body that seemed to rub itself pliantly against the body from which it was wrenching itself

81

free. Whispered goodnight wishes. And a flash of lightning as the door was opened and then shut again.

Leo stood alone in the darkness of his room, filled with sensations that made him want to compose a replay of what had happened. He opened the shutters. In the night sky above the square stood the moon. Turning your back on life is philosophical. But entering into life, thought Leo, is—what? After the first step it's—what? Leo was standing by the open window and feeling. Behind the neighbouring window Judith was standing and drinking. Is what? Lyrical. Entering into life entails the dissolving of philosophy into art, Leo thought. But this thought was once again a backward step. He would have to recompose it.

The third and last day in Venice. It became clear that this trip was a disaster but it was also a diluted disaster: time had almost stood still and disaster had been dissolved in this near stagnant water. But the time was nevertheless savoured to the last drop and in the end, when it had nearly run dry, the dregs became visible, revealing its base ingredient: when Judith was sitting over a late breakfast Leo handed her a poem. He had written it during the night after Judith had gone back to her room, in the heat of the moment, it's true, but, as regards its form, coolly and calculatedly, too. When, after countless crossings out, corrections and alterations, the three verses had exactly the same number of lines, every line was roughly the same length, the verses were completely parallel in their structure and built to a—yes, to a climax, then Leo copied out the poem painstakingly in his best, flowing handwriting onto a double page which he carefully removed from the middle of his notebook.

When the new moon rose
Over the city, God lay down
On top of Babylon. And he sinned
Between her mighty thighs.
He sunk his teeth into her full
Breasts and his hands dug
Into her soft flesh. And God
Cried out with pleasure.

When the new moon stood high
Over the city, God lay on
Babylon, and his sharp member
Ripped her belly open,

With his snout he greedily emptied
Her breasts and his long nails clawed
Deep furrows in her wet face.
    And God roared out in his lust.

When the new moon sank behind
    The city, God rose up, his sex
        Still extended mightily.
And God gazed down on Babylon,
His mother. Who lay beneath him
With bleeding belly and flattened
Breasts, her skin torn to pieces:
And God saw that it was good.

The manner in which Leo handed Judith the poem showed not just the pride of the artist but also the self-confidence that calculated into the value of the poem the future additional value of its being 'in the author's own hand'.

Judith didn't like the poem at all.

Leo was cross with himself that he hadn't waited for a more opportune moment. How swollen Judith's eyes were. No-one could read anything with eyes like those. And at breakfast even less so. She ate while she read. Every now and again she swept breadcrumbs from off the page. How can you take in a poem if a hand is everlastingly wiping across it. Writing poetry is not your strong point, Leo, said Judith. Leo thought sulkily that this sounded like: Stupidity is not your strong point.

I have something for you, too, said Judith.

She rummaged in her bag, found an envelope and eventually a biro as well. She pulled a postcard out of the envelope and wrote something on the back without taking much trouble over the execution.

The postcard was a reproduction of a Giorgione painting—Leo could vaguely remember having seen it at the exhibition. Giuditta. Leningrado, Eremitage. But it was only now that Leo realised that Giuditta meant Judith. The painting showed a woman with a sword—at her feet lay the severed head of a man. The woman had her left foot placed on the brow of the head. A bare leg protruding out of the side-slit of her flowing red dress rested on the forehead of the dead, amputated head of a man. On the back of the card it read: 'Sometimes men lose their heads. All that then remains of some of them in the picture that is passed on to posterity is the head.' Leo wasn't sure if he understood

83

what Judith was trying to say. But what it meant he understood only too well.

The last day. Judith was reserved and brusque, Leo was at a loss, uncertain and listless. An endless leave-taking. They thought they were taking leave of the city. They had to vacate their rooms in the *pensione* at midday. They then took their bags to the left-luggage at the station. And then there was still such a long time until the departure of their train. The train left at—what time? So long. Judith and Leo walked through Venice once more, walked and waited, drank wine and waited, ate tramezzini and waited, they bought souvenirs, eggs made from onyx glass from the island of Murano, and waited. What can you do with those, what's the use of them? asked Leo. Nothing, said Judith—they're beautiful. They drank coffee and waited. Such a long leave-taking, only because the train left at a certain time. The feeling you have when you kiss someone swiftly on the right and left cheeks—but spread out over eight hours. Time stood like a puddle of water in the sun. Feelings of aggression held in with difficulty. The trip was a disaster because it turned out to be a concentrated leave-taking that was nevertheless infinitely diluted. Who could stand that? Not Leo. He couldn't even stand getting his head round it. All he could grasp was that once again it was simply a question of killing time and that for as long as he could remember he had done nothing but just that: kill time. A loveless and unproductive wait at the end of which there ought to be love and productivity. But always at the end of the wait what followed was merely the start of a new period of waiting. The Rialto bridge. Leo hated walking across this bridge and being indistinguishable from happy tourists without being as happy as they. Just because he wasn't strong enough—isn't strong enough—to insist—to have insisted—coldly and confidently on the objective arrangement of his life, that is, on—oh, what the hell. And yet if Judith had been more affectionate, more loving, gentler, more committed. He wouldn't have suffered for one second. He felt like a hermaphrodite. Stuck somewhere, time standing still, somewhere between no longer and not yet. He was no longer the same and no longer the Other. And again not yet the same and not yet the Other. They walked, they strolled, they waited. Perhaps it was the shirt. His coloured shirt was sweat-soaked and dirty and stuffed in his travel bag. He was wearing his white shirt, fresh from the dry-cleaner's. The formal, white shirt underneath the bohemian green jacket—they didn't go very well together, of course. He looked funny in this combination. Leo knew this and felt awkward. Despite the white shirt he was no longer the man in the conservative clothes with the pensive gait and obvious disinterest in time and its foolishness. He was the man in the green jacket—but not any more. For, with the staid shirt underneath, the jacket didn't suit him, looked borrowed, odd. He had the blue jeans on but no longer the tennis shoes. You sweat in tennis shoes if you wear them all day long. His black leather shoes were dried out—with the aid of lots of shoe cream Leo had been able to restore them sufficiently to be able to put them on again. But walking around in them Leo noticed that they felt different now. The leather was stiffer, harder, made for a different way of walking—the leather could possibly crack. The way he walked was anxious, without that former elasticity, but also its contemplative character didn't seem natural. And when he looked down at himself while walking, the combination of cowboy trousers and traditional shoes struck him as completely wrong—they just didn't go together. Externals. Such a long time still. A cold feeling as if they were complete strangers reared up with the prospect of the time that still lay ahead, putting to flight all the intimacy that had developed between them up to then. But it was stronger and more unnerving than that experienced with strangers. For this coldness is the result of getting to know one another: the end, the farewell. This was the deep shadow cast by the brilliant light of his original attraction to her. They weren't compatible. Really not? They were both completely convinced that they loved each other, had loved each other, no longer did, had never, always would—so many fetters, but were they capable of admitting it? They drank red wine. Judith grew more affable and then conciliatory. You're not angry with me, are you, Leo, she said, because I said your poem—

Of course not. Angry? Why? Leo was touched. Read it through again some time quietly and if you still don't like it, then—

No-one has ever written me a poem before, said Judith.

Leo raised his glass, smiled dotingly and then felt the postcard in his breast pocket.

You know, said Leo, the poem's—but he didn't get to finish his sentence—Judith was talking suddenly about psychoanalysis—how did she get onto the subject of Freud?—had he ever looked into it. That didn't interest him in the least. But she talked and time passed—they walked and time passed. In the Piazza San Marco, Leo, in a sudden fit of sentimentality, wanted to have their photographs taken as a memento—by one of those photographers standing around. Do you want it with pigeons, the photographer called out repeatedly—with pigeons is typical, and frantically he shook pigeon food out in front of them, some of it over Leo—a mass of wildly fluttering pigeons descended on Leo and Judith, the air was full of dirt, feathers, dust and stench, as if they were in a glass bowl in which the unappetising residue on the bottom were being stirred up, and when the photograph was taken Leo was covered with pigeon dirt and bird droppings which, in his attempt to brush off, he merely smeared foolishly into the velvet of his jacket. Leo knew that, once back in Vienna, he would throw this jacket away. In Vienna his father's suits were waiting for him in the cupboard. He stood there like an angel that had been turned to stone. He would prefer to look down on stone angels. From his window, from his study. At home. He had made a leap, he had dared a leap. But now he stood once again with both feet on the ground. Slowly and leaning slightly forward with his hands crossed behind his back, Leo walked with Judith to the railway station. That was the end of his period as a young man-about-town, as a lover and artist.

The relationship with Judith had to be completely rewritten again, composed afresh. Until then all thought of any further work on his dissertation was out of the question. Leo knew that he could only cope with the senseless days in Venice if he could make sense of them. That is, something had to result from it all. Idea for an essay:—he didn't have any. A lot of time spent looking out of the window of his room. A lot of time spent sitting in cafés. Idea for an essay: Travel makes you stupid. Rejected. Idea for an essay: On the importance of Giorgione today. Rejected. If he had only brought the exhibition catalogue back with him. But all he had was the postcard of Giorgione's 'Judith'—that was too little to go on. He put the card on his desk, propped up against and covering the photo of Löwinger. Judith was to blame for his wasting his time with her and not only that but also for the fact that because of her he then had to kill the wasted time, too, after which he would stand there and not know what to do. He should write his dissertation. His time was running out. Starting to write. But he couldn't. He couldn't get Judith out of his head. A severed head with Judith's foot resting on the forehead. He had to rewrite the story, transform it, write it afresh, and in such a way that in the end his head would not be lying lifeless at Judith's feet. Only then would he be able, literally as well, to lift up his head. But where should he begin? He hooked his thumbs into the sides of his waistcoat as he walked up and down his room. Clothes? Idea for an essay: On fashion. Rejected—but not immediately. *Fine feathers make fine birds*. Gottfried Keller. Leo was working again. His work on Keller progressed only for as long as he was making notes on what he wanted to write, what he wanted to prove. However, when he then read the novella, *Fine Feathers Make Fine Birds*, he ran into another crisis. The novella didn't have enough in it, not enough material for the interpretation that he had in mind. A tailor's apprentice being taken for a Count—this would be far too difficult to interpret in such a way as to enable him to allude in a meaningful way to the experience he had had in Venice with the new clothes, the blue jeans, the green jacket... Green Henry! The crisis was overcome. The upshot of this was Leo's great Gottfried Keller essay. There was of course also a sub-section about Gottfried Keller's skill as novella writer, for Leo already had some notes on the subject. But—he wrote—this is not the place to go into any further detail as regards this. The main and central part of the essay became the interpretation of *Green Henry*. He himself, of course, was Green Henry. And Judith was obviously Judith. The fact that Henry's great unrealised love was called Judith was an all too tempting coincidence. On the other hand the other female characters in *Green Henry* also had such clear similarities to Judith that Leo saw Judith in each of them—in Dorothea, for example, or in Anna. Judith was obviously not so unique. This moved Leo greatly. And because of this they could all be combined as messages to Judith. 'In Keller,' Leo therefore wrote, 'every character has his or her own peculiar beauty: just as we have the sickly delicacy and fraility of Anna and Agnes, so there is also the womanly maturity of Rosalie or Judith, then there is the girlish, sturdy and pliant Dorothea with her witty and light-hearted superiority, and the calm, tough and often narrow heroism of the mother. In Keller the revelation of character entails a revelation of beauty,' always of the same, therefore. This meant that Leo revealed every female character in the novel to be essentially the same woman: Judith.

When Leo wrote that Green Henry 'attained to a maturity humanly crucial to him through his intercourse with Dorothea,' he was stating what precisely the intercourse with Judith in Venice had meant for him: 'He now freely renounced the artistic tendencies of his youth.' That meant that Judith should not pretend that nothing had happened, for the consequences of their intercourse were only too significant. On the other hand, however, she should not infer from this anything for the future, since the only purpose that an intercourse with her could have had been fulfilled: no further qualitative leap was to be expected from any possible repetitions. No more leaps. Artistic tendencies—by this, of course, Leo meant his poem. Regarding his youth—Judith had to be quite clear about this—over and done with. Leo couldn't resist using the expression 'the bragging and extravagant inclinations' of Green Henry towards Judith—if he but reflected on what, all in all, this trip to Venice had cost—'and the first moral blunder that resulted from this,' that was obvious, no doubt about it, Judith was bound to understand this. But now everything made sense: 'Liberated both outwardly and inwardly, Henry returned home to political activity.' And so that Judith would understand what his own political activity would now consist in, Leo inserted a quotation from Hegel into the central part just to show: this is my true destiny, my socially meaningful and necessary activity, the work on Hegel, and I have written all this only to be able to resume writing my work on Hegel. Science. The comprehensive analysis of social totality.

Leo sent Judith his Gottfried Keller essay like a handshake bringing an end to the time spent together and saying goodbye. And to be absolutely certain that Judith understood the essay correctly, Leo wrote in an accompanying letter, among other things: 'You know why this work was written: because I cannot write poetry. And you know whom it concerns and who prompted me to write it.' And then the announcement of what his life would essentially consist in from now on. 'As regards what I will be doing now, which will henceforward take up the rest of my life, scarcely any intellectual and scientific initiatory steps have yet been taken (excuse the expression) *in our times*; however, the fact that I have come to this point, come to myself, I owe to you alone. What I wish to do can only be done by someone on their own; however, it is only through the deepest feelings of connectedness and AFTER having had such feelings, that being alone is possible. He who does not know what another person can mean to him, what one person can be for another, can be forsaken at the most but never free from desire, secure in a state of solitariness created for the sake of science. Only the latter can pass proudly and stoically by the open doors leading to the deceptive and paltry social life on offer and stake his whole life on one throw, his work, without losing his head. "Life", for the sake of which so many turn their backs on their real intentions, no longer means anything to such a one. "Life" and "people" are but shadows next to this, his one and only real life; what can these give to someone who looks beyond them?' and so on. It turned into a long and very heroic letter—to which Leo received no reply.

Solitariness and not a single line of his dissertation. Lots of looking out of the window, at the cemetery angels, at the dismal façade of a Viennese rear courtyard, people's shadows behind the windows opposite, the electric light when it grew dark. Not a single line of his Hegel dissertation. You really should be bringing your studies to an end soon, his father said when they met up at the *Café Razumovsky*. You should be working harder, Leo—if you should need more money for the last lap, in order not to have to think of anything else except finishing, I'll gladly give you some, but you really should be coming to the end soon, that's my one wish for you. Or if you don't want to continue your studies, then you should say so soon and then you should come and join me in the firm, take it over, but you should decide what you want—where are your glasses, Leo—you should be wearing them, otherwise you'll ruin your eyes—you should listen to what your mother says—we only want the best for you—you really should be finishing soon, and you shouldn't worry either about what will happen later, there's enough there, Leo, but now you really should hurry up and—

Things were then to happen very hurriedly in fact. Barely six months later Leo was to see his father for the last time, in hospital where cancer had wasted him down to a skeleton, but he was not to recognise his father's gaunt frame—he was to be filled with the terror of death, but also with the feeling of total alienation in the face of death, since he was to experience his father's dying merely as a picture of a dying. He was not to accept this helpless fading away into death, not be able to accept the physical living remains of his father as his father—he was to be deeply affected and yet unaffected, too, because he was not to recognise this skeleton (who was dependent on the goodwill of the doctors and nurses, and was, for reasons of discretion only, badly covered over with an old skin) as the person who had been his father in his life. He was to stand by his father's bed, but his father would not be in bed but in Leo's mind and in his memory, and then he was to go again, but be there only like the flowers in the vase on his father's bedside table. He was to speak to one of the doctors again and express his horror at his father no longer being able to recognise him, and he was to keep quiet about his own inability to recognise his father. Leo was to do this, was to do that, and so it all came about, but even when it did, it remained a 'was to', an obligation, and whatever Leo should have done—or done quite differently—everything was to be quite different now all the same: on the credit side Leo was only ever paying off debts. It was just around this time when his father finally died that Leo had cautiously approached Judith once more.

Judith got to know Leo all over again, as a helpless man now, with all the stuffing knocked out of him, without any more trace of arrogance, and lost in thought as a result of a vague feeling of failure. She hadn't received anything more from Leo since his Gottfried Keller essay and hadn't read anything more of his. She had found the essay interesting, 'talented', if that might not have sounded too patronisingly condescending, but overall she had found the interpretation far too mechanical, the description and Keller's development too teleological, Leo's evaluation of it too pedantic and the way Leo always tried to tie it in with historical circumstances with 'It is no coincidence that...,' sentences all too contrived. All the same, the essay was full of substance and showed that Leo could clearly work,—so why hadn't he written anything more afterwards and not got any further, as he related, with his dissertation either?

It was at this time that Judith first saw Leo as an old man, sitting there in the armchair at her place in his conservative suit, which he wore in a slovenly fashion and with peevish indifference, like someone who never stops before a mirror to adjust his clothing, and with his new spectacles which were even bulkier and blacker than his old ones—sitting there crumpled up, sparing of both gestures and words, a traveller returned home after a long, unsuccessful expedition which had left deep and harrowing scars in its wake. Listless, and yet full of lively energy whenever it was a question of meeting up with Judith, of seeing her again, of spending time with her, only, however, to collapse in on himself completely, once he was with her, so that he seemed incapable of even lifting the telephone receiver. He still drank only tea but now he added rum to it—he liked it best when the tea was lukewarm so that he could drain the cup in one or two draughts, with a strong shot of rum in it always, and he would then grow maudlin and tearful like a child, a senile child, Judith thought, and she was at a loss. But nothing astonished Judith more than the fact that she didn't offer any resistance to being forced into the role of mother to this child, something which took place with a peculiar consistency and logic and only with her compliance and with no change at first to her behaviour or way of life. With increasing frequency Leo would want, whenever he visited her, to stay the night with her as well—he couldn't go home, he'd say, he simply couldn't be by himself. And whenever he then slept in her bed, while she stayed awake, as always until late into the night, and worked, read, smoked, drank, walked up and down the room, and then, when the feeling would arise in her that she didn't want to do any of these things, but instead to keep watch like a mother over Leo's sleep, alert, listening for sounds, ready to respond to a call. Leo's inordinate need for sleep at that time went hand in hand with Judith's determined sleeplessness in such a way that in the end, as she realised helplessly, they both began to take it quite for granted that she was looking after him, keeping watch over him even while he was sleeping. And whenever she cooked for him, then suddenly, she was no longer the self-assured, free and independent young woman who had invited a friend to her place for a meal, but instead—... Or, whenever, after five or six cups of tea with rum, he would suddenly start weeping, would crouch down in front of her, put his head on her lap, and she—what should she do?—would stroke his hair and notice suddenly the small bald patch at the back of his head—like a monk's tonsure, she thought—and was moved to comfort him, quickly stroking his hair so as to cover over the incipient bald patch, then she wasn't the girlfriend, the lover, but was instead—... And whenever he tried to rebel, helplessly and with a beseeching cry for help—cutting a mawkish picture that was tempered only by the fuzzy edges and lack of focus with which this picture developed in Judith's consciousness every time, she looked at him aghast, as he stood there asking her in all seriousness to force him to work again, to see to it that he stayed seated at his desk—and then when she would encourage him, she wasn't—but was instead—the mother who alone and to the last stood by her child, blindly confident that he was a good boy, a decent lad, could do great things—and it was too much for her: she wasn't those things she seemed to be, and she didn't know what to do, how to react without killing him. And whenever, on nights he slept at her place, she went to bed hours after him and, completely drained and almost fainting with tiredness, felt him press himself up against her suddenly in his sleep, she felt this so diffusely and indistinctly like a dream sequence that this then was like—like what? More obscene and more underhand and more inconsequential and of more lasting effect than—

In this way a relationship finally began to emerge, nearly, very unsteadily, and in a way that couldn't last and on the understanding that a relationship had already existed which no longer existed any longer in that form. It arose, as far as Judith could see, somewhere in the immeasurably wide distance between Leo's exaggerated pretensions and his incompetence at coming anywhere near realising these pretensions. This made her wary and she didn't know whether she really wanted it. But as long as she remained unclear about it, the relationship grew ever closer. Even when Judith went to the National Library, Leo went along with her just so as not to be alone and, sitting next to her, would read and cull passages of secondary Hegel literature. When Judith worked at home, Leo would sit at the kitchen table and attempt to write a new chapter of his dissertation from these extracts, but only in order to fill the time until Judith would give him her attention again. But the new relationship only nearly developed. The problems that arose from the fact that the relationship had developed in such an insidious way, without agreement and a conscious decision, these problems only nearly arose. Judith grew only nearly panicky, and it only nearly came to it that she felt suffocated and hemmed in. Leo became blissfully happy, self-confident and productive again, but only nearly. The new chapter was nearly, only nearly finished. For it was exactly at this time that Leo's father had to be suddenly operated on and Leo was spending more time at the hospital than in the library, more time with his mother than with Judith. And it all happened so incredibly fast, and then his father died.

How are things to proceed, is the question that must now be asked. Decisions will need to be reached. They were reached. Leo's mother sent for him in order to tell him what they were. Momentarily overwhelmed, Leo might almost have embraced his mother and wept, since never again would his father, in this room, at this table—but his mother's brusque manner permitted nothing more than the usual kiss on the cheek, and even then Leo had to wait until his mother had finished some task she had obviously only just started. Sit down, Leo, I'll be through in a minute. Yes, Mama. A petitioner before his mother but without a petition and she sitting there in a stiffly correct posture as if she were being observed, not just by Leo but by a large audience, or, which for her amounted to the same, as if she were completely alone, and she took envelope after envelope from the pile in front of her, in order to put a vigorous stroke with her old fountain pen through the address and, as Leo was aghast to discover, to write next to it quite unmoved in her stupid best handwriting: Addressee deceased—Return to sender. Stroke: Addressee deceased—Return to sender. Stroke:

Addressee deceased—Return to sender. It was clear to Leo why he hated her, but why she hated him was completely beyond his understanding. What had he done to her apart from coming into the world, apart from being her son?

The days of riotous living are over now, Leo, and with them the sweet idle life, said his mother, as she screwed the top of her fountain pen back on. An animal, Leo was suddenly a raging animal caught in the motionless shell of Leo's seated body—the animal roared and tore at the walls of its prison with its claws, and it defecated and licked its genitals, but then there were two human beings sitting there stiffly and the penetrating smell of naphthalin, of fireballs bursting in a room that was heated far too spartanly, of flatulence, and stiffening with fear, while only the chair creaked. The end of my studies, that's what must be meant, thought Leo. No—he wanted to say—it would be mad to stop now just before the end, and Father wanted me to finish—he wanted to say—his last wish, so to speak, and there can't be any compelling financial reasons for me to work now, there's enough there, Father said so—he wanted to say—and that he must be entitled to it—he wanted—as part of his inheritance or whatever it's called—to say. Spit it out. He wanted to and ought to and should have. Silently he looked at his mother. Or ought he perhaps to take over the family firm? But that was impossible—he knew nothing about the business, it would be a disaster, he wanted to make it quite clear that—If Father had wanted it, he would have said so much earli—no, don't say anything—silently he looked at his mother. Perhaps the firm ran itself, the firm was established, perhaps there were long-term advance orders and delivery contracts which would guarantee a living for a sufficient period—perhaps the employees were loyal, too—they had all, as far as he knew, been with the firm for years if not from the beginning. How could his mother prevent him from finishing his dissertation, while at the same time he would prove that he could make a go of it in practical life as well, support himself. Don't say anything.

His mother now had her say. We now have, now we must, the fact of the matter is that. We will, we cannot, we are. It is unacceptable that, nothing else is possible other than. What is to be done. On the understanding that, on condition that. That is to say. That means. Nothing else is possible, unfortunately. Earlier one might perhaps have, but now unfortunately. With forewarning one would have, but now unfortunately. That is to say. Firstly. Secondly. Thirdly. Nothing else is possible. We have.

When his mother had finished Leo was no longer capable of saying anything. His imagination had once again proved unequal to the task. He hadn't been able to envisage this—he hadn't reckoned with this. What should he say? How should he argue? How should he resist? His mother had decided and had already made all the appropriate arrangements as well, had concluded so many *faits accomplis*, there was no going back any more. That was to say, going back was all that was left.

On the way back home Leo had a puncture. First he couldn't find the jack. Then he couldn't make it work. When he finally succeeded in jacking up the car, he had to lower it again, as he realised only then that he first had to loosen the bolts. The jack slipped and Leo hurt his index finger. Then he was unable to get the bolts to budge even one milli-metre. Wild with rage he threw his whole weight onto the wheel wrench, pushed and pulled with all his strength: not one of the bolts would give. Rage and then suddenly panic, the fear that the strain might cause one of the veins in his head to burst. Well, so what, he thought, but ceased his efforts immediately. He left the car where it was, went to the next phone-box, looked up in the phone book the address of the nearest second-hand car dealer, drove there on the wheel rim and sold the car, without bargaining, for the ridiculous price that the dealer offered. He then took a taxi home, holding with his left arm, and pressed to his chest, his father's black briefcase that his mother had given him, sucking all the while the cut on the index finger of his right hand, his hands black with dirt from his attempts to change the wheel. I'll get blood-poisoning as well, he thought, felt he had it already and that he was as good as lost. Once home he spent a long time washing his hands, cleaned the wound carefully, bandaged it up with a handkerchief. He then walked to the nearest chemist and bought some iodine and sticking plaster. Finally he sat down at his desk with a large glass of rum. For several minutes he then sat completely listless, drinking, staring at the desk, drinking. With Hegel's *Phenomenology* open at the section 'Pleasure and Necessity'. A few pages with extracts and notes. When had he written those? His father's black briefcase. Gior-gione's *Judith*. A sudden eruption of his unspeakable despair. With a sudden and angry movement of his hand he swept the Hegel and the pages of excerpts off the table and gave a great sob. The thump of the book landing on the floor—so unnaturally loud. A blurred look at the briefcase, at the Giorgione picture. Leo took fresh paper out of the desk drawer and started a letter to Judith.

'It would be hard to work out how many letters to you this one makes, which must count as a last and final leave-taking—but if I had some energy left in me, you wouldn't now be hearing anything more from me again: I would drag out my empty, miserable life and it needn't interest you how bearable I find it, and I don't want it to interest you either. Now I must write to you since you will be receiving these lines along with the news of my death; I must write, because I have—perhaps— meant enough to you (and because there remain enough memories of the times we have spent together) for it to be not completely indifferent to you why I am taking my life, a life that everyone found to be of value and from which, without any exaggeration, some success was confidently expected, not least by myself. It is perhaps an overblown vanity and terrible overestimation of my worth—and if this is the case then forgive a weak, sick and confused human being—but I sometimes think when I reflect on what I'm planning that when you learn about it from other people, without of course knowing the motive (no-one will know this, you can imagine) you may, in your great and beautiful goodness, reproach yourself, may think that you are the cause of what has happened, that I might have been saved if you had behaved differently, that . . . in short (I don't want, as I said, to rule out the possibility that this may well be enormously overestimating both myself and what I may mean to you), in brief, I don't want you to do this. And for this reason I feel obliged to tell you why I cannot bear this life any longer. I will be brief.' There then followed a long look back over his life, beginning with the time before he first got to know Judith ('the Ice Age', Leo wrote, total solitude, unproductivity), and then the time when he did. ('I became a different person. A good person.') He wrote about his sudden ability to work ('I began to get used to this situation') up to their trip together to Venice ('Life, the life I had long suppressed'), the doubts that followed as to whether he was suited for life, could enter into it ('But a youth like mine was cannot be forgotten'), the end of this period, his triumphant breakthrough into a life at one remove from life: 'All the goodness in me ceased, withered away root and branch. I became bad, cold, cynical, malicious. Bouts of intellectual intoxication followed. Books and thoughts affected me like opium. There were weeks when I was (intellectually) richer than I had ever been in my life, during which great, powerful and wide-ranging thoughts came flying to me in great flocks.' And then the evening when the opium dream faded, from which time 'the tears of abjection' began. A 'period of personal betterment and catharsis', Leo wrote, during which, through the deepest self-doubt,

95

through the most radical focussing on his ego and on his innermost possibilities and limitations, everything is overcome in a last great trial—overcome in order to be finally transformed into an objective necessity where work becomes identical with meaning, and ceases to be a biographical reflex; in which work 'no longer shows any trace, any imprint of the personal misery left behind and, by way of this, of personal preferences, of personal prejudices—in short', wrote Leo, 'the painful breakthrough into objectivity.' ('I don't need to spell it out to you how much I am indebted to you with respect to this last period.')

Leo was thinking of the weeks he had spent almost daily at Judith's place, how he had wept, how she had comforted him, of his apathetic, trance-like states, how he and Judith had sat side by side in the library, how he had brooded dreamily over his notes at the kitchen table, how he had cleared away all his papers whenever Judith had cooked. From all of this something had emerged, something had really emerged finally—Judith's self-determined, self-confident manner, this had moved him, and then—Leo wiped his eyes with the back of his hand and continued writing.

It was just at this time, Leo wrote, that his father had become ill and eventually died. And it was a tragic irony of fate that his father, a weak and soft man all his life, who had never had anything but the flimsiest sway over him, should of all things through his death gain a sudden power over him, as he put it, and that his father's death should have deadly consequences for Leo. 'On the desk in front of me, while I am writing these last lines of mine, there sits a black bag, like a miniature coffin—it is my father's briefcase. This bag contains that which will uproot my fundamentally plant-like existence, tear me out, lift me like a violet out of the meadow, kill me—and there is only one way I can prevent this from happening: by laying hands on myself.'

Leo leant back, undid his shirt collar. He had now written so much and yet had still not explained his reasons for the proposed suicide. Now, just as he had finally got round to it, he felt drained and happily exhausted, like at the end of a productive day. Besides, writing to Judith (in his imagination speaking with her) had manifestly so calmed him that the writing had effectively ruled out his killing himself that day. Scrapping the idea altogether won't of course be possible, he thought sulkily and despondently. But he didn't want to write any longer, he wanted to talk to Judith, tell her everything. He wanted to spend his last days with her. The letter was never posted.

Leo was lucky: he rang Judith and got through to her first go. And she, alarmed by his funereal voice and dark allusions, said she was willing to meet him straightaway.

I don't understand what's so terrible about having to go back to Brazil, said Judith.

They were sitting in the *Café Sport* and Leo didn't know what irritated him more: the noisiness of the place or the way in which Judith dismissed the tragedy of his life so lightly.

Don't you see, he said, everything I've learnt and which I've worked for is suddenly supposed to count for nothing, my life an anecdote of no significance, everything I've ever aspired to, what I planned to do with my life, my goals, all shot to bits, and by an external chance event which has absolutely nothing to do with me and what's important to me—it's mere chance that my father bought some pieces of land there in São Paulo and that he died so unexpectedly and—

Why chance? said Judith. Your parents certainly didn't go to São Paulo simply by chance but because they had to escape fascism and the fact you now have possessions in Brazil is a thread in the tapestry of world history, and Judith gave an ironic smile.

World history, said Leo contemptuously, world history—that's not world history, at the most a footnote to world history, and he stopped short. Then he continued: And me, what about me? It could be important—not perhaps in the context of world history but you know what I mean—if I were to be able to continue and finish what I wanted to do, what I've started, but no, I'm to be simply uprooted from my existence, transplanted somewhere else where I'm supposed to do something completely different that I'm not equipped for, I mean, really— He shook his head. My father was always patient with me. My mother never. When my father died I expected my mother to say there's no more money now for my studies, even that she might force me to go into the business. I expected all that. But when she put my father's bag on the table and said: Everything's in there, Leo, the plane ticket—the flight leaves next Sunday—all the papers and documents relating to the plots of land father bought in São Paulo, an envelope containing in dollars the start-up capital that will enable me to get settled again in São Paulo, and I'm now supposed to sell all these plots of land, for why wait around, it must be sorted out now, she's got her hands full with the firm in Vienna, arranging for its sale at the best possible price—well, I knew then it was all finished, over and done with now—I'm to become an estate agent instead of a philosopher, with my work on Hegel—

But why, said Judith, I don't understand why. You can write about Hegel anywhere surely, in Vienna, in Moscow, in São Paulo, it doesn't matter one bit where you are, if you really want to do it. The exile of parents means exile for the next generation, too, and they are in exile wherever they are. Here or there makes not a jot of difference. The question is: Can something come from exile? And the answer to that was provided on many occasions a long time ago. Where's the problem? Get yourself a lawyer who can sell the land on your authority—you can busy yourself with it a little but you'll have enough time to finish writing your dissertation, and when it is finished you can come back and submit it. If that is what you want.

Leo had not seen it like that till now. On the other hand, however, he still couldn't. If he'd been able to, he wouldn't have been the person he was. And what about me? he didn't say. How am I supposed to get used to a completely different life and at the same time maintain my own real, essential life, he didn't say, when you're so woven into my life that on any street corner, it doesn't matter where, I can barely hold myself back from bursting into tears because just the memory of something you said to me, it doesn't matter what, reverberates in me? he didn't say. And even if I were ever able to write something again, as real estate dealer, then assuming the greatest scientists gave it their recognition, this would be completely worthless to me, since you would not be smiling and looking at me while I told you all about it, he didn't say. Or would you come with me? he didn't ask. Would you take care of me? he didn't ask. Take care I don't lose myself? That I work? See to it that what you said comes true: that you share my exile with me? he didn't ask. Would you be willing to rescue me?

He couldn't ask this—it was too obvious he couldn't ask this, even if he wasn't sure whether what came across from Judith was almost relief at the fact that he now had to go back to Brazil for an indefinite period. I hate my mother, he said.

In that case you should be really happy to be getting away from here, said Judith, for this way you're getting away from your mother, too. Judith was in fact becoming a touch impatient. Firstly she had another appointment imminent and Leo's complainings and demands for comfort looked like stretching into eternity; secondly she remembered only too well how often Leo would wallow with her in *saudades* for Brazil and it was therefore incomprehensible to her why Leo should feel his return to Brazil to be such a terrible catastrophe; and thirdly she found the helpless and miserable way Leo seemed to surrender to fate basically repellent.

And if you really are completely opposed to the idea, she said, then just don't get into the aeroplane. You tell your mother, no, I'm not flying, I'm staying here—you send the black bag back to her and *fim do papo*.

Leo was shocked. No, that's impossible, he said. The firm in Vienna and the plots of land in São Paulo, there's no getting round it, a solution must be found now. With my father gone, we can't simply continue running the firm and managing the Brazilian plots, we'd lose every-thing. No-one's qualified, no-one's in a position to do that, neither my mother nor I. There's only one solution: it must all be profitably liquidated. My mother wants to invest the proceeds and from this a monthly income can be drawn—one has to live off something. You can't say it doesn't interest you and then expect to live off it. Yes, if we'd thought about this earlier, if we'd seen it coming, but who would have thought my father would die so suddenly—I mean, what else could one do now, there's no other option.

Leo's face was very hot, as if the sun were burning down on it, and this echoing noise that he heard, like the echo of a laugh amplified many times over: what do you want to be? An engineer?

No, a philosopher.

Judith looked at her watch. One last bit of morale boosting. What's important is a good lawyer. With this amount of property there's no other possibility. You'll see, it'll all work out very easily. You'll have lots of free time, time to ponder. The lawyer'll do it all anyway. You're lucky. A privileged life. You'll be able to do what you want. Send me everything you write. You know I'm your most devoted reader. I have to go now. Another appointment. Yes, I'm afraid so. Fixed up some time ago. No, too late to put it off—impossible.

Tell me.

Yes?

I—

Yes?

I'd like—A final request. Would you—a parting gift, so to speak—would you make me a parting gift?

What sort of gift?

Leo found himself in a plainly feverish, trance-like state—nothing mattered to him now—that is, everything mattered to him now—no amount of embarrassment and self-abasement mattered to him if by these means he could rescue what was for him the most important thing: a feeling of self-assurance. If he could now say and get what he wanted, he would then be able to anchor his aspirations and interests in all waters of life, he knew that now as clearly and plainly as in a dream. An anchor. He wanted to be able to do that. That had to be the concluding and the starting point. Then he would be able to fly.

A Walmen-like look, a few words muttered almost hoarsely in his aroused state.

Judith smiled. Yes, we could do that. When does your plane leave?

In four days. On Sunday.

Well, then, let's say Saturday night, the last night before your departure?

Is that agreed, then?

Agreed.

Will you come to me?

Yes.

Leo spent the flight from Vienna to Frankfurt dozing. He hadn't slept a wink the night before. At Frankfurt airport he drank three beers just to be able to sleep through the rest of the journey as well. But when he finally found himself on the plane to Brazil, he was so agitated that he still couldn't get to sleep. He didn't know which feeling was stronger, more bitter: hatred or self-pity. Hatred.

The special delivery letter the afternoon before. He had even tipped the man who brought it. And then just a few, terse lines. Judith's talent to be terse and affectionate at the same time. Being and appearance. How long he had stared aghast at those lines. Judith's beautiful handwriting, flowing, harmonious, confident, unlike his where the letters bent in all directions, falling over themselves—Judith's handwriting was a performance of symbols forming perfect lines like so many identical ballet dancers, all pointing one leg in the same direction at the same time—a perfect choreography that any handwriting expert would have applauded enthusiastically.

He was not to be angry, she'd written, but the chance had come up of going to Paris for a few days with an acquaintance, the accommodation there would also cost nothing, and she couldn't turn down such an opportunity to get to know Paris—this he, Leo, would certainly understand. She was setting off today and so wouldn't be able to come to him. She was sure that he'd sort out his affairs in Brazil successfully and hoped to hear from him soon. Lots of love, *aquele abraço*. Judith. The pen a sword, a foot resting on the man's head. Dull hatred. What is love? He hadn't been able to sleep all that night, his last in Vienna. What price a promise? Despite the large amount of rum. The chance has come up. Perhaps it was all that tea that had kept him awake. With an acquaintance. He walked up and down in his room nearly all night, marched almost the whole distance from Vienna to Paris. Was he less than an acquaintance? Such an opportunity. Costing nothing. Not for him—no eating of the coveted fruit for him. He'll sort out his affairs successfully. But he couldn't sleep. Lots of love. Open the window. Float down to the angels—rise in the form of an angel? He flew through the air. To Brazil. Leaving everything behind. The beloved and the behated. The letter. A line. A line had to be drawn once. Addressee deceased. For Leo Judith was now dead. Everything would be different now. Could it become any more demeaning, any more disappointing, any more ineffectual than it was? No. He was flying towards something better. Flying home. Everything would be better. As long as the incentive was strong enough. The strongest there was. Hatred. But he soon forgot this. He was too far away. Far away from what? He'd forgotten.

Such a lot to do. Find a flat. At first he lived in a hotel on the Avenida São João. São Paulo's show street from the thirties. Since then it had gone to seed and downhill. The town had grown too fast. All who could manage to do so had given up on São João. It wasn't built for the chaos of modern traffic. There were no parking places. In time all the classy addresses moved away from it. From the nearby bus station the immigrants from the poor north-eastern regions poured in, took over the district, filling the cheap bars, lying on the street, begging, pouncing on people. Wives and daughters offered their bodies. It was the 'Sewer Stretch' with venereal diseases guaranteed—several times Leo came close to giving into the temptation of spending the equivalent of five or seven dollars on some brutal, cold lechery that didn't promise as much as it would deliver—yes, *beleza*, let's go, no, changed my mind, escape back to the hotel—it wasn't lust followed by fear, it was the vanity and despair that he brought along with him, yes, I want to get syphilis, the entrance ticket to genius, and then fear. That was on the route he took from the bar in the Rua Vitoria on the corner of São João to the sugar cane rum in the hotel bar. The fear remained, the craving for genius melted away and disappeared. What a noise. Day and night. From the Avenida Amaral Gurgel to the Avenida São João below the Duque de Caxias one gigantic building site. They were building a flyover to take traffic more quickly over the show street, former pride of the city, a motorway over this dungheap between the classy district of Pacaembu and the now so haughty Jardins. This was where Leo lived at first, in the São João, days spent driving and running around flat-hunting, evenings with a beer or two in the Rua Vitoria, or two or three beers in the *Brahma-Bar* on the corner of São João and Avenida Ipiranga—three men, sixty-year olds at the very least, one of them a mulatto, played waltzes at the back in the restaurant—in the bar in the front sat old gentlemen in threadbare suits and women, eating cheese cubes and olives, who looked like brothel madams out of a novel by Marcos Rey—that was the *Brahma-Bar*, though with the best draught beer in town—and on the way back home to the hotel the whores, so apathetic that they didn't even speak to potential suitors—Leo spoke to them, or would almost have done, and fled into the hotel. The hotels here were the cheapest, though still having the anachronistic splendour and generosity, the nobility and luxury, albeit gone to rack and ruin, of the hotel blocks typical of the thirties. A worse and smaller room in what was now a better district would have cost double the price. Leo felt no fear—the sounds and smells were familiar to him from his childhood and youth, but somehow more radical, brutal and arresting, and for this reason they were strange to him. But this strangeness was where his origins lay. Was there something else, something he'd brought with him? He had forgotten.

The most immediately important thing was a flat and as quickly as possible. He was on his legs throughout the day. From estate agents to addresses and then back to estate agents. Advertisements in newspapers led him from prohibitively-priced palaces to reeking rat-traps. After two weeks he lost patience and rented a small house, which even had a small garden, in the Brooklin district, but not in respectable and peaceful Brooklin velho, a clean neighbourhood, but in Brooklin novo, which was between the two large and noisy arterial roads, Avenida Vereador José Diniz and Avenida Santo Amaro: a pretty little house, and yet very cheap, right between two nearby factories, the chocolate factory Lacta and the munitions factory Alvo Ltda. The contract for the lease was for a year. It was not extendable. After this date the house was due to be pulled down to make way for a tower block such as were sprouting up everywhere in this neighbourhood. Leo wasn't planning to stay there longer anyway. The little house was a godsend. Its own garden. Cheap rent. Conveniently situated for travel along the two big avenidas. He bought a second-hand car. He bought a bed and a stove, a fridge, cutlery, crockery, glasses, a table and armchair, an iron and a deckchair for the garden. In the evenings he sat down in his deckchair in front of the house. There were even orchids in the garden. Depending on the direction of the wind, it either smelt of chocolate from the chocolate factory or of gunpowder from the munitions factory. He hardly ever thought of Judith any more—when he still did, it was most likely on the gunpowder evenings. But the truth was that he had no time and no desire to think of her: whether she had a boyfriend, of course she did, the one she went to Paris with, wonder who it could be, a man, a phantom, some capable fellow with no genius, and it's all like falling off a log, just like with Judith, and what could she be doing now, he didn't waste time thinking about, finishing off her studies, of course, with the same effortless diligence with which she managed to do everything, in the proper time and in the proper way, so completely effortlessly, but what is won at no great cost no-one misses when it's lost, that also was clear and cost no effort to realise—if he tried to imagine them, Judith and this man, no picture came, there was nothing for him to begin to make a picture of in his imagination, it was too far away as well, a completely different world and he also had far too much to do in his own world, so he didn't give Judith a second thought, let alone write to her. And Judith didn't write either, where would she have written? She didn't have Leo's address, and she didn't try to picture to herself how he was living now, what he was doing, all the things he had to do, selling plots of land of course, but what that actually meant—selling in São Paulo plots of land some of which were acquired as far back as during the war—this Judith didn't try to imagine. Her impression was that Leo didn't make contact with her for one whole year, but, if you were having to sell plots of land, a year was a day in Brazil and who has ever managed to sell several plots of land in one day?

In order even to begin to sell the real estate, Leo first needed the *certidão negativa*, the certificate from the Revenue Office showing that the property did not owe any tax and that there were no proceedings pending. To get this, however, more exact ground plans and title deeds were needed than those Leo had in his black bag, for, as a result of the enormous growth of the city over the previous twenty years and the new land demarcation system brought in by the modern city planners, the ground plans in the old contracts were far too imprecise, open to question and difficult to reconcile with the way things looked now. Mr. Adhemar Pinto Neto sells Mr. Oskar Singer the parcel of land that runs from Old Mill Lane as far as the stream that flows into the river Pinheiros. Where was this plot? A motorway had been built by the river Pinheiros, Old Mill Lane no longer existed and of the streams flowing into the the river Pinheiros there were no signs whatsoever. On the basis of the drawing attached to the contract, the position of the land could in fact be more or less reconstructed, including the fact that it had indeed once belonged to a Mr. Adhemar, long since deceased, but if this really was the plot of land, then it was clear that the good Mr. Adhemar had sold it twice. Leo now needed the certification showing that his father really had paid for the purchase and only then could the second sale be contested. Verification of this, however, could not be found among the papers in the black bag, only a note to the effect that the purchase money had been remitted. The bank which had transacted this remittance had in the meantime closed down, of course. Evenings with the smell of chocolate in the garden, beer and rum— impossible to think of anything else.

Another plot of land that Leo's father had acquired had in fact had a sale prohibition order, since it had earlier been German property which had been confiscated in the war by the Brazilian government. Entries in the Land Register proved to be falsified. On an incontestably reconstituted plot three thousand people lived in a tower block that had been erected with planning permission obtained illegally. On yet another piece of land a huge *favela* had grown up over time and the attempt to pay off the *faveleiros* so as to get them off the site deteriorated into a month-long farce: for every five who moved out, ten new ones moved in and waited for the pay-off. Leo's lawyer, who had been recommended to him by the judge, pocketed bribes from both opposing sides in the legal battle and took an actively robust part in dragging out the proceedings. When Leo noticed what was going on and finally switched lawyers, the old lawyer surreptitiously sold one of the plots a second time by means of the power of attorney which he still had from Leo, who then had to begin another legal action in order to annul this sale. Evenings with the smell of gunpowder—from a distance the never-ending roar of the two *avenidas*—rum—not one thought in his head—

104

such an immense tiredness that even looking at the orchids proved too much of a strain—closed eyelids, nothing behind, no light whatsoever—to bed—and the next day more racing about, lawsuits, government departments, lawyers, reports to his mother—off to the police station with an envelope full of money so as get them to evict the *favela*—but this also came to nothing. The police arrested three *faveleiros* and took them off—three more immediately moved in.

Evenings with the smell of chocolate—no thoughts of Judith—a new lawsuit against the owners of the tower block concerning bribes paid to notary clerks to carry out the falsifications in the Land Register, as a result of which the legally correct state of affairs is restored—everything just to obtain the *escritura definitiva* with which and only with which it is possible to sell the real estate—what is a year? Every month his mother sent two cheques: a smaller one 'for living', a larger one 'for the costs'. The land that had once been on the edge of or outside the city some-where between São Paulo and Santo Amaro was now worth a fortune because of the new city expansion—São Paulo and Santo Amaro had grown together and Santo Amaro was now incorporated. Property speculators queued up to see Leo: do you have the *escritura*? The land by the Pinheiros river was discussed as an ideal site for a shopping centre—with *escritura* you could name your price—all costs would be justified. It was going to take years.

One gunpowder evening. Another additional problem now arose: the first year would soon be up and Leo would have to look for a house again, move, make the necessary arrangements.

He seriously considered simply taking a small, cheap room in a hotel again just to spare himself the strains of house-hunting. What more did he need apart from a place where he could sleep? What was the point of a long and complicated search for accommodation only to find yourself at the end of every stressful day sitting there alone, going to bed alone? Wasn't it going rather too far having all these rooms, your own kitchen, your own garden, just so as to be able to lay your tired head down on a pillow at night? With no-one calling by—who would call after all. It was true, even a cheap hotel room would definitely work out to be more expensive than renting a small house or flat, but—What did he spend on himself, 'for living'? And São João was not that much louder than this garden in Brooklin novo with the roar of the traffic from the two big *avenidas*, the screaming of the birds and the perpetual thunder of the aeroplanes landing not far from there at Congonhas airport. The noise didn't disturb his peace. Only peace disturbed his peace—so much the better then if he wasn't continuously made aware of it. Did Leo have no friends, no girlfriend? Wrong. Regina. He had got to know her in the *Concorde*, one of the bars in the *Boca*, the nightclub and red-light district in the city centre. How gentle she was—that was what Leo yearned for, but he couldn't understand how someone could be gentle for money. He went to the *Concorde* again and again to seek out Regina but he couldn't bring himself to go with a prostitute. Regina's black shoulder-length hair, her light green eyes and prominent cheekbones reminded him forcefully of Judith—her slim, wiry body was just how he remembered Judith to be, just as impersonally, but Leo didn't give a moment's thought to thinking about Judith. A prostitute. He just needed a little bit of love now and again and why did it have to be emotional if it was all right just physically, but he found it a grubby business having to procure her each time. Every occasion he saw as a sign, every occasion was the last occasion. Regina's teeth were in a horrific state. Small, rotten black pegs, cavities which forced her to smile always with her lips pressed together, and she someone who so loved laughing. Leo took Regina to a dentist and paid for a total restoration of her teeth in four sessions out of the money reserved for his costs. After this she didn't take any money from him again. Whenever he came into the *Concorde*, she immediately went with him to a hotel for the rest of the night. The atmosphere in the one-night hotels in the *Boca* with their everlasting red velvet and mirrors over the beds so irritated him that the next time he took Regina back home with him. But her mere presence in his house, in the early morning above all, and the shyly respectful, almost devoted way she turned everything upside down in the house so irritated him that, on the next occasion he went with her, it was to the hotel again. And so this arrangement continued by turns. She called him *paixão* and—although he spoke perfect Portuguese, he nevertheless had a slight Viennese accent—*meu gringo*. He called her, absentmindedly looking out into the garden, *florzinha*. With her newly crowned teeth Regina was even able to change at last from the *Concorde* to the *Locomotiva-Bar*, the best nightclub in the *Boca* where she could earn more and was even given regular medical examinations. In this lay the success of the *Locomotiva*, for which the clients were happy to pay higher prices: the certainty that the girls who worked there were not only the most beautiful but also carried a health guarantee. Whenever Leo came, looking gaunt, hunched up, elderly, with his bulky spectacles perched on the end of his nose or pushed back up into his hair, with his hands kneading each other behind his back, then, sticking out like a sore thumb, he would be greeted by the waiters like an old friend and Regina would then decline all offers and run to him instead—*meu gringo, florzinha*. What perplexed him were the signs of morality, fidelity, honour which she accorded him. She threw everything into confusion. Anyone, she said, can have that from me but here, she said, only you can come in. But you surely can't get any pleasure from that, said Leo—oh yes, I can, said Regina, because I love you. *Paixão. Florzinha.* Leo was irritated by all the palaver that this necessitated—he couldn't just roll around on top of Regina any more, get himself into a frenzy of self-oblivion on top of a body lying beneath him which he experienced no more than as a matrix of fantasies with which he then could fuse. Lubrication had to precede everything, with oil or cream, and then he had to go slowly and carefully until she said *aí sim*, and, kneeling, he had to adjust his position all the time, and when it was all over run to the bathroom and wash, wash straightaway. You can get love so straightforwardly, if you don't feel love, he thought; if you did, it was then so complicated. Never again, he thought, am I going to get myself into this situation, never again—what am I doing.

One week later Leo went again for the last time, just one last time, to Regina. Shortly after this he went away with her for a weekend by the sea, to Guaruja, the *praia grande*, of course, that was the finest according to Regina. She had a child, a three year-old son. And where's the father? A shrug of the shoulders and: Can I bring the child along? A nod of the head. How happy Regina could be. How she sprawled out on the beach. Beautiful to see. Leo would later kick himself that he had never watched her more closely, more consciously, had not savoured her. All the time it was as though he were looking through a veil. He couldn't look at her without seeing himself with her from the outside and then everything seemed ridiculous and embarrassing to him. He protected himself by means of a veiled look. As a result everything was more shadowy and abstract, which was true, too. Regina was so happy that she bared her teeth. Leo was startled. Eating oysters at this beach bar—it wasn't a bar, more like a hut on the beach. And when the large, fat mulatto who had earlier opened the oysters for them came to clear away the shells, Regina said: no, not this one, that was our first oyster, I want to keep it as a souvenir. Then I'll clean it up better and wash it for the *senhora*, he said. Leo looked at Regina, her happy face—behind the veil a threatening, flashing shadow. One tooth after the other. And then, examined in the light, in the sunlight, looking openly now behind sunglasses: that's far too kitsch, he thought, that smells of chocolate. That was Regina. Gunpowder—that was Judith. He didn't think for one moment of thinking about Judith. But if he did, then he saw her pale and shadowy, a black mask over her eyes. A thief in the night forever plundering only herself. Because she always ran away. And there she was, gone again from his thoughts. Too much sun. Leo had a headache. Regina was wrapping up the cleaned oyster shells in a paper napkin. It seemed to him he had spent half his life with her. That was the problem: he was always only capable of half a life with anyone. Not even half a one. Even if he had led a double life, that together would not have made a whole one. Scarcely enough air to breathe. The breeze from the sea brought him the smell of chocolate. Sweetcorny, kitsch, stinking to high heaven. Beautiful chocolate brown faeces, the sign of extra special affection. For the others can have everything else as well, but it was precisely that that he wanted, what all the others had, and only then, when he had that, would he want a little more. Regina smiled at him as if she wanted to hang doggedly onto him. Suddenly Leo understood, or thought he understood—he was completely lethargic, not one muscle twitched as he thought that he would like to knock her teeth out, give himself a box round the ears—it was just a thought that did it. Get married. Only in this way would what was for general use also become exclusive. But on the other hand. Why not? There would be peace then. The child was highly-strung and well-behaved. You could put up with that. There would be a home life. He would be able to come back home and there'd be a life. And anyway, was he harbouring any great plans for himself. No, it struck him suddenly, none. But what would they talk about? And the very next day Leo and Regina could no longer talk to each other. They were on the *praia grande* and Leo was desperately building sandcastles with the little boy. The boy was beginning to love Leo—he literally jumped at him, a small crawling animal coated in sand like a schnitzel is in breadcrumbs—so in need of affection, like himself. Are you sure he's asleep? Of course he is, come! And Leo felt the teeth he'd wanted to buy himself out with nibbling on his earlobes—*paixão*, where's the cream? I can't, thought Leo—suncream in the day, vaseline at night, the grinding of teeth— I can't. *Florzinha*, whispered breathlessly—he no longer dared to breathe—the smell.

108

Leo extended the weekend by one day but only because he felt lazy as regards the return journey to São Paulo, was worried about the returning traffic, and had a headache from a rum-drinking bout. Not to mention his lumpen aversion to lawyers, judges, the notary clerks, who were anyway not waiting for him. Now Regina was quite certain: he loves me. The boy was already calling Leo *pai*. How else was Regina supposed to understand her *gringo* if he didn't say anything? He was building sandcastles. Regina also didn't say anything when Leo next came into the *Locomotiva* again six weeks later. She ran to him, kissed him tenderly and gave him an immaculate, open smile. *Meu Gringo. Florzinha.* It was laughable. Stupidly corny. Leo didn't want anything more to do with it. He didn't even want to go to the hotel with her any more. Leo sat down with Regina in an alcove of the bar and gave her a lecture on Hegel. Her smiles evaporated. Bravely and with round eyes she tried to listen to him, until he was so drunk that he could only drawl. Then he staggered out, vacillating between a feeling of triumph and the need to be sick. The fragments of his double life didn't fit together. He never went to the *Locomotiva* again. And when Regina went round one day to call on Leo at his house, he was no longer living at that address.

And did Leo have no friends? Wrong. Löwinger. His picture on the desk for all those years in Vienna. What did it show? Not a particular person but the ideal picture of a person, what people should be like, according to him. But how complicated love is when it is fulfilled. His first visit. Leo, who was at home nowhere, would at last be able to return home. But he knew immediately without daring to think it: this man is not my friend. Löwinger embraced Leo, said, my boy. He embraced him long, opening his arms stiffly again and again and, before Leo could free himself from the strong smell of after-shave lotion, patting him again on the back, pulling him back into the embrace, from which four or five times Löwinger only *seemed* to release him. He led him into the drawing-room, displaying a degree of affectionate warmth that only a father wanting to establish a friendly relationship with his son might have, but in such a way that it should remain always a hierarchical relationship: one that the first wishes to bring about for his happiness and that the second must accept for his happiness, with the result that both forms of happiness are identical only in the mind of the father. A struggle for recognition without struggle. Someone like Löwinger who always wins, who can no longer recognise that recognition requires a loser, carries perforce such a struggle into that realm where he can finally embrace the loser as his equal, because he was such a one before the struggle: on the battlefield that is only bloody because it is the battlefield of your own flesh and blood. That sounds more complicated and simpler than it is, but that's the way Leo felt it— he didn't think this, he felt it to be so. Didn't they talk about Leo's doctorate, about Hegel's *Phenomenonology*, about the Master-Slave chapter. Later. But from that first moment on Leo felt instinctively: this beloved and respected man is not my friend, he is a father, a father again—after the weak father now the strong father. Without asking what Leo wanted, Löwinger simply called for some port because he liked it so much himself, and poured Leo a glass, too—Leo might perhaps have preferred a coffee, so that he would be able to explain away to himself the beating of his heart. Leo would have confided in a friend now, eagerly unburdened his heart, but he answered Löwinger's questions in a polite, in an unreally polite way. Unreal to talk politely with a father about the death of your father in measured phrases—yes, really tragic, so sudden. And about his mother, so far away in space and time, desire for her far away, on the part of both father and son, but the wistful question and the desired answer—yes of course, things are tough for her right now. But she's very strong. Good, said the strongman, the father. And your doctoral thesis? Nearly finished, said Leo, but he'd had to stop work on it unfortunately because everything had happened so suddenly, with his father, and the fact that he'd had to come here, but he would certainly be finishing it, that much he owed his father.

Yes, you must, said the father—a sip of port and some words Leo didn't understand immediately, a gesture—what did it mean? Leo had to struggle so hard to concentrate, port in the early afternoon, the drawing-room filled in his memory with the excited buzz of voices but now merely resounding with the unnaturally loud echo of a faltering, restrained conversation, gestures that had no meaning, wordless inflexions. But the meanings emerged in the course of time, conversations in the drawing-room, conversations in the library, dinner together, sitting in an alienating, bleak light with an old man who has everything and who now as a matter of course lays claim in addition to this: the confidence of a younger man he calls 'my boy'.

110

Moles on his hand, a way of gesturing that appeared more and more like that of a marionette master, so harmonious, so commanding, as if everyone were suspended from strings attached by magic to the ends of his fingers. And the voice which only *appears* to come from far away but is in fact used to travelling far, a ventriloquist's—the puppets echo him by reading his lips, lips which barely need to move any more.

I'll arrange for you to meet George Abutre de Maganão—he's Brazil's greatest Hegelian—he could be a useful contact for you in your work, said Löwinger, and Professor George was already sitting there, visibly manipulated by the powerful, imaginary strings, a timid little mannequin who lived off the fact that Hegel had never been translated into Portuguese—he ate and drank as much as was befitting, nervous because he was not familiar with any of the secondary Hegel literature that had appeared since 1958 when he had been Visiting Professor at Konstanz in Germany, so defensive that he didn't once notice that Leo was not really very familiar with it either. Everything Professor George was wearing was too big for him: he continually had to stretch and elongate himself in order to appear out of the ends of his clothing, and even then he always looked like a pile of crumpled up garments that had been chucked carelessly onto an armchair. What was most absurd was his jacket: it was so stiff that the Professor still seemed to be sitting there rigidly, even when he fidgeted about. Such uncertainties were completely unknown to Professor Hans-Friedrich Schröder, German Visiting Professor of Philosophy at the University of Porto Alegre, a tall, slim, blond gentleman who by contrast was shoved into clothes that were too tight, a close-fitting shirt with buttons stretched to bursting, a pair of drip-dry trousers with no waistband pleats and with an artificial leather belt of the sort that always came with such trousers. He spoke non-stop in that careless accent that seems to make a German dialect out of every language in the world, but he was the only one who had a father at least, Hegel, the father of the Prussian state. And Löwinger? One might have been tempted to underestimate him: an old gentleman who scarcely said a word, who sat there motionlessly, only his fingers moving now and again, tapping one after the other on the arm of his chair, so inconspicuously, so seemingly without purpose that it might have been merely a sign of repressed impatience and boredom, but Leo could not rid himself of the impression that this was Löwinger playing with the puppets. And Leo himself: he wasn't at home here, not even here—he wasn't in control of himself either—he didn't fidget his feet. Please, Senhor Leo, said a young man who, as Leo was astonished to observe, was always taking notes, could you please tell us what significance Brazil or South America has in relation to Hegel's concept of world history?

It can't be true—none of it can true—Leo was certain he was dreaming—no, he wasn't, he could never have dreamt up such a thing. He wished he were somewhere else. Where? In Judith's kitchen? No. In the National Library in Vienna? No. In a one-night hotel in the *Boca*? On the beach? In the garden of his house? No. He carried this madness around with him and wherever he was he set it going. It can't be, can't be true. How Löwinger looked at him. Leo lowered his eyes. He now saw Löwinger's hand, saw the middle finger slowly rise and then tap the arm of the chair, then slowly the index finger, rise and fall, then the middle finger again—both fingers began to move together rhythmically.

Veja bem, said Leo. Hegel's central category is totality and that has to be understood, especially today, in such a way that—. It is clear that today no qualitative development remains restricted any longer to the area where it takes place. The speed of life nowadays. Our technological age. Modern means of communication. The world's getting smaller. Everything is beamed from one place to everywhere else. So quickly that soon it will no longer be possible to say where it began exactly. It was now becoming clear that—. The world is one whole. It had become so to such a degree. What was thought up yesterday in—just an example—Vienna, can today change Brazil—just an example. Hegel's category of totality, of the whole that alone is the truth, assigns Brazil its proper place as well, as part of the whole. That is to say. That means. You could also say. Today the world spirit is no longer at home anywhere, not in any particular place. One place would be only a small part of the whole. Nowhere at home any more. Not here either. But why should it not appear here, too? The world spirit has become a conqueror and discoverer, like Cabral was. It reaches out towards new continents.

Towards all of them.

Very well put, said Professor George.

Perhaps the world spirit is paying Brazil a visit right at this moment, *quem sabe*, perhaps tomorrow something will happen here in São Paulo that will take place at the same time in, let's say, Berlin—Professor Schröder nodded—and in, in, in Paris—just an example—that wouldn't surprise a Hegelian.

Quite correct, to be sure—Berlin, said Professor Schröder. Someone said 'very interesting.' Löwinger nodded. Leo leant back, his shirt sticking to the sweat on his back.

And two days later in the newspaper people could read about that afternoon in Löwinger's drawing-room, in an article—a compliant wriggle of response from Löwinger's strings—with the bizarre title: 'The World Spirit Visits Brazil', with a photo of Leo, the 'important Hegel specialist from Europe' who was 'on a visit to our city,' 'he reported on the highly interesting results of the latest research,' Professor George Abutre was quoted as saying, who, it was mentioned, was making every effort to secure for Leo a Visiting Lectureship at the University of São Paulo.

It was ridiculous and embarrassing, this Leo both knew and felt—the article caricatured what was already a caricature, and the photo—Leo had been completely unaware of it being taken—showed him lecturing, surrounded by Löwinger's guests—so ridiculous, so pretentious and false—Leo sweated nervously as he read the article, it was so embarrassing—he read the article again and again, he didn't read it, he stared at it, at home in his garden on a gunpowder evening. Löwinger himself was of course nowhere to be seen in the photo, his grey eminence, the puppeteer, there was only the photo on Leo's desk, and that resulted in a false picture. But when did Leo sit down at his desk? Now. He tore the page out of the newspaper—just be rid of it!—put it in an envelope which he addressed to Judith. He didn't ask himself why. She had to see he hadn't given up, that he was famous already in Brazil as a Hegel scholar. My dissertation, he wrote, is as good as finished. At the present moment I'm working on a series of Hegel lectures for the University. Didn't Leo ask himself whether Judith might not possibly see through this dreadful yarn? No. I'm doing fine, he wrote—my lawyer is dealing with all the land-selling business, so I have lots of free time which I'm trying to make use of. It makes me shudder to think how I frittered away my time in Vienna, but here in the Brazilian 'jungle' I have found my path and made good progess along it in the meantime, he wrote. Oh, if only you were with me on this path, he didn't write, then I'd be really getting somewhere. He wrote about Löwinger, a friend whose goodness and affection it would be impossible to write about impartially. Why did Leo write all this—be shot of this page from the newspaper, seal up the envelope quickly without reading through the letter again, and one last visit to the *Boca*. On the way he posted the letter and bought another copy of the newspaper so that he too would have the article and be able to keep it safe somewhere.

But Löwinger was not a friend, that Leo knew—his good offices on behalf of Leo were not the favours of a friend but were rather a kind of militant protectionism. Such a man always has a sound reason for what he does. Did Leo know what this was? He tried not to think about it. My boy, you need a different lawyer, and it was Löwinger who placed his own, the best, one whose loyalty had been tested over many years, at Leo's disposal, as a matter of course. And the documents from the bank that in the meantime no longer existed, these Löwinger procured through his connections, genuine or falsified, Leo did not ask—he needed to send reports of success to his mother and so everything took its course. And then there was always the *salon* by means of which Löwinger systematically conducted a political campaign of contacts and connections which were to smooth the way for a rapid career for Leo in the intellectual life of Brazil. Would he be prepared to write an article for the *debate* page of the *Estado* newspaper? Would he give a lecture in Porto Alegre? Leo declined every offer. A larger study project which he had to have finished by the end of the year, he said, was taking up all his time—only when this was behind him would he be free to take on other tasks. Leo squirmed with fear, with wind, but Löwinger praised him when they were alone: You did well there, my boy—it makes you more interesting and more desirable. People only desire the things they cannot so readily obtain.

Leo suffered, didn't want to admit it to himself, but he was starting to feel aggressive towards Uncle Zé, the way he sat there, a protected monument, like a piece of statuary, Zahradnik's masterpiece, a white-haired god to whom you had to pray because he had power over life, death and the after-life. Feelings of aggression at the way he spoke almost without opening his mouth, barely moving his lips, as a result of which everything he said, even the most banal words, acquired the character of a liturgically intoned utterance of universal validity, didn't appear to come from any particular pair of lips, certainly not from lips that didn't move. And every time he disagreed strongly with anyone, he did so in this drone and under the cloak of agreeing: if someone expressed an opinion Löwinger couldn't share, then at first he would say 'you're quite right' or 'absolutely' or at the very least 'mm!', then pause briefly as if he were weighing what had been said with the view to reassessing it—it was thus worthy of consideration!—only then to say exactly the opposite in such a way as if he were simply expanding on what had been said, and that was that, he'd have them know. This conciliatory way of his of stating the irrefutable must have been at the root of Löwinger's incredible career in Brazil because it satisfied so comprehensively the basic need of the Brazilian, if not of every, mentality: it's up to one person to decide but everyone else may be deemed to have been right.

However, Leo didn't want to be right in this way, not under conditions that were clearly no longer correct: this was no longer the Uncle Zé he had loved from his childhood, it was now just his generally revered icon, his publicly admired portrait, his monument erected in a vain market-place. And the exclusive nature of the affection that Leo himself experienced was also directed at an unfortunately false picture of himself, the one on display: the philosopher, the Hegel specialist, the promising young intellectual. He didn't even feel young. And since he had arrived in Brazil he hadn't done any intellectual work, hadn't read anything, written anything—that was over and done with. Hadn't written anything: the regular confessions—why confessions?—communiqués written to his mother overtaxed him already so much that, despite the fact that her voice alone filled him with hate, he switched to telephoning her. This way at least, after communicating the most important information, he could break off the conversation by remarking on how expensive long-distance calls were.

And Leo began to avoid Löwinger's *salon*. He no longer picked up the phone when it rang, or, when there was no way round it and Löwinger did in fact get hold of him, he then invented trips he had to go on or illnesses he was suffering from at that moment. And finally he withdrew from Löwinger with the same excuse he had already used once in front of him: his all-important study, his doctoral thesis, which required his total concentration, he had to pull back from things for a while, as much as he regretted it, as much as he enjoyed visiting Uncle Zé, but he wanted to, had to, he said, finish this work.

Well done, my boy. Now he had his peace and quiet, had it as never before. Löwinger put his machinery into motion in order to relieve Leo of all obligations, all necessity for movement, for any action with regard to the selling of the land—from Löwinger's lawyers to Löwinger's errand boys, from Löwinger's chauffeur to Löwinger's cleaning ladies, they all formed a net to catch anything that could disturb Leo's concentration. Now Leo could really have got down to work, but he was not able to and he hated Löwinger for taking from him even the possibility of being able to distract himself by visits to the law-courts,

115

the *cartorio*, the lawyers, or even the supermarket. The contract on his house ran out and the bottomless lethargy into which he'd sunk also made him incapable of looking for accommodation. He didn't need to either. Löwinger placed a small house at his disposal. On the property in Morumbi where Löwinger lived there was a small gatehouse near the road—this had just come free, or had been made free by Löwinger, Leo hadn't quite understood which. This was now his new address. And so it was that Leo, shunning Löwinger's company, became his totally shielded protegé, tenant and neighbour. However, before the move, it so happened that Leo found in his post the letter he had sent Judith. With a line through the address and underneath: Return to sender, addressee—and Leo couldn't read the next word: departed? deceased? The postman's illegible signature, the date, the stamp. Leo's first impulse was to tear open the letter, just as one does in fact with a newly received letter. As if it contained more specific information. But Leo knew, of course, what this envelope contained and the key information was written on the outside—no secrecy on the part of the postal service—namely, that Judith hadn't received what he had sent her.

Departed or deceased? At first it didn't seem to make any difference to Leo—either way Judith was out of his reach. But he wanted to know. Thanks to Löwinger Leo had so much free time, and now at last he had something to do with it. A visit to the Austrian Consulate in São Paulo. There he could find a Vienna telephone directory. Leo copied out the addresses of all the people he knew in Vienna, however vaguely. Judith's address as recorded in the directory was, of course, the old one. The next day Leo spent at his desk. Once again Judith had driven him back to work. He wrote dozens of letters to Vienna, asking everyone he could if they had ever known Judith, could still remember her, were in touch with her, had heard anything from her, if they knew someone who knew her, could ascertain something of her whereabouts, if they could set inquiries in train with regard to this, and so on and so forth. He wrote to everyone, asked each one to let him know about Judith Katz, he needed to contact her urgently, it was important, please, thank you for your trouble, how are you by the way. These days spent at his desk, which he hadn't used in such a long time, were happy ones. He served up the most remote acquaintances with pearls of the epistolary art, more and more joyfully and boldly as he went, all of it fictitious, phantasies, outlines of his life which he recounted as if they were chapters of a real and exciting autobiography, but it was his life, his world, in its most successful phase, which was why it was in fact true, above all the question: Have you heard anything of Judith? Leo grew in spirit during these days, felt suddenly so strong that, despite the fact that he had initially ruled it out, he even wrote to Lukas Trojan.

Thoughts about a possible appointment as university lecturer. That should be the logical continuation of his commentary on Hegel's *Phenomenology* and—Leo just wrote and wrote without stopping, with one sentence leading into the next—that could only be a continuation of the *Phenomenology of Spirit* itself. That was how the idea first arose. Out of a mood, a flattering, fictitious portrayal of himself, the punch-line to a letter, an idea born of rum. Leo was drinking rum. This idea appealed to him immediately and he straightaway put it into action. In his *Phenomenonology* Hegel describes the development of consciousness from the most primitive level up to Absolute Knowledge. But the development of consciousness didn't come to an end at the same time as Hegel came to the end of his *Phenomenonology*—it has unquestionably continued to change and develop. In what way? What new forms has consciousness acquired? That was what he wanted to recount, an adaptation of Hegel, from Hegel's death to the present day. He was surprised no-one had done it before. But wasn't this vitally necessary in order to introduce the concept to the contemporary world and bring philosophy truly to an end. He wanted to, he had to undertake this task. Brazil being so removed, he wrote, made it an ideal vanishing point from where a true picture of what was essential...and Judith? Heard from her, still in touch with her?

Leo wrote for days on end—at last the house had become more than a place to sit in the evenings wrapped in a particular smell, more than a place to sleep merely after a day spent in dull torpor. And then? Nothing. Everything had been done and again it was a question of waiting. He was sitting at his desk again when he picked up Giorgione's picture of Judith which had its place there, looked at it and stowed it away in a box shortly before the desk was loaded into the van and taken away. The first night in his new house Leo slept badly.

There was a stench in the room—what a stench. A provocative one—it provoked Leo into wanting to be sick, but also provoked, he thought—not without a certain irony yet with distinct nervousness— supernatural aspirations. It was obvious that the pervasive smell was, very clearly...what was it? Sulphur. Pitch and sulphur. When Leo had gone to bed he had noticed the smell faintly and vaguely, as if it were wafting in from far away, from a canal perhaps or a factory nearby—he had of course learnt to live with such olfactory inconveniences at his old address. But was it at all likely for there to be a factory near there, in the respectable suburb of Morumbi? Supposedly not. But what did he know? He had closed all the windows tight, something he'd got used to doing the previous year, so now nothing could come in any more. But the smell became stronger as a result. Leo didn't think seriously, of course, of a manifestation of something made flesh, of a devil's pact now offered to him and which he would naturally enter into. They were simply daydreams, not even dreams, associations made in the dark, for he couldn't sleep because of this irritating stench. He turned on the light and immediately started to look for the real cause of the stench, for a scientific explanation, as it were, without any understanding of the relevant science. He knew as little about chemistry as he did of literature—which was why his Faustian associations were so dry and abstract that they failed to frighten him. How did sulphur smell? Where could the smell of sulphur in this room come from? Was it pure sulphur he could smell—sulphur only? Or was there another smell mixed in with it? What kind was this one? A sicky smell, Leo sniffed, a smell of death and decay. Leo had never smelt a corpse, though, even that of his father. How had his father smelt when he saw him for the last time in hospital? Not good. But what did that mean. And memory, after all. He remembered how often he'd reflected how difficult it was to remember optical impressions, but primarily smells. Father. Are you here. Of course not. What do you want of me. Do you want to tell me something. Of course not. A stupid phantasy. Nothing to be seen apart from what was in fact to be seen, this room that was still so strange and unfamiliar to him that he couldn't visualise it when he turned the light off again.

Leo's hair stood on end from tossing in a sweat to and fro in bed. He was now scrabbling around through the room on all fours, inspecting every nook and cranny. Perhaps some rotting animal lay in a corner of the room, a dead rat behind the cupboard. Nothing. Couldn't be, either. Does carrion smell of sulphur? No. Though Leo was familiar neither with carrion nor sulphur. But it stank in this room, of that there was no doubt. Perhaps the window wasn't shut tight. No, it was. The bolts were so tight he sprained his finger opening the window. He stood there, with drooping finger, groaning softly by the open window, and the fresh night air flooded in. He enjoyed the cool fresh air, breathed in deeply, cooled his hot, sweat-soaked body as he leant far out of the window. The stench definitely didn't come from outside. But from where, then? He smoked a palomitas, an aromatic Brazilian cigarillo he'd made the acquaintanve of a short while before at Löwinger's and which he'd now bought for himself. Fifty in a pretty little wooden box. Palomitas have a slight chocolatey flavour. The smell drowned the stench in his room. Almost. The smell of chocolate. Almost. Was it possible he'd caught syphilis? For a moment he stiffened—happily. Regina. No, not from Regina. That would have been banal. The smell of decay. Judith. Yes. Deceased. Still infectious. He smoked. Nothing to be seen. The smell of tobacco, but it stank. He put out the light again. He could still see the swathes of smoke in the dark, night-blue light of the room. But they didn't assume any shapes. They drifted away like the swathes of mist in a cemetery. Stone angels over the graves. There, Judith, no, more monumental—he was almost asleep. He sat there as rigidly as a statue, without moving, speaking without moving his lips, I hope you'll like it here. You? Yes, me. Now you belong to me. You belong to me. Löwinger smiled.

It must have been the cold night air and the fact that he had stood so long at the open window bare from the waist up and covered in sweat—that must have been it. Leo had caught a cold. Feverish, he had to keep to his bed, sweat it out, drink tea, couldn't smoke any palomitas. You thought the devil appeared to you, my boy—wonderful. An exciting experience, though. It doesn't matter in the least whether something is really there or not, as long as you experience it. I envy you. Life becomes boring when you're old, I'll be honest with you, my boy. When you have power and experience, the excitement ceases, you can't put a foot wrong any more. Eradicate stupidity and bad blunders and you make a wrong move, for there are always some who hurry immediately to change the conditions of reality in such a way that you find that in fact you made a right move. But those aren't devils, they're boring, mediocre little spirits who always appear with neckties and shirts that are too tight and the sum of their desires is to have shirts that are never too loose. A demonic apparition. Delightful. What form did the devil assume? Mine? Surely not! Did he sit by your bedside like I'm doing now?

For the first time Löwinger's lips moved. A smile.

A joke, my boy. I'm sorry you've had to put up with this stink. Before you moved in I gave instructions for the rooms to be thoroughly cleaned and well aired. I really thought that all traces had been removed. Traces of stupidity. But the smell really is more stubborn than I thought. You can still smell it even now. Not you, of course, with your cold. You must get better quickly, my boy. You were ill so often over the last year. There was a period when you were ill all the time, whenever I telephoned. And yet you don't look that delicate. Your sensitivity probably. Sensitive people are always prone to illness. It'll take a while till the smell disappears completely since the windows have to stay shut now of course for as long as you're ill. A very stimulating smell, though only when set against the background of your story. The original story of this smell was unsavoury and stupid. What? I'm just going to tell you about it now. Last year I put this house at the disposal of a young painter, as an atelier. I often do this when I'm convinced about someone. The young artist gets board and lodging from me here and some pocket money. No, nothing in return. If I like what he paints, I buy the paintings from him at a realistic price. It's the art market that gives me something in return. Because in the end, if I have been right, then these pictures were gifts, so to speak. Martin Daher—you know him by sight—he was often up there in my *salon*—a taciturn young man—gives the impression of being more pensive than he is. Yes, that's the one. Drink some more of your tea—you're so croaky, I can barely understand you. Well, he was the one who lived here before you. A year ago he had a highly regarded exhibition, highly regarded by me. So I set about promoting him. This fellow has talent, I thought to myself, and I was right—this fellow will come to something, and there I was wrong. The mistake is not important. A gallery owner bought the pictures from me that I had from Martin at absurdly high prices—pictures that I now wanted to be rid of because I had realised my mistake—just because I had promoted him, that was guarantee enough for the dealer that something would come of him. The next thing he does is to create a huge media circus around Martin in order to ratch up the prices and people are already saying I was right again, I had recognised Martin Daher's importance before anything about him had appeared in the papers. The truth is I made some money by mistake. And this dealer now has to sort out his mistake. For you see, Martin Daher only has talent. Do you know what the difference is between someone with talent and a genius? Someone with talent has the sulphur delivered not by the devil but by a chemicals firm. In other words, genius is a fiend, talent a scoundrel.

Again Löwinger twisted his mouth into a smile, but he remained otherwise as stiff and motionless as a monument—no, he didn't, he crossed one leg over the other and swung it to and fro. Leo sighed in relief. Löwinger might have interpreted this sound as a groan and concluded that the conversation was putting too much strain on the patient. But he didn't even notice. He seemed to be listening to something far away, from where his voice came. And what he heard there amused him. A joke, he said. Leo was sweating.

So I let Martin Daher work here in peace and quiet. In peace and quiet.

Löwinger sat motionlessly on Leo's bed without moving a finger. I never came over to have a look at what he was doing. Never. I don't do that. Now and again I invited him to dinner. He'll say, I'm sure, when I should come and that I should come, I thought. If he is an artist then he will need someone with artistic expertise. Will need someone to explain to him what he's doing. An artist can do the right thing with ingenuity and ease and without knowing it's right but if there isn't someone with artistic expertise to tell him it *is* right, if he continues not knowing it is, then suddenly he'll do the wrong thing. I waited. Artists aren't solipsistic. That's an old wives' tale. They are ignorant, believe you me. They have hundreds of ideas and don't know what to do with them, other than do something with all of them. In getting to grips with artistic expertise, which is what they seek to do, they concentrate truly and effectively on what is correct for the first time. That's what had to happen. I was ready. I waited. From the prudish stories he told over the dinner table I was able to deduce that Martin was not an easy person, a painter who lacked confidence, was full of scruples, at odds with himself, who tried out all manner of things first before getting down to painting a picture. Genius doesn't entail being in a constant state of trance, during which you spontaneously do only the right thing all the time, no, that it is not, believe you me. Masterpieces painted in a day, brilliant compositions noted down without a single correction in a few hours, novels that flow from the pen in two weeks, poems tossed off in an evening which reflect the feelings of a whole epoch, these are the exceptions and for the most part these genius stories aren't even true. The general rule is, the truth is, that genius is far removed from the artist himself because it lies so incredibly deep down inside him. He first has to learn to conjure it up, as it were. Genius must first come up out of the artist, and then step up and confront him. It is this ruthlessness that he must find his way to. He must work towards getting the devil to appear to him, as it were. You, my boy, have got nearer to that than Martin Daher. Martin is a madman, not an artist. A talent that doesn't work on releasing genius but decorates itself externally with lunacy. Nothing will come of that. That much is clear to me now. He lived here and painted for almost a year but never showed me anything, never invited me to this house that I'd put at his disposal, never discussed any work on the easel with me. But I was patient. Now and again I looked at the pictures that I'd acquired for his first exhibition. Very fine demonstrations of talent. Somewhat exaggerated in their frantic desire to make a statement, but in execution, technique, composition and colouring most striking. Demonstrations of talent, please note. Nothing more. Sadly. One evening at dinner I noticed that Martin had eczema on his face and hands—scabs and moles. And his clothes and hair were giving off an unpleasant smell. I spoke to him about it and he confessed he'd been experimenting with new materials. At the beginning, he claimed, he'd unfortunately been careless, which is why he'd got these skin problems. Now, however, he was able to handle the materials and the eczema would certainly disappear soon. He'd made, he said, good progress converting to his new technique and soon he'd have a series of paintings—Soon? I said and confessed to him my irrepressible curiosity, asked whether I could now take a look at this work that he said was on the point of emerging. He squirmed and made excuses that with all the understanding in the world I couldn't accept. Finally he agreed. After dinner we went to his atelier, over here. There was a pervasive and repulsive stench. Drink your tea, Leo, even if it's not that hot any more, the honey will do you good. So, and now stop drinking, otherwise you'll choke when you hear. Do you know what that madman had done here?

Löwinger clenched his hands into two fists—and the marionette which had lived and worked in these rooms collapsed in on itself, and lay broken on the floor.

Martin had begun to repaint famous battle paintings in the history of art—'The Battle of Ivry' by Rubens, 'The Alexander Battle' by Albrecht Altdorfer, 'The Battle of San Romano' by Ucello, 'The Battle of Waterloo' by Allan and so on. No, not copies. He painted the scene from the same visual angle but depicting the next day. The sequel, as it were. Before—After. Instead of troops marshalled in their positions he painted mountains of corpses. Instead of horses thrusting forward energetically he painted cadavers. Instead of idealised landscapes, he painted fields of carcasses. But always on the basis of the detail and the composition of the original painting to which he was referring. The tips of precisely those lances that in the 'Alexander Battle' look like little pennants he drags down into the filth of a blood-drenched soil. What did you say? Where the stench came from? Wait, I'm about to tell you. Painted corpses don't smell, you think? You're right. Supposedly. But the madman put all his so-called artistic ambition into it, sought out a method of making them stink in fact. I'll tell you in a minute. The madman began to expound to me—to me—that art had always idealised life, but ought to show the truth. What is the truth? The picture of truth? In the midst of this penetrating and encompassing stench he began to talk about the military dictatorship here in Brazil—we lead such seemingly pleasant lives but what is the real truth behind this. People are tortured, but tortured in cellars, no-one sees it. People disappear, suddenly they're no longer there, no longer visible. Invisible political influences on our country that no-one admits to or comments on, from the USA, from Germany. He told me endlessly about all the things that were not visible, were hidden, and which were therefore beyond all possibility of being portrayed. There I was, standing over there in the corner with a handkerchief over my mouth and nose, while the madman lectured me. The truth is, he said, that a painter today who no longer wants to be subject to any authority would have to exhibit a white canvas and nothing more. To which I say: He does indeed need to find a metaphor. Voilà, he says, here it is, and points to the stinking dung-heap of his paintings. The logical metaphor is war. What dominated here was a war waged by self-styled heroes and national saviours against people. That's all very fine, I say, but why does it stink so dreadfully in here? The truth of war, he says, is not the hero, the victor, but death and the misery of the many. I've known this, he says, since my twenties, from experience and from art. But why does it smell so much here? That's the truth of Brazil, the smell of corpses and decay. Can you paint a stench? No. Yes, he can. The result of a long period of experimentation. The message: Don't let yourselves be taken in by your heroes—it's not just motorways they build. Whoever looked at his pictures, said Martin, would have to turn away, because of the spectacle of death and decay and because of their stench. They wouldn't even allow of a voyeuristic examination just because of this stench. This would liberate the eye—which seeks to aestheticise everything—open it to reality, to the truth. In short, do you know what this madman experimented with in these rooms? He mixed chemical substances, mainly mercaptane and tiophenolen, which are sulphur compounds with an extremely offensive smell, with his oilpaints, adding the remains of cadavers which he had purified into a paste—the wretch had even experimented with faeces. He tried out valerian acid, anything that smells unpleasant. And he found a mixture that was practicable, to use his words—practicable. Which he could apply to canvas and which at

123

the same time developed a long-lasting stench. And then? What do you mean, then? I threw him out. The man's crazy, a charlatan, raving mad. He talked non-stop, scratching at his scabs all the while. Besides, you needed somewhere to live. Imagine buying a painting by Daher. You'd have to move home. Imagine you have an art collection. One painting by Daher would reduce the collection to a stinking dung-heap. Imagine a museum. You would only be able to visit it with special breathing apparatus. That's quite mad. I held my handkerchief over my nose and said he had a week, in a week's time he should kindly return the keys of the house to my estate manager. What? Perhaps he's right? Artistic truth is exaggerated normality, not abnormality. The young man was abnormal. Polluting a house is not art. You should get some sleep now, Leo. You must get better. Your work. That's important. I know. I'm never wrong. Almost never. You wanted to know why it stinks here and I've told you. But it's not as bad as it was. It's dissipating. By the time you're better it will have gone. I beg your pardon? That's right, my boy, but the idea had nothing going for it, absolutely nothing. Art, in fact, has nothing whatsoever to do with ideas. Art lives by the laws of beauty. And if it wants to depict the horrific, then all the more must it live by this tension between what is most terrible and the beauty of appearance, the apparent beauty into which art turns it. And it must endure this tension in its form—its form, mind you, and not through tricks that it sets up outside of itself. Quite apart from this, you cannot separate art from the uniqueness, originality and incomparability to which it is wedded. It's also in this sense, therefore, that we're talking of originals. And even though every original work of art constitutes incidentally a dialogue with tradition, with the canon—incidentally, mind you—if art wishes to be no more than a paraphrase, a quotation, a dialogue with other particular works of art, then it founders immediately. Works of art that seek and assume comparison with others, instead of resisting all comparison, these are products of the cobbler not works of art, products of the cobbler, believe you me. Go to sleep now, my boy, and if you need anything, let me know.

Soon Leo had nothing more to complain about. This was the most painful period. What was he to do? Weeks went by during which he just let things drift. Two or three appointments at court where his personal appearance was considered advisable. A few social events at Löwinger's, a private dinner with him from which he didn't back out for the simple reason that he didn't know what else to do with himself and his time. Visits to the cinema, to the bar. A few superficial drinking acquaintances, people who were so very pleased when he arrived and didn't notice when he didn't. You're pale, my boy—you're working too hard. You need some sun and fresh air for a few days. Three days by the sea in Guarujá where Löwinger owned an apartment. Now and again the odd letter from Vienna. No-one had heard anything of Judith. The mild chocolate smell of the palomitas, the fading smell of sulphur. Every day the close perusal of the newspaper. Whenever a concert at the *Teatro de Cultura Artistica* was advertised that looked set to become the talk of the town, Leo was there. Though, after the concert, he preferred in fact the pianist in the *Baiuca Bar* just around the corner from the theatre. Ah, you are of Austrian extraction, said a lady at Löwinger's one afternoon, who dabbed her lips with a napkin after every bite of a roll, so you must have also seen the Vienna State Opera ballet at the *Teatro Municipal*. Leo had seen it. It was so beautiful, so delightful, my husband and I love waltzes. That I can understand, said Leo.

The match between the two city football clubs, São Paulo and the Corinthians, written about nervously for days beforehand in the paper: Leo was there. Following this he heard heated discussions in a small bar in Pacaembu near the stadium. The winning goal, some declared excitedly, had clearly been *impedido*, clearly offside. The referee a criminal, the linesman bribed—*impedido* they shouted again and again, *impedido*. You'd have to look at it again, suggested one man, to see whether really at the moment when the ball was passed—They were level, shouted another, *impedido, impedido*. Amazed, Leo drank his beer. He didn't understand the problem. He knew the word *impedido* only in the meaning of blocked—a road can be *impedido*—or impeded, occupied—a person invited by someone can excuse themselves by saying they are *impedido* at the time of the suggested meeting. Hey, doctor, one man called, what do *you* say? The majority were clearly for *impedido*. No doubt about it, said Leo—*impedido*.

To his astonishment it was precisely this question that was discussed the next day page after page in the newspapers. I saw it with my own eyes, Leo said when he was buying bread in the *padaria*, a clear case of *impedido*.

On one bleak and listless evening spent at home Leo remembered how once in a conversation with Judith he had polemicised against life.

125

Life, he had said, was merely the process of being absorbed into that which happens anyway. The essential thing was the deed—this was what he wanted to use to shore up against life, he had said. Leo wept when he thought of this. He was of course a little drunk and alcohol made him tearful. No earthly sign of any deed. He wasn't up to it. He was fully absorbed in everyday outer events and was nevertheless not living. Not even that. Life. Leo had put on a few kilos. He was getting podgy. Not from eating. He only ate hot meals when he was invited out somewhere. On his own he had never lived such an ascetic life. A piece of bread and butter whenever he suddenly got hungry at home—maybe two. It was the alcohol. He drank too much beer and rum. He wanted to numb himself. He couldn't stand doing nothing, hanging around, every day discovering anew that he didn't know what he should do with himself. He was no good at being a good-for-nothing, he thought a touch coquettishly. A rum idea. How was he supposed to sleep at nights, too, without the rum. The alcohol settled on his hips and stomach. And his face became rounder, his head appearing now much bigger. Soon people would be thinking he had hydrocephalitis. Leo hated himself now as well whenever he looked in the mirror. That wasn't him. That wasn't the person he saw in front of him whenever he looked at himself from the outside without a mirror. So conical. The large cranium, the narrow weak shoulders, and then the broad hips and stomach. And from the side the thin arms and delicate hands. Ridiculous. He ought to change his life even if it didn't amount to one. Every day, or nearly every day, he said this to himself. You must change your life. Work. For weeks he said it to himself. Uncle Zé inquired how his work was progressing. A new qualitative stage, Leo explained—he was now at one with the subject properly for the first time. Whatever else he was doing, he was wholly preoccupied with thinking about his project.

One day the boredom, the self-disgust and despair at his restless apathy were so great that he actually did return to work.

Not really of course. No-one writing something serious simply sits down at the desk and starts to write.

Leo hadn't brought nearly enough secondary literature with him to Brazil. He was missing so many important books needed in order for the work to have any meaning. No amount of time or trouble was too great when it came to getting hold of these books. At last he had something to do. Tours of the city. To the University library. To the library of the Philosophical Institute. To the library of the Institute for Germanic Studies. To the German bookshop in São Paulo. He even paid Professor George a visit. When he got home in the evenings he was too tired to read the books he'd struggled back with. And when he had exhausted all the possibilities of acquiring Hegel literature in São Paulo, he then sat despondently in front of the heap of books—when was he supposed to read all this? He read novels. Or went to the movies. He had to wait until the books he'd ordered from the German bookshop arrived. But things were how they were. There was nothing to be done. No matter what he did. Whether he read or not. The distraction tactic. Dinners with Löwinger. Drinking, sleeping. Things were how they were. The unwritten laws of life. He couldn't give life any new laws, couldn't lay down new ones even for himself. What difference did it make whether he worked or not. There's someone who thought and wrote and changed the world. That's a long time ago. The chances of being as influential with such an approach are clearly over. Otherwise the interpreters, explorers and commentators of this philosophy would surely still be influential, effective and of generally recognised importance today. Dozens, hundreds of people have expounded on this philosophical work, sacrificed their lives to gaining an expert knowledge, to giving an exposition of this work, even to demonstrating its continuing contemporary relevance. Leo contemplated the thick volumes on his desk. What have they changed? Nothing. What have they brought about? Nothing. I haven't even read them—that's how little. And how many people have worked for years whose work I don't even know? What have they produced as a result of their years of industry? Nothing—I don't even know their names, often not even that of the chairholder at some philosophical institute. Leo realised slowly that the one book he was looking for, a very different book, didn't exist—this would in fact have been the book he wanted to write himself. Since he hadn't written it, he couldn't find it. He wanted to find it so that he wouldn't have to write it any longer. Since he didn't find it, he couldn't write.

I must accept this, thought Leo. I no longer want to write this book. Something or other has changed, something in me has torn. I must rid myself of this task—only then will I be able to get some idea as to what I really want to do. It seems to be all over with Hegel. Over and done with.

Now he had something to do again for a few days. He had to take the books back that he had borrowed. University library. The Institute libraries. Professor George. Cancel the orders at the German bookshop. He said he was prepared at all events to take those books that had already been sent off from Germany. Furthermore, he bought a whole pile of fiction in order to placate the exasperated salesgirl at the bookshop. He even bought Pontopiddan's novel, *Lucky Hans*, the famous dead stock of the German bookshop: the only book still left from the stock when the bookshop was started and which had never been bought till now. A skittish conversation ensued from this that led to dinner with the salesgirl. For the first time he didn't say to a woman he was taking out that he was writing a book about Hegel. In answer to the question 'what he did in life', he said he was an estate agent. He was amazed to observe that this increased his attractiveness. That's at least how he interpreted the fact that subsequently everything went very smoothly that evening.

Theresa, the girl from the bookshop, had no understanding for 'these eternal students'. What is it we want from life? she asked. Just peace and quiet. And what do students do? Stir up trouble and unrest. They can study, she said, but they don't. They just make a lot of hullabaloo. Did you read, she asked, what happened at the University of Brasilia? I don't understand it. Leo agreed with her. He was tired. Everything was so simple. This was what life was like. You agree and then you're right. Justice is administered according to unwritten laws as a result of which all people, after agreeing with each other, quite simply love each other. Leo didn't know why, but that's how it was. She had had to work since she was twelve years old, said Theresa, she had always worked. But students, they don't want to work and don't want to study. If I were able to study, I wouldn't go out onto the streets and demonstrate—what would I be doing on the street? You're completely right, said Leo. Can you understand why they do that? said Theresa. No, said Leo, I don't understand it either.

At breakfast Theresa's understanding had finally come to an end. She read the newspaper, giving Leo a tired and oddly disappointed look as she turned the pages. Or did the look only seem disappointed? Why should she be disappointed? Every time Leo thought he ought now to say something, Theresa would disappear again behind the paper. Leo was irritated that she was reading the paper. Not because he would have preferred to talk with her. He would have preferred to be reading the paper himself. He was used now to reading the paper at breakfast. But he hadn't quite been able to bring himself to do this now as Theresa was there. He'd thought he really ought to pay her some attention. And then she goes and reads the paper. All at once she exclaimed: Look at this then—come off it, an estate agent, *porra nenhuma*, what a fibber—a famous prophet, that's what you are, well, I never. In the paper there was a long article about Leo with a photo beneath which was written 'Archives'—it had already appeared in this newspaper once before: Leo holding forth at Löwinger's, surrounded by the *salon* guests. The article reported that Leo had predicted, down to the most exact detail and in the presence of a whole load of witnesses—the author of the article was also present—the events of this year of 1968, the student unrest in Paris, Berlin and Brazil. Even the centres of these historic events—'Paris, Berlin and also Brazil were named precisely in the notes I took of the comments made by Leo Singer months ago' wrote the author of this article. Deriving from nothing else other than from Hegel's historical dialectic. Logically deduced. Professor George Abutre, also a witness: 'This is no surprise to a Hegelian.' The question arises whether Hegel's historical philosophy has not only a surprising actuality but also even allows insights into the future which and so on and so forth.

I don't understand it, said Theresa.

Nor do I, said Leo.

I don't believe you, Mr Estate Agent—come off it.

The first thing Leo had to do was change bakers. In the *padaria* where he'd shopped till now the man behind the counter began to plague him with the pools. He wanted Leo to tell him the results of the coming football matches. He could see into the future, after all. Using a scientific method. It was in the newspaper. And Leo had already proved it to him once before—he'd predicted that São Paulo would win against the Corinthians with an off-side goal. He remembered exactly. Please, doctor.

Next, Leo even had to move out of his house temporarily because of the people ringing non-stop at his door, journalists from newspapers, magazines, the radio and television—above all, though, the countless believers who flocked to him as to a soothsayer or miracle healer. He moved up to Löwinger's house where a guest room was put at his disposal. From his hiding-place Leo watched the clusters of people forming below in front of his gate-house, followed the growing media hysteria of which he was the centre, even though it was Professor George who, since Leo couldn't be contacted, served the sudden general interest in Hegel's historical philosophy with articles and comments here and interviews there. Professor George, who was visibly enjoying being suddenly in such demand, proceeded always with the same routine: first he explained in the most simplified and general way Hegel's historical dialectic, then went on to hint darkly at its consequences for the immediate future, in order then finally to express at great length his regret that Hegel's *Phenomenology of Spirit* was still not available in a Portuguese translation, which, if this deficiency were finally resolved, would satisfy the legitimate curiosity of the public considerably better than he was able to do. And since Professor George knew exactly that the interest of the public essentially concerned Leo and that the interest in himself would persist only insofar as he succeeded in continuing to stir up the interest in Leo, he garnished his comments regularly with favourable words about Leo Singer whose 'priceless service' was this or that, whose 'illuminating comments' had clarified this or that darkly alluded to problem in Hegel research—this leading, however, to all the Hegel quotations with which Professor George interlarded his remarks being attributed to Leo and becoming household words. So the Governor of São Paulo, installed by the military, loved 'those pertinent words of our Professor Singer: What is actual is rational'. The student left-wing insisted on the 'cunning of reason' and on the fact that, 'as Professor Singer has proved, reality cannot withstand ideas.' No self-respecting journalist lost the opportunity to introduce his one-sided, page-long leading article with 'Leo Singer's incontrovertible words: 'Truth is not simply the opposite of error: it is both.' And the most popular TV presenter replaced his clichéd 'The show must go on' with Professor Singer's wise words: 'The essence must appear!'

In the domestic politics sections of the newspapers the possibility of Leo entering politics was discussed. He was being talked about, they said, as adviser to the Governor, but the tolerated opposition party was also making every effort to get Leo Singer to work with them, which was only logical according to what was reported as emanating from opposition circles, for, after all, they had the future on their side. In the culture and science sections the newspapers vehemently demanded the long overdue translation of Hegel's Phenomenology and produced on the sports pages a bogus interview with Leo, in which the scientifically deduced prophecy was put into his mouth that Brazil would without any doubt win the football World Cup in 1970.

The philosophy students vehemently demanded a Visiting Professorship for Leo, something which Professor George, in view of how he had earlier represented himself, could not exactly ignore. His argument that a Visiting Professorship would be hard to get accepted by the university bureaucracy at that present moment was demolished as a result of the curiosity that had seized the other faculty members. A written invitation from the faculty was sent to Leo to give a lecture at the Philosophical Institute—following from this, and given a continuing interest, a Visiting Professorship might also be possible.

Leo accepted the invitation. The guest lecture seemed to him to offer the only possibility of escaping in a sensible and reasonable manner from the incarceration of Löwinger's palace. To have written, simply turning down the invitation, indicating that the interest in his person arose from a misunderstanding and the interest in Hegel from a completely erroneous conception of his philosophy, for which reason he could satisfy neither interests, would have served only to have kept him in his hiding-place until grass had grown over the affair—for who knows how long. Furthermore, such a refusal would have aggravated his incarceration, for he would assuredly have incurred Löwinger's incomprehension, if not his hatred, had he done so. There was no question: the misunderstanding had to be cleared up publicly. The lecture was the opportunity to do it.

I'm proud of you, my boy. You've stirred things up. Are you certain you really haven't sold your soul? I'm sorry, a joke. No, you did everything just right. Didn't grab the first opportunity but waited for the best. Worked hard, too. If you wait and carry on working at the same time, then the right moment comes and you're prepared. That's what I myself have always practised. I wasn't wrong about you. There's this feeling of certainty about you and the unbending consistency that marks out the great spirit. You've been working a long time. I'd so like to read something of your work. Well, whenever. Now you can garner the fruits of your work. A mistake? You're right, my boy. A mistake on the part of others. But you are right. That's what counts. For one man to be right requires others to be mistaken. The success of the one always entails the error of the others, mark my words.

Leo simply couldn't talk to Löwinger. Couldn't get him to understand. Leo wanted to keep Löwinger at arm's length and now he was living under the same roof with him, was Löwinger's sole property. Leo didn't want to know anything more about Hegel—he had cut short his work on Hegel and just at this moment a Hegel boom takes off and Leo becomes the most sought-after Hegel expert. He had come to the conclusion that Hegel was history, that busying oneself with Hegel

131

was a meaningless, backward-looking exegesis, and now Hegel is seen by a wide public as the most up-to-date philosopher there is, with whose help you could even obtain power over the future. Leo had always dreamed of becoming an important man, of influencing history, changing the world, and hardly had he given up this childish dream than he found he'd achieved a public importance for which he was completely unprepared and which would in truth have given him considerable influence if his nerve—since none of it was true any more—hadn't failed him at the prospect. He couldn't tell Uncle Zé this—who wouldn't hear him out—he couldn't handle it, handle Uncle Zé, who was rubbing his hands proudly and getting his marionettes moving at the same time to pull off a coup that he thought would be all to Leo's good. Leo wanted to escape. Clarify things. Discuss things sensibly. He didn't want Löwinger to be disappointed with him, to hate him. If that happened, then he'd rather many people were disappointed with him, hated him, for this might lead some at least perhaps to understand, to grasp what had happened and to say something apposite. The guest lecture. When Leo accepted the invitation, then true stature was his for the first time.

Since the summer vacation was just round the corner, a date was fixed for after the holidays: October 2nd 1968.

Time enough for Leo to prepare. Time enough to ask himself always the same questions. What should I say? How should I say it? Ladies and gentlemen, we are gathered together here as a result of a misunderstanding. What was the nature of this misunderstanding? To explain I must begin at the beginning. Or another opening. Ladies and gentlemen, you are expecting me to enlighten you as to how one can acquire power over history with the help of Hegelian philosophy. I would first like to give you a brief summary of the contents of the Hegelian system, chiefly, though, of the *Phenomenology of Spirit*, about which so many misleading things have been written in the newspapers recently. The summary follows, the elaboration of the most important categories. And then I could ask: what could be done with this now, please? Could one deduce from this future historical processes? No. History didn't stand still with the final full-stop of the *Phenomenology*, and all the historical changes since then are of course not reflected in the *Phenomenology;* furthermore, the whole of history from Hegel's death up to today can certainly not be described by means of Hegelian concepts alone—never mind the future. But how was it then, the students will ask, that you managed to arrive at a concrete and precise prediction simply on the basis of Hegel's categories? I didn't. It just said that in the newspaper. But why? Why would the newspaper have invented that? And there was said to have been witnesses. Our Professor George. I don't know why that was written. Uncle Zé. I can't talk about Uncle Zé. I can't. I'd have to. Clarification. Clarification comes before a fall. They'll despise me. No-one will accept that, no-one will understand. Not one. I scarcely do. No, I'll have to begin differently. No summary of the contents of *Phenomenology*. That would be like a Hegel lecture again and I don't want to work on Hegel any more, explain Hegel, talk about Hegel. I wish to explain to you why. You want to study Hegel's *Phenomenology*, call for its translation and from this you expect to gain for yourselves social influence and power over history. This expectation is a great error, to which I too succumbed. My experience, however, is that it is absolutely not necessary to study *Phenomenology* for years like I did. No-one will achieve social influence by these means—yes, but haven't you yourself proved the opposite, Leo Singer—aren't all eyes on you, aren't your words on everyone's lips, and the expectations that society has of you, are these not of the highest order? A misunderstanding—I will explain—But if I really did succeed in clearing up this misunderstanding, they'd refute me all over again! I'd have become an historical force. The interest in Hegel would be extinguished in a flash and it would be my historical achievement finally to have brought it about that Hegel does not in fact get translated into Portuguese, or at least not for a long time. Not like that, then. Quite differently. Nothing would come of it— and something must. But no more quotations from Hegel. Ladies and gentlemen. Leo marched through Löwinger's garden, no longer a child or boy hero practising the conquest of the real world in an imaginary one. Bent forward, hands behind his back, a man of the hour who was stepping out of the world of the upper bourgeoisie, out of Löwinger's house where he remained a stranger, in order to sound the depths of his own being in the loneliness of this garden.

A completely passive, indifferent, forlorn existence, resting thus under the shade provided by this tree, dreaming unassumingly like Oblomov in his bed, and idling away the indistinguishable days until his hair grows grey, until the grave looms.

And then, leaping up, he ran through the garden, a phantasising fighting-cock again—Ladies and gentlemen—a Don Quixote who had read the great tales of a bygone age, the images of the world drawn up by Idealist Philosophy, and who was now spoiling for a fight with the mental windmills of a new age.

And again it was Judith who brought Leo back to his desk—to the desk this time that Löwinger had had set up in Leo's room—again it was Judith who freed him so he could work and who brought his wretched, unproductive and phantasising existence to an end.

Judith is dead. Leo had to read this part of Lukas Trojan's letter several times until he understood it, until he grasped that simple fact that is so hard to conceive: that there is no more hope and no possibility any more of seeing this human being again, that that life, both in itself and in connection with others, is irrevocably concluded and at an end, as far removed as those dead of past epochs who have been dead longest, even further away than the remotest future. Over and done with. What wasn't already over and done with in Leo's life. But this time: over and done with.

Regarding Judith's death, wrote Lukas Trojan, there was only very little he could report. He himself had not been in touch with her for a long time. He had simply found out through a friend of a friend of a friend... that she was supposed to have taken her own life, a tragic story, but he unfortunately hadn't been told anything more as to the background and reasons: depression probably, wrote Lukas. A tragedy—he was very sorry he didn't know enough to be able to tell him anything more precise. Hoping to hear from him (Leo) again, mainly though to read him—'Your project to write a sequel to the *Phenomenology* promises to be extremely exciting'—he remained etc. etc. Leo didn't understand. It was a mystery to him. How? How did Lukas find out? Then Leo remembered that in his letter to Lukas he had in fact rambled on, to himself really, about a sequel to Hegel's *Phenomenology*. Over and done with. It was so hard to grasp. Leo tried to picture to himself something, anything, to do with this news that Judith was dead. But he couldn't manage it. Hadn't he himself once written a farewell letter to her, a farewell to the world, and hadn't he too come close to— and now she. It was true. He shuddered as if he himself were dead and cold. In his head there was blackness. Night. Sleep. Was that how Judith died? In her sleep, the sleep that she feared so much was destined to be the cause of her death. Didn't wake up again. Will never wake up again. Wake out of sleep. Out—and over. But why? Sleeping pills. But why? An accident, perhaps. A mistake. If you fight against sleep as much as Judith did, then perhaps you can no longer get to sleep any other way than with the help of sleeping pills. And taken along with alcohol it could result in—Now she would never wake up again. And he too will never be able to go to sleep. From fear. In sleep everything comes back, the past is there again, suicidal and murderous phantoms that night after night kill themselves and others, Judith, a spirit, a ghost from whom he'd never freed himself, never again will he be able to get to sleep. He groaned. A cry, almost. His lower jaw vibrated, tensing itself like with a boy who wants to weep but is not allowed to. A tight, strangulating feeling around the neck and throat, a tightening, a pressure as if they were pushing against each other. Now his whole head vibrated, a heavy vibrating that swung back and forth because his face was so bloated. I'll never be able to get to sleep again, he thought and continued to think it as he slumped forward and into sleep, completely inebriated with rum, his head, fuzzy with palomitas, dropping onto his arms on the desk-top. At this the postcard print of Giorgione's 'Judith' fell over with scarcely a sound, scarcely any movement, ghostlike. Leo jerked his head up. What had happened? The woman, who had been standing there upright with sword in hand, had sunk down and the head of the man, which had been lying at her feet, had risen, raised itself and was now looking down at the woman lying in front of him.

For days Leo didn't feel at all that he was working. 'Working'—that had become a demanding occupation fraught with emotion, obligation, heroic intentions, futility and, in the end, pointlessness, over and done with. But now the work was taking place in him, coming out of him. Only after several days, on noticing the sheets of paper that had piled up, did he suddenly think with excitement: I'm working. What was he producing? The Giorgione print was lying somewhere underneath the many sheets of paper on which a new picture of Judith was emerging, the first great declaration of love to her and a homage to the time they had spent together. The text begins with the words: 'Heavenly are the days'—that's what it says word for word, flowing along naturally, no corrections, no crossings out, 'are' and not 'were' and not 'have been'. From this opening it's already clear: now the truth is coming out. Leo quite simply let it happen in the text, whereas earlier he had always suffocated it with his great theoretical claims in the process of writing. And the reason for this change? The trance-like condition he allowed himself for the first time as he wrote. An acutely-felt freedom, both in the painful and joyful sense. Freedom from—(this sentence can be completed in a variety of ways). A moment of thoughtlessness, then, experienced with great emotion. Or none of this and none of that, but simply the alcohol? Whatever. The truth is: heavenly are the days he had spent with Judith, but they weren't heavenly, they haven't been. They are now, in his memory, in his need for retrospective idealisation, in this moment of writing. They are now untaintedly happy, innocently sublime and pure—that is, heavenly. But they are irrevocably over and done with, dead—that is, heavenly. They are history and, as such, redeemed in the present. 'Heavenly are the days,' Leo continued: 'for whom the starry night-sky is a map of practicable footpaths, and whose ways are lit by the light of the stars.' Those days, then, days which were over and done with and which for this reason gave rise to such feelings of heavenliness, were ones when Judith and Leo had oriented themselves by the stars and not by the concrete landmarks of their daily life. What were these stars called? Hegel, Dostoyevsky, Kleist, Sterne—the last being well and away the first and most brilliant of Judith's gallery of superstars. They travelled only those paths lit by these stars of the human spirit and consequently found every path they walked along enlightening. 'Everything is new for them and yet familiar, adventurous and yet safe,' this sentence, in the light of the above, is immediately clear—'The world is wide but like your own house'—this incorporates an allusion to Löwinger's house and then to his garden, which represents the world. However—'There is a harsh line between the world and the I,' and herein lay the problem, the solution to which (the salvation and liberation of which) this brilliant text made possible for the first time, and was expressed already in the opening words: that these days were indeed heavenly, the days of your youth, if not your childhood—over and done with.

Line after line, page after page, day after day Leo wrote, employing this lucid ambiguity, speaking to himself in this veritable dialectic, unravelling a truth that was completely unthinkable without the lies on which he had wanted to build not just his life but the influence he would have on future generations as well. Even as he was writing the text, he wanted of course to idealise things but he also showed openly and clearly the false bottom by means of which he carried out his sleights of hand, and through this he did in fact come close to the truth, which is the whole. And this is no empty illusion, no merely compliant quotation controlled by limited interests. This truth, properly understood, is a wound in the kind of human thinking that makes us feel comfortable, and everyone, as far as they are able, puts a plaster over it. But Leo wouldn't have been Leo if he hadn't come along in the end with the thickest possible plaster of paris. You make busts from plaster of Paris. Galleries of ghosts. The ambiguity of the text, raising a monument to Judith under the pretext of freeing himself from her, soon toppled over into another ambiguity, namely dealing with a philosophical-historical problem under the pretext of doing just that. Leo generalised the description of his 'heavenly days' into an exposition of those historical epochs Hegel had called the Age of 'Ethical Life', by which he meant Antiquity, and described its sublation in education as the Age of Legal Status. Hegel, the *Phenomenology*, that was in fact Leo's bag of tools, as it were—he had no other, there was no other way for him. And even though Judith was the subject, she no longer figured. And even though Leo's own story was the subject, it certainly no longer figured in this philosophical-historical exposition: his story was cunningly and point-lessly hidden in its belly, his work a Trojan horse before the gates of a Potemkin village, a mere façade. It isn't necessary to report all this. After days of working Leo became *conscious* of the fact that he was working and consequently began really to work—that is, to hide in an academic way and in the actual writing every thought either already put down or remaining to be put down. Leo's description of the 'ethical world' was free of the kitchen smells he'd experienced on evenings at Judith's place and which he certainly thought about while he was writing. He wrote about the 'security' of this world in which 'all the doings of the soul were meaningful and rounded', in which the purpose was directly given and in which human beings formed a spontaneous, beautiful and natural community. The paths they had to tread may sometimes have been unending but they were never lost from sight down abysses since both paths and goals were directly given. From home to the library, from the library to home, into the kitchen, from the kitchen to the bedroom, those the longest detours—this he did not write. The greatest ideas were yoked to the service of the smallest moral point, the smallest problems led on to the greatest world revela-tions, and feelings of depth were readily at hand if you simply looked down out of the window and into the courtyard at the stone angels below—this he did not write. 'Homogenous world', was what he wrote, 'spontaneous totality of Being'.

'The act of knowing,' he wrote, 'is but a removal of obscuring veils, the act of creation a distinguishing feature of visible, eternal beings'—here the faintest whiff of the kitchen was most likely to be discerned: wasn't it always the case that Judith would cook when he was copying out excerpts from secondary literature on Hegel? 'Virtue a full knowledge of the ways' that led to Venice—where the path of virtue was abandoned very quickly indeed.

And there was not one whiff of the gunpowder and chocolate of his Brazilian evenings in Leo's description of the age of Education, even though this was the period he'd been pondering on relentlessly when describing 'Education'. There was 'no longer any escape from transcendental homelessness,' he wrote, 'from loss of security' and with all the plainly frivolous longing for it, for now 'neither goals nor ways were given directly.' A rift had opened up between Man and men, between Man and the world. The 'Individuality'—this was the pseudonym he had chosen for himself in the text—became 'problematic', it lacked any obvious meaning and sought at least some artificial meaning in the great expanse of meaninglessness. Boozing and smoking, gazing gloomily into the night, his head full of thoughts in the subjunctive mood—this he did not write. That which earlier could be immediately taken for granted has now become a desideratum, is outside and alien to the individual, a demand that the individual can no longer fulfil. The 'inclination' to 'appropriate every kind of thorough-going educational material' in order, in this fashion, 'to constitute one's own being' has become completely 'abstract'. This obligation is wretched and riddled with holes—and then again and again the same central statement: 'Obligation kills life,' a statement of such purity that not even the smell of sulphur clung to it any more, the fading of which smell enabled Leo to achieve such clarity.

It turned into a fine text, of which Leo was justifiably proud and which put him on cloud nine. Leo developed and deepened his thesis, finally taking his cue from all those novels that he'd been reading latterly, during this period of futility and homelessness—novels read out of despair and boredom. And if, as a result of this, his work became a small autobiography, a very private spiritual history, then, for this very same reason, it was no longer this at all in the end. Now it was his first valid exposition of a central passage from Hegel's *Phenomenology*, namely from the section about the 'Sublation of Ethical Life in Education', and at the same time a boldly constructed entrée into the theory of the novel, a historical-philosophical essay concerning the forms of the great epic. At the end of the day Judith was only a nameless dead person lying buried beneath this text. It was her memorial; never named, her name took on a certain uncertain longing, became a reference to a homeland to which this work was a last farewell, with tears of joy which, in the text, were brushed away as tears of sorrow and mourning.

Here you have a truly ruthless—selfless and sulphurless—piece of writing, Uncle Zé, was what Leo didn't say of course when he handed Löwinger his work to read. Löwinger was reassured and relieved, as he weighed the typed manuscript in his hands: Leo really was working, that was the main thing. He hadn't been wrong about him. He's on his way. And he, Löwinger, would set up the finishing post and see to it that the public were there by the finishing line as well.

Leo felt Löwinger's relief, felt it as if it were his own—some of the pressure in the Löwinger house had now eased off and his leash became noticeably longer. He could do and not do what he wanted without his feeling badgered in the evenings at the end of supper as to how the work was progressing, as to when there would finally be something to read, as to whether these long walks in the garden really did help concentration or whether sitting longer at his desk, and a greater obsession with his work there, wouldn't achieve better results—my boy.

Leo walked in the garden all day now and in the evenings Uncle Zé praised his industriousness and the progress he was making with his work and instructed the gardener to see to it at all costs that Leo's concentration was not disturbed.

But inside Leo things were still working away. And one day while lying under his 'Oblomov tree' he even received 'enlightenment'—this anyway was the expression he would use when telling Judith about it. He'd been thinking about his lecture at the Philosophy Institute. The day was drawing ever closer. What should he say? How should he say it? Leo was so thrilled about the work he'd just completed that he first toyed with the idea of summarising this and giving it as a paper for the lecture. 'The Sublation of Ethical Life in Education.' The central passage in Hegel's Phenomenology' or something similar? But was that what the students wanted to hear? Weren't they expecting something altogether different? Yes, but that arose from a misunderstanding. But he wasn't to blame for this misunderstanding. But he'd have to clear up the misunderstanding, that was his task. Ladies and gentlemen, with the help of Hegel's *Phenomenology* the futue cannot—Leo was looking up into the crown of the tree—how old could this tree be? A hundred years old? Here is a tree—that's all I know. What kind of tree is it? A tree. I don't know what I can say to the students—perhaps the following: With the help of Hegel's *Phenomenology* the future can—be deduced very effectively—Leo leapt to his feet, looked in bewilderment at the palms of his hands as if he were carrying a mirror—I, yes I can, you can, as long as you've read *Phenomenology* thoroughly enough, then you can very easily look into the future, logically deduce it, of course, it's obvious, I—Leo jumped up into the air—can—Leo leapt up and clapped his hands—look into the future—Leo began to run, making sure that every syllable that he shouted out coincided with the sound of his feet hitting the gravel: I-can-see-in-to-the-fu-ture. The gardener in amazement stopped cutting the hedge, the cook went to the kitchen window, leant out and looked astonished as Leo ran by shouting, and the chauffeur, on seeing Leo's ecstatic outburst, wiped his brow in consternation with the cleaning cloth he'd been using to polish Löwinger's black Galaxy.

It had suddenly struck me, he would tell Judith, that I had experienced the inverse process, the reverse development. I had sublated education into a new ethical life. Wasn't I now living in perfect harmony with the outer world? Had I not given up all claims to being special? Wasn't the road ahead and my destination clearly before me? I was heading in the direction that everyone else was heading in: where everyone one was heading I could gather from the newspaper. Did I now want to be something different from what others were, even if I towered head and shoulders above them? I wanted to be able to sing along, not call the tune any more. Didn't the misunderstanding arise from the fact that it was true but that I didn't know it then? Everyone shouted *impedido* and so did I, that was all. The abstract treasures of education I'd become estranged from were no longer mine, and the new consciousness, the sense of *impedido*, was not yet in place. That was all. That needs to be clearly understood. Then everything suddenly became clear to me. No rift any more between me and the world, between me and other people. Only the unwritten laws of life, of the market-place and of metabolism. I was one of many, nothing more. And your death, Judith, hasn't it made all sense of personal entitlement meaningless, rendered obsolete every desire, every obligation? Everything was the way it was. Without the desire for anything more. And then the decisive question. Does this regression belong to me alone or isn't it much more likely to be a general thing? Look around you, Judith, no question but that it is general. Let's leave Löwinger's garden, I thought, and consider Brazil. Dictatorship. Hasn't the dictatorship

140

brought about a new unity of the individual, the family and the state? Was that not its aim, its task? Is not this expressed in the dictatorship's propaganda: 'Brazil! Love her or leave her!' The dictatorship created this unity brutally, in a criminal manner, admittedly, but what it has created is, strictly speaking, a condition of ethical life in the philosophical sense. The subsuming of the individual into the community, the clear issuing of all directives and objectives, the general binding force of unwritten laws—the written ones, those of the constitution, were rescinded by the dictatorship. Ethical life, no question about it. The signs weren't good at the outset, I grant you. But ethical life nonetheless. Do you see, Judith, that was my enlightenment. In the dimension of world history we are experiencing a regression. Only in Brazil? No. Brazil is lagging well behind. The fascisms in Europe managed it long ago. And Stalinism? A variant affected by fascism—we must stick to the point, we can differentiate later. There's no doubt about it. It's quite clear that—If we were now experiencing education being sublated into ethical life, precisely the reverse of how Hegel described it, we can conclude from this that—? Yes. You see, suddenly I saw the future and the end of history before me, in the crown of the tree I was looking up into, so to speak. I saw the future in my hands because I have it in hand. In two fingers. I need only to leaf through pages, leaf back through Hegel's *Phenomenology*. The *Phenomenology* ends with 'absolute knowledge'. What has happened since then? How have things evolved further? What's clear is that the present can no longer be understood by means of the concept 'absolute knowledge'. Consciousness is no longer, no longer at the stage of 'absolute knowledge'. So a regression has taken place. Now, turning to ethical life again. That is. That means. In other words. Now we can deduce the future quite easily, we need only to read the *Phenomenology* again in the reverse direction, backwards to the beginning and we'll be able to predict point for point, chapter by chapter, what's coming, what the next stage, the one after that, the last stage will be, the goal, the actual goal of history. That's how he would explain it to Judith. But now it was all a bit higgledy-piggledy in his head, while he practised already the arm movements to accompany his explanations as if he had a whole auditorium of people in front of him. He ran excitedly to his room, grabbed hold of his edition of the *Phenomenology* and rushed up and down declaiming and gesticulating. He didn't notice when he bumped against the table-leg, nor when he charged into the side of the bed—he didn't connect it with anything, it didn't elicit any further associations. He was already imagining his lecture, began to declaim,

141

ladies and gentlemen, he stuttered and babbled, as if transported, which state he helped along by means of a bottle of rum he'd put for safe-keeping in his desk. That moment when the tide of history changed direction, he couldn't deduce the reason for it—he put this question in parentheses—it was immaterial as regards the lecture—he didn't want to get stuck in the past—with his eyes on the contents page of Hegel's *Phenomenology*, he marched directly into the future. Ladies and gentle-men, what awaits us now at the next stage of evolution? There is no doubt that . . . He forgot all about dinner.

Löwinger was informed that the young gentleman had, after some strange fits that day, late in the afternoon, gone charging into his room. Löwinger went to have a look. The door to Leo's room was ajar and Löwinger peered in. He saw some stockinged feet, a man's back—it was Leo—he was rolling about on the floor, jerking, tugging at his shirt, making sounds, a long 'Ah' and 'Lazenginmen'—he was no longer capable of standing and walking, he was lying on the floor, still holding forth in a babble that horrified Löwinger and suggested he had seen the devil in person. He went back to the dining-room. Lay only one place today, he said, my boy is not well. He never ate so slowly as on that evening. Each mouthful he chewed never-endingly. Pushing the saliva-soaked paste back and forth in his mouth, he couldn't decide whether he had been witness to Leo's genius or madness. Finally he pushed the plate away, lit a cigar and drank some port. If he is mad, he thought, I'll kill him.

The dogged industriousness and plain spirituality that Leo evinced over the following days reassured Löwinger. Leo's euphoria and self-assurance grew and with it Löwinger's curiosity and commitment as well. Tomorrow something incredible will happen, said Leo on the evening before his lecture, you'll see, Uncle Zé—tomorrow I'll be famous.

What happened on the 2nd of October 1968, the day of Leo's lecture at the Philosophy Institute, went down in the history of Brazil as 'The Events of Rua Maria Antonia'. After Leo's agreement to present himself for the first time before the public with his sensational thesis, the media interest was huge. Löwinger will have made his own personal contribu-tion, too. All the main newspapers and two of the important television channels turned up for Leo's lecture. For this reason the events are particularly well documented.

Professor George had insisted on fetching Leo and taking him per-sonally to the lecture hall. There were good, egotistical reasons for this generous act of kindness. Professor George, as organiser of the lecture had co-ordinated the inquiries of the press and television, was in a state of high excitement because of the widespread interest and, in order not to be forgotten, wanted to be photographed and filmed continually at Leo's side from the very first moment.

There are hardly any parking places right by the university, said Professor George It would be best to park here and walk the rest of the way. It's no distance.

That's very convenient, said Leo, as Professor George was locking the car—a cemetery so near to the university.

Professor George gave a start.

Yes, said Leo, you see, today a few treasured old ideas will have to be laid to rest.

Leo was in the best of moods. Swinging his briefcase with gusto, he turned into Rua Maria Antonia, with Professor George next to him who, in his effort to remain constantly at his side, was walking with one foot on the pavement and the other on the road below the curb, a limping comparison that forced itself upon Leo continually.

Just in front of the univesity they were brought to a halt by a camera team—a young man reached out a microphone towards Leo—Professor, he said, would you able to sum up briefly for our viewers what your lecture today will be about?

What I have to say, I will say in my lecture, answered Leo. Before that there's only this I can say: what I have inside here—he raised his briefcase which contained only Hegel's *Phenomenology*—will be like a bomb exploding.

Leo smiled and the reporter grinned as well. Like a bomb, Professor? Do you think that is the reason why there is such a strong police presence here?

Professor George was standing very close to Leo with retracted head and raised shoulders as if he wanted to disappear into his jacket.

Leo stammered, What sort of police presence?

Over there, said Professor George, just take a look. Only now did Leo see the large building diagonally opposite, around which a police cordon was formed—police cars were driving in and out through the arched entrance to the building—it looked more like the barracks, the police headquarters.

Is that the university? Leo asked.

Not ours, said Professor George—that's Mackenzie. On the Rua Maria Antonio here there are two universities next to each other, the

Philosophy Faculty of the University of São Paulo, that's the building next door, number 294, do you see, and then as I said Mackenzie University, a private university, which is there where the police are standing—why are there so many police standing there?

Ah, a private university, said Leo—and that's also its Philosophy faculty?

Well, actually, said Professor George—Mackenzie provides a training chiefly for engineers and—

There, you see, said Leo to the reporter, the police presence has to do with the neighbours—perhaps the engineers are more stupid than the police allow. Grinning happily, Leo looked at his watch. Excuse me, gentlemen, my lecture! And Leo stepped across the road in the direction of the Philosophy Faculty building.

Mr Singer! cried Professor George, running after him. You shouldn't have said that—we have so many problems with the Mackenzie people, the relationship, very competitive, all the resentments, you should—

Oh, put it out of your mind, Professor George. Tomorrow everything will look very different.

The Faculty building was full of people—Leo began in fact to get a little nervous now. He asked Professor George if he could retire for ten minutes to his room so that he could gather himself a little and concentrate.

Reading the contents page of Hegel's *Phenomenology* from the end to the beginning, Leo tried to memorise his lecture but he couldn't manage it. In his head he planned headlines for next day's newspapers, fantasised about a chapter of a Leo Singer monograph—he looked out of the window—so many people on the street, dozens of police in front of the neighbouring building, State police and military police—cars sounding their horns aggressively pushed through the throngs of people who were running this way and that across the street—now the police were beginning to bar the road to traffic—why? Why wasn't Leo concentrating on his lecture—this lecture would change his life, he had to concentrate—Ladies and gentlemen—Leo could only think ladies and gentlemen and he looked down in astonishment at the street below. Outside the door the sound of voices grew louder and louder, the door opened, Professor George's head in the crack, a questioning look, Leo nodded and, in a business-like manner and without seeing anyone, was already hurrying after Professor George into the lecture hall, which was bursting at the seams, all the seats full, more students sitting on the floor between the first row and the lectern, students standing along the walls at the sides, at the open door a whole bunch of people swelling out into the passageway.

Leo was drenched in sweat by the time he had finally worked his way to the lectern—a generalised murmur and buzzing of voices that died down as Professor George was speaking his introductory words: how fortunate he regarded himself that Professor Leo Singer had found the time, even though he was working at this moment on a very important study which demanded all his time... Leo nodded, he had a lump in his throat, and on his forehead cold sweat, which, with trembling hand, he wiped off with a calm and pensive gesture—he put on his spectacles, looked into the audience and suddenly became very calm. He knew that this audience belonged to him, this day belonged to him, the future belonged to him. He drew a deep breath... might therefore ask Professor Leo Singer to begin his keenly-awaited commentary, said Professor George. Leo rose, opened his case, took out Hegel's *Phenomenology*, opened it at the contents page, looked into the audience and said: Ladies and gentlemen.

At this moment the three windows of the lecture hall shattered into a crashing, clattering hail of stones and Leo then saw—in the space of a deathly quiet intake of breath that turned immediately into a deafening shriek and into universal panic—a bottle, like in a slow-motion film, flying in through the window nearest to him. The bottle had a burning piece of cloth stuffed into its neck. Quietly and in an oddly languid way the bottle flew almost gracefully into the room, shattered against the wall opposite the window. Had the screaming already started by then or was it only now that it began? Later it was to seem to Leo in his memory as if it had all happened in complete silence, a film with a damaged soundtrack, and only now had the sound suddenly returned, a high-pitched roar just at the moment when the flames shot out of the wall like so many tongues. The louder the screaming became, the more flames there were. Now three or four Molotov cocktails had exploded in the lecture hall, a commotion in the space which gave the impression that all the students, egged on by fanatical shouts and according to some secret code, were seeking to change places with each other. Leo stared fixedly into the audience—ladies and gentlemen—to his right Professor George was hitting the wall repeatedly with his beloved jacket, the fiery writing on the wall. Leo staggered down from the podium, over to the window—hadn't he looked out into the street again a quarter of an hour ago? Hadn't he seen just ordinary people going about their business? And police? So many military police? How could the police tolerate—?

Leo was standing by the window, next to him a bearded young man who was shouting repeatedly: The Mackenzistas! Leo hadn't yet managed to see anything of what was going on in the street when the boy crumpled up with a cry, holding his shoulder—*meus deus*, what's happened? said Leo, looking round for help. Then he saw, like bullet-holes bursting on the walls, like—because it seemed so unreal to Leo, he searched for some comparison, like, like, like? Now Leo threw himself onto the ground. Not because he was frightened. Not because he was gripped by panic. It was simply that there was something in him that forced him to throw himself onto the ground, while another part that remained standing, so to speak, watched him do this and was astonished to see him scrabbling over the floor. But it's possible this astonishment took place only in his memory, when in the following days he saw in every newspaper that photo in which he was seen lying on the floor with his hands over his head.

Leo lay on the floor wondering what might happen to him. In the midst of all the panic reigning there, the thought that anything could happen to him seemed completely unreal. Really happen. After all, he had spent his whole life dealing only with theoretical questions. Then a tear-gas canister exploded in the room. Leo held his handkerchief closely against his nose and mouth.

In one corner Professor George was sitting on the floor and sobbing as he contemplated the burn-holes in his jacket. Leo crawled over to him. It's the tear-gas, said Professor George, rubbing his reddened eyes, the tear-gas. Come, said Leo, we've got to get out of here.

At the entrance to the building there was such a lot of shouting and shoving of people pushing to get out, and then to get back in, that Leo completely lost his nerve. He struck out savagely with fists and elbows for fear of being knocked over and trampled on. At the same time he had to fight against the impulse to let himself simply sink under and die in the stampede. Professor George tugged Leo away to one side—they heard that the police were using water cannon to drive everyone back who wanted to leave the building. But why, asked Leo, why?

Come to the rear entrance, said Professor George.

146

But they couldn't get out of the building there either. Anyone here stepping out of the rear entrance immediately came under fire from the roof of the neighbouring building, Mackenzie University. Through the open door they saw a dead student, his body strangely twisted, lying half crooked, half hanging, one hand in the wrought-iron gate that separated the small front garden of the university from the street. From their elevated position the Mackenzistas controlled the area between the building's exit, the iron railings and the entrance gate like guards in the watchtower of a prison camp.

And again and again the throng of people in the corridor in front of the rear entrance swelled, almost shoving those standing further to the front outside, these then setting up a cry and pushing back in—some shots were fired and everyone scattered, flying back down the corridor.

Leo and Professor George now ran up again to the first floor and into George's room. They barricaded the door from the inside and together shoved a cupboard in front of the shattered window. Then Professor George sat down at his desk, Leo sat down opposite him on the visitor's chair and they waited. After two hours Leo had run out of palomitas. The fighting lasted another eight hours.

It was only in the course of the following days owing to the reports appearing in the papers and on television that Leo first understood what had happened. At Mackenzie University, and chiefly in the Technical and Social Science faculty, a militant, extreme right-wing student group had formed calling itself BACK (Brazil Against Communist Killers). It was this group who were responsible for the planning, organisation and execution of the armed attack on the Philosophy Faculty of the University of São Paulo. The philosophical orientation of the State University was traditionally considered by the Mackenzistas and, above all, by the members of BACK, as a breeding ground for Marxism and so was the target of childish acts of aggression. Up until now, the Rector of the University of São Paulo said on television, the rivalry between the two universities had taken the form of idealogical pranks—who would have ever imagined such an act of lunacy possible? BACK had regularly daubed the Philosophy Faculty building with slogans like 'Communists out!' or 'Back BACK—Back Brazil!', had disturbed a meeting of students of the Philosophy Faculty with chanting, and Mackenzistas had always vilified philosophy students in the pubs around the university. This foreign agitator's lecture was the trigger, said a spokeman for BACK in a press conference, that brought the anger and indignation of the students to a head. He then explained how you could see the

147

villainy of left-wing agitators in the way they pretended to want to have a perfectly harmless debate, about some problem in the history of German philosophy, for example, when in reality it had to do with a huge brain-washing exercise in disguise, which was then spread far and wide by the media to our credulous and trusting people. He reminded people that Hegel was the teacher of Marx and that it was Lenin who had said that Marx's 'Kapital' couldn't be understood without first studying Hegel's *Phenomenology*. The true significance of this lecture could be measured against this. Furthermore the lecture was announced in such a way that it couldn't but convey to our people with their gullibility as regards makumba, magic and, at the same time, university professors, that what was being taught here were scientific techniques giving, as it were, magical power over the future. The people, however, were not to realise that this future, ostensibly brought about by science, was to be communism. The armed action was for this reason pure self-defence, an act of counter-resistance to a communist putsch attempt as well as one whereby the population were disabused, and BACK, therefore, thanked the police for their support.

In reply to the criticism that the police had permitted the destruction of a public building and made common cause with its destroyers, the Chief Superintendent of the police pointed out in a press conference that on that day it had not been a question of protecting a building but of protecting human life and restoring law and order. The task of the police had been, he said, to de-escalate the conflict and this they had finally managed to do. Why were the students of the Philosophy Faculty prevented from leaving the building with water cannon? Didn't this action prolong the conflict unnecessarily and result in many more being killed and wounded than would have been the case if the philosophy students had been able to leave the building and escape from the attacks of the Mackenzistas? No, quite the contrary, said the Police Superintendent, for in this way it had been possible to prevent the conflict from shifting to the streets and spreading as a result. The wisdom of this action could also be seen from the fact that that those students who had escaped from the building before the water cannon started had subsequently set fire to the parked cars of innocent citizens. Why had the police used Mackenzie University as their base—didn't this point to complicity with and support for the attackers? Quite the reverse, said the Superintendent, this showed the unpartisan attitude of the police. The base was in fact, and quite objectively, the best for the necessary operation from a strategic and tactical point of view, for from there the police had

148

the optimum command of both universities. Why hadn't the police disarmed the Mackenzistas if they were already stationed in their university—surely this would have ended the fighting more quickly? He hadn't been able to disarm any Mackenzistas, said the Police Superintendent, because he hadn't seen any armed Mackenzistas. And where did the bullet holes outside and inside the Philosophy Faculty building come from, and the tear-gas canisters of North American origin? That was the work of communist agitators for the purpose of propaganda, the Police Superindendent said, and he reminded everyone of the television interview with the foreign professor when he boasted of having a bomb in his case.

So ended Leo's career as Professor of the Philosophy Faculty. One week later the military closed all the universities in the country. Four weeks later Löwinger had the street-front façade of Leo's little house, which had been daubed with slogans like 'Communist pig' or 'Gringos out', cleaned and repainted in an immaculate white. All talk of the events in Rua Maria Antonia had petered out by then, Professor George had emigrated to Paris, Hegel was once more a foreign word to scratch your head over, the future was the business of soothsayers and out of the hands of the media, and Leo was completely forgotten.

And you'll be a professor yet, my boy, no question of it, said Löwinger. The chances, the possibilities of your becoming one are now even greater than before, much greater, mark my words. This conversation took place in Löwinger's library ten days after the above events. The yellow ochre light. The solidity of the materials in the room. Wood, glass, leather, brass. The atmosphere of a meeting of war veterans. Defeated warriors who had not been able to rescue anything save what was in the end the most important thing, namely nothing real: the regimental colours to which they had stood loyal. The idea of a career born out of the spirit. One of the two veterans an invalid Leo. Erstwhile Professor—almost, that is. In the meantime he understood what had happened and yet didn't understand. Something was missing. As if a limb had been severed. And the other, highly decorated. Löwinger. From today retired bank director. An early pension. He hadn't fought it. When the generals turn up, there's only one thing for it: click your heels, about turn and dismiss.

You don't want to be a professor anymore? You're absolutely right. No sensible person now, during this dictatorship, wants to become something. It would mean becoming a collaborator. And then, when the dictatorship came to an end, you would be completely discredited.

Then you'd have blown all your chances. You know, my boy, he said, people say that if a fellow does everything right, he's just lucky. One stroke of bad luck and then they say that that was a wrong move. But for the very same reason a real wrong move can sometimes be a stroke of good fortune.

Löwinger was drinking port and smoking a cigar, his beloved Dona Flor, his harlot, for, as he had explained to Leo, it made everyone happy, both the lover of light and of dark tobacco, and its glow lasted exactly one hour. Leo had only just established his own preferences: he drank rum along with a beer. And he smoked palomitas. A childish indulgence, was Löwinger's opinion—the taste of chocolate! I sometimes have the impression that the palomitas taste of gunpowder, Leo had replied. It's a tobacco that's really in tune with the times.

Both men's hair was combed back straight and slick. Löwinger's hair was white. Leo's hair was heading in the same direction. For the first time you could see white streaks in his hair.

And do you know what the mistake was? asked Löwinger. The mistake was to believe that at this time, under a dictatorship, you could have a career of any significance. Imagine if everything had gone well. You would now be a professor. And when the dictatorship steps down, which could happen tomorrow, you'd be discredited, dismissed from state employment and unable to make anything of yourself again. And that's why the mistake we made was a stroke of good fortune. For later use you now have the proof that you were persecuted and obstructed in your career plans for political reasons. Such people will be much sought after. Those who are untainted, who haven't collaborated with the regime. Then everything will be open to you. You were lucky, my boy. Things are going splendidly. It could all happen tomorrow. Keep yourself at the ready. You must carry on working, quietly preparing yourself. And you can do that, you've got everything you need here. You mustn't be depressed. You must be happy. Your day will come. Sooner than you now think. There's a smell of faeces and sulphur in the air, isn't there? Yes. The great men are beginning to whiff badly. All we have to do is to cover our noses and simply wait. Cheers, my boy.

Löwinger was a man not given to many words. But when he was with Leo he loved to talk. In the younger man sitting there quietly and attentively he saw himself, just as he would always sit quietly and attentively. He loved seeing himself in Leo.

150

I never had anything against the junta on principle—that you know, my boy. I am a realist. And therein lies the difference: the military are not. They confuse today with yesterday. Today they're at the helm, tomorrow no longer. Today they hold in check those struggling for redistribution, which would prove ruinous, and that's good. But tomorrow they'll bring about bankruptcy and have to step down because there'll be nothing whatsoever left to redistribute. Every dictatorship till now has had to step down for this reason. One has to be ready for this. They've showed us who's boss. So? That's reality. They're the bosses. Today. Tomorrow these same bosses will have to pack their bags. And the lackeys now have to carry on working away quietly. Because today they are lackeys and because tomorrow they'll need to be standing by. Tomorrow things will depend on what they know. You must carry on working, my boy.

In the meantime the ash on Löwinger's cigar had grown so long that it threatened any minute to drop onto the floor. Leo watched this nervously. Löwinger was quite unaware. Leo jumped up to hand Uncle Zé an ashtray. At this, Löwinger, who, while he spoke, had been sitting until then as motionlessly as a statue with a taperecorder behind it, made a startled movement which caused the ash of his cigar to fall to the floor.

Leave it, my boy, he said. I'll have that cleaned away tomorrow. Löwinger's enforced retirement didn't bother him. It was such a long time ago that he had last taken a holiday, he said. His wife had been alive then. And it hadn't been a real holiday. He was on the telephone the whole holiday for reasons of business and his wife had organised a non-stop round of social evenings, to which she invited all the important personalities who happened to be holidaying at the same resort. Basically a continuation of the wearisome business dinners that took place all year round, except these were mellowed by virtue of the colourful summer dresses. From a business point of view things did come of it but a holiday was the last thing it was. Now was his first real holiday, he affirmed. Not retirement, mark you, but a holiday. Watching everything disintegrating from your armchair. A real pleasure. His successor, said Löwinger, will set about embezzling for all he's worth, work away to line just his own pocket because he knows only too well that he'll never accumulate the required number of years to be able to draw a pension. This man had done everything to get where he now was. In Löwinger's shoes. The worst possible mistake. He, Löwinger, was sitting in his armchair, calm, elegant, recuperating and waiting for the new starter's

151

gun. And the starting line, so it would transpire, was right at the tips of his toes.

From among the generals a gentleman became president who was fond of riding. A fool to whom the historical task fell to make the dictatorship impossible in the end. He wouldn't, he said, expect his horse to stable in the *favelas*. The minimum wage, whose level he had fixed, was good grounds, he said, for shooting yourself. Society began to seethe.

Work, Löwinger told Leo. You must get ready. It won't be long now. For the first time Löwinger was to be seen in his garden every day, early in the morning. Tomatoes were his special love. Tomatoes need to be watered very early in the morning. A drop of water on one of the fruits when the sun shone could prove fatal. The drop had the effect of a magnifying glass and burnt the fruit. The fruit grew plump and red and full of life if you did everything right—the least little mistake and they didn't stand a chance.

The gardener was sacked and a new one employed in his place. The old gardener hadn't understood that tomatoes were fruit. Paradise apples. He had put them in the same category as vegetables.

The cook was sacked, a new one employed. The cook had always peeled the tomatoes. Just as she had been used to doing for years. She hadn't understood how much trouble it took to see to it that the skin of the tomatoes was flawless, how much pride this afforded. Work, said Löwinger, it won't be long now. You must get ready, my boy. Our lords and masters will soon have to step down—their decisions are becoming more and more irrational—it could even happen tomorrow, even tomorrow, mark my words. The strange thing was that Leo was really able to work well. He read and copied out extracts in a conscientious fashion. He wrote plans for his great opus which he had arranged on such a large scale that as far as he was concerned the military could remain at the helm for years yet. Löwinger's everlasting 'tomorrow' made him almost nervous. He rewrote the chapter synopses of his book. He rewrote them several times. Then he ditched the lot. There was still so much he had to read and study. He had learnt from the earlier events that whoever studied Hegel could understand Marx's *Kapital* and that was clearly an explosive state of affairs. So he studied Marx. And hadn't the year '68 shown that the task and possibilities of changing the world had not become in the least bit obsolete? History hadn't yet come to an end. That he had understood. Even though he didn't know how he could bring Marx's historical teleology and his own together in his mind, he nevertheless felt that his old theme was now doubly reinvigorated and fraught with contemporary significance: the question regarding the laws governing historical movements, the question: How do I change the world. He had only one fear: that the junta might step down before he had understood everything.

He thought of Judith, of course, as he was writing. He had always done so. One thing was different, however: the fact that he was so miserably happy that she was dead. This lengthened everything he read, thought, wrote, because it continued to be addressed to Judith and so into infinity. He wasn't obliged, impelled by a *finite* desire for mastery, to finish his work today so as to be able to put her address on an envelope tomorrow. The goal of his daily work was now situated in infinity, there, finally, where his work was to begin to come into its own.

He had cut the head of Giorgione's Judith out of the postcard print and placed it in a round and shiny brass frame on his desk. It looked like a saint's image. An idealisation that rendered any further material idealisation obsolete. The saint's image enabled him to feel a convenient kind of melancholy which immunised him against every real pain, every real irritation or disturbance in his life, for what was all that compared to the great loss he had already had to bear. And the saint's legend enabled him to experience a convenient and minor fervour that gave Leo the feeling in everything he did that he was doing it in the spirit and in memory of someone, and for someone, without there being any danger of being contradicted, rebuffed or of failing in this or any other relationship. This little saint's image on his desk was therefore a kind of battery which miraculously fed with energy his need to be a tragic and profound being, while he was able to transfer this energy into all conceivable kinds of activities, meaningful or banal, with growing joy and happiness. Leo began in actual fact to love his life. He was able to work and he enjoyed the carefree quality and the surprises that his life as an eternal student brought with it. He wouldn't have said an eternal student but rather an independent scholar. He enjoyed the simple diversions and changes of routine which he treated himself to, something he was able to do without any difficulty, without brooding any more on the point or pointlessness of them, on their success or failure. And he enjoyed his daily routine, the peace and regularity, the feeling of being discreetly privileged which pervaded the Löwinger household, the way Uncle Zé had thoroughly ritualised every aspect of it. Leo noticed that he felt a strong affinity towards all this: the meals together, the talks they had in the library, the salon afternoons spent with all kinds of people and which always passed off in identical fashion but were nevertheless so stimulating, the walks with Uncle Zé in the garden, two gentlemen bent slightly forward, hands behind their backs, the crunching of the gravel on the path. Leo's love of the kitsch and of solemnity was neither reined in nor fostered there, this love simply providing a basis for his existence, on which everything that went on crunched so prettily, like his steps on the gravel, without there being any need for discussion. And when Brazil won the World Cup the joy then seemed to embrace everyone as if they were all one, the individual, the family, society, all directly related to each other. Leo thought that he'd been right all along: the condition of morality had been finally restored. Of all the people who had put up pictures like saints' images in their homes, pictures of those relations, boyfriends or girlfriends who had disappeared and were dead and about whom they knew nothing more, Leo was the only one whose happiness was untroubled.

It was then he received the telegram from Vienna. His mother was seriously ill, it said. She was in hospital. She wanted him to come to her immediately. Leo folded up the telegram, pushed it under a pile of books on his desk. No. He looked around as if he were frightened someone might have seen him reading the telegram, receiving it. He was alone in his room, of course. His breathing was laboured. He walked around very carefully, as if on tiptoe, so that the floorboards wouldn't creak. He wasn't there. The telegram wasn't there. Hadn't arrived. What telegram? He didn't want to go back to Vienna, especially not now. Wasn't he supposed to be selling the plots of land? Negotiations had reached the critical stage. Contracts had already been exchanged for the plot of land on Campo Bello, with a down payment received. The net proceeds would cover all the expenses and legal costs incurred up until now. And the sale of the land by the river Pinheiros was on the brink of being concluded. Only one piece of paper was missing. But this was as good as in his pocket. According to his solicitor. The potential buyer, Shopping City Construction Company, had offered a sum that would make him independent for the rest of his life. Was this the time to leave the country? Yes, of course, there was always the solicitor. Power of attorney. But that wasn't all. He was writing, he was reading, he was working on a regular basis. Something was beginning to come of it all. He liked living the way he did now. It had taken a long time but now he had the life he had always wanted. And was this now to come to an end again, before it had hardly begun?

Was he to let his mother uproot him once again from the soil where he'd only just begun to put down roots? Give up everything once again for a life that didn't suit him and that he hadn't chosen? The life of a sick-nurse. Ministering to an old woman he hated. Who, being as tough as she was, was quite capable of taking years to die. No. He hadn't heard anything. What had Judith said? If you don't want to, then just don't board the plane, end of story. Never again will he board a plane and fly away from himself because of his mother. She asked him to come, please. Please. In his whole life he had only ever heard his mother say the word 'please' whenever she had said to him: What does one say, Leo? Say please nicely.

Never, ever, had his mother asked him for anything. Whoever it was who went to the post office for her to send this telegram—her solicitor probably—was free in their use of language. It was of no concern to him. Let her disinherit him, Leo thought—all the money from the sale of the business in Vienna, there'll be quite a pile coming from that—his mother spent nothing, played bridge all day, that was all—and for penny stakes. Won thirty pence. Lost forty pence. Day in, day out. And when she went shopping to the Rochusmarkt, she would then haggle over twenty pence when buying two apples. Pence. Let her disinherit him. He won't go. He's got the land. Worth millions. If all goes well. It will go well. End of story. Leo really didn't respond to the telegram. Not a word to Uncle Zé, no phone call to Vienna, let alone reserving a flight. The news of his mother's illness? What news? No, it never came.

A week later he had a strange dream. He dreamt he was a child again. Tied to the table-leg with the washing-line. Suddenly Maria, the maidservant, came in and untied him. She was smiling. As she was freeing him, she took on the form of Judith. That was the last time you'll ever have to be tied up, she said, because now your mother will never come back again.

Leo woke up. It was three o'clock in the morning. In Vienna it was now eleven o'clock at night. He couldn't ring anyone up at this hour. Shortly after midday he telephoned his mother's solicitor in Vienna. He'd only just received the telegram today, said Leo—incredible sloppiness on the part of the postal service.

Your mother, said the solicitor, died last night. Regarding the burial, he said—

You arrange it all, said Leo. I give you full authorisation. I wish my mother to be cremated—please arrange for the urn to be sent to me here in Brazil. The urn will be laid to rest here. After all Brazil was very much at the centre of my family's interests.

And as regards the will of the deceased, said the solicitor—

Please let me know in writing. I first have to digest the news of her death, I'm sure you'll understand.

First came the letter from the solicitor itemising his mother's estate, to which he was the sole heir. Leo was rich. There was no doubt of that. The scheduling and figures in the letter were abstract. No matter how many times he read through them Leo wasn't able to say, Wealth brings happiness. Nor, Wealth does *not* bring happiness, strangely enough. Leo read though the letter again and again. As regards the figures his imagination failed him, but words like 'your deceased mother' or 'the testator' repeatedly aroused in him a knotted feeling of joy closely related to schadenfreude—as closely related as mother and son—however, the feeling didn't spread out in him but somehow stayed in the dark, enclosed in a black cyst, as if he had to go through the motions of mourning so as not to awaken suspicion. What sort of suspicion? He hadn't killed her, for goodness' sake. Perhaps because he hadn't flown to Vienna. From the outside, however, the stiffness of his joy could be confused with that of mourning. He now spoke to Uncle Zé. My mother has died suddenly, he told him. It came so out of the blue that there wasn't any time to fly to Vienna and see her once again. Then came the next bolt out of the blue: Uncle Zé wept. He stood up and put his arms round Leo, holding him long and ceremoniously. He could scarcely speak. When the moment is right, said Löwinger, I wish to talk about your mother—but not now, not now.

The next day he helped Leo draw up an investment plan for his capital. Leo wrote to the solicitor in Vienna giving him the appropriate instructions. The final point: his mother's apartment. In this instance Leo chose not to take Löwinger's advice. He wrote: I hereby authorise you to sell the said apartment including all the furniture. Including all the ancient sweets, liqueurs and piles of wrapping paper in the chests— this he didn't write. Including all the furniture. Leo trembled a little when he read this again, folded the letter finally and put it in an envelope. What caused this trembling? To tremble with joy, that's what you say—Leo thought that this was the first time he really knew what it was like to tremble with joy. In fact, he experienced such a strong feeling of triumph that he half spilt the rum he was now pouring out for himself. That was what he had firmly resolved and stuck to as well: first the letter to the solicitor, and only then the rum. He was beginning to feel calmer now, though the feeling of happiness remained with him, remained and blossomed even more. Even his headache began to lift. He now wanted to buy some new clothes. He drove into town and wildly bought everything that was light and airy, very fashionable and disgustingly expensive. It was the first genuine impulse arising from his feeling of triumph: while celebrating the death of his mother, he wanted to walk about disdainfully, happily, wearing something that hadn't been previously lying on Mother's 'commode'.

Leo looked a little like a parrot when he drove to the *Boca* that night to celebrate. A green linen lounge jacket, a pair of blue, light cotton trousers narrow at the waist and flared below, a silk shirt the sales lady described as 'aubergine' in colour, and white, lace-up shoes made of soft light leather.

The new clothes suited him perfectly. His feelings, his intentions, his fantasies were, in precisely the same way, also motley-coloured.

He spent the night in the *Boca* at the Hotel Castor. With a girl from the Concorde Bar. Both drunk on a hideously expensive cheap Brazilian champagne. The red lighting on the ceiling of the hotel room. Leo lay on his back and stared into the red light without blinking until his eyes hurt, until he felt his retina was dyed red forever, blood-red, fire-red, glowing sun-red, eternal sunrise-red. Another bottle, *meu bem?* Ja, *benzinha*. Leo felt the girl's hands, the way she manipulated him—*gostoso*, she said. Leo put on his spectacles. What are you doing? I'm putting on my spectacles. What do you need your spectacles for? I want to see better. Well, you're a funny one. The champagne. The pop of the cork, a cry. And a scream as the lukewarm Spumante frothed over—Leo shook the bottle, and the spray shot out, the girl went on screaming—the urn, thought Leo, that's the way he should shake the urn, scatter the ashes over the ground. They drank from the bottle, the girl pressed her wet body against Leo—mirage, she said, everything's just a mirage, *gostoso*. He ought to scatter his mother's ashes somewhere, thought Leo, give them to the wind, to the earth, irrevocably, gone forever, his mother's ghost could roam the world, as far as he was concerned, and not find anything you could call a last resting-place, nowhere where you could visit her and read the dry dates of her life. *Gostoso*, said the girl. He should drive out of São Paulo, into the interior somewhere, no houses, no people, scatter the ashes under a glowing-red sun, dancing at the same time, dancing under the sun, fire-red, white heat, it should be a festival, the scattering of the ashes in no-man's-land, no people, no houses, just him and the sun. Mirage, just a mirage, said the girl, and she giggled. He ought to plan it out, ought to wear his new clothes, not mourning clothes, festival clothes, he ought to laugh derisively, sing, no, not sing, just laugh, and drink champagne from the bottle. Mirage. Where did you get that word from? Leo was so drunk he thought he might pass out any minute. What word? the girl asked. Mirage. The girl was sitting astride Leo, watching him as he lay under her with his large black spectacles, his eyes closed—give me the urn, he said. What urn? I mean the champagne. You're a funny one. The girl looked at Leo and laughed. You're absolutely right, he could only babble weakly, almost without moving his lips, mirage, yeah, yeah, seeing is believing. See you again soon, said the girl. Leo had fallen asleep. The girl got dressed, took all the money from Leo's briefcase and disappeared.

The urn. Now it was standing on Leo's desk. This time no little peck on the right and left cheeks, Mother, even though this urn is as hard and cold as your cheeks were. Urn. Leo had imagined an urn would look very different. This one here was a small oval container made of sheet-iron, sealed with an aluminium lid which was embedded in the iron container and held in place by means of two aluminium clips, like the lid of a tin of paint. On the lid were name, date of birth, date of death, date of cremation and cremation number. He should be having a shower now, shaving, changing. He stared at the urn. He was feeling euphoric, of that there was no doubt, but in such a particular way that he had to keep urging himself to remain feeling euphoric. Finally he had his shower, shaved and dressed. He had to tell himself what the urn on his desk meant. He now had so much money that he could spend his life as—as what? as whatever—spend his life like someone able to pick and choose what he did. A private scholar, perhaps. Private scholar. And he was free. Free from—from everything that could keep him hard-up, restrict him, force him into a life that didn't suit him. Free— so what, he should be setting off—the journey there would take him a good four hours. After studying the map he had decided on Buri, a little hamlet in the interior of the country. Around about it there was nothing marked on the map—a few estates—for miles around nothing but the odd country house perhaps. He shouldn't forget to take a screwdriver with him. He was then to set off, hung-over in a euphoric kind of way. Was to keep wanting to stop but then drive on. Journey more than four hours, with an urn and a screwdriver. Burí. The main square with the church. The railway station. A junction. Unmade-up road. Burning heat and dust.

The car jolted and lurched over the holes of a country lane. A fork in the road. Leo stopped the car. A wooden signpost. So weathered with the paint peeling off, and faded that the words were illegible. It was simply an arrow pointing left. Where to was indecipherable. Leo went right. Some wooden stakes were sticking in the red soil as if someone had begun once to build a fence there. Dry, dust-covered grass. Some clusters of pale pastel green. Not a human being in sight, not one animal, not one house. A few clouds passed across the sun. The sunlight broke rhythmically through between the scudding clouds. Leo's hair stood on end—it was the wind, a hot rush of air that now abated. Leo stood still, the urn in one hand, the screwdriver in the other. He wrinkled up his eyes. He was weeping. Why? Don't you say: tears of joy? Tears. Sweat. With the back of the hand that was holding the screwdriver he wiped the sweat from his forehead. He felt sick. He should have brought something to drink for this festival. He was then to open the urn, undo the clips with the screwdriver, snap them free from the urn. Next he was to prise off the lid of the urn with the screwdriver, was to look into the container curiously, holding his breath, sweating— the sun, the excitement—the ashes there, like one imagines ashes to look, simply ashes—is that supposed to have been a human being? His mother. That could never have been a human being. Tears. Why did Uncle Zé cry? He was to breathe deeply. He was to lift the urn up suddenly and decisively and tip it up with a tossing movement of his arm.

If you want to scatter ashes, you should not throw them up into the air, least of all against the wind.

Leo had his mother's ashes in his hair, on his face where they stuck to the sweat—weren't there ashes even in his eyes and mouth? He spat and snorted, wanted to vomit. He had Mother's ashes on his shirt— stepping back in panic he rubbed his hands all over it, smearing grey streaks into the shirt. He tore his hands away from his body, lifted them up, stood there as if he wanted to surrender himself to some higher power. How nauseated he felt. He didn't dare to swallow. He kept clearing his throat, spitting out the saliva that gathered in his mouth. He wiped his face with the sleeve of his shirt, and again froze with shock. Weren't those ashes on his shirt sleeve as well? Didn't he wipe the film of ash and sweat into his eyes? Water. There was no water there. He looked down at himself with his arms spread out either side of him. He was still holding the urn in his left hand. His beautiful new shirt, his beautiful new trousers. His mother had ruined them. The urn. He dropped it now as if it were red hot. He ran back to the car, ran as fast as he could. He was crying. The tears at least cleaned his eyes. He had to drive home immediately. Why on earth had he driven so far? The car didn't start. Desperately he kept on turning the engine but nothing happened, just a strange scraping sound that got weaker and weaker.

Leo had inherited more money than he would need in his life but he drove an ancient old second-hand car which you could see was about to give up the ghost any minute. Give up the ghost. Why was he so impractical? He'd bought himself a new shirt but not a new car. Leo would have dearly liked to have screamed. Help! Far and wide not a house, not a human being to be seen. He climbed out of the car again and began tramping along the earthen track again, now on foot. The fork to the left. Perhaps in the not-too-distant future some kind of dwelling would appear in the direction that the weathered signpost pointed to. After walking for two hours Leo came to a beautiful country house. In front of it a swimming pool. On the edge of the pool lay a middle-aged lady sunning herself—two teenage children were playing with a ball and then jumped into the water. Leo approached the *dona de casa*, still or once again with his hands half raised, pacifying—not himself—appeasing: he wasn't a tramp, a suspicious creature, dripping with sweat. Leo made an effort to adopt a particularly polite manner of speaking, and he explained his problem. A trip. The car. An accident. He needed help. A mechanic, a breakdown van, a telephone. He apologised for his dirty appearance but he'd tried to repair the car himself but to no avail. He looked down at himself and his nausea made him black out for a second. And when the blackness lightened he saw crystal clear water, still through a greyish black, streaky film, water where you could see right down to the bottom. The water moved gently, at which the ground appeared to sway slightly—wonderful clean water in a huge bathtub. I got quite a shock, the *dona de case* said later, when Leo was sitting together with the family—(the *fazendeiro* had meanwhile returned home)—in borrowed swimming trunks and with a cold beer in his hand. Before I could say anything, she told them, the gentleman jumped into the pool and went under. And when he came back up he began to wash himself just like you do in the bath—I mean, that's how it looked, his hair, his face again and again, I mean, for God's sake, I thought, he must be—I mean, the gentleman must have sunstroke, I thought, I was so flabbergasted.

And let me assure you once more, said Leo, it may have subjectively looked to the *senhora* as if I jumped into the pool but objectively I fell. I simply fell in. The long walk, the heat, I was getting desperate, my brain was reeling. Objectively I fell in, he said again.

You see, Leo would tell Judith, I had got to the point where, contrary to my earlier resistance, I now really wanted to plunge into life, would have liked to have moved about in life, a perfectly normal life, like a fish does in water. They say you learn to swim when you're thrown into the water. Suddenly I was the one to be thrown in. And it wasn't some wild and dangerous stretch of water I was thrown into but instead a luxurious swimming pool, as it were. And what was I forced to conclude? I can't swim and will never learn. Whatever the situation, whatever happened, all my attempts to find my place in life, to take part in life, both on the public and private levels, were scuppered and sunk, so to speak, without trace. No sooner do I get the chance to hold lectures at the University—and I fight tooth and nail to do it—than the University is closed down. I arrange a trip to the country which I look forward to with immense pleasure and what happens—my car breaks down. No matter whether I jump into life or am pushed, in reality I have only ever fallen in and found I couldn't swim, simply couldn't learn. It's important to see this clearly. That's my life. I am free, rich, innocent. Isn't that a lovely, safe paddling pool? Of course it is. But my experience is such that I can already see in the unruffled surface of a paddling pool the irrational power of the tempestuous seas. So I prefer to sit on the edge of the pool, he would tell Judith, not jump in anymore. I sit on the edge of my own life.

And so Leo simply went on living without changing his life. There was nothing to change because it wasn't a life and couldn't become one, as he thought. He became neither more pretentious nor less so. On the one hand, he didn't want more luxury, pleasures and diversions just because he could have afforded them. But nor, on the other hand, was he willing to give up his ambition to change the world with his writing just because there was no possibility at that moment of making a mark in some form or other. He sat in Löwinger's little gatehouse and worked. He read, culled passages from what he read, made notes. At some point he would begin to write. The book. The opus. He could do this while completely set apart from life. And then this was to go out into life in his stead. And change everything—life and the world.

Meanwhile large sums were transferred round half the globe, from Vienna to Zurich, New York and São Paulo. Instalments were diverted from these cities to Munich, Pretoria, Tokyo, which resulted, strangely enough, in interest accruing in London, Santiago de Chile and Montreal—it involved batches of shares, currency speculations, forward transactions, company stocks; investments in real estate and gold; wheat and umbrellas, copper and orange concentrate, banana purée and diamonds, petroleum—shabby materials. Leo had no notion as to what was happening with his money—Löwinger did it all. He trusted him. Punctually at the beginning of every month a certain sum arrived from somewhere or other (Leo didn't ask from where), a kind of pension—it arrived at a *cambista*, a black market exchange dealer in Rua Direita in the city centre, where at any time Leo could withdraw the whole amount or part of it in cruzeiros at the blackmarket exchange rate of the day. The blackmarket rate was on average fifty percent above the official conversion rate. Using all the experience and help of the international contacts he had acquired during the course of his career as a banker, Löwinger organised that part of Leo's capital that was in the form of interest-bearing investments, without knowing that at the same time Leo, set apart from the world, was studying Karl Marx's *Das Kapital*. And Leo dreamed of writing a book that would travel the world, without knowing that his fortune had been doing just that for some time.

Leo's inheritance from Vienna and the proceeds now coming from the sale of the land Leo owned in São Paulo altered Löwinger's life. This old financial shark, at home in all the money markets the world over and who, regarded as politically suspect, had been robbed of all his offices, dignities and functions by the Brazilian military, was now able to

162

feel, after his tomato-cultivating intermezzo, that he was once more the director of a bank—the sole customer and partner of which was Leo with his fortune. To this he committed all his time, energy and intelligence. The tomato plants shrivelled up. After a time he wouldn't have been able to say where in his huge garden they had once been. Tomatoes. That was something you bought at the market—that was the cook's job. And you didn't just put them in the bowl—you needed to prepare them first by blanching them, of course, and peeling them.

And the everlasting and comforting admonitions that 'tomorrow's the day', that the military would 'step down tomorrow', that Leo was to 'prepare himself for tomorrow', his everlasting 'tomorrow' with which Löwinger had sprinkled Leo, like the water on his tomato plants—this was all over: he said 'soon', then 'the day will come' and then spoke not a word more on the subject. The dictatorship seemed set in stone and was moreover young compared to that of Salazar and Franco. Löwinger wasn't bothered, for the business that he now ran with all his energy didn't affect this dictatorship in any way, on the contrary. He had the peace he needed, he exploited the latitude for commercial criminality that the dictatorship offered like no other system, and played as well with the inflation that the military caused in Brazil, so that even more profit accrued.

And now that Löwinger was representing Leo's interests on an international scale, he soon began to concern himself with Leo's inner needs as well. You have never introduced a girlfriend to me, my boy, and yet you're at the age when you really should be starting to think about marriage. Do you have a girlfriend? Why don't you invite her round? Or have you got—and he smiled mechanically as if were pulling the corners of his mouth apart with his fingers—such a wide choice that you can't make up your mind? You can speak freely with me, my boy. Grand, I mean, children are an important, enriching addition to life, they give you a goal, a meaning, you know why you're working. In this respect I—well, never mind—you must, I mean you may fully rely on my impartial advice, my life experience, my—why don't you invite your girlfriend round?

Dinnertime with Uncle Zé had meanwhile become rather an awkward affair for Leo, like going home to your parents to eat. Here was a father you loved, you avoided, you depended on and deceived. Leo wasn't that taken aback. But he saw clearly that he stood in need now of a good lie. For the last thing he wanted was for the salon to be awash all the time with various daughters—Löwinger was quite capable of having

163

them parade in and parade out until he fixed on one, all for Leo's good—Leo pictured this possibility with ghastly clarity and then thought that the human being's power of imagination with regard to the future was stronger than the ability to remember the past—an idea for an essay—then he reflected as to whether this thesis was correct—then he thought, Nonsense! and wondered whether—

Why don't you answer, my boy?

Leo looked at Uncle Zé, postponed till later all his thoughts—he had to hurry now, a salon full of so-called matches had to be avoided—quick, a lie. He did, in fact, said Leo, have a girlfriend, one he was even thinking of marrying perhaps. She was called Judith. Unfortunately it wasn't possible for him at the moment to enable Uncle Zé to get acquainted with her as she was staying in Vienna because of her studies. However, she would be finishing these very soon now and coming to Brazil and then he would, of course—it went without saying—introduce her to Uncle Zé.

As he said this, it gave Leo a stab of pain because in this lie there was truth, this being that he would have liked the lie to have been true. Which was why the lie had come so easily to him. Löwinger inquired as to what she was studying, asked Leo to describe her, tell him about her, and he was soon convinced that Leo really was completely besotted with this Judith. This restrained Löwinger for the time being from all his well-meant matchmaking attempts: Leo obtained a stay of execution. Six months perhaps, a year perhaps, two perhaps, perhaps by then Löwinger would even have forgotten the matter, and if not, then Leo would modify and elaborate his lie and win a further stay of execution, and in a few years, who knows, the whole business would have resolved itself.

Cinemas, bars, trivial adventures in the *Boca*, occasional dinners with Uncle Zé, now and again a salon afternoon, the odd weekend by the sea in Guarujá. Otherwise reading and copying out, note-taking, draft attempts, screwing them up, writing out fresh extracts. Leo could only think of Judith and he felt such a strong pain that he had to work, work at the pain, work it off; the pain came in bearable doses, wasn't so strong that Leo couldn't work any more because the pain rendered him speechless, or because, alongside the immensity of the pain, what he was doing seemed yet again trite. For at the same time Leo felt happy, he was free, independent, had complete security, had his little pleasures, and since he lacked for nothing he was able to convert his happiness into work where it was perpetuated in the joy of toil, but his happiness wasn't so great that it rendered him speechless because, alongside the intensity of his happiness, what he was doing seemed to him to be nothing but a weak, meaningless imitation, a pale shadow. No.

It could have gone on like this for years, without anything changing, and so it did. The story might have come to an end at this point, if it hadn't begun again from the beginning. And this had to happen because not everything was resolved yet.

In 1972/1973 Leo lost a part of his wealth, but that was all he learnt, no details, that was Löwinger's job—he had speculated badly over oil prices. And when is your Judith coming, my boy? Very soon, said Leo, she has nearly finished her doctorate.

In 1974 nearly all the various land sales in São Paulo had been wound up. In view of the recession and economic crisis prevailing, the Shopping City Construction Company had forced the price down considerably but in the end the price that was paid and which covered Löwinger's speculation losses was a fair amount. Löwinger became more cautious. I don't want to probe, my boy, but isn't your girlfriend supposed to be finishing her studies soon and coming here? Very soon, Uncle Zé, very soon I'll be able to introduce you to her.

In 1975 the last piece of land was sold, the one that looked unsellable because a *favela* had grown up on it. Löwinger had lost patience. After having insured himself against sanctions by means of a whole raft of bribes—even the governor had taken half a million—he got bulldozers to smash their way into the corrugated roof shacks, broke the resistance of the *faveleiros* with a few gunshots from *cangaceiros*, bandits he had hired, the *favela* was razed to the ground, armed guards set in place and after no time at all the land was divided into lots and sold at a profit. And Judith? Soon, said Leo, she'll soon be here. Systematically Löwinger withdrew Leo's capital from all risky and speculative transactions and put it in simple forms of investment guaranteeing long-term and assured returns on his money, which, though not spectacular, were nevertheless gratifying.

Tomorrow, tomorrow—in a manner of speaking, that is. It's just her orals she has to do still, her finals—you can get ready now, Uncle Zé, said Leo in a tone that lacked conviction. Löwinger's questionings were now putting Leo under some considerable pressure and he resolved, the next time Uncle Zé should ask about Judith, to kill her off, so to speak: he would tell him she was dead, he didn't know the details, suicide apparently. Why? Impossible to know from so far away—and then he would get a last stay of execution, perhaps a year, during which he'd successfully manage to turn a deaf ear to Uncle Zé's attempts to cheer him up—a year of mourning. This was the last possibility he had of embellishing the lie and through it he would have arrived at the truth. But for the time being he continued saying: Tomorrow! She's packing her suitcase. The ticket's booked. Tomorrow!

Leo felt like a liar who'd been caught out when his lie turned out to be the truth. What do you say to someone you thought was dead and who is suddenly standing there plainly alive at the door—just as you had promised they would.

You weren't hard to find, said Judith. I knew Löwinger would know where you were. So I drove here. And then I rang at this gatehouse to find out if anyone knew where you were or if I could speak with Mr Löwinger—and lo and behold it was you who opened the door.

A slim woman in Leo's memory, Judith had become well and truly skinny, had aged noticeably: hard lines, wrinkles round her mouth, her hair thin and lustreless, and the shadows round her eyes—'her little mask', as Leo had called it—had all the appearance of a tattoo. Her large nose, her large mouth, the disproportionateness of her features, these now no longer seemed to be distinctive characteristics that enormously enchanced her overall beauty, but instead were the consequences and symptoms of growing old. This moved Leo—he stared at her and in her features that were so changed he rediscovered that face of hers he knew and loved—she was beautiful, no doubt about it—Leo found Judith beautiful. And all of a sudden he knew that if she really had been dead, he would never have been able to have endured and got over her death; if, in believing she was dead, he had converted this loss into a fantasised mourning, a fantasised freedom, a fantasised productivity, a fantasised life, a fantasised little world of his own, then this had arisen from a profound lack of fantasy, for if he had really been able to imagine for one moment what her being dead would have meant to him, then none of that would have been possible for him. The last few years had been nothing but a frantic flirtation with the imagination, the product of an artificial mourning for speculative purposes, which had been waiting for one thing only, to be refuted and abandoned. Fundamentally he had lived his life in a way that suggested he had never for one moment taken the news that Judith was dead literally but only figuratively, as if he had thought to himself frivolously: she's dead for me, hoping secretly at the same time that one day she would be standing at his door and saying: Here I am again—and here we are together again!

Suddenly, then, he was struck by a well-nigh blinding realisation, by the light of which it now appeared obvious to him that, objectively, he must have always known that Judith was alive and would return to him.

But why? Why had Lukas written that she—?

Judith was blinking in the harsh sunlight—at last she held up her hand to shield her eyes and said: Why are you staring at me in such amazement? Did you think I was dead?

The joke was in bad taste. Judith didn't know of course that this was what Leo had believed. Leo now came to life: making an array of polite movements all the while, he invited Judith in, led her into his sitting room and, after a series of enigmatic gestures, threw all scruples and caution to the wind and took her in his arms in a moment of sudden decisiveness—it was an expression of spontaneous joy at seeing her again, the awkwardness of which made it almost authentic. And when, to his own surprise, he found he had managed this, he then imitated Löwinger's manner of embracing (this time spontaneously but all the more calculatedly) by continually pulling her to him again whenever he seemed to be letting her go. He felt her cheek against his, her shoulder blades under one hand, the back of her head and her hair under the other, and then finally her delicate upper arm in one hand, the small of her back beneath the other. He smelt her smell, he tasted particles of her sweat when finally he pressed his lips to her neck, and everything that the palms of his hands, his senses of smell and taste, and his eyes told him, everything seemed immediately familiar and yet so strange, so familiar once but all too strange now, never really familiar and so not really strange now, and in the space between these discrepancies there was room enough for any amount of sentimentality and pathos, for endless rapture, endless amazement. Judith was touched. Iced tea? You bet. Leo fetched the carafe from the fridge, poured some out, adding for safety's sake a generous dash of rum to his own glass. He needed some dutch courage as quickly as possible and yet he didn't dare to ask her how the rumour could have arisen that she was dead. This question remained unasked, a hidden bomb towards which all his nerves ran like burning fuse wires, and Judith couldn't smell the burning, all through the years she couldn't, until the bomb detonated.

167

Highly delighted. These two words were not merely polite froth—Leo could clearly see that they really did express in the most precise way what Uncle Zé genuinely felt when Leo introduced Judith to him. Highly delighted, as only Uncle Zé could say it. Leo admired the natural precision with which Löwinger made form and content coincide: obligatory politeness with true feeling. Leo was proud of him, a father who makes quite an impression on the son's girlfriend without— and Leo was convinced of this too—putting her under any pressure. And he was proud of Judith. The way she allowed herself to be appraised without the least sign of being intimidated, and at the same time did everything correctly without needing to dissemble. In other words Leo was proud of himself. He had done everything correctly. He had what he wanted as regards the circumstances of his life. A peaceful and trouble-free routine which, far from disturbing his purposes, furthered these greatly. The happy and uninterrupted flow of his work over the past months were proof of this. But not only were the objective needs of his life taken care of, now the subjective ones were as well: he had the woman he wanted. He had her here within reach again at least. With her being within reach, he could reach her at any given moment, meaning, in the final analysis, conquer her. Incontestable. And with her he enjoyed complete recognition of his life for the first time—something he had at the moment in one form through Löwinger. But that was recognition that counted for something. Public recognition would be bound to follow on from this private recognition in the form of the impact his book would make. And in this way the circle was closed. For his book could not fail to take shape as a result of the perfect orderliness of his life. It was a closed-off life system. Life as it should be lived. The ground beneath his feet. Total economic security matched by security as regards the economy of his emotional life. Everything subordinated to the overall purpose of his life. Just as his wealth didn't lead to his living a life of luxury, since he was able to regard it merely as the material guarantee of his scholarly life, so did he view love in the same way. For him it wasn't the source of incalculable, sensual rapture but rather a power source for productivity. He looked amorously at Judith. Being creates consciousness. This is the foundation over which he will now build the arching superstructure, the last complete philosophical system.

The actual consummation of philosophy. If he were to lie down on the floor now on his back with his hands behind his head, he could almost believe he'd be able to see it arching over him already, rather in the same way as an awning is raised. Leo could not believe his luck. He had been objectively right here, too: it really was thanks to quite a bit of luck that everything now—what? Leo thought: has turned out so well. Everything has turned out well. Nothing will be able to upset him any more now.

Dinner, with all due marks of affability, passed off so correctly that Judith could barely swallow one mouthful—she wanted only to drink, to lose control by drinking, to destroy all control. Leo and Löwinger made such a perfect ensemble that you could almost have confused the one with the other. Not a friend with his uncle, not father and son, not two generations, but twins, or at least a minimalist edition of a *pas de deux*, two people whose movements, gestures, idiosyncrasies, reflexes, intonation were completely synchronised, even down to the way they looked at you. They sat opposite each other, both on the long side of the table—Judith had been given 'the place of honour', 'the place of honour', as they had both said, at the head of the table—she watched the two of them, turning to them each in turn, so that it must have looked, as she herself thought, as if she were slowly shaking her head from side to side in amazement. Putting down their knives and forks and dabbing their mouths with the large cloth napkin—this was, as it were, the signal that they wanted to say something. The one who put down his napkin and picked up his knife and fork again was handing over to the next speaker. While one of them spoke, the other chewed. The discrete mouth and jaw movements of the one who was speaking were barely distinguishable from those of the one who was chewing—it seemed to Judith as if the two of them were literally taking every word out of each other's mouths with their napkins, like little mouthfuls passing back and forth from one mouth into the other. Even the most banal of statements from the one were pleasurably and thoroughly chewed over by the other after the former had given him the word to do so. Judith had thought at that moment when she'd first seen Leo again that he had just come from the dentist and was still suffering from the anaesthetic, but now as she observed Löwinger she understood why Leo scarcely opened his mouth when he spoke. The way they both wielded their cutlery, the way they both raised their wine-glasses to their lips, the way they chewed, swallowed, dabbed their mouths, and whenever they did this last at the same time, they then both pointed at the other with their napkins in order to allow the other to speak, after which Judith had the distinct impression they were speaking in chorus. Perhaps this Löwinger didn't exist at all and Leo had only put up a mirror in front of himself, pointed to his mirror image and said: I've already told you a lot about him.

Can I, said Judith, have some more salad, and she stretched her hand across the table towards the salad bowl, which was at the other end of the table. Keeping her arm outstretched, she cupped her elbow in her other hand as a support, as if she wanted get herself into a position so that she could hold her hand stretched out across the table for as long as possible, and she grinned at Leo provocatively.

Leo went rigid—Judith saw the shock in Leo's face for a split second terminating in a fearful, wide-eyed look—then he reached in a panic for the salad bowl, but just at this same moment Löwinger, too, said: But of course! and also reached for the bowl so that the two of them in tandem conveyed the salad to Judith's plate, siamese twins attached to each other by the bowl. They both smiled but Leo's smile turned into an uncontrolled, explosive giggle, a giggle of relief which this time could not return to the smile that its mirror image was demonstrating. It's nothing, Uncle Zé, I'm just so happy that Judith is here again. After this everything returned to a relieved correctness, for Löwinger's smile, whenever it strayed from Judith to Leo, seemed to be saying: a good choice, my boy.

Everything had turned out well, but only in Leo's mind. For in reality he had not conquered Judith yet and had not yet written his book. And so, as he stepped through this closing part of the story, Leo was forced to see that he was suddenly back at the beginning.

Look at that, said Judith, you've got a spanking new *fusca*. Yes, said Leo, shall we drive down to the *Bexiga* for a pizza?

Leo had the whole story in his head, from this beginning to the fondly imagined end. He thought in all seriousness that, in order to make it come true, making it conscious was enough. While eating their pizza he had already finished reminiscing about their time together in Vienna and was now describing how things had gone for him since he had arrived in Brazil, telling the story in such a way that it was leading with growing compulsion to the question which Leo was able to put finally—at best by implication—with the third bottle of wine: whether Judith would like to move in with him. He had after all, so ran the moral of his story, been living with her, so to speak, during all the years of their separation, that is, in that he had constantly thought of her, in that what he had begun with her, and learnt from her back then, had continued, along with the fact that he had always expected that she would return to him. Leo leant back and lit himself a palomitas. He was impressed with himself. He had spoken superbly, in such a way that all the episodes, as they unfolded one by one, together made perfectly mind-blowing sense—each seemed a vitally necessary stage out of which the next one was logically bound to develop. The germinating seed, the urge for growth, the leaves arising from this, then the buds that hint already as to meaning and purpose, these being finally revealed in all perfection in the fully unfolded blossom. This plant image was wrong, Leo thought—Judith didn't figure in it, or at the most as the one who plucked the blossom. Leo now grew nervous. Why hadn't Judith said anything for so long? He felt as if she were picking off the petals one by one and consigning the consummate rationality of the life he had offered her to the absurd irrationality of a love oracle instead.

Up to now Judith had hardly said a word, certainly nothing remotely at any length. And now she also said in the end just one word: No. She reflected for a moment, wanted to add something but Leo was talking once again. He was talking because he thought he hadn't in fact expressed himself properly, hadn't spoken with enough conviction, and he talked as if his life depended on it, went on and on talking in order to wash away with a torrent of words the shock and extreme irritation that Judith's terse reply had provoked in him, but it was no use—he grew more and more nettled and at a loss. You will admit that, he said again and again, and: No, wait, let me finish, let me finish, and he went on talking finally just to put off and put off the moment when she would definitely confirm her no—let me finish, he said once again, thinking at the same time: I'm debasing myself—never again will I tell anyone so much about myself. Leo was forced to see that this new beginning was far from being the beginning of a consummation. This time he really was thrown right back to the beginning again. Back to square one again: the wooing, the waiting, the nervousness, the moments of euphoria and of irritation, the hate. But that wasn't all. Everything in his life was now suddenly thrown back to the beginnings. The organisation of his private life—brought about finally by a steep ascent in his development, since it had enabled him latterly to work without interruption—his habits and the everyday little securities that he had formed over years and which had propped him up and even given him some satisfaction—all of this had now returned to those

171

former uncertainties and inabilities. He lived only in the narrow no-man's-land between the expectations he had of Judith and his frustration when these weren't met. Any thought of uninterrupted work was now out of the question. The harmoniously symbiotic life in the Löwinger household was destroyed. Now just as at the beginning Leo again became aware that Löwinger was not a friend to be trusted. That hadn't mattered anymore lately. The walks in the garden, having dinner together, the time spent chatting in the library, the conversations in the art collection, the salon afternoons, all this had given rise to a system of co-ordinates whose limits Leo had thought he no longer had to go beyond. For contained within them was that happy minimum which sufficed to enable him to pursue his phantasies and his work, and at all times be affirmed in everything he did, so that not the slightest doubt as to the meaningfulness of all this had been able to emerge. Now, however, Leo would have had constantly to re-address points which were not contained within this system of co-ordinates—he wanted nothing else, thought of nothing else, and the result was that the whole system, as practicable as it was, collapsed again. He couldn't talk with Löwinger any more. He began avoiding him again because what he had to speak to him about irritated him. He would never have been able to say to Löwinger: The truth is that I thought Judith was dead. He would never have been able to say: As long as I thought she was dead, I was able to work wonderfully. Never: But even when suddenly there she was again, the devil knows why—The devil, my boy? I'm sorry, I was joking—I still had the highest expectations: the woman I love so much is alive! But I can't tell you, Uncle Zé, how rampant her life is in its constantly changing needs, moods and desires and yet she doesn't want to give this life of hers meaning and content by means of a sensible way of life with me. There's no doubt whatsoever that her life suffocates mine, suffocates my work. If the truth be told, Judith is too much alive.

He couldn't tell Löwinger that he wasn't working any more, that all the preparations and spade-work had ended in nothing. The last years were most definitely productive ones: Leo had read and copied out extracts, had formulated his thesis very precisely, completed the conceptual side of his work and how it was to be elaborated. Löwinger would have said: Now write it, my boy. And if Leo had tried to explain how, because of

Judith, he couldn't, Löwinger would have said: Then you must forget her. But that would mean also forgetting everything he had worked at until now, including especially the book as well. For the book is the revelation of the hidden totality of life, that is: it is wrung from life. The book doesn't arise out of an obliviousness to life but rather from the fact that its rationality arranges even the chance events of life into a meaningful order.

One shouldn't forget, Uncle Zé, that Judith didn't turn up again just any old time but exactly on the day I had wanted to begin the actual writing of my book. This shows with blinding clarity what Judith means to my life on a deeper level, the role she plays in the system of my life: she personifies the arbitrariness of life, chance. She is life incarnate and I love this life, love life as much as the next man, of course, no question. I can't tell you how much, Uncle Zé. But for the sake of my opus I must overcome it, that much is certain. For this reason it was not by chance that Judith appeared again on that day of all days and sat down in my study. For on that particular day when I had decided finally to start writing my book, once again on the agenda for me, objectively and historiologically, was the question: opus or life. But Löwinger used to talk about artists and philosophers like you might about bees who build their honeycombs as a matter of course, and he was the beekeeper, who, as interpreter, strained the thick sweet honey from their creations. Leo clammed up whenever there were literary discussions in the salon about the greatest cultural achievements of history—in his case he felt only the pain that was necessary to bring them to birth. He clammed up whenever he sat in Löwinger's library, thousands upon thousands of books and each one, as insignificant as it might be, a completed work, a victory and he had nothing to set against these dust-covered jibes at his ambitions. And the quite unbearable dinners when with such understanding Löwinger praised Leo's absent-mindedness as an expression of the obsessiveness with which he was now working and which cut him off from the world.

Again and again, whenever Löwinger wanted to invite him, when he pressured him to come and have dinner with him again, to show his face, Leo used excuses like the ones he had made formerly. The gatehouse seemed to distance itself from Löwinger's house as if it had slipped its moorings, floated away from the mainland and was now drifting out to sea at the mercy of unpredictable currents. Leo couldn't swim. He clung to Judith, in panic at first, then with increasing apathy.

173

Leo tried to rediscover in Judith's face the face he had once fallen in love with—there it was, he could see it very clearly but it was at the same time strangely ravaged, as if Judith had had some dreadful, destructive experience. What could it have been? What had she been through? Without him. It must have been something touching the roots of her life, some mortal blow, thought Leo, and paused in amazement in the middle of holding forth. Death. Had she experienced it—her death? Quickly he went on speaking. He was talking about his work, his sequel to the *Phenomenology of Spirit*, which was to take the history of consciousness up to the present day and bring it to an end. It sounded as if he were working at it every day—the truth was that he talked instead of working. He lectured about what he had written, but in truth it was what he would have liked to have written if only he'd been able. He elaborated theses to her as if they were the results of a process of long and painful hours of reflection, whereas in truth they had only just occurred to him that moment. His book progressed only orally, and yet it didn't, for everything that was said was lost and forgotten again afterwards. Not even in Judith's arms could he manage to place his book before his inner eye. He wanted to give himself to his book in the midst of Judith's caresses, to experience it imaginatively taking shape but quite physically. He sought exciting thoughts in excitement, tried to find in rhythm the rhythm of his language because he thought that through this the possessed mind would come to a climax and find fruitful release. But he remained speechless, almost wordless. He closed his eyes, he opened his eyes, but all he saw, knew, could think of was Judith and then he would let her name slip from him—Judith! he said and froze in shock as if he had betrayed himself after some act of infidelity.

He was in reality unfaithful when he wasn't doing any work and yet said 'Book!' all the time when with Judith. But to talk at least about his book, again and again, relentlessly, was the only way for him, in the life he now led, of preventing his project from sinking without trace. Since his book, however, didn't exist, wasn't even approaching existence, he immediately elevated it into myth. And so he would talk, say, about his Oblomov tree, beneath which he had been 'enlightened'—and just in case Judith should wonder at seeing this man she had first got to know as an anti-life Puritan, tied to his desk, now suddenly lying voluptuously for afternoons on end under a tree dreaming away as the mood took him, well, she'd have to realise that he had learnt in the meantime to unite desire and necessity in total harmony. Leo gave a momentary start when he said 'tied to his desk' and quickly said 'dreaming' immediately afterwards. The dream. Judith hadn't just untied him from the dining-table, as he had dreamed it, but from his desk, too. But that was just a very brief flash of a thought—he had hurriedly gone on talking so as to unite desire and necessity in total harmony. It wasn't true what he said of himself in fact, but the aim of his lies was true: he wanted to create the thing he was talking about. If he wanted to conquer Judith, then he wouldn't get very far with his everlasting polemics against life, that much he had grasped. With his lies he systematically produced a false picture of himself—but wasn't propaganda allowed, if in the end it turned out to be the truth? Leo honestly believed that through Judith he would finally become what he was cracking himself up to be already: brilliant, hard-working and yet a great connoisseur of life's little pleasures.

But in Judith's experience it wasn't that Leo himself wanted to become a different person but rather that he wanted *her* to become a different person, that is, available, predictable and under his thumb. Because she systematically resisted this, she appeared to him chaotic and irrational. He didn't understand it. In his opinion it would have been 'systematic' to be able to build on everything he'd established with Judith, instead of always having to fall back again to stages already passed before. Whenever Judith spent the night at Leo's, he would then assume, if they were meeting up again the next day, that she would naturally want to repeat this. But she would say: Do you think you've taken out a subscription for me, Leo, or what? Whenever the two had met up with each other three days in a row and had made arrange-ments again for the next day as well, Judith would then ring up just before the appointed time and call it off. She wanted to be alone, she would say. When on the following day, and after a dreadful night, Leo had got his headache more or less under control and was considering, with a defiant look at his desk, whether he shouldn't draw some con-clusions from the absurdities of this life, then Judith would ring and say that she absolutely had to see him straightaway. And Leo would jump in his car without a moment's hesitation. He didn't understand Judith. He didn't even understand her when she was very clear. Once he had invited her for a picnic under his 'Oblomov tree'. It was a beautiful sunny day, one that made everything appear easy and effortless. Despite this everything went badly wrong. In Leo's life not even the weather matched the course of action that he expected from the fine literature he'd read. He had really put himself out. He'd even specially bought a picnic basket so as to be able to carry the provisions through the garden in style. Judith must see that he knows how to live. Really live. For style and form bring control and order to life. But not one word about the horrendously expensive, beautiful basket passed Judith's lips—she probably took it for granted that, if he invited her for a picnic, he had the appropriate accoutrements. The first problem was that a huge ants' nest was discovered under the 'Oblomov tree'. Judith asked sarcastically if this really was where he always lay down. The ants' nest wasn't here before, Leo said. I don't understand, where did it appear from? It takes no time at all, said Judith. They're industrious creatures.

But sudden changes in the weather also take no time at all, especially in São Paulo. By the time they had decided on a different place, black clouds had started to gather threateningly in the sky above. A strong wind blew up and the tablecloth that Leo had just spread out on the lawn was swept up into the air and blown along for several yards. So Judith and Leo made a dash for the gatehouse, which they reached just as the first drops were beginning to fall. But the deterioration in the weather had lifted their spirits. They found everything very amusing and laughed a great deal. Lucky it rained, thought Leo, for now they were having their picnic in his bed. Then came the next misfortune. Suddenly Leo received this powerful look and he began to snuggle up to Judith. She let him have his way, even pressed her body against his finally, with her eyes shut, opening them again only when Leo took the plates and food off the bed, put them on the floor and said: We'll carry on eating afterwards!

Judith got up, straightened up her clothing and said stiffly and with a metallic ring to her voice, as if she had to don a suit of armour now because her skin had been flayed: I wouldn't have minded at all if, instead of the word 'afterwards', you had used the nice little word 'later'.

This was precisely what Leo felt to be capricious and irrational—he couldn't understand Judith, but went on believing it was just a question of his having to make himself clear to her. Desire and necessity. A love that found expression within the context of an orderly shared life and the book. She must surely see that. He talked and explained—every time they met he never stopped explaining. So as to convince her of his opinions, to make his actions or omissions plausible to her, and, last but not least, to prevent there ever being a silence when they were together. For Judith never said a thing. The thought of being together with her and not a word being spoken was most unpleasant. As if they didn't have anything to say to each other. All his efforts would have thus come to an end but not attained their goal. Again and again Leo resolved to sound Judith out the next time, to get her to talk, let her have a say. But then, when he did meet up with her again, it was he who began talking immediately, waking happily out of the lethargy of his loneliness and, as he talked, new ideas and thoughts would come to him continually which he absolutely had to elaborate on and take to their conclusion. Delighted by the stimulating effect Judith had on him, he would regularly finish up with the great questions of philosophy, literature, mankind, instead of with her. In retrospect Leo again failed to understand why Judith, who would discuss films or books with vigour, revealed so little of herself, so that for him everything was somehow mired in vagueness and uncertainty.

Leo got not one inch further with Judith. Her love was not to be browbeaten, nor indeed was the productivity that was meant to arise from this love. On the other hand he also wasn't able to transform the disappointments she caused him into work, for Judith didn't in fact cause him any disappointment, it was just that she simply didn't react to his deceptions. One day he gave her to read the piece on 'Ethical Life and Education' that he had written when he thought Judith was dead. As regards the circumstances surrounding the origins of this work—heavenly are the days—he said nothing, of course. He wanted to impress Judith with the lucid beauty of this long essay but he also wanted just as much to pull the wool over his own eyes with regard to the productivity of which, as was observable, he was thoroughly capable. 'Was', it's true, but in the act of taking this work out of the drawer, he also seemed capable of it now.

Judith never commented on this work. After a time Leo grew impatient and was on the verge of enquiring as to whether she had liked it when he was struck numb with horror by the thought that her silence could be due to something he'd be better off leaving well alone. It was possible that she had realised that he hadn't written the essay just now but a good long time ago and, what was still worse, that it constituted an attempt to endow Judith's death with a fine meaning. As always an attempted advance had turned into its opposite. He had given Judith this essay to read because he had hoped that her enthusiastic praise would rekindle his ambition enough to bring about as soon as possible a new piece of work of the same quality. At the same time the expectation was that Judith's enthusiasm for what he wrote would extend to his own person. A new quality in their relationship would have thus been attained. Instead of which he himself now kept quiet about this essay so as not to have to address something to do with the past that was best kept in the dark. The essay, the only longer piece of work he had completed, disappeared beneath her silence and, instead of being able to build on it, it was as if it had never been written.

It sometimes seemed to Leo as if he were not just thrown back always to the beginning with Judith but even further back beyond the beginning. Their love had had, after all, a certain naturalness at the beginning and there had been the belief that out of this a life of solid productivity would unfold. This could no longer be taken for granted now. The fact, however, that Leo continued to concern himself with Judith, met her at every opportunity, was always there for her, resulted solely from the automatic nature of the situation, which was that he would have been at a total loss as to what else he should do. He wasn't anything other than merely a rich man. He had forgotten how to work. With Judith he could at least talk about the work he imagined—in this way it continued to exist as a parameter by which the work others had really done could be measured, work which, when discussed and criticised, they even drew pleasure from. If Leo hadn't had these aspirations to master and improve the world, it would in fact have been a pleasant life: he had no financial problems; now and then he would read some philosophical literature and fiction which he would then discuss with Judith; they cultivated little pleasures such as visits to the cinema, meals in good restaurants and heavy drinking bouts in bars. But his identity would have completely collapsed if he hadn't always wanted more. He dug in his heels, even though his advances became ever more sluggish and stupid, until all they boiled down to finally were his efforts never, if possible, to leave her side. The man Judith had once wanted to take in her arms had become an overexcited, frightened and tired child running alongside her and tugging constantly at her sleeve because it wanted to be carried.

The senile child. He was now turning forty and looked fifty. Puffy with drink, he drank when he met Judith, so as to relax, and he drank when he couldn't relax, so as to deaden himself. He had put on so much weight due to alcohol that none of his suits fitted him any more. He got a tailor to make him half a dozen new ones, which in no time at all looked as if he slept in them. His trousers now no longer did up round his stomach, so he forgot that he had a stomach. He had become short of breath due to his smoking, so he hardly ever went for walks. Whenever for Judith's sake he did go, then he would walk very slowly with his hands no longer behind his back but crossed over his chest, his shoulders hunched up, his head bent far forward. His hair was turning white; this didn't bother him to begin with, but it became worryingly thin as well; every morning he saw a mass of hairs on his pillow and startling amounts of hair covered the washbasin and shower tray. After smoothing down his hair meditatively, he would find wisps of it between his fingers. When Judith remarked once that his monk's tonsure could now be seen very clearly, he took fright. He didn't want to forfeit his attractiveness to Judith for such a banal reason, risk throwing away his chances. And wasn't a good strong head of hair a symbol of strength? So now he had his hair dyed black and drove three times a week to his hairdresser in the Jardins to have his scalp massaged with a tincture which was supposed to strengthen the hair roots. From then on his hair looked a little greasy but he interpreted the slightly oily feel on his fingers when he carefully touched the back of his head as a sign that his hair was already stirring into new life. This was enough to restore his self-confidence to some degree, though only on the condition that he avoided looking in the mirror. When after a shower once he slipped on the tiled floor of the bathroom and, in an instinctive attempt to grab hold of something, tore the mirror off the wall and smashed it, he didn't buy a new one. He was now fully immunised against any kind of self-criticism. The thought that he might not have much time left didn't enter his head. He'd only just begun after all. Yes, only now in fact did the beginning lie before him.

But the beginning slipped ever further into the distance. He finally succeeded in taking the one step forward he had longed for: Judith now declared that she was in fact willing to move in with him. It would transpire that this step, too, was a step backwards.

It was in the course of one night, and after she had once again rung Leo and cancelled a meeting they had arranged, that Judith made her decision to take up Leo's offer and move to his place. She had wanted to be alone. She was in her apartment in the Rua Pamplona, which she had rented overhastily and with little thought, immediately after her arrival, so as to have her own four walls and some peace and quiet as quickly as possible. Not least because of Leo, too, who had assailed her with reasons why she should move in with him and who then couldn't be dissuaded, however, from driving her in his car from estate agent to estate agent and from one suggested address to the next, only to cast a disparaging look around every flat they visited and to observe how much better off she would be with him in his house. She had signed the contract for this flat simply to bring this tiresome discussion to an end. That was a mistake. She had seen flats before this one that were a lot more appealing and would have certainly found a better one after it. Not only was the noise from the street far too loud but, most importantly, it was also too small: basically just one room, for the so-called bedroom was so tiny that it served only as a walk-in wardrobe. But from the first she had also seen an advantage to this: a sitting-room without a bedroom would be ideal for a chronic insomniac like herself—sleep would thereby lose a lot of the threatening aura it had for her. But since there now had to be a bed as well in the only room that was available, this room was far too cramped for her to be able to walk up and down freely and easily, as she was accustomed to doing during her sleepless nights. Every step she took she had to swerve out of the way of a piece of furniture—as a result she walked in a tottering, swaying way, but inasmuch as she would drink one vodka after another during this pacing up and down of hers, the walk was, as it were, in character. She'd been living there now for nearly a year. She had to decide soon whether she wanted to extend her contract for a further year. The rise in the rent that the landlord had announced was absurd, but even if, as was to be expected, he were to be open to reason, the flat was still overpriced. Flat. It was a cell she lived in. But that wasn't the reason why she was to decide to move to Leo's. For she would have had a substantially larger room even in her parents' house. And she hadn't wanted to stay there either. She hated this cell emotionlessly, if that is remotely possible. Its outward crampedness was in the end insignificant for her. It was unreal. On all the walls she had hung rows of mirrors—the walls appeared to the eye to open and to push apart their actual distance from each other many times over.

The real cell was inside her. The cell of her locked-away memories. There were too many for one room, in which even a coffin had to be accommodated. All her thoughts and feelings, in order not to bump into anything, had to swerve at every step and appear to totter. That was why the tiny flat she lived in wasn't the real problem. It had nothing to do with her existential confinement. The outer expression of this she saw rather in her body that had grown even thinner and scrawnier. This was the connection that frightened her. The walls of her body, so close to each other that there didn't even seem to be enough room within them for the volume of air needed for a deep, releasing breath. When she stopped in front of one of her mirrors and observed herself closely, the mirror didn't mist over. She was wearing a white towelling robe. Her black hair hung in damp strands over her shoulders. It was absurd to compare Leo with Michael. She knew it. It hurt her. She had been having a shower—so as to feel fresh when Leo came to pick her up—when it happened again. She had been soaping herself pleasurably, her hands gliding over her body with unbridled anticipation, when she froze because she suddenly realised that she had forgotten for a second who she was going to meet. It had been a moment of spontaneous anticipation which had not related to Leo. She had felt like this, that's how it had been, whenever she was about to meet Michael. The stream of water rinsed the foam from her skin without her moving. Because her actions had been basically so insignificant, she hadn't been paying attention, had bumped into a memory, a feeling as if that memory were real, and now an all too real, unbearable pain. She turned off the water, tore open the door of the shower cabinet as if she couldn't breathe. The hot steam immediately filled the tiny bathroom and misted over the mirror. Without drying herself off, she ran into the sitting-room, went to the telephone, rang Leo to tell him not to come. For a further few minutes she sat helplessly by the telephone, then she put on her dressing gown, poured herself a glass of vodka and began walking up and down in her cage. She knew that, as always, she wouldn't be able to bear it, being alone and waiting for sleep. Everything is going to begin again from the beginning and it will drive her crazy. On the other hand there was no way she could see Leo now and so pretend everything was all right. And to speak openly with him was quite beyond her. Not only because she could hardly get a word in edgeways with Leo. She couldn't tell him something for which she didn't have the words. A banal story would result that could only provoke unbearably banal reactions, stupidly verbose attempts to cheer her up or a wounded helplessness which would only serve to mirror blindly the helplessness she herself would feel when communicating the incommunicable. It was unfair. Unfair to Leo, whom she couldn't get involved with. And it was unfair of Michael to get in her way still. Michael—he was the object of her thoughts, the one she had to sidestep in the to and fro of her thinking. Leo. It was so stupid. She didn't love him. And he didn't love her. Even if he was always maintaining he did. But she knew Leo better. For him it was more a theoretical premise which he started out from. Leo's love with all its commercial breaks bore the same relation to love as a television programme did to to real life. That was the problem. There was no simile possible for love, no image, no way of describing it. Nothing can be said about it.

She had got to know Michael—it was round the time when Leo left Vienna—and it was real love. Full stop. Out and out love leaves you speechless, just as out and out nothing does: death. Limitless happiness and limitless pain elude all description. That's why literature was full of descriptions of love. Because people who don't know love want to write it into existence. Everyone who loved was immediately struck dumb. Judith was convinced of this. That was why there was no way she could read any other literature than that which dealt with failure and not with fulfilment. This literature shrinks back from its goal, doesn't go stomping straight for it, because the goal, the greatest happiness, cannot be reached by means of a method—it can also lurk in the shadows. Like death.

Judith drank another glass of vodka. As she wound her way between the furniture, her manner of walking took on an artistic quality. She smoked one cigarette after the other. Ashtrays were distributed throughout the room, and she lingered briefly by each one in turn, in order to drag on her cigarette long and greedily while watching the ash grow, which she then tapped off. She had always warded Leo off, but not because there was no love in this relationship. You couldn't make love dance to your tune, least of all demand it from another. It would be absurd therefore to break something off just because it can't be perfect. But perhaps she was afraid that with Leo it couldn't be any different either. As a repetition it was too dull, as an anaesthetic too weak, as an escape it didn't take you far enough away, not to mention the descriptive and defining opportunities it gave Leo—yes, that was it: too many words were possible, quite apart from the many words Leo already had.

On the other hand what was she to think? She hadn't really got involved with Leo yet, after all. What will he do now? Work probably. Will say he did tomorrow, that's for sure. All the same she could count on him for affection, respect, interest and a remarkably unswerving loyalty. That was amazing. Loyalty. It wasn't out of loyalty to Michael that she didn't want to throw her lot in with Leo. That would be absurd. Loyalty to the dead. She wanted to live. Death is a scandal. Why a person would want to bring it upon themselves she will never understand. Someone who loves. There he was again. Michael. She would have stayed in Vienna because of him, would never have seen Leo again. But she had returned to Brazil, was with Leo again, whom she sometimes couldn't bear to see because she kept on seeing Michael, that ghastly picture of him that she carried around with her inside and that she would only be able to destroy if she destroyed herself, something she fundamentally could not do, as a result of which this picture was slowly destroying her life.

Quickly Judith emptied her glass, poured herself another, took one swig from it. She looked in the mirror in front of her with an obstinacy that was her attempt to armour herself against what this obstinacy already expressed: the horror she could no longer suppress at the picture she could no longer close her eyes to, even when she closed them. The horrified expression on the face she saw in the mirror was just one part of the picture that opened out into a room in which Michael was hanging from a piece of washing line tied to an overhead light hook—Judith turned aside, took a few steps, bumped into the armchair, the reading lamp, the table—Michael must have climbed up onto the table to tie the line to the light hook, then the loop round his neck, then a step. She stopped still. She would always have this picture and never an explanation for it. That there had to be a reason for everything was a heresy, if not the reason for all suffering. Causality was terribly overprized. The search for causality always takes you over dead bodies—your own in the end. What she had experienced was so devoid of reason that it deprived her life afterwards of all reasons. They had both been short of money, had too little for a larger flat where they could have lived together. That was no reason. He had moved from his rented room to her place. They were happy. Easily said. But true. She had moved into the bedroom with her desk so that he could turn the sitting room, which got more light, into his studio. He painted, was studying at the Art Academy. He didn't get anything from his parents. That was no reason. He subsisted by working as a night porter in a one-night hotel. That wasn't good for him. Judith was prepared to go out to work. The money her parents sent her was not enough for two and for the third, the art. The paints, the canvas, wood for the frames, all the working materials, the contribution to the costs of the gallery and to the catalogue—that was important, his first solo exhibition. The kind reviews the exhibition received didn't sell many paintings, though. That was no reason. There had been positive reactions, after all. From then on Judith gave Portuguese lessons at the Latin America Institute. She had been working that evening. She came home. She opened the door to the sitting room. Michael had planned, after lengthy preparation, to finish a new, larger picture that day. Judith was looking forward to this picture.

The picture. There are no words for the shock and pain she felt. She saw herself walking through the room, endlessly multiplied, just like she saw herself now in the many mirrors in her little *sala*—in her horror she was as if scattered, fragmented into so many bodiless and lifeless ghosts: there was the Judith who was looking for a suicide note, the Judith who was looking at the sketches which he must have been working at immediately before, designs for the large panel painting he'd already started on—the sketches presented scenes from the one night hotel—the idea was to show the shrillness of social normality when that normality removed its masks and travesties in a secluded place, or was allowed to show them for what they were—there was the Judith who went on standing there and looking—later she was to ask herself over and over why she had stared for so long at the dead body hanging there, exactly as if she had wanted to imprint this picture on her mind—but there, too, was the Judith who cut him down from the rope, the Judith who attempted to resuscitate him, as far as she knew how to resuscitate someone, and the Judith who finally stripped him naked. There was no farewell note, no explanation on paper for the inexplicable. The big and, moreover, unanswerable 'why' disintegrated for Judith into a variety of 'whys', as if she could obtain an answer by blurring them all together, whereas the details—each single one as unanswerable as the totality—only served to cruelly exaggerate the incomprehensible horror. Why, before she had left, had he said he was determined to finish the picture that day, a picture of which, however, apart from a beginning, there was nothing to see? Finish? Why, before he did that, had Michael put on some of her clothing? He was wearing Judith's blue knitted dress, one of her favourite items of clothing during the colder times of the year—she had so liked wearing it, had worn it so often that she always saw herself in this dress whenever she thought of winter in Vienna. Underneath Michael had been wearing a bra which he hadn't, however, been able to fasten at the back, and one of her stockings. The police were not to see him like this. But not naked either, with this jutting out erection, which she couldn't connect with anything other than shame. She put a pair of his under-pants on him, that would have to do, she had already overtaxed her strength. Not because touching a dead body disgusted her. She was still surprised how little she felt, touching a dead body. She would have liked to have told him this, if later he had come to life again. The fact that she could not tell him this or anything else either any more, that was what was terrible. Why did he do it, even though he knew she was pregnant? Then there was the Judith who went to the phone and rang the police. Past, present and future collapsed into a unity. What Judith had seen, she saw still and would always see. As if what happened were captured in the form of a monumental, gruesome painting that she had to stare at forever. Until the rotting stench of the picture became hers, too, while she expired with her eyes wide open. She died as long as she held her breath, as if she could breathe through her eyes. The sigh she gave as she did breathe in again, when nothing else would do, was a small, tortured scream. Her rib-cage now rose and sank rapidly and this brought life into the picture. Did she not see herself picking up the phone? So she picked it up. She rang Leo. No reflection preceded this. She didn't have to think and mentally put into words what she now saw with a clarity that already contained the decision. She had to survive this picture, get life to paint over it, or she would die in front of it.

Leo's speech was a little slurred, just as Judith's was, who, while waiting to be connected, had quickly drained her glass. Leo please come immediately—can you come over? I'll come. How long will you be? Three quarters of an hour. Please hurry. I'm on my way.

Judith crouched next to the phone, frozen with pain and fear, and waited. Why had he done it. She didn't understand the patience with her that Leo was able to muster. But perhaps this was what saved her. The patience which was intended to turn her into a sacrifice on the altar of his ambitions. It didn't matter about the ambitions. Suddenly Judith saw the grand gesture with which Leo believed he could direct the world as the brandishing of a paintbrush that could perhaps paint over the picture she could no longer bear to look at. In this picture was the scream of fear of her own death. Judith, who was cutting down from the rope a corpse which was wearing Judith's clothes. The clothing was stretched, the corpse was somewhat fatter than Judith. At the time she had been four months pregnant. They had both been looking forward to this child. If there was an explanation for Michael's action, then Michael would never have taken the action. It was just because there was no explanation, just because there was absolutely nothing, not even an explanation, no

185

reason whatsoever, that Michael had been able to do it. That meant, though, that the child, too, no longer meant anything to him. When Judith, while waiting for the police, thought about the child she was carrying, she knew immediately that she didn't want to have it. The child of a man for whom it had no longer meant anything. Of a man who was lying there in front of her like a makumba doll and in her dress as if he were merely an instrument by means of which she was to be cursed and her death, in fact, conjured up. It wasn't Michael who had killed himself. It was a doll meant to represent Judith that had been hung up in her flat. She had to move out of the flat immediately. But where had Leo got to. She had to get out of her cell. She drank another glass of vodka. Alcohol deadens what kills. Not everything and not completely. But a little of almost everything. She gave a short giggle—it sounded like a mixture of a suppressed sob and a gasp for air. She froze. It was spooky, making noises when completely alone. She had begun, in her state of shock, to have conversations with herself. She asked herself questions, gave herself answers, and in these every potentiality was more real than reality. But on the subject of this question she would brook no discussion: she couldn't bear this child. She saw before her now the synthesis of herself and Michael that this child was to have been, the man with the appearance of the woman, and she would see this synthesis forever in this child. She couldn't bear this death. Only the death of this child would be able to remove this death.

She had moved out of her flat without taking with her a single piece of her furniture. She rented the first furnished room to hand. Terminating a pregnancy in the fourth month in Austria was out of the question. She didn't dare to discuss with doctors the possibility of an illegal abortion. She was frightened she might get reported and so be forced to see the pregnancy out. The girlfriends and acquaintances she spoke to split into two camps: the first tried to convince her she should have the child. A job, a new meaning, an emotion, which would allow everything that had happened to recede into the distance. The others gave her tips how you could apparently bring on an abortion: hot baths, jumping down from the table several times, inserting parsley into your vagina. For a week she pondered these pieces of advice. Then she climbed up onto her table and jumped. Even before she fell to the floor, she gave a cry of terror. She had felt a tightness about her neck, as if a noose were abruptly pulling together. She didn't know what to do anymore. She began to think she would only be able to kill this child by killing herself. That was the curse. But she wanted to live, to be free of the death she had seen. All that was meaningless. If the shock of seeing Michael like that hadn't brought on an abortion, then parsley wouldn't do it either. She made systematic enquiries among her circle of acquaintances. Time was pressing. She was in her fifth month already when she got the address and telephone number of a doctor in Hungary near the Austrian border who carried out illegal terminations. An early morning train to Sopron. A dilapidated house on the outskirts of the town, black with the soot from the smoking factory chimneys, which made Judith think of crematoriums. A surgery visit in the basement with no daylight. Walls painted with green oil-paints. A doctor in a white coat, his face grey, his hair yellowish. No receptionist, no nurse, no other woman, just herself and this man. He indicated that she should undress and lie down on the white, metal slab couch. He counted the money—then he washed his hands. If it were to hurt, Judith was sure she wouldn't cry out. The situation was as eerie as in a horror film from the silent movie era. She screamed as she had never screamed before. The walls began to shimmer and to sway, seemed to turn red, then violet, black, then they were green again. She had two hours in which to rest, then the journey back to the station and then the train to Vienna.

Heavy bleeding began in the night. The next day she had a high fever. She nearly died as a result of the abortion. It was the one and only time in her life that she longed for sleep to come. She survived. Death, she thought finally, was overcome. She swiftly completed her studies and with a degree of concentration that suggested nothing else in the world existed. That was indeed why these studies held her interest: so that nothing else in the world would exist.

Finally the return to Brazil. She thought it would be the ultimate return to innocence. Nothing in Brazil would remind her of Michael. Even as she thought this, she was packing him in her suitcase. In Brazil there was nothing for her outside of what she brought with her: with her literary education she could find no work and with her memories of a dead man she could find no entry into life. While the pictures in her head continued into infinity between the mirrors of her apartment, she experienced Löwinger's house or that of her parents as flat, illusory worlds, the stone backdrop of the city of São Paulo as nothing more than a Potemkin village exaggerated to a maddening degree and put together from a mass of huge gravestones. She couldn't bear it. She had to give life a chance. She thought this in these words. She thought the formulation was rather kitsch. She examined the glass in her hand. These thoughts she had! Kitsch. So what. She drank a little and thought again, emphasising every single word as she thought, as if she had to memorise a difficult formula: give life a chance. She shouldn't forget it. She stood up and looked at herself in the mirror. She wanted to give up this woman she saw there. With her thumbs and forefingers she massaged her swollen eyes. She wanted to give up this torture-chamber she lived in. Slam the door shut from the outside and never return. She had to try. Leo didn't love her—she didn't love him. He'd never be able to wound her fatally. But by enmeshing her, as firmly and persistently as he did, maybe a net would form which would not allow anything threatening to slip through into her life any more. Maybe. Maybe that was a good thing: that way there was no love at stake. At stake in the game that was so hard to win. Maybe that was why Leo's loyalty was so solemn. Because it was pure loyalty, without love, completely artless. This loyalty will suffocate everything. Even death.

She ran to the window and leant far out to see if Leo was coming. Fear gripped her suddenly. She lived on the ninth floor. Rua Pamplona below was swaying and coldly flickering in the white headlights and rearlights of the cars—the thought came to her briefly that they were all ambulances, collecting the corpses of people who had jumped out of the windows. So many windows belonging to so many little apartments. So many cars. Coming to the rescue of each person. Every ambulance arriving only after it has happened. Quickly she shut the window. She yanked open the front door of the flat and looked out at the lift door to see whether the little red light was shining and the lift was in use. It was free. Through the glass pane of the lift door she looked into the lift shaft. The cables weren't moving. She stared at them for a few seconds longer, then ran back into her apartment without shutting the door, ran into her so-called bedroom in which there was just one cupboard with glass doors, seized a holdall and began throwing items of clothing into it. What else? Shoes. She had three pairs which she thrust into the bag. Jewellery? She had just one pearl necklace from her mother. Here it was. She was just about to drop it into the bag when she hesitated, then finally straightened up and put the necklace on in front of the mirror. Round her neck. For Leo. She waited tensely to see if something would happen. All she saw in the mirror was her thin neck and the necklace. That was a necklace round her neck. Perhaps Leo would like it. Slowly she let her towel bathrobe slip down off her body. Then she rummaged again feverishly in the cupboard, decided on a dress and a blouse which she then put on. She ran into the bathroom, fetched her wash-things, which she also stuffed into the bag. She was just doing up the zip when she heard steps in the sitting room. Leo had arrived. She went out, put the bag down before his feet and said: Does your offer still stand?

Leo had pictured this moment very differently. Happier, more euphoric, more triumphant. Now he was taking back home with him a drunk who was sitting apathetically on the front passenger seat, looking out of the side window and not saying a word. Even though he had always been sure that sooner or later she would move in with him, the inexplicable suddenness of Judith's decision was nevertheless distinctly weird. And, on top of that, this lethargic, dejected and resigned impression she gave. He didn't know...what? He drove as if their way were lit only by the light of the stars, slowly, uncertainly—he, too, had drunk far too much. Not as much as Judith, though. The state she was in irritated him. Once home she could barely walk straight. On the other hand he had seen her drunk often enough before—it didn't mean a thing. The important thing was that he had brought her home. Everything now ought to seem new to him, new and yet familiar, adventurous and yet as safe as houses. He held her firmly round her shoulders as he led her into the house. Leo decided to take the situation for what it was. It was one that occasioned the greatest joy, of that there was no doubt. However, if, strangely enough, he didn't feel this joy, he was then obliged to cling to those things where the joy was apparent. Judith didn't want to go to bed straightaway, she wanted another drink. Of course. She wanted to celebrate. Perfectly natural. You're right, he said, we have to celebrate. He happily went off and fetched a bottle of rum and two glasses. Judith sat there in his armchair, strangely dislocated and looking around her with glassy-eyed astonishment, as if she had just awoken from a dream and didn't know where she was. Leo looked around as well: it moved him to see the room, as he believed he did, through Judith's eyes—and he was pleased to note that she could have done a lot worse. Welcome to my home, he said—cheers. Judith emptied her glass in two gulps and crumpled up. She hadn't fallen asleep—she'd fainted. Leo carried her to bed, undressed her and lay down beside her. In his excitement he naturally couldn't get to sleep for a long while. Holding his breath, he carefully placed his hand on Judith's stomach—Judith didn't react. She lay next to him like someone dead, and Leo was happy because he felt so much life in him, so much talent, energy, the highest of hopes. His concept of what life was really about. Now there's no question but that it will blossom freely. No more getting lost on the flat plains of an aimless existence. Cautiously he let his hand play over Judith's body— she lay there like a corpse. Before him Leo saw his *oeuvre*, his book, not a lifeless object but rather full of life for whoever reads it—he looked at Judith in the darkness, an enigmatic text, a source of knowledge for whoever could correctly interpret her. He'd start work tomorrow, straight after breakfast. He remembered suddenly he didn't have anything in the house for breakfast. First thing in the morning, while Judith was sleeping it off, he would quickly drive to the shops and then get some breakfast together before she woke up. Ham and salami and cheese—no, not cheese, Judith didn't like cheese—and fresh, hot rolls, and champagne, of course, champagne, and to go with this some caviar, too, of course—where could he get hold of some caviar—he'd never bought any before—perhaps in the fish market. Or perhaps oysters— but he didn't have an oyster knife—you just couldn't get the things open with normal cutlery—oysters were out of the question—it's possible he could hurt his writing hand when opening them—something that had such slippery iridescence as oysters suited girls like Regina but not Judith—smoked salmon, perhaps. And freshly squeezed orange juice of course—fruit generally: mangos, melão, carambolas, grapes and an abacaxi, of course, in memory of the beginning of their love— no, no abacaxi, no reminder of the quarrel that time in the bath-tub— fresh figs would be better. It had to be a banquet, the first breakfast of their life together. And he'd have to lay the table particularly beauti- fully—Judith would have to be bowled over—a white tablecloth, can- dles—no, no candles in the morning. And after breakfast down to work. A little later, a communal break, in bed. No, bed better straight after breakfast, when feeling rested and fortified, with all the high spirits that would doubtless come to the fore over breakfast—to fall teleologically into each other's arms in order to make up for what the late hour, exhaustion and alcohol did not permit now. Yes, yes, definitely, into bed straight after breakfast—all the better, for then he'd be able to work afterwards without a break—of course—Judith will be delighted—it was too late today to celebrate fittingly, however much Judith might have wanted it—but tomorrow, tomorrow there'll be a feast.

Leo thought he had only just fallen asleep when Judith woke him. Wake up, Leo, you can't stay in bed forever. Leo was completely confused—he had thought his mother was talking—you can't, you can't—alive still in dreams, a lifelong echo—Leo rolled over in bed, opened his eyes and saw Judith standing in front of the bed and buttoning up her blouse—How come Judith . . . oh, of course, Judith.

How late is it, then? Far too late, said Judith—come on, get up, we've got loads of things to do, we've got to do so much shopping—I'm really looking forward to it—

That's right, said Leo, and sat up, we haven't got anything in the house for breakfast—that's what I actually wanted—

We'll drink some coffee on the way in a *padaria*—come on, do get up now—

What do you mean on the way, on the way where? He rubbed his eyes—he had a stinking headache.

It wasn't to get better all day: in the chaos of the traffic through which he struggled with Judith from one furniture store to the next; in the showrooms, in which he had to run behind Judith, who wanted first to get an overview, and where it smelt so aggravatingly of paint, impregnated upholstery and airspray; in front of hundreds of cupboards, shelves, tables, upholstered furniture, where he hadn't the faintest idea for what purpose they needed such things. Everything was totally incomprehensible to him, even though he hadn't been able to offer anything to counter Judith's arguments: that now they were living together they should furnish the house jointly and in a way that was appropriate to their joint needs; that she would otherwise see herself always as a lodger, or at best as a welcome guest in a strange house without ever being able to feel really at home there; living with Leo, she said, had to be more than just having a few items of clothing in his cupboard and a second toothbrush in the bathroom. What would Leo have said to that? That she could of course furnish one of the rooms in his house for herself alone and exactly as she wanted? That wasn't an argument after she'd already said she didn't want to feel like a lodger. And if she were to go about things in a calmer and more considered fashion, wait until they'd lived together for a time, then she would have a better idea as to what they might change and add to in the house? There would have been no point suggesting this to her: she was positively bursting with energy and the compulsion to do something.

191

Anyway, he'd thought, this would have just postponed things—it would be better to get out of the way today and straightaway what was clearly unavoidable but which later would be all the more inconvenient when he was in the middle of his work.

His work. Three weeks later this seemed to him further away than ever before. Each and every day he drove through the city with Judith to large furniture stores, to highly repectable interior decor firms, to cheap little furniture shops, to antique dealers, rag-and-bone men, carpenters and even to the private addresses of foreigners who, because they were returning to their own countries, had advertised the sale of their household effects. His house was full of prospectuses, catalogues, preliminary estimates, finance plans, furniture magazines—but two thirds of his own furniture went missing. Judith had arranged this with Löwinger, to whom, at the end of the day, the furniture there belonged. In countless shops Leo looked at sofas and tables, listless and open-mouthed because he didn't understand why these were better than the sofa and table he already had, and he had to lend a hand with the removal of his sofa without his having grasped why, if they were obliged to replace it with another new one, it had lost its useful-ness. Judith had charged his account for two cupboards while he'd been standing in front of the showroom piece unsure as to whether he liked the look of it at all. And why two—didn't he have one already—just one more surely would be enough for her clothes. Please, Leo, they wouldn't go together, she'd said, or do you want separate bedrooms? Her feverish bustle and irritation paralysed him. His own home had become unfa-miliar to him and, with every piece of furniture that was delivered, he once again felt barely more than a guest in Judith's house, a helpful old acquaintance who was giving her a hand to push the furniture around because she wanted to see in what position they created the best effect. She organised the disposition of the rooms without discussing it with him, taking for granted that he would agree and so give her a free hand, feeling as he did that it was all too much for him. It drove him nearly crazy, her covering all the walls with mirrors—he felt this hypertrophic love of Judith's for mirrors was pathological but told himself he'd actually known about it before and that, for this reason and regarding this point of all points, he ought not to complain. Even in the bedroom over the new bed—far too soft—she had had a mirror fitted on the ceiling, in which he could see himself lying alone and exhausted, while Judith was still drinking and smoking in the *sala* and studying brochures instead of coming to bed.

Objectively, and this he couldn't fail to see clearly, the experiment of moving in together, contrary to his expectations, had turned out to be a step backwards. Instead of all preconditions being settled and his being able to begin his book, new preconditions had been created which first had to be clarified. It had certainly been a lot better before. Hadn't he been able to read regularly at least? Since Judith had moved in he hadn't had anything to do with books apart from clearing them from his old bookcase and arranging them on the floor. When the new bookcase was finished he would be able to put the books back. And when was he supposed to read anyway? While trying out chairs in the furniture stores? Hadn't he had lovely, stimulating discussions before with Judith, about films, literature, philosophy? In the last weeks they had stopped going to the cinema—he was always too exhausted in the evenings. And what was he supposed to discuss with her now? The latest technological developments in kitchen gadgetry and hi-fi systems? Colour theory with particular reference to curtain materials? The aesthetics of built-in cup-boards? And hadn't he been able, before she moved in, to get a little affection from her—only occasionally, it was true, but in retrospect a lot more frequently than he could now? Since they had been living together, she was more distant from him than ever before. Here he was, lying alone in this bloody bed that they'd absolutely had to buy because two people need a wider bed and because you absolutely have to have a bed with a drawer underneath for the bedding, while she meantime was sitting or walking up and down in the next-door room and simply didn't want to come to bed. Should he perhaps don a loincloth, the one pictured in a glossy brochure on curtain poles, and, vaulting into the *sala*, do a Tarzan to her Jane and take her by force? He was at his wits' end. Nothing productive was coming from their living together and what they had had before had disintegrated. With difficulty he still managed to drive to the hairdresser's once a week to have his scalp massaged.

He heard steps in the *sala*. Was Judith actually coming to bed now? No, she had put on a record, her beloved Ataulfo Alves—and now she was walking up and down again. He hated her, though he told himself continually it wasn't her but the situation they found themselves in that he hated. For the time being. He clung to this last little expression with all his might. It was only because of the future prospect that this expression promised that he put up with everything with a stoical composure, as he saw it, and with no hint of opposition. Should he, right at the outset, allow bad-tempered discussions and petty squabbles over questions concerning furnishings to destroy the feeling of triumph he felt at her moving in with him, along with the hoped for consequences that this would quite definitely bring in the medium term? No. Judith's intoxication with interior decor couldn't last forever. And then—and this he had to keep clearly in view—Judith would feel at home in his place and would settle down happily. With his eyes firmly fixed on this future he turned a blind eye to the days that passed and which he called the preliminaries. He thought it sufficed during these preliminaries to show, if possible, no irritation, annoyance, impatience and exasperation and to avoid all disagreements and fights so as not to endanger the harmony which would be able to develop productively once all the preconditions had been definitely clarified. Whenever Judith cooked, he would sit in the *sala* and dream of how he would soon be looking through his notes at the kitchen table and keeping Judith company while she cooked. He didn't notice later the way that Judith would signal how much she longed for him to have things out with her—he only saw what still needed to be done in the house and never saw that Judith also had other needs—he believed that, whenever she suggested things that they might do together, she too was thinking of the future and so he ignored everything with a lethargic and tolerant nod. He was most at a loss on Sundays when all the shops were closed. There seemed to him to be no point in beginning work, since he wouldn't be able to continue with it the next day, and so he would sit around disconsolately, looking enviously at Judith while she read, and would finally suggest driving into town and doing some window-shopping. They might see a dining-table on display which Judith might finally bring herself to decide on, and then on Monday they'd need only to drive down and buy it and the matter would be settled. Relieved not to have to sit around aimlessly and emptily at home, he would, however, be immediately embittered again to see how his life consisted only of driving to and from furniture stores, and would console himself by thinking of Judith's gratitude for the fact that he'd once again shown himself to be so co-operative.

All at once everything went very quickly. Leo got the impression that Judith, too, wanted to put all this home-furnishing business behind her. Gradually all the items of furniture were delivered. Six weeks after Judith had moved in, Leo found himself in a house where nothing else could be changed anymore, unless you were to change everything again. He breathed a sigh of relief. The time had come. At breakfast he spoke about his book for the first time again. Then he withdrew into his study like a child who has finally been allowed to open a parcel whose precise contents he already knew. He looked lovingly at the typewriter, the new bookcase, the chaise longue that Judith had said she thought looked so right there. He polished the shade of the brass standard lamp, he sharpened his pencils and set them out in orderly fashion on the desk. He arranged his folders which were full of extracted quotations, delighted to see how industrious he was being already. What should he begin with? What would Judith be doing in the meantime? It was very quiet in the house, so quiet it made Leo nervous. Had Judith gone out without saying anything because she hadn't wanted to disturb him? Surely not. Leo immediately ran out of his room to check up on her. She was sitting on the sofa in the *sala* and gazing into the air. Leo stopped by the door, perplexed for a moment, then went over to the side table, picked up the box of palomitas and said: I'd forgotten these. Judith didn't say anything. So, said Leo, I'm just going to get down to some work. Yes, off you go, then.

Leo ran back into his study and lit a cigarillo. He looked absent-mindedly at his writing desk. What was up with Judith? Why was she sitting around so absent-mindedly? Now that everything was all organised. She should surely be content now. He looked in the bookcase for Hegel's *Phenomenonology*. It took a while before he found it. The books had been arranged in his bookcase any old how. The books had been arranged any old how before as well but he had always known roughly where to find what. This lack of order was completely new, one in which he couldn't find his way around. He had to introduce a system into his bookshelves—there was no question of his being able to get down to work until he had. He cleared all the books from the shelves and piled them up on the floor. He thought about what system he should choose. Alphabetical according to author's names? If he did this, then Hegel, whom he needed every day, would either be on the top shelf, which he could reach only with the aid of a chair, or, if he began backwards, on the lowest shelf where he would have to slide about on his knees. The numerous volumes of Goethe's complete works would have shoved Hegel down to the second shelf at least, in the former arrangement, but he didn't have a full set. He therefore tended to favour an order based on partiality. Those books that were important to him within easy reach, those needed less frequently above these, those not so favoured underneath. On the other hand, although his bookcase took up one entire wall of his study, he wouldn't possibly be able to squash ninety percent of his books on the middle shelf. Besides, it wouldn't be a system either—it would once again raise the question as to what order he should put the books in. And he shouldn't forget Judith's books either. The decision to put all their books together into a library was, after all, the reason why they had got a joiner to build this massive bookcase for them. When they had first cleared the books away, they had bundled both his and hers together, which was why he now didn't know where anything was. He certainly couldn't separate the books again and put hers down with the unloved ones. Such a separation would defeat the whole object of having a joint library. He gazed helplessly at the empty shelves along the wall and at the piles of books on the floor. He pulled open the door and called for Judith. Her suggestion to arrange the books according to subject area and, within one subject, historically, that is, according to year of publication, was of course the most sensible system. That's what I thought, too, he said. But why did she have to be so waspish and brusque with him, and then, when she went out, why did she have to slam the door so hard? He pulled open the door and shouted after her: I only asked you because— after all, it's supposed to be *our* library, he thought, closing the door again—she doesn't want to listen. What had got into her? Why couldn't she show a fraction of the patience that he showed towards her? And why couldn't she state clearly what it was, when something got on her nerves? She spread a nervous unrest and a feeling of uncertainty which destroyed all attempts to concentrate. How was he supposed to be able to work like this? He hated Lukács—he had just picked up a volume of his. Should he put his *Aesthetics* in the Philosophy section or did it belong more in the Art Theory section? Did *History and Class Consciousness* belong to History or to Political Theory? And what about Lukács writings on literary sociology? The History of Literature or the Sociology sections? The Young Hegel must surely go under Secondary Literature on Philosophy, if it was a question of the relation between dialectics and economics—but strictly speaking he'd have to put him with those things he'd need to have constantly to hand for his own work. But there was no way he could split up an author's works into five subject areas— six, for somewhere he also had Lukács' political writings. Politics—that, too. This idea to separate them into subject areas was quite clearly a nonsense—it manifestly went against his universalist idea of spirit. He threw Lukács *Aesthetics* back onto the floor and stamped his foot—not really, of course, but inwardly, so to speak. Judith! he shouted. Work was out of the question as long as this chaos with the books reigned in his room, an insoluble problem—out of the question until he could find out what was wrong with Judith. What was eating her?

For days on end Leo circled round her, was shooed away continually with tired movements of her hand like you would a fly that was drunk with the heat, or he was at best tolerated by her, like market conditions you can do nothing about, like the heat they were currently sweltering in and which had invaded the house as well, as if someone had taken a deep breath and held it for a long time so that all life seemed to stand still. Conversations Leo would try to have with her would break off so abruptly it was as if he were helplessly trying to tune into a radio station, twiddling the knob all the while but always getting only a few scraps of words and then a prolonged background roar. Uncle Zé, Leo said, had invited them both for dinner. I can't work, said Leo, what on earth is wrong, Judith? What's the matter with you, asked Leo, why are you so—he couldn't think of the word. Her short answers didn't explain anything and Leo didn't improve matters either by trying to analyse her behaviour in the belief he was expressing his feelings sympathetically. You're like my mother—she also used to always say that Löwinger... My mother never took my work seriously either, always thought it absurd, too, that I... My mother would also sit there stiffly and self-righteously all the time, never troubling herself as to whether my father or I...

In the hall of mirrors where they lived Leo felt that her isolation was doubled and found it unbearable, but whenever Judith went out, then in the mirrors Leo saw his own multiplied into infinity. In the bedroom, in the living-room, in the kitchen, in the bathroom, everywhere he was immediately encircled by his mirror image, as if by some third person who was unknown to him. Where he had come from, how he'd got in, he didn't know, this old man (which he certainly wasn't), a stranger who, on the pretext of imitating him, in fact gave him his cue all the time, until Leo was able on his own to mimic the gestures and bodily movements, the melancholy lassitude, this bloated despair, this puffy, bowed-down appearance, this fidgety fellow now so thin on top, with his sharp-nosed, thin-lipped troubled air, this weakling with his look of perpetual astonishment. In the mirrors Leo became like this other one, this other Leo who demonstrated how to insert a cut-glass wall between your self-esteem and your appearance, a wall through which you can't get a hold of yourself any more, you always appear to be the wrong way round, until, that is, you go around the glass wall, become the other one and from there just continue looking out from the mirror—at nothing.

Once when Leo was lying side by side in bed with Judith, he reached up with his hand towards Judith's reflection and saw with horror only his own hand reaching out towards him from above.

My girlfriend, said Leo, while looking thoughtfully in the mirror as the hairdresser massaged his scalp, has put up mirrors like this everywhere in the house, in every room—it's driving me crazy but there's no use talking to her about it.

Interesting, said the hairdresser—you must relax your scalp and neck—they're completely tensed up. Don't screw your forehead up all the time—yes, that's right—you see.

I expect, said Leo, that as a hairdresser you're probably professionally au fait with mirrors. You work in front of them every day. On the other hand, though, what would you think if your wife were also to plaster the home with mirrors and then wasn't able to offer you any explanation— I mean—

I see, said the hairdresser, so she doesn't say anything. She can't say anything, either. Do you know what a taboo is? Yes? Well, there you go—she can't explain it because it's got to do with a taboo. I bet she has anal problems. Don't get me wrong, said the hairdresser—and please relax your scalp—what I'm saying is purely scientific. I'm doing a course in psychology at the moment. It should be a part of every hairdresser's training. You wouldn't believe how often problems with your hair have emotional causes. I would never be able to give my clients the treatment they expect if I knew nothing about psychology. You'd never believe the stories I hear at work from my clients. It all boils down to psychological problems. And if I weren't able to deal with them, my clients would never come back again to have their hair done. Look at the way you always push up the muscles in your forehead—and your neck is rigid with tension—here, can you feel? Like concrete. This totally undermines any attempts to solve your hair problem. The sturdiest hair roots would never withstand this. How do you expect the blood to be able to get into the scalp when you're as tense as this? Yes, that's better. Purely psychological your problem, I'd bet my life on it. Perhaps the problem with your girlfriend irritates you as much as it does because it unconsciously touches on a fear you have, that is, that something from behind, as we say, that something is going on behind your back and hence the continual tension in your neck muscles. Yes, that's much better—let yourself go. Had you ever thought that we can hear something going on behind us but can only *see* what's going on in front of us? I thought not. You've shut the thought out deliberately.

198

Because otherwise you'd always be forced to think that something might come up from behind you without your ever seeing it. That causes anxiety. So best not think about it. A clear case of repressed anal sexuality. And now the anxiety has settled in your neck. It's quite a business, you know, this anality. It's number one, so to speak, on our course programme. It's unbelievable the things people do wrong with their kids, which then wreck them for life. There are whole books about it by psychologists, you wouldn't believe it. I've thought a lot about it. It became quite clear to me that that's the central problem. Let's look at it for a moment. The anus is, strictly scientifically speaking, our most enigmatic means of production and communication because we ourselves can never observe what's happening there. In the oral and genital phase we are of course brought face to face with things that are always there in front of us. This is not the case in the anal phase. That's terrible, of course. In spite of this, the first things that we as human beings produce, we do from the anus. But we can't see how we do it. Production takes place there behind our backs. We see it only when it's all over and done with—the term is: 'objectified', because anyone could have done it. When a child is sitting on the pot, you wouldn't believe how absorbed it is unconsciously with this question. You can bet your bottom dollar on it. Many people never manage to reach a normal genital condition because they can't solve the anal problem. Relax. I tell you, I've see a thing or two. Dona Gaetana, the blonde *senhora* who was cut by Maria, over there in the front—yes, she was sitting there, that's the one—well, you could see for yourself she's quite clearly anorexic. She can't keep anything down, brings everything up again straightaway. It's perfectly clear—what she puts in her mouth she can see, so it has to come out of her mouth, too. The anal phase, completely out of control. And do you know what she told me? Wherever she goes, she's always bumping into things because she's forever turning round and looking behind her. As if she were frightened that something might happen behind her, that something might come up to her from behind without her seeing it, so she says. And do you know what she's actually frightened of? Eh? I'm sure you do. That something might happen behind her—yes? Exactly—that behind her, where she can't see, something might come out, somewhere she can't accept because she wants to have things going into and coming out only through her mouth because there she can see what she's doing. You see, that's how it is! A never-ending problem. She's getting better now, now she's having treatment. I advised her to try eating in the dark for a time so that she gets used to non-visible processes. I didn't get that from the course, that was more my own idea. In my profession intuition is the key thing—specialist knowledge alone is nothing, you need intuition, I always say. Is your girlfriend very thin? There, you see, just as I thought. Pure intuition. Perhaps with these mirrors of hers she wants to protect herself from the great enigma as to what is behind her. Ask her one day if she has a problem with things behind her back. Perhaps something might emerge—I mean, she might then start talking perhaps. You'll see. Has your girlfriend set up a mirror in the bedroom, too? Thought so. In bed your girlfriend is probably—strictly scientifically speaking and between you and me—probably suffering from a totally anal fixation. Am I right? Please relax your scalp. I've seen a thing or two. A mirror next to the bed and above the bed, that's something I see only with people who are suffering from a totally anal fixation—but totally. They want to solve the problem as to how things can go in and out of them there, where they themselves can't actually see it happening. The genital human being doesn't need a mirror. He's got everything in front of him in full view. Senhor Leo, your scalp—please relax. If ever by chance you're passing a bookshop, take a look in—you'll find an amazing amount of books on the subject, for beginners, too—wouldn't hurt to find out a little about it. I've seen a thing or two, I can tell you. Sometimes I get the impression that unconsciously people don't think about anything else other than their anal sexuality. The stories I hear at work here. Anyhow, the way I see things, you should broach the subject with your girlfriend. For the sake of your scalp if nothing else. There must be a reason for this continual tension. You'll see—Freud explains it. Next time we'll also have to touch up the colour again, by the way. There, do you see, when I comb your hair straight back you can already see a light-coloured down growing back again a little. The little tonsure at the back here has stabilised. Hasn't got any worse. You must always remember—relax, relax.

On the way home Leo seriously wondered whether there was any point at all in working scientifically if scientific efforts led in effect and in practice to hairdressers' tormenting their clients. This mirror theory was the most absurd nonsense. On the other hand, was psychology in fact a science? Clearly not. His hair stood on end, his scalp was pleasantly coursing with blood—he loved this feeling when he had had his scalp massaged, he loved the slightly oily wetness on his fingers when he ran them through his hair, and he loved the smell that his fingers then had on them. He felt like a long-haired young lad and caught himself looking at himself with satisfaction in the rear mirror of the car.

When he got home he saw a delivery van in front of the house, saw two men under Judith's direction carrying into the house a narrow, very tall object which was in a brown cardboard box.

It's great you're here, said Judith—look what I've just bought.

She got the men to set the box down in the *sala*. She hadn't been so animated and in such high spirits for a long time. Immediately the men were gone she began to open the box. Now I'll show it to you, she said, I'll set it up for you now—you'll see.

A wooden frame around dark glass came into view—it looked like a window about the height of a man fixed to a wooden base so that it could stand freely in the middle of the room. Leo didn't have the first idea as to what this object was supposed to represent. Was it a mirror? But if that were the case the glass was too dark. A window? But what did you need a window standing on a base in the middle of the room for? Judith hurriedly cleared the packaging material to one side, took Leo's hand and looked at the object with visible joy. You know Roberto from the *Persona* bar in the Bexiga quarter, she said—he made that. He calls it the mirror of self-knowledge—other people call it the magic mirror as well. It's fantastic, you'll see. It works very simply. Come, take your clothes off. Leo was seized with an enormous excitement, a dazed feeling of sheer happiness. The spell was broken, her lethargy and depression overcome, his patience and far-sighted understanding of her situation had paid off. He couldn't imagine for one moment, of course, what this so-called magic mirror might mean but this would soon be made clear. What seemed crucial to him was the liveliness and excitement with which Judith undressed and urged him to do the same, her mysterious agility, which seemed to be leading towards the revelation of all secrets—he felt infected by Judith's excitement as he stepped out of his trousers—this was clearly the beginning of... the beginning... Forget it, just the beginning at last.

The principle is very simple, explained Judith. The glass reflects but becomes simultaneously transparent if light falls on it from the other side. She darkened the room, lit two candles and put one of them into Leo's hand. Now go and stand in front of the mirror, she said.

Leo saw himself. He looked a little ridiculous, he thought, naked with a candle in front of a mirror in a darkened room. Judith walked around the mirror with the other candle and positioned herself behind it. Because of the candle she was holding, the mirror became transparent as well—Leo still saw himself but saw Judith, too, at the same time. She laughed. Move about, Leo—do you see? So, what do you think?

Leo looked, and didn't know what he ought to say.

If we move deliberately, she said, carefully—do you see?—we can synchronise our bodies in the mirror—yes, that's right. You always have to take your cue from the other person's movements. I can be your reflection, you mine—our two reflections can melt into a common one. Look! Do you see?

Leo saw how his body in the mirror seemed to permeate Judith's, to unite with it—his movements seemed to emerge from Judith's, to continue them, and hers his, despite the fact that with the candle in his hand he moved rather stiffly.

Let's concentrate just on our faces for a moment—but don't go too near the glass, Leo, you're misting it up—yes, like that.

His face and hers, his and her eyes, his and her nose, his and her mouth, all were made to coincide in the mirror—both faces seemed to melt into one, into their common, ideal face, as it were. If he were to ask himself, Am I that? then he would have to affirm, Yes, that's me! But at the same time it was definitely Judith, too, Judith's face, quite distinctly. That's really—fun, he said, on one note. Suddenly she bent her head so that hers slid out to one side from the common head and in this way the common body had two heads, his and hers. She slid her feet apart—now they had four legs, the outside ones hers, the inside ones his, at which his sex, starting to become aroused but also confused, as if it wanted to return to him, arched away from Judith's stomach and towards him. Look, said Judith, we can stroke each other—careful, always along the surface of the skin—but we can also dip into each other, penetrate each other, come out of each other, but everything one of us does with the other, he does with himself, too. They now went back to the position where their bodies appeared to be fused into one and whenever one of them moved, it was a mutual movement, each was able to complete the movements of the other with his own, take them a step further, move within the other's field of movement and then return once more to total superimposition.

Leo realised that in this mirror he was seeing exactly what he had been longing for for years, had always wanted to experience. It was the solution to the riddle. And a new riddle at the same time. How could it become real, what he saw—how could he really experience, feel on his own body what he now only saw in front of him? He'd have to be able to walk through the mirror, take a step through the glass and seize hold of Judith.

Not too close to the glass, Leo—watch out!

Leo stepped back, shaken, and asked: What is this supposed to show? That union and fusion are a mirage?

No, no mirage. It really happens, don't you see? But the fact that it's a trick—*that* is true.

With this she blew out her candle and Leo could hear only her ghostly laughter behind the dark surface of the mirror—in which he saw himself again, standing there alone.

He wanted to walk around the mirror, go to her—No, Leo, stay there, stay on your side, please. That's just the problem with union, he heard her say as he stood there stiffly, they say you have to, as it were, 'see the light', understand how the union works. Without light you can't see anything of the other person, do you see, even though they may be within reach—if there weren't a glass screen in between. Blow out your candle. What can you see?

Myself, said Leo.

That's how it goes, said Judith. You're naked and you can see your wretchedness, I am covered up and hide my wretchedness—(she came round from the other side of the mirror fully dressed, having put her clothes back on meanwhile behind the mirror like behind a screen)—and suddenly nothing fits anymore. It didn't work, Leo. You know what would've been really lovely with the trick? To have been able to pick out which movements of which person fused with your own. But it didn't work in fact.

I don't know what you mean, said Leo—it's quite clear that—

What? What's quite clear, Leo?

The only thing Leo could think of saying were the words: But I love you.

Judith moved out the same way she'd moved in: with just her hold-all.

Up until the moment Judith had packed her bag and left the house, Leo could have given any number of affecting lectures on how his life until now had been particularly fraught with pain and suffering. Ten minutes later he couldn't have even conceived the word 'pain', let alone consider it as a concept which might describe the feelings he was experiencing. He was, so to speak, senseless but with his eyes open. He sat there as if he had been thrust back onto his seat, catapulted backwards by a superhuman force. Night fell. Through the large window of his *sala*, as through a cockpit window, he saw the moon. The earth lay immeasurably far behind and with it the laws, too, that pertain there in the world. The law that everything that happens in life can be interpreted in different ways—no longer valid. No amount of interpretation could in any meaningful way change the fact that Judith had left him. The law that wonder is the beginning of philosophy—no longer valid. His wonder didn't have a single thought in its head. He didn't understand the world any more. He was in a black space which swallowed up every scream even before he could let it out, before he could even think it.

Everything looked very different in the light of day. Things once more assumed their natural shape in the mirrors on the walls.

Simulation of reality. The words slid off the silvery surfaces that only *seemed* to open out to reveal depth.

This house Leo was in was not a house but rather the objectivisation of a mental building in which everything was meant to be taken care of. One thing had not been taken care of: that it wouldn't work in practice. Personal happiness based on living for what is essential and from out of which a comprehensive consciousness of the world was meant to result. Something inexplicable had happened. The inexplicable. Irrationality had intruded. The unexpected that couldn't have been part of one's forward calculations. As if a nod made at some sensible thought had set up a movement in the air which had increased to a storm wind which had devastated everything.

On the walls, many mirrors. Like the broken pieces of what had once been one large single mirror but now was shattered. Fragments that no longer reflected anything of general validity, they showed only the last splinter of Leo's broken existence: his expression of private pain. Not even that. His expression was no different from the somewhat ridiculous one on the face of a drunkard blinking in the light of a dawn he hadn't been expecting for a long while yet.

Leo couldn't stay in this house, a house that wasn't his any longer but had become Judith's. He couldn't bear the thought of living in her place without her, in a private museum of the illusions he had constructed from his life with her. Judith had to arrange for her furniture and her mirrors to be collected. Leo felt that the assumptions he had made regarding life had been devastated so radically that for a split second he was surprised to find that the telephone was working.

The person who answered the phone in Judith's old flat was a stranger. When she had moved in with Leo, Judith had terminated her contract and now someone else was living there. A servant girl answered the phone at her parents' place. There's no-one at home, she said. Senhor Ricardo and Dona Ruth have gone out. And Judith? Judith doesn't live here any more, said the girl, but I can give you her number. Leo wrote it down and then for a quarter of an hour stared at his own telephone number on the note-pad. He carried the magic mirror into the kitchen. He wasn't planning on cooking just for himself so he wouldn't see it here. For a moment he considered pushing all the living-room furniture into the other rooms and setting up the bed here. Then at least one room would have been cleared and he wouldn't have to look in the mirror hanging over the bed the moment he woke up. But he felt too drained of energy. Besides, he thought, he could sleep lying on his stomach.

He drove into town.

Two weeks he spent wandering aimlessly around town—he drank coffee and pinga in *padarias*, ate sandwiches in snackbars whenever he got hungry and nodded off in dark cinemas whenever he got tired. At night he got drunk in bars, enough so as to be sure he would fall asleep immediately he got home. On two occasions he was so drunk he couldn't drive home and so spent the night in a cheap hotel in the centre of town. He considered going away for a while but he couldn't do that, he thought, until Judith got in touch. He had to talk with her, come to some agreement with her regarding the removal of her furniture.

No, said Judith, I don't want the furniture, I don't need it. But it's yours, said Leo, I don't want it either. It's actually yours, said Judith, you paid for nearly everything—I would never have had enough money to pay for all that. But I only paid for it, said Leo, because you wanted it—I would never have bought it just for myself. He almost said: I was happy with things the way they were before.

He was silent for a moment, nonplussed. Twilight was fading over the square—he'd met up with Judith for a talk in the *Pari Bar* on the Praça Dom José Gaspar following her surprise phone call. More and more people were pouring out of the surrounding office blocks round the square—passers-by strolling in different directions turned into a broad

205

stream of humanity—a flock of pigeons flew up, circled the monument in the middle of the square and disappeared behind the crown of the old, overhanging rubber tree that stood in front of the city library. Above the library on a tower block behind it, neon writing flared out, at the end of which there was a neon star, some kind of brand sign— Leo saw it as an asterisk referring him to an footnote that would explain what was puzzling about his unspoken sentence. He dropped his gaze— there was the library, a multi-million-volumed collection of annotations—would he ever be able to find there the one annotation? He saw himself in the midst of books and that was when he saw the precise footnote that explained his sentence: He had been happy in the midst of his books, the way it had been earlier, during the time he had thought Judith was dead. He had been capable of happy, continuous productivity because he had had an inexhaustible incentive, a longing, in fact, that it seemed he could not fulfil. He had known—clearly right at the outset: what he needed in order to work was a condition of perpetual longing. His mistake was his need to realise what he longed for, when it had suddenly seemed possible to do so. From this arose his theory about living for what is essential, and this had had a negative effect on life as it really was. The attempt to put it into practice and really live together had destroyed both the theory and the life together: his work, because he had sacrificed it for the fulfilment of his longing; his longing, because he fulfilled it; his fulfilment, because it had become empty and devoid of work and longing. In the longing for love you can think, but you can neither love nor think in the longing for thought. Mirrors were, in relation to thinking, a metaphor for reflection, but in relation to life and the one you love they are nothing more than plain mirrors in which all you can do is to gawp dumbly. He had walked out of this paradise— which he had at least been able to conceive—in the very moment he had imagined he was really entering it and had slammed the door shut behind him.

Leo rubbed his eyes—they were hurting as if he really had been reading small print. So there was no doubt whatever that his problem lay not in the fact that Judith had moved out but that he had really wanted her to move in. Could that be true? Could a theory destroy the lives of people who wanted to realize it?

Leo, what are you thinking about—what's this problem you have with the furniture? Why don't you leave everything as it is—you've got a wonderfully furnished house, you've got your peace and can work to your heart's content.

206

Yes, sure, said Leo, heart's content—leave it like it is, yes. Tell me, can you remember my interpretation of the beginning of Hegel's *Phenomenology*, the story about the mirrors that philosophical consciousness sets up in order to explain the problems of reflection to simple consciousness—do you remember?

Yes, I remember, said Judith.

And?

And what?

Leo looked at her and wondered whether she really didn't understand what he was thinking of or whether she was just pretending. Suddenly it didn't matter to him. It didn't alter the problem. The problem had to do with the efficacy and realisation of thinking. Whether her countless mirrors on the walls were the conscious realisation of his philosophical metaphor or not, either way it was *her* realisation and therefore *her* destruction and therefore mindless. He had started to unfold his potential before managing to find a way of doing so in a full and realised way.

He had come to this meeting with the intention of somehow unburdening himself of his hatred for Judith and it had gone even before he'd been able to give expression to it, even before he'd been able to throw reproaches at her, just because of a confusing thought that strangely anaesthetised his feelings. The strangest thing of all was that now he might have to direct his hatred against himself. Why hadn't he written and just dreamt of Judith—why hadn't he carried on working and writing with all the energy of his longing? Why had he put the writing and thinking aside—just so that he could conquer Judith? He felt almost reassured when he did in fact begin to feel angry with Judith, angry at the callous satisfaction written all over her face and which he found so incredibly stupid—satisfaction that he wasn't remonstrating with her and that he appeared to be dealing with her like a dear old friend with do-you-remember questions—nonsense, that wasn't what he had meant. Yes, he hated her, hated her because there was no going back from the mistake he might possibly have made, and, if it really was a mistake, then it was a mistake with a good reason, and therefore even the mistake should have worked. If it is in the very nature of practice that things never work, then it would have been up to him to make sure that they did. By taking control, by suppressing all opposition. Everything's false anyway, so why not raise the mistake straightaway to the level of a principle, a premise that does not allow of any questioning? He was far too soft. You can only be soft once there is no more opposition. Why didn't he stand up, go to the *Boca*—he could get there on foot from here—haul Regina out of the *Locomotiva Bar* and marry her. A perfectly normal love story—it didn't matter who he loved or whether he loved—anyhow, no-one with any sense could put up with the overinflatedness bound up with it one way or another, which was why it was prettified only in bad novels and films. But it works, people breed, they fall out of the arms of people they don't love and into the arms of other people they don't love and they call the experience happiness. Leo asked for the bill. Come, he said to Judith. Where? Come, he said—he was standing in front of her now and trying to grab her by the wrist—she refused and said: No, I'm not driving to your place. To your place, said Leo—my place is yours. He tried once again to pull her crudely towards him but he appeared so ridiculous to himself that he let her go immediately—he couldn't do it. I'm not normal, he thought, while she was saying: What do you want to do, Leo? Make me feel sorry for you? I'm sorry, he said.

The next day he could only remember one thing about that night, during which he'd got so drunk that he'd once again had to stay the night in a hotel: that in some bar or other in the *Boca*, where naked girls danced in front of mirrors, a tall, gaunt man with an enormous Adam's apple had stood at the bar next to him.

When Leo got home next morning totally hung-over, he looked briefly round the house, then left again, driving to the corner of Avenida Vereador José Diniz and Rua Vieira de Morães, where he had often seen these lorries for hire parked and the drivers lounging around, waiting for removals or transportation work. He was in luck—there were vehicles there. He asked the first driver he saw to follow him back home in his van, as he had a job for him. Leo led the man through the house, explaining to him that he was to remove all the furniture, all the mirrors, all the other objects like lamps, curtains and so on, with the exception of the books and clothes. The clothes cupboards, too? Yes, of course—just lay the clothes out on the floor. And this bookcase, as well? It's screwed to the wall. Unscrew it, said Leo—everything's got to go, whether it's screwed on or not, except for the books, clothes and the contents of the desk. The stove on the kitchen, too? Not the stove. Nor the fridge, either. Anything else not? Apart from those things, everything. Everything must go. That's OK, said the man. But it's more than one lorry load. Anyway, I'll need someone to help me. That'll cost a bit more. What's more it depends on where I have to take it all. Where you want, said Leo—my offer's this: as payment for clearing the house you can keep everything you take away.

The man looked at Leo in bewilderment and somewhat mistrustfully at the same time, then looked around him once more, said, *Tudo bem*, we'll do a good job, just leave it to me, boss, we'll do you proud, and paying me the way you said, *tudo bem*, boss, no problem. He drove off to fetch his mate, with whom he returned a little later and immediately got down to work.

What I was meaning to ask you, said Löwinger—Leo was sitting in his salon, smoking and drinking port with him. Leo looked at him, waiting for the question, but Löwinger was silent, his mouth half-open as if he were about to continue talking, but he didn't, struggling painfully for a long time, his pale, watery eyes seeming to be turned inwards into the interior of his skull in order to hunt for the words—the expression on his face bore a look of such helplessness that Leo was horrified. How terribly old Uncle Zé had grown. He was now fragile and emaciated, he seemed to have quite shrunk, his head looked disproportionately large on top of his thin, wrinkled neck and frail body. His complexion was yellowish, his hair, too, even his white shirt was stained yellow—Leo felt sick—he thought of urine, thought he could smell it—Uncle Zé is incontinent, he thought, his whole bed must be soaked in urine—he rolls about in it without noticing—why doesn't anyone help him, why doesn't he pay someone to help him. And why isn't he saying anything—he was about to ask something. Finally Löwinger continued: Are you disappointed, my boy? I mean because everything has turned out so differently.

Another pause, but only a very short one this time—now he continued talking so hurriedly, it seemed as if he were frightened of being misunderstood, though Leo hadn't understood a thing, being frightened only that he may indeed have understood him.

Everything's turned out very differently from what I'd thought, said Löwinger. People are far too patient—patience is a bad characteristic, mark my words. It enables people to drag things out unnecessarily long, during which time common sense, instead of coming into its own, is fed continually with hope only. Common sense doesn't keep indefinitely—in time it spoils. Patience, believe you me, is the greatest enemy of common sense. A pause. Was talking a strain for him? Leo found listening a strain, too.

Leo took his hatred with him everywhere he went. Full of loathing, he had left the two men clearing his house on their own and had gone up to Löwinger because it was so clearly written on their faces, especially on the driver's, that they thought they'd bamboozled Leo, this idiot whom they'd allowed to pay them with furniture as good as new for a service only a fraction of its worth. The habitual downtrodden air of the driver had given way to a downtrodden air put on for Leo—the way in which he'd said 'boss' to Leo non-stop was like a music-hall comedian's rendering of a tradesman, impudently chummy—the fellow made himself shrink, thought Leo, because he felt bigger already, a major entrepreneur in the making, who could already see himself buying another second-hand lorry with the proceeds from the sale of the furniture. Leo would have loved nothing better than to have planted a fist on the driver's smirk. Listen, he'd have loved to have told him, you'll never get out of the shit-hole you're in, not you. You with your stinking backside of a brain, you'll never be able to sell this furniture for a good price because everyone will think, with your looking the way you do, that you've stolen it. In the end you'll be hung out to dry by some back-street dealer and there'll be nothing left of your magnificent, ill-concealed visions of the future apart from a couple of extra bottles of pinga and a few unusual bits of meat in your otherwise usual bowl of rice and beans. Which he hadn't said—instead: Watch out for the books when you dismantle the bookcase. Woe betide if anything happens to the books. He had then tried hard to look stern and masterful—he could have punched the man in the face—and had left.

And now Leo was in Löwinger's house and again writhing with hate. Hate because Uncle Zé was forcing him to feel pity for him. He didn't want to feel pity for Uncle Zé. He also had a right to be pitied, but even that he didn't want. This talk of patience and common sense that Löwinger was getting carried away with seemed muddle-headed to Leo, a painful sign of degeneration. Leo thought of his father, when he'd visited him at the end in hospital. All shrivelled up and caved in, a mere caricature of the picture he had presented in life. Everything that had marked Löwinger out before, that had lent him a majestic stature and powerful identity, now gave him a cranky air, was painfully

210

embarrassing almost. The way he moved his left hand which he'd extended and stretched out over the arm of his chair, as if strings were still attached to his hand but which he now made strange and repeated efforts to throw up into the air as if he were trying to snatch back that which had long ago wrested itself from his influence and become autonomous but now continued to move in a carefree and unruly manner beyond this house and its park, while here, inside, it was deathly quiet, even when he spoke, as if this man who scarcely ever moved his lips were literally only thinking aloud thoughts of unbelievable powerlessness.

For a while Leo hadn't been listening. He came to with a jolt only on hearing he was expected to say something—what, what was he supposed to say? They looked at each other questioningly, then Löwinger went on talking again. We deceived ourselves, he said, I thought they'd soon go, but they're still there, they'll be there forever. Leo swallowed hard—what in God's name is Uncle Zé talking about, he thought—who is still there? The junta is bankrupt, said Löwinger, but people are far too patient. Now the President is promising *abertura*, a slow transition to democracy—slow, note—they're bargaining very shrewdly on people's patience—this patience will lead one day to no-one being incriminated any more. All those who have collaborated with the dictatorship will then have deserved well of the slow re-establishment of democracy. The transition will be so slow and seamless that it'll stay the same—all those who have committed crimes under the dictatorship will be able, as heroes of *abertura*, to carry on committing their crimes. You need only patience, the patience of others—then you can go ahead—in order to stay put. Intellectual probity won't count for anything any more, too much water under the bridge, common sense—Löwinger made a gesture as if he were throwing something away and began to cough, a coughing fit that jolted his crumpled body up and down helplessly until he was suddenly sitting there calmly again, pressing a handkerchief to his mouth and spitting out the phlegm into it. The whole effect was like a cruel and disgusting parody of the elegance with which he had always dabbed his mouth with his napkin at dinner before beginning to speak. He was silent, recovering from his coughing fit.

Leo could now no longer resist feeling overwhelmed with pity—for himself. It came so suddenly and powerfully that it was a raging grief that he felt. He suddenly saw in Löwinger—and this was what shocked him—himself; he saw for himself for the first time the similarity that, without his knowing it, had given rise to much comment in Löwinger's circle of acquaintances. He didn't sense this similarity because Löwinger reminded him of his mortally sick father and because he therefore saw Löwinger as his father and himself as his son, who thus necessarily looked like him. No, it was much more a spiritual similarity that Leo saw, a similarity that for existential reasons could engrave itself as a likeness on the way people actually appeared; now, because Löwinger was powerless, without influence and isolated, because he appeared to be foundering, ageing quickly and helplessly Leo found himself again in him. While the men below in his house were taking the mirrors off the walls and carrying them away—these mirrors in which he had recently seen himself so often that he had a clearer picture of himself than he would have liked—he saw himself again now more than ever before in Löwinger, as in a mirror—a half distorting, half magic mirror, however—which opened up to him the hideous perspective of the future that he, too, no longer had. In a gesture of embarrassment full of numb fear extending right into the tips of his fingers, Leo ran his hand slowly through his hair—no reassuring feeling of body and thickness—he saw the sparse white strands on Löwinger's head and through them his shiny scalp. The fact that Leo had to look at Uncle Zé and couldn't feel that he by contrast was a young man, full of strength and hope and with all the time in the world before him, that he was without power and influence solely because he had only just reached the foothills of an ambitious ascent—the fact that instead he was sitting there opposite Uncle Zé, as like opposite like, or that at least he felt this to be so—this made him demented.

He wanted to get away, to get up and go.

They've also robbed you of your work and career, said Löwinger. I miscalculated, I thought it would be to your advantage that the junta made teaching at the University impossible for you. But time goes by and nothing changes and suddenly it's too late. Are you nevertheless still working?

Yes, said Leo.

Good—intellectual honesty needs time, but time also destroys the conditions which would have been receptive to intellectual honesty.

Uncle Zé, said Leo—he wanted to say he had to go—he couldn't stand it any longer.

Perhaps you would give me something of yours to read again, said Löwinger—I'm sorry, I interrupted you—I'm not letting you get a word in and yet all I want is to hear you talk.

They looked at each other, both of them at a loss—again this impression of a mirror—Leo couldn't bring himself to say that he wanted to go—he tried to force himself to stand up—he wanted to escape from Löwinger and from himself and yet he couldn't leave either Löwinger or himself alone. Leo's attempt to stand up resulted in his crossing his legs—almost simultaneously Löwinger did the same, cleared his throat and said: Would you like to tell me perhaps why Judith has left us so suddenly?

Mirrors! said Leo, so suddenly that he himself was taken aback, and then uneasy—We've separated because of the mirrors. It's hard to explain.

She put up mirrors everywhere.

We never saw anything of each other.

Only via the mirrors.

It was definitely the mirrors.

One of them in particular. The magic mirror.

Difficult to explain.

I looked into it. She looked out of it.

She had a theory regarding this mirror.

The theory wrecked everything.

That people can see each other in the mirror for what they are.

That's what she thought. I think.

I hated Judith's mirror.

People are becoming so alike that all of a sudden you have to be by yourself.

Leo was now rid of all the mirrors. The house was empty. Everything had been taken away. The next thing he had to do was to be rid of his hatred. Through his work. In defiance of everything that's happened and what it might signify. Perhaps hatred was a better spur than longing. It forces you to be pitiless in the face of reality, to be critical instead of utopian. Leo looked around him. The empty house was a new beginning. That's the way he had to see it. One thing at least had become clear as a result of the collapse of his utopia, of living with Judith, and that was the problem he hadn't been able to solve before. How did this complete reversal come about—why did the mind step back from its consummation and return to its starting point? Because the mind aspires to realising itself in practice. That is what he had learnt. The episode with Judith had had a purpose, in fact. He didn't need anything more. Everything else had been cleared up. The realisation of philosophy was the beginning of its end. That was how he would have to begin his work. And the central, pivotal point would be the sublation of education in ethical life, the brutal and dictatorial insistence on error, until this error becomes in practice a matter of course. And in the end total mindlessness, the general and blissful spread of stupidity into infinity. The title of the work: *The Phenomenology of Despiritualisation. The history of vanishing knowledge.* He would now have to write this work, which reflects history since Hegel and conceptually captures the present. But where? On the floor? There was nothing left in his house—not a single table or chair, nothing that might have made it possible to write. His clothes were lying on the bedroom floor—books, paper and writing implements were lying on the floor of what used to be his study. And in the middle of the *sala* this pietà was now standing, a grotesque wood-carving on a pedestal with red cladding; how Leo had cringed with embarrassment when Löwinger had ceremoniously foisted it on him. Leo found it primitive, almost ludicrous in its exaggerated, literally wooden pathos. Fourteenth century, according to Löwinger, of Rhenish origin apparently. Now that there was no longer this excess of furniture, Löwinger had said, this sculpture would really come into its own in Leo's house and give his study a completely new character.

Leo had wanted to shake himself free from the absurder aspects of his life and to order it according to the strictest principles of reason and yet there he now stood in a house devoid of any furniture and in the midst of which stood a pietà whose worth was equalled only by its ghastliness.

That afternoon at Löwinger's was, so Leo thought with a renewed rush of self-doubt, fundamentally a cruel intensification and continuation of what he was trying to bring to an end and to leave behind him. After his feeble attempt to explain that the mirrors were to blame for his break-up with Judith, Löwinger had nodded and, after pondering briefly, had said at last that he wanted to show Leo a picture that until now he had withheld even from him. Leo had thought that Uncle Zé wasn't able to make anything of his explanation or didn't want to probe any more, which was all right by him, since Judith wasn't a subject he was keen to press. But at the same time it had irritated him that Löwinger was obviously no longer capable of staying with a subject—no doubt a sign of degeneracy. The long corridors in this huge house. Up the large staircase, another corridor, a narrower staircase up into the attic where Leo had never been before. On the way, Löwinger's tirades against the treacherous acts of revenge on the part of the junta— he was ordered to pay insanely high tax arrears, property tax, dues going back years, as if they had only just tumbled to the fact, now they didn't need him any more, that he was well-off—extortion, pure and simple—they've got their eyes on my collection, he said, they want my art collection. And they'll have it, he said. I will be donating my collection to the National Museum—not all of it though, please note. Unbeknown to them, I will retain the real works of art, he whispered conspiratorially with a yellow grin, for the simple reason that they have no idea that they exist, for they are works of art which have never been reproduced, no prints in books on art history, in compendiums, no postcard reproductions—they are, he whispered, the last originals in a world which, because of the abundance of reproductions, can no longer look at originals without experiencing them as anything more than just more copies. He shook his head. Come, my boy, I'll show you a work of art now that is really unique because you can see it here in my house and nowhere else.

Despite his slow and uncertain steps, it seemed to Leo as if Uncle Zé, supporting himself on Leo's arm, was impatiently pushing and driving him along. Leo felt sick from the smell of urine and what he believed was decay that poured out of Löwinger and mingled with the musty, damp smell of the enormous, unlived-in house. Löwinger led him into an attic room, over to a curtain, onto which, through a large, sloping skylight, was falling the intense but almost filtered light of the São Paulo midday haze.

For every work of art there is the right day to make its acquaintance, said Löwinger, and I think that today is the right day to show you this picture here. He released his hold on Leo's arm and took a step forward into the light falling down from the skylight—Leo saw Löwinger's mole-speckled scalp shining beneath the straggly hair. Löwinger pulled a cord, at which the curtain swiftly slid back, revealing a painting which was hanging there luminously in front of him so suddenly, that it was as if a slide were being projected onto a screen. Tell me what you can see.

Leo was definitely impressed but he wasn't sure whether it was by the picture or by the particular nature of its presentation. Besides, he had such bad wind that this considerably exacerbated the hatred, self-hatred and impatience he was feeling at Löwinger's wish to induce in him a sacred awe of this work of art, whereas nearly all his concentration was being taken up with controlling problems profane. He stared helplessly at the picture and wished just one thing for himself: to be as untouched by all of life's banalities as the kind of life that consists only of colour on canvas. The picture depicted a bearded man in his forties, a little on the stout side, with thinning hair, a sensual mouth and pale eyes that were

215

trying, so Leo thought, to adopt somewhat fixedly a prophetic expression. Something oppressive, though, seemed to pulsate strangely in this picture, so that Leo couldn't be sure there wasn't something pious as well in the way the man appeared, an impression that derived certainly from the strange monk's habit he was dressed in—half Francis of Assisi, half Rasputin. Leo was far from being a highly qualified art historian but he could straightaway recognise this as a picture belonging to the Viennese Modern school from the turn of the century. There was the characteristic contrast between, on the one hand, the naturalistic portrait technique, the sensitive and exact way the head and hands were portrayed, and, on the other, the radically stylised manner and stiff two-dimensionality employed for the surroundings, the clothing and the room. There was hardly any attempt to indicate the bulk and hanging folds of the habit—it consisted just of thick bundles of lines and where the ornaments ended gave the impression of the contours of the folds. Leo felt that these ornaments—gold and silver triangles with stylised eyes inside—constituted a plain and irritating attempt to pump up the picture with symbolism and meaning. On the brown, flattish background was a row of black, right-angled ornaments, though these were not continuous, as the man portrayed was surrounded by a black frame, on the inside surface of which the brown of the background and the black ornaments were not continued. Here you could see more a silvery surface, a different background that seemed to have much greater depth, although the figure painted onto this silvery surface was the main focal point of the observer's attention and so projected itself into the foreground.

Leo noticed that Löwinger was growing impatient. Before, when Leo was still a child, Löwinger had always tried on such an occasion to get him to look carefully and patiently. But this thought neither called up sentimental memories nor did it bring relief. For Leo was in the throes not of metaphysical awe but of mere stomach pains. And even if, in his impatience, he'd managed to cut things shorter, it would still have lasted far too long for him.

Could this be a Klimt? he asked.

It isn't a Klimt. It's Klimt.

You mean that is Klimt there in the picture?

Correct.

Which is why, appropriately enough, it is painted in Klimt's style?

Yes.

By whom?

216

By Klimt.

Then this is a self-portrait—but Uncle Zé—

Why was Leo making objections? Out of politeness perhaps. Löwinger clearly wanted to savour the surprise at what he was disclosing and he could only do this if Leo went through the motions of being sceptical:—But that's not possible—everyone knows only too well there isn't a single portrait of Klimt, that he had a thing about self-portraits, said so as well and gave his reasons.

Yes, said Löwinger, everyone knows that only too well.

Leo asked him how the picture came into his possession.

That's a long story, said Löwinger. If, though, by your question you're implying I might have been duped by some forger who knew how to imitate Klimt's style to perfection, then let me put your fears to rest. This Klimt is genuine. You know that in the last resort I decide what is genuine and what is not. My judgements are recognised internationally. If there are any uncertainties and contradictory opinions as regards the authenticity of a work of art, then in such a case my expert opinion is called upon. Museums, gallery-owners, auction houses, private collectors, all tremble before my judgment. World-famous paintings, once hanging prominently in large museums like magnets for tourists, I have recognised to be fakes, and these have then disappeared into various storage depots. The 'Man with Golden Helmet', not by Rembrandt, as I was able to prove—the 'Storm at Sea', a very fascinating painting to be sure, but by Breughel? No. Not in a million years. But this Klimt is genuine. No question of an error here. I could sooner prove that all the other pictures by Klimt, including 'The Kiss', were painted in fact by Klimt's mother-in-law.

Had Uncle Zé gone mad? Or had he always been and Leo noticed it only now because his picture of reality had now become more unerring, clearer, freed as it was from particular hopes and longings? Leo didn't know what to say. Uncle Zé, after all, was the only human being remaining to him, the only one he could go to, talk to still, put his hope in, so he had thought. Was he now to have no-one? The loss of Uncle Zé's former power at the bank, his social isolation, his age, the depressing living conditions in this spooky, echoing house, could all this rob a man of his reason? Or was it the other way round: was it power, wealth and the influence bound up with these that had made him slowly mad, to the point where he could no longer distinguish between himself and the world and between his interests as a collector and artistic truth and the art market? And was it only now that his true being, powerless and without influence and with no gold and silver habit, stood naked and wretched before the gaze of the observer? Was that possible? What should all this mean? Why was he showing him this picture? Just because of that? Because of this stupid gold and silver, almighty habit-of-power, in which Klimt was supposed to have painted his self-portrait? Leo didn't doubt for one minute that it had to be a fake, Löwinger's emperor's new clothes, the work of a cynical craftsman commissioned by a madman.

You're completely right, of course. That is indeed the truth of the matter, is it not, as you rightly noted, said Löwinger, who had stepped back out of the light, so that his face seemed to have darkened and to be overlaid with a patina. There is indeed no self-portrait of Klimt. On the back of this picture its title is recorded in Klimt's handwriting, namely: "Portrait of my reflection", he said. The black frame there is a mirror, of course. It's hanging on this brown, wood-panelled wall. The black ornaments are inlay work in the panelling. So it's a reflection. What's irritating as a result is that, although Klimt is looking out of the picture, you as the observer don't have the feeling he's looking at you. Yes, even though his gaze is directed at the observer, he doesn't appear to be in the least bit aware of an observer. The explanation for this puzzling impression lies of course in the fact that this is a reflection: Klimt is looking out of the picture, looking at himself. Diametrically opposed are the ornamental eyes on his habit, which, bent at every imaginable angle because of the hanging folds, express an all-encompassing seeing in all directions, an all-knowing grasp of every angle of vision—and this has no connection with how the artist happens to look, his physiognomy, but belongs instead to his external environment, his outward situation, the composition around him, to his form. That's how it is.

He now contemplated the picture silently, when suddenly the light from above began to drain away, perhaps because the sun had moved or because of a cloud. At almost the same time Löwinger pulled on the cord again and the picture disappeared behind the curtain. Löwinger took Leo's arm and, supporting himself on him, led him out of the room. There they sat down on a group of chairs from which they could see this pietà—now in Leo's sitting-room. The impressions Leo had now received began to impinge themselves painfully, like a gust of fear whipping up and swelling inside him. Löwinger would now continue wrangling about Klimt, possibly, and then get onto the subject of Klimt's 'Judith' and as a result make a link between this portrait in a mirror and the name of the woman who had encircled him with mirrors. Was his past to stare out at him from everything that still lay ahead of him but, as it were, the wrong way round as in a mirror? Leo was looking helplessly towards the pietà, labouring painfully with his swollen inner life, when he noticed that Löwinger had already been talking again for some time.

...have something in common, do you see, Leo? Klimt's picture painted in 1907, that is, at the beginning of the 20th century, and this pietà from the 14th century—these artists can have nothing in common in terms of attitude to the world, life experience, knowledge, intentions, external reality—these two works of art are in no way comparable in terms of subject matter, purpose, material, form, and yet something connects them with each other that is characteristic of all art throughout all time. And for every individual who learns to see it, this reconciles him to history and to life, and, at one and the same time, makes it impossible for him to reconcile himself to life until such time as this life has returned once more to the state of paradise. Now, it is—he got up and turned on a spotlight that lit up the pietà—let me put it like this: Before, with Klimt's portrait, we spoke about the contrast between the concrete physignomy of the subject and the composition or form. And now look at this pietà and you see this same contrast and its synthesis depicted here too, in quite a different way, mark you, but it is the solution to the same problem. Look at the faces, the anatomy of the bodies. None of it looks right here—from a naturalistic point of view, please note. You could say that everything about it has failed crudely— and yet in no way can there be any question of technical ineptitude. The contortions are dreadful indeed but, taken as a whole, horrifically beautiful. You might say that the artist wanted quite consciously to turn a blind eye to the—yes, to the particular nature of what he was giving form to. Just as with Klimt's painting the particular, individual gaze of the artist falls back onto itself and the gaze is only liberated to the world by means of the formal, in this case ornamental, resolution of the picture, so here too you can see with this sculpture how the figures are redeemed from the particularity of their selfhood by means of a formal configuration liberated from nature, and how at the same time the objectivity and generality of the subject is redeemed from its human remoteness by means of the crude execution of the wounds and the pain. That, I think, was what I wanted to say to you, my boy. Nothing that comes to meet us in life has greater significance. The world can go to rack and ruin and we wouldn't notice. Unless a better one arose. The only thing of significance is what is both of general significance and what simultaneously pertains quite concretely to the individual. That is the hallmark of art: that a work only acquires meaning if it becomes a seeing, hearing and feeling organ of humanity in the consciousness of the one who contemplates it—Humanity in each and every individual human being.

Löwinger voice was ringing clearly again in Leo's ear, as he now looked at this woodcarving in his empty *sala*. Had Löwinger really said all that? Perhaps, in order to get acquainted with the sculpture and give its existence in his room some meaning, Leo was now trying to fill in scraps of Löwinger's words with his own verbal sequences. Leo himself could no longer remember very exactly. He'd sat there so lumpishly as Löwinger had been speaking. Got a shock and woke up with a start only when Uncle Zé had said he wanted to make him a gift of the sculpture.

Why wouldn't you be able to accept it? What do you mean, it's too valuable? Its value will certainly not be any the less for being in your house. Besides, I'm an old man—things of material value, wealth, these no longer mean anything. But if nothing else, accept it as a loan. This would give me a lot of pleasure and you wouldn't need to be embarrassed by its value, since it wouldn't be a gift. Put it in your study. In that bright space without all those pieces of furniture it will come into its own and give the room a completely new character. Perhaps its presence will have a positive effect on your work.

Leo's work. First thing tomorrow he wanted to deal with the problem of having to re-establish proper working conditions. He found a bottle of vodka still in the fridge and three bottles of beer. In this way he managed to sleep on the floor that night, fully-dressed and with his jacket shoved under his head as a pillow. I must remember that, he thought before he fell asleep: outwardly a refugee, inwardly someone returning home. Home, finally—meaning, infinitely far away from the world, from its banal necessities, from the petty circumstances of one's personal life.

First, thought Leo, he had to get himself a desk. Until then work was out of the question. He looked around him morosely. He would dearly have liked to have sat down now, or lain down, but where? On the floor again? He was stiff all over and his muscles ached from a night of sleeping on the floor. He rang Löwinger's house and asked if he could have his old bed back, the one that had been taken away after Judith had moved in. Löwinger promised to have it brought down to him that same day. Did he need any more of the old furniture? No, nothing, said Leo, at the most, the clothes cupboard, otherwise nothing else. The desk? No, but the kitchen table, perhaps, and the chairs that go with it. Thanks, said Leo—apart from that he really didn't need anything. Why didn't Leo have his old desk brought back, too? He could have got down to work straightaway. No, actually. He needed, so he thought, an innocent desk. Not the same one he had only ever stared at apathetically, waiting for Judith to move in with him and release him so he could work. Simply seeing his former desk could possibly arouse in him again the feeling he had had then of being completely incapable of working. On the other hand, looking for a new desk suitable for his work and then buying it would also be the first step towards resuming work. He had to create working conditions for himself that were wholly rational. Leo decided to make the living-room his study. It was the largest and brightest room, the only one with two windows. What did he need a living-room for? He wanted to work, not live, live somewhere—what is that anyway, 'living somewhere'? What do you actually do? This room was, moreover, the first you came into when you entered the house. If it was a study, then it would be immediately clear that this is a place where work is going on. The room had to be furnished strictly functionally, of course, really minimalistic—nothing that didn't contribute to the work should be allowed a foothold. Only in an uncluttered room would the mind be able to concentrate and not be distracted, would be able to blossom freely. Leo stretched and, rotating his shoulders, tried to massage the back of his neck. The pains in his muscles were so aggravating that he would have dearly loved to have lain down on a comfortable sofa so as to release the tension. But there was no sofa there any more. Nothing except this pietà. He looked at the Man of Sorrows almost enviously, lying there resting in the lap of the Mother of God. Leo pulled himself together—he had to tackle this question of a desk. Where would be the best place to put it? In the middle of the room? That would be the outward expression of the fact that his work was uncompromisingly at the centre of his life. It would make the room smaller, though, and this could possibly cramp his style while he was working. Perhaps he ought to push the desk up against a wall. But then he'd always be staring at a wall while working. The walls. They were in a terrible state with those hooks everywhere that the mirrors had been hanging from—Leo even thought he could see the shapes of the mirrors in the form of somewhat lighter patches on the walls. All of a sudden there they were again, restored before his eyes, the mirrors he had had removed. He tried to look closely and see nothing but he couldn't manage it. At all costs the very first thing he had to do was have the walls repainted, he thought, that was certain. He fetched the telephone book and rang up painters and decorators in the vicinity, until he found one who was ready to come round immediately and give him an estimate. Leo was impressed with himself. How active he was being. Not even his extremely poor physical condition could rein in his elation. If he went on like this, he'd definitely make swift headway with his work. While waiting for the decorator, he smoked palomitas. The smoking made him dizzy—he hadn't eaten anything. The ash fell onto the floor. Leo hadn't reckoned with the ashtrays disappearing, too, when the house was cleared. It didn't matter. He wouldn't be sleeping on the floor any more, and besides, after the decorating he'd have to have it cleaned anyway.

The decorator arrived. Leo quite consciously set about showing him who was boss, so as not to let himself be made a fool of again. He'd learnt from his mistake. No more civilities, no more open-handedness. He wasn't going to allow any workman to grin stupidly at him again like the van-driver had. This he owed to the fact that his feeling of self-worth had been restored. Leo gave the decorator curt instructions as to what he was to do, asked what it would cost, disdainfully brushed aside the decorator's estimate, offered a fee markedly below this and stipulated that the work had to start that day.

Not long after this he had to get on the phone again to find another decorator.

Again the waiting.

In the meantime Leo himself was struck by the absurdity of the situation. In his head there was a masterpiece that he couldn't put down on paper because there was nothing in his study apart from a terrible wooden sculpture. His work would change the world but he couldn't write it because the world was the way it was. Full of insolent workers on whom he was entirely reliant for the creation of the requisite working conditions.

Finally Leo was so enfeebled by hunger, weakened by pain, dizzy with smoking, and with his head reeling so much, that he felt himself to be completely at the mercy of the verbal outpourings of the next decorator who arrived.

The *Senhor* shouldn't forget, the man said, how expensive just the materials alone had become—despite inflation, he said, he would do the job for the *Senhor* at the old price but the increased costs of the materials he would have to pass on to the *Senhor*—he'd do it for the *Senhor* at a really good price, a special price, for first-class work—the *Senhor* will be pleased, he said, without looking at Leo, continuously appraising the rooms, with a finger scratching here, running across the walls there, tilting his head worriedly, thoughtfully—a difficult job, but he'd do it. There was no way he could begin immediately, he said, he'd got contracts, was sought after for his excellent work, but in three weeks he could guarantee—well, if that was too late, yes, he understood the *Senhor*, perhaps he could solve the *Senhor's* problem, you can always find a *jeito*—the job here wasn't so big—it could be done in a day—he could let him jump the queue, slip him in, the day after tomorrow, on Sunday—everything taken care of by Sunday evening, but only if he didn't have to repaint the doors as well, doors took up a lot of time and would make the business dearer. Leo lost his patience and accepted the decorator's offer. Sunday, no doors. Leo broke off negotiations over the price when the man began to use the number of children he had to feed as an argument, which was why he couldn't work for free, the *Senhor* will understand that, he also understood the *Senhor*, which was why he was doing it at a special price.

The only satisfaction Leo had was that he managed to so pressure the man that the agreed price was only fractionally higher than the estimate the first decorator had given.

Now the desk finally. After a greedily devoured snack that graced his stomach first with cramps and then brought on his wind again, Leo drove into the city centre, to the Avenida São João. When he'd first come to São Paulo he had noticed a second-hand store very near the hotel he'd lived in then, the biggest such store he'd ever seen. He was confident that he would find a bargain there, a solidly-made, second-hand desk that would suit him down to the ground.

The *Olixão* second-hand store was a huge, dusty warehouse in which it appeared as if the entire possessions of an average-sized town that had suddenly given up the ghost had been unceremoniously dumped. Leo pushed his way through the corridors and tunnels between the pieces of furniture piled on top of each other in towers and the stacked up household effects and, filled with repugnance at all this junk and its desolate appearance, was about to turn round and leave when a salesman addressed him and asked if he was looking for something in particular. Perhaps it was because of Leo's aching limbs and his exhaustion combined with his perplexity at this unsavoury place that he mumbled something about a comfortable armchair, a sofa, too, perhaps, or even a suite of chairs—a sofa, Leo repeated, almost beseechingly—he wanted nothing better than to get out, out into the daylight, to sit down somewhere and gather himself once more. The salesman led him triumphantly to a leather suite, which was, he averred, excellently preserved and beautiful, though it was buried beneath an upturned dining-table and a ponderous clothes cupboard. What he could see of the bulky, crude settee with its dirty black leather was enough for Leo: he thanked the man but said he wasn't interested and attempted to leave the store. But this the salesman would not allow. His experience told him that Leo belonged to that category of customer who, once ensnared, believed the only way he could get himself out of the situation was by making a purchase. Suddenly there were two more men on the spot who, on a swift command, began removing and levelling off the mountain of furniture, while the salesman explained to Leo at length that he had to see this complete suite, that he'd really like it, it wasn't a problem. The musty atmosphere, the dust, the smell of sweat coming from the salesman were beginning to make Leo feel ill, and the dull, yellowish-brown light in which the motes of dust were dancing and the cigarette smoke of the workers was curling depressed him. In his efforts to keep out of the way of the workers, he kept on bumping into things, as a result of which he felt completely hemmed in, in a narrow cell whose walls were closing in on him. Buying this bulky suite of artificial leather was out of the question, of course, but the paring down of the furniture revealed two armchairs for which Leo showed a pretended interest in order to distract the salesman from those ghastly chairs he was making such a song and war-dance about. To test them out, Leo sat down on one of them—it was surprisingly comfortable. Sighing with relief, he stretched out his legs and rested his arms on the upholstered arm-rests. Leo closed his eyes—he had no desire to get to his feet again. Ouro Preto, he heard the salesman saying, the chairs were from Ouro Preto, that baroque town in Minas Gerais, genuine Brazilian baroque. They'd make a really lovely suite together with the two-seater sofa in the same style that's also here somewhere, he heard the salsman saying, heard the banging and shoving and grating of the workers' latest manoevres, heard their quiet, labouring groans, brief commands, heard the noises getting quieter and quieter, seeping into the cotton wool which his consciousness seemed now to consist of, heard suddenly almost too loudly a triumphant, 'Here it is—isn't it a gem.' Leo opened his eyes. The sofa was in front of him. He contemplated it a long while, as if he were trying to recognise it again. He put his glasses on. Now he was once more alert. Even an extremely functionally furnished study needs a comfortable suite of chairs, thought Leo, for reading, for short

224

periods of relaxation after hours of hard work. He began to like this suite of baroque chairs, not just because in his consideration they seemed to go well with the pietà—as long as you weren't a purist, of course, as regards style—but also because, owing to their lightness, they wouldn't overburden his room. They were also in quite good condition—the red silk material of the upholstery at least wasn't torn. Leo inquired about the price. The salesman sat down at a desk in order to work out some complicated sums on his pocket calculator—which Leo didn't follow because this same desk was now taking up his whole attention. It was a fine bureau with a curved roll-top, exactly, as he now realised, what he'd actually been looking for. In his enthusiasm he remembered a quotation which moved and uplifted him: The moral hero makes discoveries even when he is not looking because his aims are for him immediately manifest. He had written this, and approximately in these words, years ago, hadn't he, when he was writing that piece on morality and culture, at a time when he'd thought Judith was dead. What he thought he'd lost, what he'd made a note of already, was there again and he could build on it. That meant he could work again.

I'll take this desk, said Leo. And the chairs? asked the salesman. Leo got up, contemplated the armchair he'd been sitting on with gratitude—he felt more rested, stronger. I'll take those, too, of course.

In his sudden elation he even found a round, metal-clad table as well, which went fairly well with the suite of chairs. For a small fee, the salesman assured him with much forelock-tugging, the furniture could of course be delivered. The following Monday was the agreed day.

The walls brilliant white, innocent once more. The furniture delivered, the desk put in place. Did Leo feel stirred into action? Yes. He went out to celebrate. It was already too late to start working that day. He had to begin in the morning, Leo thought, straight after breakfast—the day had to be innocent, too. He trawled the bars, thought it wholly appropriate that the beginning of his celebration coincided with what they called the 'happy hour'. He drank only the best, at first champagne, then imported bagaço instead of the Brazilian pinga which he normally drank. He drank far too much, like someone who wanted to forget. Judith. It didn't once enter his head to indulge in a sudden melancholy, an inexplicable, vague depression. He didn't want to forget, wanted much more to try to remain aware, to remind himself all the time that he was celebrating, and why he was. The drunker he became the more stubbornly he repeated to himself a phrase which, when he was completely befuddled with alcohol and had forgotten everything, he had nevertheless managed to make a mental note of. He recited the phrase triumphantly like a magic formula that would open the gates of paradise: Tomorrow begins a life of substance.

The night porter at the little hotel in the city centre knew Leo of old, didn't understand what Leo had said, it didn't interest him either—without a word he handed him a room key and turned back again to his lottery form.

When Leo got home the next day he had the most frightful headache. On no account could he allow himself to slip now into self-pity. In this respect he was very hard on himself. He forced himself to analyse the situation sensibly. It was clear he had to sacrifice this one day to putting himself back on his feet again physically, so as to be able to get down to work tomorrow, rested and in full vigour.

He had to sacrifice many more days. Again and again it transpired that the conditions necessary for work were not yet right and that as a result further time and money needed to be spent. His books were still lying on the floor in the former study. These now had to be put in his present study. But where? On the floor again? He couldn't work like that. There wasn't any order. With the books lying around like that he'd always be tripping over them and spending hours finding the particular one he needed at any given moment. First he had to separate his books from Judith's. This separation was long overdue. Nearly every book he picked up made him wonder how he could have so idealised this woman once. Decadent literature like Sterne, Proust, Kafka, or camp-followers like Machado de Assis, or decadent camp-followers like the late Erico Verissimo. It was dreadful. It seemed to Leo as if he were thumbing through Judith's inner life, the true nature of which was manifest here in black and white. This job took him a long time, a whole week, because he'd always start leafing through and reading Judith's books and feel so poisoned every time by the texts, by the sentences Judith had underlined and by memories of Judith that he had to stop work, go out, clear his head, go for a drink, in order to be able to continue the next day. Finally all Judith's books were sorted out, packed up in boxes and stored in the old study. But there was still a lack of real order in his present study. His books were still lying around on the floor. This problem had to be solved, he realised, sensibly and once and for all—this half-cock solution would only serve to hold him back completely. He remembered a shop in the Avenida Ibirapuera where, when accompanying Judith on her furniture shopping frenzy, he had noticed there was a particularly wide range of bookcases and shelves. He had to see this thing through to the end, thought Leo, and drive to this shop. After all, he had come to an historic point in his development, a crossroads: he was finally free to work. Now he could do everything exactly right or exactly wrong. It couldn't be a coincidence that his work, a study in Idealist Philosophy so to speak, compelled him to seek out ideal working conditions. He shouldn't out of indolence try to duck out of this 'compelling tendency'. Besides, he thought, overcome suddenly by a very strange mood of half euphoria, half melancholy, besides, an end was now really in sight: this would be the last item he had to buy. So he drove to this shop and there found two bookcases which, like his desk, were built of mahogany and would therefore, he felt, go well with his desk. The bookcases had glass doors which would protect his books from the dust. The glass doors had a backing of stretched green silk, something that Leo also found extremely sensible: in this way the books were removed from his sight and could therefore never discourage and dishearten him just because they were concluded works, whereas he was only just starting on his. In these cases his books would finally become what he really wanted them to be: not just concluded works but excluded, that is, locked away until such time as he needed to consult them. He bought the bookcases—they were delivered the very next morning. Leo spent the remainder of the day sorting out his books. While dusting and arranging them on the shelves, many of these books he opened and began to read, standing at first, then sitting comfortably on his sofa with his legs up on one of the chairs—for a moment he was so happy that suddenly he couldn't carry on reading but instead just looked emotionally at the book he was holding in his hands. Night fell and there were no more books on the floor—the study looked in fully functional working order. Leo walked up and down smoking palomitas, picturing to himself how, first thing in the morning and in this room, he would be starting to write. The wooden floor creaked. This irritated Leo. This creaking could possibly disturb his concentration. His work. Nothing should be allowed to disturb him. He tried to keep his thoughts exclusively on his work. *System of Science*, thought Leo, by Leopold Joachim Singer. *Last Part*, he thought, the *Phenomenology of Despiritualisation. A History of vanishing knowledge*, he thought, conceiving it so intensely over and over again until he saw it in print before his inner eye on the cover of a finished book. He had to carry on thinking, for these thoughts were highly pleasurable for him. He now saw editions of this book in the bookshops, saw on the spine—Singer—*Phenomenology*—on a host of shelves and bookcases, a huge range of them he could see—the ones he'd seen the previous day where he'd bought his two bookcases. Shelves of all sorts and styles—an ideal public library in the world somewhere. All the shelves were empty because they were waiting for his book which excluded all others. Now the shelves were all full, full with copies of his book. Then immediately empty again because of course everyone was reading his book, in a rapt concentration which was collectively so powerful that there was only one sound in the world: a rustling noise—a creaking... The floor didn't creak as loudly in some places as in others. Leo paused in irritation. He knew it. This floor was going to distract him, send his thoughts off in the wrong direction. He now walked around the room systematically, testing it at every step, rocking on the balls of his feet so as to determine which were the boards causing the problem, those creaking the loudest, and where the boards were firm beneath his feet and made little noise or none at all. He wanted to find the ideal path of thought through this room that he could walk up and down when he was working without being disturbed in his concentration. After a while he gave up in despair. There was no negotiable path. He wanted to look out of the window thoughtfully like the heroes did in comparable situations in the literature he knew—and he saw himself. He hadn't reckoned with that either. At night windows became mirrors, an irritating fact of life that would completely destroy his capacity to work, and, what was more, during those all-important evening and night hours when, like all inventive people, his creativity was at its peak. A solution to this had to be found instantly, otherwise work was out of the question. Without a moment's hesitation he went out and stayed out until he was so drunk and tired that he was able to fall asleep.

The next day Leo drove to *Jotapetes*, the biggest fabric shop in town, confident that he would immediately find some suitable curtain material. He felt drained and despondent. Nearly all his energy was used up already before he had had the chance to convert it into work. And here he was again on his way to a furniture store. He whose calling it was to write a book about the end of history was incapable of creating the preconditions which would enable him to begin. He felt like he was on a wheel where despite all his efforts he remained stuck in one place. It was Judith's fault, of course, that was indisputable. It had all started with her furniture-buying frenzy. It was she who had shoved him onto this wheel. And now he was obliged to drive back and forth to shops all day in order to solve problems with furnishings and fittings. No, he thought decisively, one more investment—these curtains that he could draw across the reflecting panes of his windows—and then he'd have escaped Judith's wheel and would be able to make progress with his book. Confronted by the enormous range, Leo stood there so blankly that he was totally at the mercy of the overzealous bonhomie of the salesman and thus let himself be talked into buying some exorbitantly expensive material made of red silk. All the same, he thought, the colour and the material did go well with his suite of chairs. In addition he bought some rolls of thick carpeting also in red because matching up the colours seemed to him the only consideration that would lead to a quick decision. The making up of the curtains and the laying of the fitted carpet was to take a week. Leo spent this time in bars and saloons where he sat as if he were in a waiting-room.

When he was finally standing once again in his study, he was horrified. There was far too much red in this room. He shut out all associations. No doubt he'd get used to it, he thought. In no time at all this oppressive dominance of the colour red wouldn't shock him any longer—soon it would appear as a natural and fitting expression of his world. He just had to keep all thoughts of hell-fire or blood out of his head at all costs and instead think of nothing—sunrise at the most— what was new—think of progress, the progress that he'd now definitely be making with his work. At least the floor wasn't creaking any more. He couldn't be reflected in the windows any more. And besides, when- ever he looked up from his work, he would have to concentrate on the innocent, smooth white of the walls. The walls. That was now the next problem. Leo noticed that the walls were riddled with cracks and flaws, which he immediately began to examine with extreme nervousness. The coat of paint had begun to bubble up and flaked off in sheets the size of his palm if Leo so much as pressed on it a little. Clearly the decorator had taken little care when scraping off the old paint or hadn't done so at all, which was why the new paint that had meanwhile dried now had nothing to grip on. This was a catastrophe. Leo couldn't bear the thought of having it repainted once more. But it couldn't stay as it was. For days Leo ran around desperately, wondering what he should do. Finally he had a decorator come round specialising in wallpaper. He chose some paper with thin green vertical stripes—the green was meant to provide a contrast to the abundance of red in his room—what's more, it matched the green silk behind the glass doors of the bookcases. Leo kept a continuous eye on the work of the decorator and his assistant so as to make sure they didn't bungle anything. When the work was finished, he didn't feel relieved, strangely enough, but felt instead almost a little sad. If only his work could be as straightforwardly physical as that of these workers! He had enjoyed watching the two men, had soon come to envy the way they plainly understood what they were doing, how the actions of their hands, the techniques they used, immediately produced clearly visible results. If only he could scoop things out of his head like the decorators did the paste out of their buckets—if only he could roll out his theses as easily as they did their wallpaper—if only his theories regarding the world could be displayed so convincingly and self-evidently as these immaculately papered walls. Leo pulled himself together and contemplated the walls with the stern look of one who now had to move on to some work of substance. But what if it should get on his nerves seeing nothing but green stripes on all the walls? Stripes of all things. Weren't they reminiscent of prison bars? Was this comparison appropriate or didn't it much rather unsettle him? After days of reflection and then searching he found a lovely large Gobelin tapestry which he mounted along the side of the room where the suite of chairs was. A definite improvement, but not perfect yet. The ceiling, which hadn't of course been papered, was still bare and scored with cracks. Leo bought a chandelier in the Venetian style and if he were none too sure whether memories of Venice gave him that much pleasure, nevertheless the chandelier immediately drew attention to itself whenever he looked up, and in this way the problem of the cracked ceiling was in some measure resolved. Was he able now to begin work? Not yet. The predominance of the colour red continued to bother him. There was far too much red in this room—the curtains, the fitted carpet, the uphol-stery of the sitting room suite. The problem with this was that he only had to see the thick gouts of clotted blood on the pietà and each time he was unable to shut out the impression that in this room he was wading in blood. This was, of course, absurd and couldn't continue. He bought a thick green carpet, the same green as the stripes on the wallpaper, and spread it on top of the red fitted carpet.

The room now had a very remarkable character. It was, thought Leo, definitely not the ideal study that he had pictured. On the other hand he had never pictured his ideal study in any detail. It had furnished itself, in the course of which it had developed a dynamic all of its own which he, with the things he bought, had merely gone along with submissively. Leo stood there not knowing whether he should be relieved that the whole furnishing and decorating business was now happily over, or dejected and perplexed because this was now the result. If this room now presented the ideal working conditions that the work he planned had demanded, then in this case he wasn't sure—he hunted for the words in his head—he wanted at all costs to avoid the thought that he then wasn't sure how convinced he was still of this work... Then the telephone rang. It was Judith.

For a second Leo immediately felt a weight descend on him when he heard her voice. It was nothing, a straw, but the last one before his back finally broke. How he was? He was so outside of himself that he looked for the answer outside of himself, too. He looked around. There really wasn't anything more to do in this room. He saw the Man of Sorrows lying covered in blood on the woman's lap.

You know how painful my work is, he said. But all the preparatory work is finished—I just need to write it all out. Leo would still not have admitted to himself, though he sensed it certainly, that none of this was true any longer.

Judith wanted her books back. She had meanwhile found and moved into a small house—in Brooklin, very near the munitions factory where Leo had lived earlier. She had settled herself in more or less completely—all she was missing were, in fact, her books.

Leo offered to bring the boxes of books over to her by car. Judith's house. In the *sala* there was nothing but a two-seater sofa in the middle of the room directly underneath a naked light bulb dangling from the ceiling. On the floor a record player along with some records. In the bedroom just a bed and a cupboard. In the second bedroom that Judith was using as a study stood a desk and a chair. That was all. Just put the boxes down on the floor here, said Judith—I'll find the books in them I need as and when. Leo looked around and would have dearly loved to have cried out: Yes, this is where I shall stay. He didn't want to drive back to his own house ever again. His own study now seemed perfectly ridiculous. He had wanted to eradicate all traces of Judith in his house and had thus created conditions which didn't suit him either. Here by contrast everything was like—

Would you like a *cafezinho*, Leo?

Yes, please, he said—Judith went out of the room and Leo sat down at the desk. Yes, that's exactly how it was. Just as he'd imagined it, if he'd been able to imagine something. At the same time it shouldn't have been necessary for him to imagine it. For hadn't he, too, originally lived like this when he had come to Brazil? In such spartan conditions as suited him and in which his mind no doubt could blossom, something that didn't happen back then only because at first he had had his hands full exclusively with the sale of the various plots of land. And the smell of gunpowder. The smell of Judith. Leo would have liked to have wept. His eyes actually grew watery—he blinked his eyelids quickly a few times. He was at home here—and would never be allowed to be. He had returned to the beginning but not in order to be allowed to begin again but only in order that he should see that he had done everything wrong. If Judith hadn't moved in with him, but he instead were now to—here with Judith—

Wouldn't you have liked to have had your furniture? Leo asked when Judith came back in with the coffee, put the tray on the desk and, in the absence of a second place to sit, stood herself next to him.

No—what for, said Judith—what I've got here is quite enough for me. This is the furniture I had in my room, in my parents' house, my childhood furniture so to speak—I don't need anything else.

Leo felt a tiredness which he thought he would never again be able to shake off because it was the last great tiredness. At home he would—what else?—go for a walk in the garden, would think, There is the hiding-place when I played *Lampião*, and here is the Oblomov tree, which I lay beneath when I was dreaming of an academic career. And whenever he called on Judith, he would sit in a spartanly furnished house in Brooklin with its smell of gunpowder—here his grown-up life had begun, away from his mother for the first time, sentimental dreams of a great love affair and great success. And Judith, too, had returned to this point—this here was basically the room she had had as a child, just uncoupled from the parental home—here she had dreamt of Vienna and whatever—whatever the two of them believed still lay ahead of them was over because they were still living only in the memories of the time when it really did lie ahead of them. Just one thing missing—the *Café Sport*.

Not far from her house, in the Avenida Adolfo Pinheiro, Judith had discovered a bar that had opened only a short while before. The *Bar Esperança*. She wanted to show it to Leo. They could have a drink there together and a chat.

About old times?

Why not?

Yes, why not?

The *Bar Esperança* belonged to a Viennese, as a result of which it had very quickly become the meeting-point for Austrians living in São Paulo. So, like the *Café Sport* in Vienna, except antipodean, its clientèle were mostly foreigners. The regulars divided into two groups which basically consisted, on the one hand, of Austrian business people, entrepreneurs, employees of multinational firms and, on the other, of artists and intellectuals, this being because Oswald, the landlord, was himself a painter highly regarded in São Paulo. He had been able to acquire the bar with the sale proceeds of his pictures after a much-acclaimed exhibition. After several drinks, which regularly led to competitive drinking bouts, a harmonious understanding reigned between the two groups, an understanding as to their own superiority to the natives, contemptuously referred to as the *"Brazis"*. This harmony fell apart after increasing inebriation and led to mutual exchanges of jeering and abuse. The artists reproached the businessmen with a cultural and intellectual ignorance which surpassed even that of the illiterate *Brazis*. They laughed at their nouveau-riche attitudes, how they would import rustic little taverns from Austria in order to impress the *Brazis*, or how they would deferentially accept the invitation of the fatuous Austrian consul to a guest performance of the Vienna Boys' Choir so that they might then be congratulated afterwards on Austrian culture by the wives of Brazilian millionaires. The entrepreneurs, on the other hand, jeered at the lack of realism and the economic ignorance of the artists who would all be forced to join the *Brazis* in the *favelas* if it weren't for the various subsidies or grants they received from back home—the intellectuals they described as parasites and lunatics addicted to abstruse idealogies which didn't work in practice, practice being what they, the businessmen knew about best, of course. These discussions ranged back and forth within an area that encompassed statements beginning either, on the one extreme, with 'Man ...' or, on the other, with 'You prat ...' The effect of further consumption of alcohol, administered with a regal flourish by Oswald, was a renewal of brotherliness which expressed itself in mutual congratulations on how far superior they all were here to the 'primitives' when it came to life experience, and in joint, merciless diatribes against the provincialism of those compatriots still living in Austria. By closing time a strange, general euphoria had finally established itself which, in a maudlin and complacent way, drew its sustenance from the happy knowledge that, being at home nowhere, they were therefore everywhere an élite. In short, what was pursued in the *Bar Esperança* were the perfectly normal activities of privileged expats, and any thinking person would most certainly have taken flight instantaneously.

In this bar Leo was to become a regular.

The atmosphere of the bar had something seductive about it for him which he could not resist. As strange as it may sound, this bar was as if made for him. For the first time in his life he felt himself to be universally acknowledged. In this bar the chance events and failures of his life arranged themselves into the picture of a triumph which he celebrated daily until closing time. He was, in fact, the only customer who was regarded as an authority by both camps and so, as it were, by the whole world—the world of this bar, that is. The business community accepted him as the protegé of the banking veteran, Löwinger, and as someone who had made himself a fortune as well. And the intellectuals accepted him not only as someone on intimate terms with the legendary art-collector, Löwinger, but also as the battle-scarred champion of Critical Theory, someone who, as was only too well remembered in these circles, caused quite a stir a while back with avant-garde theses about Hegel and who today still would have no trouble lecturing on any given problem.

It wasn't long before Leo acquired the nickname of 'Professor' in the *Bar Esperança*, by which the intellectuals expressed their recognition of his intellectual prowess, and the business community their recognition of his business career. For the former he was a free spirit, for the latter an economically successful man and Leo could not help but respond to this with pleasure—a pleasure, however, which evaporated the moment he got back home after closing time, this accounting for the fact that it was only then that his craving for the bar grew in earnest.

Once, when he got back to his house in the early morning still drunk on the good cheer he'd brought home and was standing in his study, which was so dusty that he could have written with his finger on the top of his desk, he thought to himself that this study was the only piece of work he had truly completed. My masterpiece, he thought. He ought actually to open it to the public for an entrance fee as the materialised expression of the impasses of an intellectual existence. Or, he thought, as he poured himself a rum that was supposed to smash down the door that led at last to sleep, or he'd have to try and sell the room to the Museum of Modern Art.

In the cold light of the next day he wouldn't have found this thought so funny anymore but with any luck he would have forgotten it again by then.

As regards Judith, the most terrible thing happened that Leo could have earlier imagined: a kind of thick-skinned friendship emerged in which all that had happened in the past and that had resulted in one break-up after the other now functioned as a sort of dependable cement. The *Bar Esperança* in fact became for Leo the great stage on which the real charade of his life would at last be enacted: Leo and Judith appeared there like an old married couple, which they had never in reality been, an alliance of two pensioners who had decided to let the young ones have their turn now and who would discuss how well these were doing but only on the firm and mutual understanding that they themselves were still spry enough to grab the wheel back at any time should the need arise. A sham, this unity: they knew each other only too well, enough to know that neither had ever been in control of any sort of wheel—and this knowledge resulted in their sniping at each other with cynical remarks which, when they got too near the bone and painful, would topple back into melancholy protestations of love.

They would even go to bed together occasionally, not without questioning each other in a playfully aroused way when undressing as to who among the younger customers in the bar that day had taken their fancy, after which, hurt and angry, they would then try to get to sleep, their backs turned to each other. Judith began to take cocaine—she quickly came to depend on this drug which made her blissfully happy and which, and this was the most important thing, seemed to free her for a time from the sleep she so much feared. Leo remonstrated with her, which she, pointing to his alcohol addition, refused to accept. Both grew thinner and thinner, Judith from the cocaine, Leo from his drinking—it was as if they had decided to concentrate solely on disappearing slowly from this world an ounce at a time.

Judith had given up hope of ever finding work relating to what she'd studied—she made her living by giving German lessons in a language school. Alongside this, but without entertaining any aspirations or hopes in connection with it, she had started to write a study on Laurence

235

Sterne, perhaps to maintain her self-respect, perhaps, too, simply as occupational therapy, something to fill up her sleepless hours with. Leo saw this, of course, as historically logical: after reverting to her childhood nursery room, he said, it was clear that now Judith had to re-read her favourite children's book.

Leo had given up his ambition to write his sequel to Hegel—he contented himself with his stool of Philosophy in the bar, which gave him the feeling at least that he was somehow fulfilling his ambition. What a pity, said Judith—for fifteen years the world has waited in vain for Leo to change it for the better.

It was a union of decay, which they lived on and which lived off them.

Saying goodbye on the street outside the bar after closing time: Judith ran her fingers through Leo's hair and asked if he was still having his scalp massaged. Yes, he said, and pressed his face to her neck, kissing her, so that he was no longer looking at her but could see her as he remembered her. That might well have been the end, since it could have stayed like this until the end, if a new visitor to the *Bar Esperança* hadn't turned up.

A sensation marked the beginning of Leo's and Judith's acquaintance with the newcomer. It was a pistol shot—though, in the end really just a sensation. The evening was, if anything, rather quieter than usual in the bar to begin with, apart from the fact that Leo and Judith were squabbling. Judith had taken a line of cocaine in the lavatory, which Leo had immediately noticed on her return to the bar. She came over as being hyped up in a fidgety sort of way, which greatly irritated Leo. It was an intoxicated condition that he couldn't see as being on a par with his rum habit, a pulsating feeling that made you nervous, an illegal intoxication. He was about to tell her off again when the door opened and in rushed a wretched-looking man of about thirty with a gun in his hand. Nobody move! he shouted. He stood there, legs apart, swinging the pistol back and forth in his outstretched hand. He was wearing a faded tee-shirt, torn jeans, gym-shoes. His hair was almost matted. His skin, probably light brown in colour, had taken on a dirty grey hue, like the façades of the houses in the industrial areas of the city.

Recently hold-ups like this had generally been on the increase in Brazilian cities. Misery was growing. Many no longer saw any chance of getting work and a regular income. A sufficient income. There was no unemployment benefit. Hold-ups in restaurants were less risky than in banks. The *desesperados* who took money and jewellery off the customers in the bars had something to eat wrapped up for them as well in the kitchen and didn't think that they were doing anyone any harm this way. Afterwards the victims would drive back in their cars to their beautiful houses or apartments and the next day, if they so desired, they would go to the restaurant again. These people weren't victims. This man was a victim.

There was a deathly hush in the bar. Although everyone had heard or read about such hold-ups, each one of them, as they would later assure each other, was nevertheless taken aback. This hold-up was doubly unusual: first, because it took place in this quarter of the city where there was hardly any night-life, and secondly, because it was one man by himself. This man could never keep all the customers under control all the time. He wanted cash, watches and jewellery. He put a plastic bag down on a table—everything in there, quick! He took a few paces back towards the bar counter, indicating with frantic, swiping movements of his weapon that everyone standing by the bar should leave there and go and join the others. Slowly one after the other these walked around the man, who suddenly swung round again nervously, probably because of a noise, and pointed the weapon at the customers by the tables. At this moment he was standing directly in front of Judith with his back turned to her.

I would never have done it, she said later, if I hadn't taken cocaine just a moment before. I was too fast to be able to control myself—the idea, the feeling of invincibility and the execution, they all happened simultaneously. She became a heroine with a bad conscience. Because she felt sorry for the man and because she realised only later the danger she had put the other customers in.

She picked up a bottle of pinga off the bar counter and hit the man over the head with it.

Everything now seemed also to happen simultaneously: the bottle smashed into pieces, the man collapsed, a shot was fired, a customer cried out and also collapsed. Then everyone was shrieking.

The armed man no longer posed a danger. He was lying on the floor unconscious and with his head bleeding. Oswald took charge of the weapon and called the police. Everyone clustered around the customer who had been shot—he was a young man who no-one knew—he'd never been in the bar before. He was lying on his back with his head leaning against the wall, one leg drawn up and lying across his other thigh, his arms crossed over his stomach. He looked as if he were sleeping, with his head propped up and lower body hunched as if his bladder were near to bursting. It was assumed he'd been shot in the abdomen. Judith felt sick and sat down.

He's alive! she heard someone shout. He's alive! He's alive! We must put him in a different position—he could suffocate with his head like that. For God's sake don't, that would be far too dangerous if he has internal wounds. That's right, that's right, we must leave him like he is until the police come! He doesn't need the police, he needs an ambulance—have the ambulance people been notified? We'll suffocate him like this—I did a course in first-aid and—No, don't—Please—On your head be it—I can't see any blood—he's not bleeding at all. That was Leo. Judith got up and pushed through the throng of people. At this moment the young man opened his eyes and, half astonished, half embarrassed, smiled. Whispers. Carefully he got up and looked down at himself. It was now as quiet as it had been at the beginning of the hold-up. No-one moved. Are you hurt? Leo asked eventually.

Don't know, said the man. The gun went off and I then felt a blow here on my side and, my head, he said, rubbing the back of his head. He opened his jacket and examined his left side—Here, he said—there was nothing to be seen, no bullet-hole, no blood. That's funny, he said, I thought—and, and it threw me back—he was rubbing the back of his head again—I must have hit my head against the wall and then I don't remember anything anymore. At least, he said, now looking at his jacket—here! I don't believe it. I really don't believe it! On the pocket of his jacket there was a small, barely visible hole—he put his hand inside the pocket and drew out a book which, as everyone craned forward to see, did indeed have a bullet imbedded in it. Leo recognised the book immediately. It was Hegel's *Phenomenology of Spirit*. The black paperback edition with the comprehensive appendix of information that Leo himself owned.

The shocked and dumbfounded mood that had reigned now resolved into relieved and downright hysterical laughter at exactly the moment the police came in.

The two policemen were soon to understand the reason for this peculiar mood. Shaking his head, the younger one kept on examining the book with the bullet-hole. Has this Hegel fellow, he asked finally with a grin, has he written other books? Something for the heart, perhaps? I mean I'm always worried a bullet might get me in the heart.

In a flash a police van was ordered which took all those who'd been in the bar to the nearest police station where the *bulentinho de ocorencia* had to be made out. In the harsh, neon-lit atmosphere of the police interview

238

room, faced with the two officials at their wobbly desks and antediluvian typewriters, a hung-over mood soon set in. An open door looked out into a corridor where men were continually being dragged or shoved along. Staggering drunkards or half-naked transvestites. Judith's eyes never left this door—she had the impression she was looking through a camera which, chaotically zooming in and out, alternately pulled faces towards her and hurled them from her again—beard stubble, mouths with teeth missing, blood-shot eyes. Leo was standing next to Judith, caressing her hand soothingly all the time—he was worried they might discover that Judith was up to her eyeballs with cocaine. A total stillness seemed to reign in the room, even though there was a continual stream of questions being put and answers given and the two officials were banging away on the keys of their typewriters. After the *Bar Esperança* this must be the Bar of Good Hope, said the young man who'd been shot. One or two thanked him for the attempt at a joke with an attempt at a smile. When everyone had been interrogated and the *buletinho* had been signed, each one saw to it that they got away as quickly as possible.

Suddenly Leo, Judith and the young man were standing alone on the street outside the police station. How about another quickie somewhere near here? asked Leo. Absolutely, said the man—I couldn't imagine anything else right now. That was the beginning, no, not of a friendship, it was the beginning of a relationship.

They found a small bar very near that was still open, a kind of garage, in which there was one of those typical chrome bar-tops with bolted down bar-stools. In front of this on a concrete forecourt, as it were, were a few metal folding tables and chairs brown with rust and with the last remnants of yellow paint. The bar was exactly opposite the huge, brightly-lit Jotapetes department store, which Leo ignored, however. They ordered half a dozen quails and some beer.

The young man was called Roman Gilanian and came from Vienna. He was twenty-six years old, a little older than Leo had reckoned. He was a talented young man—Hegel's *Phenomenology* in his jacket pocket! But he wasn't too serious either.

Doesn't bear thinking about what would have happened, said Judith, if you hadn't had that book on you. It would have been my fault then that you—

239

Perhaps there'll be another opportunity to become your victim, said Roman, giving Judith a bow and a wide-eyed, childish look.

Well, said Leo, clearing his throat nervously, what I was going to say—Leo felt impatient. He wanted to know more about Roman, what he did, what the significance was of the fact that he was carrying Hegel's *Phenomenology* on him.

Roman explained that he'd arrived here in São Paulo only a short while ago. He was working at the university.

Was he teaching philosophy, Leo asked.

No, said Roman, he was teaching Austrian literature—he was a Lektor in the German department.

And you read Hegel for pleasure? Leo asked sceptically.

No, come off it—if you could show me how to read Hegel for pleasure, I'd be grateful, said Roman. It's a strange story, I'm afraid, he continued—you wouldn't believe me. On the other hand, after what happened today—

Tell us, said Leo. Yes, do, said Judith.

All right, he said. The story happened recently in Vienna, shortly before I left, and I was involved only on the fringe of things really. Once a week I would play football with an amateur team. With contact lenses, of course, he said, as he noticed the surprised looks they gave his thick spectacle lenses. Anyway, he said, it was all just for fun, a joke— basically a lot of amateurs none of whom could kick. With one excep- tion: our goalkeeper. Bloch—that was his name—had earlier been a well-known goalkeeper with a club in the first division, but really he wasn't ambitious enough to make a career of it, make money out of it. He was a brilliant goalkeeper with superb reflexes but—and for the story I need to mention this in advance—he never struck me as having any imagination. Quite the opposite. Those who knew him could tell you it would never once have entered his head to compare himself as a goalkeeper to a tiger. The Tiger of the City Recreation Ground or such like. Nothing of the sort. For him a tiger was a tiger and a goalkeeper a goalkeeper. He was, by the way, a fitter by trade. Not exactly a job that excites the imagination. Do you know what a fitter actually fits? There you go. Anyway, the story began after a match where we'd won, only because Bloch hadn't let in any goals. He had managed to catch or deflect the most impossible and unstoppable balls. As a former profes- sional he was, of course, a trained goalkeeper, much better than any- thing other amateur teams could muster, but on the other hand in friendly matches there are considerably more hopeless situations for a

240

goalkeeper because the defenders, generally podgy and opposed on principle to kicking, are always making mistakes and giving the opposite team's strikers one chance after another, which even clueless amateurs can exploit and which the goalkeeper has no hope of saving. So I dare maintain that not one of today's top goalkeepers in the world, not Dino Zoff or Sepp Maier, not Friedl Koncilia or whoever, could have saved our team from a losing goal in that match. After the game we went as usual to the pub. Some players from the opposing team came along, too. You can imagine how much Bloch's outstanding performance was discussed, how fulsome the praise. Then Bloch suddenly said: There's no art in catching leather balls. We thought for a moment that he wanted modestly to play down his achievement but then he began saying something about mind and matter, that reality couldn't hold its ground against the mind and so on—I was still puzzling over his manner of speaking when he said that absolute knowledge must, therefore, control reality absolutely. Everything in the world worked according to one and the same principle, said Bloch. There was, so to speak, one single mind or spirit which made itself felt in political life just as much as in religion, art, morality, in social life, trade, industry and also in sport. This absolute Mind brought forth everything that was objective out of itself and held it quietly in its power. So in other words, said Bloch, if the material world is under the direction of the Mind, then the mind, if it advances forward to the absolute, can do what it wants with matter. It could hold even the most aggressive matter quietly in its power. He could prove this very easily, he said, and not just with a leather ball. At this Bloch stood up, drew a revolver and held it above his head. You can imagine the consternation in the pub. Watch, said Bloch, someone will fire at me and I'll catch the bullet with my teeth. He happened to be standing next to me and so he pushed the revolver into my hands, walked away a few paces and cried: Shoot at me, come on, fire. I couldn't do it, of course, I couldn't just simply shoot at him. I was standing there helplessly with the weapon in my hand when a player from the opposite team called out to me that I should go ahead and shoot, the weapon was probably not loaded. Not loaded, cried Bloch, rushed over to me, grabbed the revolver and fired a shot at a picture hanging on the lounge bar wall of a belling stag in the forest. The bullet tore a hole in the picture, in the middle of the stag's body. There you go, said Bloch to the young fellow who had doubted the weapon was loaded, it's loaded! But neither stags nor pictures have minds, as you know, and I'm afraid that you, too, don't stand a chance against a bullet either, pal. He then pushed the revolver into his hand and said: Go for it and shoot—aim at my face. He turned round and walked to the end of the dining area where we were sitting. Despicable, by the way, the reaction of the others, myself included. Some of them simply wanted a free-for-all and shouted: Shoot! Shoot! The others, for whom the whole thing was a bit weird, just sat there stolidly not budging an inch nor saying a word. No-one made a move to take charge of the weapon and unload it, to pacify Bloch and his challenger. There was a lip-smacking fear in the air as if this were a film show only. Bloch stood there, head raised, hands on hips. The lunatic fired. Bloch made a snapping movement with his mouth and, with his lips drawn back wide as if he were giving a forced laugh for a photographer, came to us at the table. Between his teeth he was holding the bullet. He went from one person to the next, laughing in this absurd fashion so that everyone could see it. Then he took the bullet out of his mouth—Morons! he said, and left.

Naturally a heated discussion followed on the heels of this. Probably only the first chamber was loaded with live ammunition, was the conjecture soon reached, the second was a dummy and Bloch put the bullet he had on him in his mouth when in our excitement we hadn't been looking. But, went the objection, he couldn't have known that I wouldn't fire directly after the first challenge—then the bullet in the first chamber which smashed the picture would have had his name on it. The discussion went back and forth. Finally, Peter, the slowest and dreamiest of all of us,—he, by the way, was our sweeper, and the reason why our goalkeeper, Bloch, was always kept so busy—that day Peter had even been responsible for a penalty—well, Peter said that he could imagine only too well how material things could suddenly lose all meaning for someone, that they could become mere words that no longer meant anything over and above themselves. Bloch didn't catch a bullet with his teeth, he said, but rather put a word into his mouth. The word bullet. Look, said Peter, I can do it, too. And he took a ballpoint pen out of his jacket pocket—hence the name *ball*point! he said—and wrote the word bullet on a beer mat which he then put between his teeth. With a coy look and with the beer mat in his mouth, he looked around him at the company. Everything now dissolved in laughter of relief. You ought to go on the stage with that trick, Peter, someone shouted, at which the merriment further increased. Then in that case a revolver is a ballpoint, another shouted out—and the stag a beer mat, shouted yet another—everyone tried to go one better than the other and to go on flogging the supposed joke. But the landlord is a landlord, said the landlord and he demanded compensation for the wrecked picture and the damage to the wall. Well, I don't need to go into this any further. All this jocularity, which everyone loudly used to soothe their feelings of impotence, didn't make this experience disappear for me at least. I couldn't get the episode out of my head and so I told a colleague from the Philosophy Institute about it a few days later, some-one I often liked to to chat with. He naturally didn't believe my story. Great piece of fiction, he said, really funny. I swore to him that I'd really experienced it, seen it with my own eyes, and asked him again for his opinion, assuming that it really had happened. Well, in that case I'd say it was a trick, he said. He looked at me thoughtfully and asked: You really didn't cook this story up? No, I said. Do you know what the oddest thing about it is? he asked. That the man's name is Bloch. Do you know the German philosopher, Ernst Bloch? He wrote once that there were fundamentally only two real authors and they were Karl May and Hegel, all the rest were just mixtures of the two. Yes, and the story about the man who can catch a bullet with his teeth—I know it, it's Karl May—it appears in the short story, *The Magic Water*—and this explanation involving the Absolute Mind reminds me of course of Hegel, of the *Phenomenology of Spirit*.

You can imagine how amazed I was. That was the reason, then, why I bought the Hegel—and the Karl May book, too, of course. The whole thing was a total riddle to me. I knew for a certainty that Bloch really was called Bloch. I looked up in the Karl May story how this trick with the bullet between the teeth worked and I decided that on the following Sunday, when we were to play football again, I would talk to Bloch about it. But he didn't come. Nor the week after that. No-one knew why he wasn't coming any more—no-one had his telephone number. I was feeling pretty sure I wouldn't hear of him again when, a few days later, I read about him in the newspaper. A fitter by the name of Bloch, it said, had murdered a cinema cashier. 'The brute was unemployed,' one newspaper reported—so much for the language of our press. A few days later the end of Bloch was headline news in the Austrian press. Bloch had fled from Vienna but was recognised—it led to a chase, during which, thanks to a major police operation, he was surrounded in Regelsbrunner Au, just outside Vienna, where he'd obviously been wanting to hole up somewhere in a copse. The police, while combing the area, finally discovered him—a few warning shots were fired in an attempt to persuade Bloch—who in desperation had started to run for it—to stop and surrender. It said in the paper that despite the hope-lessness of his situation Bloch wouldn't heed calls from the police to give himself up and even returned fire several times. Finally a police officer aimed a shot at Bloch which killed him. The body was lying face down and when the police turned it over to examine it, they saw that his lips were drawn back as if he were about to laugh. And between his teeth he was holding the fatal bullet. Bloch had been hit in the back of the neck—the bullet had driven through the neck, penetrated the cavity of the mouth and come to a halt between his teeth. The police officer who had fired the final so-called coup de grâce justified his action, according to the newspaper, on the grounds of self-defence since, as he was reported to have said, Bloch was after all armed to the teeth. Yes, well, said Roman, since then I've been trying to read Hegel, and this story somehow caught up with me again today, too. Leo was, of course, thrilled by the story, even if he wasn't sure whether he could really believe it. Nevertheless, the events in the bar that day proved that the most improbable things could indeed take place. Leo wanted to believe the story. Moreover, in time Roman became more and more credible since he was obviously a specialist in experiences which, in general at least, were rather incredible. Once he fell off the bar-stool. He wasn't even drunk. He'd just been rocking back and forth on the stool and suddenly lost his balance. Some days later, though now really drunk, he ran out of the bar and across the street paying so little heed that a car had to make an emergency stop so as not to run him down. The car stopped half a metre short of Roman who leapt to one side in an alarm out of step with real time, while a car coming up behind drove with a crash into the first. Two of the bar clientèle were witnesses and these went straight back into the bar to relate what they'd seen. Then on another occasion Roman went to the seaside with a female colleague for the weekend and on the way the car fell off a bridge and into a river. Not a scratch. In the bar he showed Leo on his return a photo of the crumpled car. Shortly after this there were a number of days during which Leo waited in vain for Roman to appear. Where on earth can he be, he said to Judith. I rang him, Judith explained. He said he's got syphilis—he has to take penicillin—

That can't be true, said Leo, meaning that it couldn't be true that Roman was taking penicillin. Syphilis still had for Leo an aura of genius—he would never have dosed himself to try to get rid of it.

Yes, said Judith, he—yes, well—he tried out one of those cheap tarts in front of the university. Anyway, he says he's not overjoyed at the thought of standing in the bar and not being able to drink any alcohol.

And why are *you* drinking only mineral water today? asked Leo. Because I don't want to drink alcohol every day, said Judith. I'm not an alcoholic like you.

Oh, do shut up, said Leo.

Whenever Roman stayed away it unsettled Leo considerably more than when Judith failed to put in an appearance in the bar. Roman's particular allure for Leo was the fact that he taught at the university, the fact that now, since the military regime was softening, a young man from Vienna had been invited to give lectures at the university, whereas there was no prospect of his own university career, which had been wrecked by the military, starting up again—all this churned Leo up. To make Roman his pupil, now became for Leo his one aim in life. The thought that he, a reject, might influence and form the up-and-coming generation and so in spite of everything slowly acquire an influence which cunningly and in the teeth of history would gain acceptance—this thought gave him an almost intoxicating feeling of satisfaction. Naturally in this context he also felt that all the disagreements, the marks of immaturity and peculiarities that irritated him about Roman were ultimately all of a piece and necessary. For Roman was after all not yet 'finished', and so had to be a pupil as well so that the teacher could mould him into shape and set him on the right path. The main problem was that Roman, alongside all the signs in him of notable intellectual promise, had far too much zest for life, had a plain craving for adventure. Those he was continually stumbling into automatically clearly weren't enough for him. So, for example, he decided one day he wanted to get to know a *favela* from the inside. He simply walked into one, in the "*Buraco quente*", which was very close.

No, said Leo, when Roman told him this, looking at him aghast, as if he doubted that Roman was still alive and was standing there at the bar in the flesh.

Yes, said Roman. He related how he'd even been invited to a *churrasco*. It was a mystery to Leo how Roman could have won the trust of the *faveleiros*. He shook his head. And just imagine, Professor, we're eating and drinking—drinking pitú, that dead cheap rum that comes in bottles with sealed caps—and I was already completely smashed when I realised for the first time that they'd grilled a cat. They can't afford any meat so they catch stray cats.

A *churrascinho de gato*, said Leo—ghastly—did you throw up?

No, said Roman, why would I—no-one else did either and—

The physical contemplation of misery, said Leo, doesn't lead one to acquire any new and deeper perceptions over and above the general feeling of compassion which every moral sensibility already had before. And paying a visit to an actual *favela* similarly doesn't reveal the reasons for the misery. So it was totally unnecessary. I hope you've learnt that much from it.

Yes, I don't know, Professor, said Roman—it was very interesting, anyway.

Roman's escapades with women were also bound to irritate Leo, of course. Not just because they were naïve, from the account Roman gave of them, but because they contradicted in principal Leo's picture of an ascetic mind devoted to study.

Roman told him how he'd been to the *Boca* a couple of times now. I never went with prostitutes, in Vienna—I mean it would never have entered my head. But here, he said, beaming from ear to ear, the prostitutes are far more affectionate than all the so-called normal girlfriends I had in Vienna ever were.

How many would that have been, thought Leo, thinking back briefly to his own time in Vienna. Clearly Roman's enthusiasm for the *Boca* was nothing more than an understandable need to make up for times when he'd lost out on things, thought Leo, but which, now that it was a question of deepening Roman's philosophical education, had to be put an end to.

The thought that he might run into Roman by chance in the *Boca* he was not willing to entertain. He took Roman severely to task for his tendency to idealise the girls from the *Boca*—it was only too easy in this way to become, out of principle, doggedly attached to a lie. He explained his concept of a life lived in its essentials, which was the total opposite of living life to the full, the happy-go-lucky life.

I am certainly no monk, said Leo, but—

Hence the battle against your tonsure, said Judith.

Oh, Judith, do shut up.

With his thick lenses and uncertain, angular movements Roman at least didn't look like a pin-up, Leo felt. Judith felt differently, or did she just want to give the impression she did out of sheer spite towards Leo? Sometimes, however, she showed an obvious fondness for Roman, would flirt quite openly with him and hold him completely under her spell. At such times Leo could have gone wild with jealousy. Immediately he would try to get Roman to focus his attention completely on him again, would even take him by the arm, reasoning with him. But Judith would continually interrupt Leo's lectures with barbed remarks like: Leo, you've lectured on this thesis so often now, isn't it about time you wrote it down?

Oh, Judith, do shut up.

Roman, whom a chance event turned into a reader of Hegel, was given a thoroughgoing schooling by Leo in a systematic study of Hegel, and against life. Leo showed Roman the German bookshop in São Paulo where he could obtain a new copy of *Phenomenology*. Leo held regular lectures on Hegel in the bar, tried to show Roman how you could read Hegel with pleasure, the pleasure deriving largely from Roman being obliged to arrive in his thinking at Leo's theory, as he read Hegel. Leo's theory—it really would go out into the world, carried along in the wake of Roman's academic career, it really would have its effect: a time-bomb. Leo was obsessed with this idea. Being now a teacher through and through, he would even think up exercises that he would then regularly give to Roman to do as homework.

Compare the section on Legal Status in the *Phenomenology* with Karl Marx's 'Excerpts from John Mill' and tell me tomorrow about anything that struck you particularly.

At first this relationship developed extremely happily. Roman was a man who was completely without any direction in life. He had spent the whole of his school years, as he told Leo once, in a boarding school. It was like twelve years of imprisonment, he'd said. After taking his 'Matura'—after leaving school, that is—he'd been totally unprepared for life and therefore quite unequal to it, too. He'd been eighteen years old and his heart had thumped with excitement whenever he ordered a mocha with milk in a café. He would blush whenever anyone spoke to him. He was eighteen when he went on the tram in Vienna alone for the first time. Terrified that he might get lost, he'd got someone to explain the route precisely and had discovered that he had to travel on that line to the terminal where he then had to change to another tram line. So as to be absolutely sure, as soon as he'd got on the tram he'd asked the conductor: Excuse me, please, but does this tram go to the terminal?

His university years had served to enable him to graduate and to realise that he knew nothing, but that he would have to know and understand everything in order to be better protected and to be able to move about with any independence and certainty. Leo was therefore

247

able in fact to become for Roman an authority, one who gave him the feeling he was acquiring a sensible view of the world. With such a view you could master the world—at least insofar as, for every phenomenon, you had an intelligent explanation that wasn't in the newspaper.

It wasn't long before Roman was spoken of in the bar only as 'Prof's pet'. He admired Leo, liked listening to him, was fascinated—and only ever contradicted him by mistake: whenever, for instance, he told a story—something to which he was all too prone—which to Leo's horror began with the words: You'll never guess what happened to me yesterday, professor...

Leo didn't notice straightaway and was never to understand that this teacher-pupil relationship was to turn everything in his life upside down again. To all appearances, after all, it had looked as if Leo were finally able to stand with both feet planted in reality and in this way find some measure of happiness.

His peaceful friendship with Judith, the self-satisfaction with the role of bar professor to which he had realistically resigned himself, this now came to an end. Nearly all that Judith and he ever did now was quarrel. Her ironic remarks, which before he had taken as an expression of special intimacy, now, in front of Roman, drove him to distraction. The scientific and pedagogical task that Leo felt himself called upon to perform through Roman made him blissfully happy. Whatever Judith said, Leo took as an attempt to destroy this happiness, to pull him to pieces in front of Roman and undermine his authority, to steal his attention. Leo couldn't take it, especially not when her barbs scored direct hits.

Poor Leo, Judith said once, you've got a pupil now but still no masterpiece.

She taunted him because, what with the independence and freedom his fortune gave him, he was quite incapable of starting anything—he would neither write his book nor get any pleasure out of his life. The only pleasure you're up to, Leo, is talking about that book.

Judith was always in financial difficulties. She was not able to finance her cocaine addiction with the German lessons. Even though she continually maintained that cocaine didn't make you dependent, she was, emotionally at least, soon so much so, that she even asked Leo for money. Leo, who knew what she needed the money for, had always for reasons of principle, not to say love, refused her. Now, however, he regularly and generously helped her out. For he knew that whenever Judith had money and was able to buy herself the stuff, then she would often not come to the bar for days. Where earlier her absence might have troubled him, now it suited him just fine—just as long as she left him in peace and didn't confuse Roman. Leo was only ever completely thrown whenever Roman didn't turn up. He would then immediately feel betrayed by the world, robbed of his purpose, cheated of his influence, and dragged down by a feeling of the meaninglessness of life, a feeling that had until recently been no part of his life in the bar. He got drunk more quickly than usual, reacted irritably to the idiotic conversations and quarrelling in the bar and, from being the universally acknowledged middle ground where opposing camps could be reconciled, he became the outsider who vilified everyone aggressively and in equal measure.

Leo discovered once that Judith and Roman had met up together in another bar and had both not come that evening to the *Bar Esperança* for that reason. The next day he made a scene in front of Judith—not in front of Roman, of course—which culminated in Leo's saying that Judith shouldn't forget that she could be Roman's mother.

You only say that because you'd like to be his father, said Judith, isn't that right—Roman, your son, your creation, your oeuvre. And, just as it is with sons, he is at the same time the substitute for your great book, your proxy who's now got to do what you yourself couldn't pull off.

Shut up, Judith—not another word, he screamed so loud that for a moment the bar was silent.

When Roman then came in, with his eyes nearly popping out behind his thick glasses and, standing there, began to relate something that again had happened to him, Leo was so downcast that it was only with great difficulty that he managed to steer the conversation into a sensible direction and hold forth on his theory.

Every shred of a sense of reality he had ever once had, Leo had now lost. The wisdom of age with him had been a bright but short-lived blaze. He was now burnt out and people could only stare coldly at the ashes. It wasn't only Judith who had finally had enough of him. His status in the bar was also in ruins. The way Leo courted Roman and defended himself against Judith prompted jocular and disdainful comments. And the uncontrolled manner in which, when he was alone, he would kick up a stink and rail against everyone had won him some open enemies.

The nickname 'professor' acquired an unmistakeably ironic, if not contemptuous undertone.

Leo should have seen that to some extent he had as a consequence destroyed the emotional foundations of his life. But there was Roman. Roman was Leo's hope, his hope that what he been thinking about all his life might be rehabilitated, his hope that his theory might later take root and blossom in the world. Why should Leo let the mood in the *Bar Esperança* bother him? First Roman would teach at the University of São Paulo under the influence of Leo's theses. Then he would go back to Vienna to teach there. And that was just the beginning. In his mind's eye Leo saw how, in one country after another, one inquiring generation after another were gripped by his ideas. The world would not be able to resist him.

Roman found Leo's explanations of the world really interesting. He was open to being seduced. But he found other things interesting, too, could be seduced by others, too, by Judith with her cocaine, by everything he stumbled into, blinking uncertainly through his thick glasses. He lost the urge to go to the *Bar Esperança* every evening, even though there were so many interesting things to discover there—besides, he found the professor a little too possessive.

Cut off to a great extent from everyone else in the *Esperança*, Leo was right down the far end of the bar. He was thinking. Clearly the problem was, he thought, that he wasn't able to pass on to Roman anything that was written down. There was no doubt whatever that Roman was a man who thought seriously and worked hard. For this reason he had to stick to the academic rules of the game. That meant that every thesis had to be open to verification, every quotation had to have a reference so that others could check it against the original. Very sensible, too, thought Leo, for he didn't want to be an influence only—whatever effect he might have, he wanted this to be linked with his name. The logical outcome of this was that he did in fact have to write his book. There was no escaping it. His opus. He saw it clearly before him. As a result of the lectures he had regularly given to Roman it had progressed fundamentally. It had become more concrete, more graphic, clearer in its details. Leo thought it was no accident that it was only now he could write it. He had first had to free himself from his fixation on Judith, even the fixation that entailed rejecting her. In order to emerge, his book had demanded this process of detachment.

Bill! Leo called out. It took so long before he finally got his bill that, in a mixture of fury and megalomania, Leo briefly thought of simply buying up the place and closing it down. He believed he would never need it again.

250

He didn't even stop to dust off his desk for fear of one thing leading to another until in the end he'd find himself spending weeks reorganising his study. He really wanted just one thing: to write. But after so many years during which he'd not written anything, he was completely out of practice, the routine was gone, though not to the extent he that had regressed to the stage of a naïve and untroubled beginner. He tinkered fastidiously with one sentence until it became so cumbersome and convoluted that he threw it away. He decided to begin with a quotation, a long one, and while he was copying it out he very soon grew euphoric: one sheet began to fill up—he was writing. But hardly had he closed the inverted commas when his wretchedness caught up with him again. Perhaps, in spite of everything, something might have come of it if Leo had given himself the time, if he'd been patient. But it was precisely time that he thought he didn't have. He simply wanted to tip the work out of his head and onto the paper. It had to be done immediately, while he still had Roman standing there at the ready. Time was what he had had over the last fifteen years. Now he had run out of it. In this work it was the totality that mattered. With this work he wanted to deal with the totality. He couldn't give a second's thought to anything but the totality. He couldn't accept any one sentence because each one was but one sentence and not the totality. He couldn't write one sentence without trying immediately to say everything in this sentence. And so he couldn't write one sentence.

On top of this he got ill. His chronic wind had developed into regular and severe bouts of colic which sometimes doubled him up. And he had found blood in his stools. Once again he was sitting in waiting rooms, doctors' waiting rooms. A week in hospital for the purpose of observation and examination. That was quite out of the question. A strict ban on alcohol. That was quite out of the question. He first had to finish his work. He had pages of extracts and ideas but beyond that still not one sentence. He maintained that he needed some time still to complete an extremely important piece of work, not a lot of time, just some time. The stay in hospital was postponed. He was prescribed some medicine, large capsules, one half of which were red, the other half transparent—in the latter case you could see that they were filled with little specks in various colours. These capsules looked like little confetti cartridges. What Leo did was not serious, and yet was, in a way that was almost homicidal. He swallowed these capsules, drank his rum, stood in a delirium in his study and struggled with the first sentence.

251

He thought of the talks he'd given in the bar. He had in fact already dictated the whole of his book, it was just that no-one, unfortunately, had written it down. Why was it that he couldn't manage to write it now with the same ease with which he could at any time have lectured on it in front of an audience? A numbing fear of death came over him. He wasn't yet fifty years old and yet he looked like an old man, even though his hair, which meanwhile had turned completely white, he still dyed black. In his briefcase he had a hospital admission form. If this work were now to founder, it would mean death. No matter how long he were then to continue living. All his life he had thought that the idea of an afterlife was frivolous. Now it was serious.

Perhaps it was this fear of death that suddenly found him running, as if without thinking, out of the house, getting into his car and driving to Judith's. No reflection had preceded this decision, so he hadn't rung Judith up beforehand either to find out if she was at home and whether he could call round. When he started up the car he wasn't even sure whether he wasn't going to drive to the bar. He drove to Judith's.

Slowly he drove down Avenida Morumbi, downhill past the walls that bordered the properties of the rich, who had settled up here, high over the city between the Governor's Palace and Morumbi Bridge. He went past the gap in the buildings on the left which suddenly gave a view of the sea of lights down below that was the city. In front of this panorama were the cars of courting couples strung out in a line and next to them the illuminated van of a seller of popcorn.

Leo drove slowly and with automatic movements, his head as empty as a blank sheet of paper. He drove past the fork to the right that led to Morumbi cemetery, drove over the bridge to Brooklin. He crossed over Avenido Santo Amaro and didn't turn to the right into it. To get to the bar he could still have taken Vereador José Diniz further on. But he didn't drive as far as that, only as far as Barão de Triunfo, stopping in front of Judith's house.

All of the windows were lit—Judith was at home. The garden gate squeaked. Leo's steps echoed on the flagstones of the small front garden. The front door wasn't locked. Judith wasn't in the *sala*. Leo went into the study. Judith was standing bent over her desk with her back to the door and with her forearms resting on the top of the desk. Her backbone could be seen clearly through her teeshirt. Judith gave a sudden start and screamed—her shock was so great that Leo also winced violently, as if not just he but someone else had slipped into the house unnoticed, too.

What was he doing there? Leo wondered that as well. Why had he come? Leo didn't know himself. She had thought it was over, over and done with—she wanted her peace, her peace. Leo saw at once that she had taken some cocaine. Her nose running all the time, her impatient, agitated nerviness, her movements at bursting point. What did he want here? Leo went up to her. Oh, Leo, she said, you gave me such a shock, I nearly died. She turned away from him and bent over her desk again. Leo was still looking for the words, for the reason why he'd come. It shouldn't be necessary by now to have to explain this. On Judith's desk lay dozens of sheets of paper filled up with writing, folders, open books. On one book a little mirror with white powder and a razor blade. Judith was now working away at the cocaine with the razor blade, rhythmically, fixedly, without paying Leo any attention anymore. Judith, I— he said helplessly. Do you want some, too? she asked, rolling a banknote into a little tube, with which she then sniffed the cocaine up into her nose. She straightened up and, giving another loud sniff, handed Leo the note. Ah, yes, you don't want any, do you—you've never wanted any. I'm glad, too—I haven't got much left and if I don't get hold of any new stuff tomorrow, I'll be looking for crumbs—some of it fell off the plate perhaps—perhaps when I breathed out I blew some onto the desk, perhaps onto the floor? There was something impious and taunting but also tragically self-mocking in the way she knelt down, moistened the tip of her finger with her tongue, dabbed about on the floor with it and then massaged her gums. She was beside herself. Now she was standing in front of Leo again. How white her face was, how glassy her eyes. Could Leo see himself reflected in her eyes? He could hear a very quiet whistling, short bursts in rapid sequence. Her breathing. And always this nervous agitation in her face. She kept on licking her lips, chewing on them, running her tongue over her gums, wiping her nose on the back of her hand. How her face had collapsed. Ghost-like, the life in it, staring out of a ruin.

Leo, do you have any money on you? I need money. I've got nothing left, not a single *tostão*. I'll pay you back. Really. You must help me.

Yes, I'll help, of course, I—

Go away, Judith shouted suddenly, get lost! Leo froze. I think it would be better if I—he was saying when Judith stretched out her arm past Leo and in the direction of the window, flapped her hand and made a whistling noise. Get lost, piss off, she screamed, staring at the window with her hand still stretched out and flapping it again, giving another hiss, and now even stamping her foot. Go away, you! Leo turned round and also looked towards the window. Shoo the cat away, Leo, screamed Judith—it's sitting there behind the window. It's staring at me. Why is the cat staring at me like that? What does it know? Piss off, get lost! Leo tried to take Judith by the shoulders, to give her a shake—Judith! he shouted—Leo! she shouted, backing off, please, chase the cat away! There's no cat there. There, said Judith, there it is. Judith's chest rose and fell as if it were about to explode at any moment. In the room there was a feeling of terror that Leo's sobriety made completely bewildering. He had come to be rescued. He was even quite prepared to see a cat as well, a glowing pair of slanting eyes behind the window. Judith saw a cat, he saw a cat, too, chased it away and they were both saved. But he couldn't see any cat. There was no rescue. Slowly he walked over to the window, opened it. There's no cat there.

Nervously Judith came closer. She looked out, closed the window, peered through the window pane, opened the window again.

Leo?

Yes.

If there was no cat there—

There wasn't.

Then it must have been this plant here. These two leaves here, do you see? They're the ears, and here, these two leaves are the eyes.

Yes, those are the eyes.

Yes, you see? Look, if I close the window, it reflects because outside it's dark, but this shrub, so close up to the window, it shivers, I mean shimmers in the light that shines out on it from the room. That's why it looks like—it was the shrub.

Yes, an optical illusion.

Yes.

She shook her head and was turning round when she hunched up convulsively and looked back over her shoulder again with an abrupt turn of her head. But Leo, a shrub can't watch you—we were being watched—I could really feel it. Judith's voice, which had become quieter, almost flat, grew louder again and shrill. Leo's relief turned to dust. Someone or other is looking in, she shrieked, I can feel it, I can't take it—come, Leo, let's go out and have a look around. Judith picked up her handbag that was lying on the floor next to the desk and took out a small pistol. Come on, let's go outside. Leo had to look twice before he could believe his eyes. Where did she get that pistol from— why was she carrying a pistol in her handbag? Please put the gun back, he said flatly, making pacifying gestures. Judith was looking so agitated that Leo really feared she might start shooting wildly about her. What was he doing here? How long had it been—ten minutes? Half an hour? Before, he'd been worried about having to justify why he'd come.

He stood there as in a horror movie, in which a normal person stumbles into an abnormal situation and has to surpass himself. With bated breath the audience wonders if he'll make it. Leo was the audience at the same time. But he couldn't come up with anything other than to say repeatedly 'Please, Judith' or 'Listen Judith'. Judith was beside herself—she didn't know what she was doing any more. Compared to her, Leo was 'on the ball', as they say. But in reality he wasn't. It just looked as if he was because he wasn't screaming hysterically, because he wasn't waving a pistol around. He stared at Judith, bewildered and helpless, as if there were a dark pane of glass between them, a magic mirror in which his own fear of death was reflected back as Judith's self-destructiveness and in which both fused together. Please, Judith! All at once she seemed completely exhausted and listless. She said flatly that he was right in fact, the cat really had been an illusion. She stowed the pistol away in her bag again. Leo breathed a sigh of relief. She said she wasn't feeling well. She wondered why. He tried to explain her condition as arising from the drug, which she'd clearly taken too much of, but she shook her head slowly. No, she said, it couldn't be from the cocaine, the cocaine always made her feel good, except when she didn't have any. And she'd been feeling great earlier, before Leo had come—he'd come and suddenly she'd felt sick. And how tired she was. She didn't want to be tired, if she couldn't switch things off in her head.

Judith bent over the desk again, over her mirror with the cocaine. Leo saw her stick the rolled up banknote into her nose, saw her make a jerky, forward movement with her head, then, with hunched shoulders, greedily, hectically, make the same movement again—no! he cried, that'll kill you—he made to go to her, stumbled over the books lying on the floor—she'd turned round by then—they stood opposite each other, she with her hands supporting her back, and with her trunk, which was arched forward, rising and falling like the stomach of a fledgling fallen out of the nest. Both of them were panting—never before had they panted together in such a uniform rhythm.

Leo, leave me alone, please. You turn up and I feel sick. I was tired. I don't want to be tired. Please, Leo—

Leo looked into Judith's eyes, saw her looking at him. For the briefest of moments he now saw before him the picture of Judith that he had in

255

his head, that ideal going back years, but now it began to dissolve as if after an acid attack, furrows dug into her face, wrinkles, blemishes, shadows, the contours disintegrated, Judith's mouth opened like a burst of colour slithering down. In this instant and in an almost expressionless voice she said: Stay! Suddenly she began to walk up and down in the room, hands on her hips, breathing deeply and frantically, sucking the air into her lungs with her open mouth, her hands pressing against her rib-cage, then again on her hips, rearing up with every intake of breath. She ran out of the study into the *sala*—there was more room there—gasping, she walked up and down, around the sofa—she gave a series of little cries as she tried to draw in breath. Then she sat down on the sofa but leapt up again immediately and resumed her march round the room, always with this frantic breathing in and out that she desperately sought to bring into a reassuring rhythm. The panic had spread to Leo, a full-blown infection, and now he stood there helplessly—wanting to help. But how?

Please stay, said Judith—something or other, was too much. My heart, it's tearing me apart. I mean really. I—can't take it. My heart—can't—take it. I think I'm dying. Fuck it. She whispered this, interrupted all the time by the panic-stricken gasping for breath. Such a stupid way to die—no—Leo, help me.

Leo had no idea what he should do. Judith then ran into the bathroom and he after her. She stood bent over the washbasin and splashed cold water onto her face. She pushed her forefinger up her nose, rubbed around inside it as if, at this eleventh hour and before it was too late and too much, she could still flush out some cocaine crystals which perhaps hadn't yet dissolved and penetrated the inner nose membrane. She even stuck a cotton-bud up and blew her nose several times, her face under the tap. Leo helplessly observed her clearly meaningless actions. Then Judith ran back into the *sala*, sat down on the sofa, leapt up again straightaway, pressed her hands against her chest, gasping all the while, and then again ran around the room like one possessed.

If I stand still, my heart stands still, too.

What should I do—can I do anything?

Stay here with me. What a stupid way to die.

Should I call for an ambulance?

Yes. No. Take me to a clinic. No. Leo, you're crazy. No doctor—that'd be the last thing—he'd see what was up straightaway. It's alright, it's over.

Leo couldn't stand around any longer doing nothing. He thought he could make Judith some warm milk with honey—milk was supposed to have a detoxifying effect, and honey calmed you down. Judith had milk and honey in the house. She drank it in little gulps with concentration but Leo still found her condition frightening, although at least she wasn't running about the room, struggling and wheezing. The way she repeatedly sipped from the glass and in between desperately pumped air into her lungs—it was like the final twitching of a body at the moment of death. Leo went into the study and picked up the packet of cocaine that was lying on her desk. Then he went back into the *sala*— Judith was sitting motionless and crumpled up on the sofa. Judith! She lifted her head. Is that all? he asked—she looked at him blankly, her eye sockets like plundered mines. Or have you got some more cocaine hidden away somewhere? She shook her head slowly. Good. Leo flushed the stuff down the lavatory pan, along with the razor blade wrapped in toilet paper, even the banknote she'd used. Then he washed and polished the little mirror and put it on a shelf in the bathroom. He took a towel and wiped her desk clean in case there were still traces of the drug, little dust particles that might be detected by experts from the criminal investigation department. The desk was now as clean as a whistle, no traces of life or death, just traces of work. Traces. If Judith were to be found dead here, wouldn't a post-mortem be performed, signs of toxicity found and the possibility be entertained that she'd been given poison? Won't they then try to investigate if there was a possible perpetrator by looking for indications as to who has been in the house? After pondering these questions Leo went into a blind panic, but in his actions he was strangely systematic, thorough, perfectly clear-headed, in fact. Using the towel, he wiped all those places in the house that he had touched—nothing escaped him, he forgot nothing. He erased traces even before he had done anything. He was seized by a manic fear of discovery, and the fact that this fear of discovery was not preceded by any deed didn't reduce the fear but instead gave the deed reality. But at this moment Leo didn't yet think or know this. Right now he kept on looking towards the window to see whether anyone was looking in from the outside and could see him here. Someone or other was looking in and watching everything, Leo could really feel it. Rubbish. A delusion. He asked Judith how she was. Not good, she said, but it was getting better. What was he doing there? I'm just tidying up a bit, he said in an exaggeratedly loud voice, and then more quietly: what else am I supposed to do? All his movements he performed for an observer, wiping things down in the most casual way he could, in an unsuspicious, perfectly natural manner—he even tried to polish the door handle as if it were the most normal thing in the world.

The crisis was over. When Leo looked towards Judith again, she was lying on the sofa and breathing more peacefully. I think it's passing, she said. Should he put her in bed?

No, she said. She wanted to remain lying the way she was. And she asked him to stay with her still, just in case. She had spoken these words in a quiet, choked voice—she then closed her eyes. Leo stopped in front of her and observed her, saw her rib-cage rise, fall, rise, fall, as if this were caused by the blinking of his eyes, his blinking at this lifeless marionette with its waxy complexion and oddly turned-in feet that had been thrown onto the sofa.

Strangely enough Leo didn't feel relieved to see that she had calmed down. What should relieve him about it? This accursed, emaciated body? This burnt-out shell—all that remained of a longing? In ruins like his hopes, which she had destroyed as she had her beauty, like she had herself? She had brought it upon herself, this pitiful state—something to which she had absolutely no right, it seemed to Leo altogether too self-righteously. No compassion, just disgust and loathing. She'll sleep it off, thought Leo, she'll recover, she'll start eating again tomorrow and as soon as possible start taking that poison again—she'll carry on tomorrow where she left off almost for good today, and she'll have her will-o'-the-wisp thoughts and not the least awareness of the real world, thought Leo, not of him, not of herself—she who's become the least thing in the world, whom nobody will desire any more, whom nobody will long to hold in their arms—but she'd prefer to destroy her life than live with him, thought Leo. A piece of shit always fancying herself cut out for better things, indestructible and pure like a diamond buried under coal. No, no compassion, only—

He was looking now at Judith's throat, at the artery throbbing there lightly, Leo had to concentrate very quietly in order to see this throbbing—Judith's sweat-soaked hair curled about her temples, her delicate, almost transparent eyelids covering her eyes like gelatinised tears—Leo now felt moved, thought it was love again that he felt, moved because of the care of which he was capable while he looked at her. Judith opened her eyes—for three or four dogged seconds she returned his gaze, eyeball to eyeball. Then she sat up slowly and asked: why did you come actually?

I felt a longing for you, said Leo.

She smiled and gave a deep breath. Leo, I think I've managed it again. She patted the seat of the sofa next to her—come and sit down beside me.

Leo sat down, slightly tensed. He didn't dare touch her, irritate her with his physical proximity, with words—he looked at her stiffly but didn't see anything, saw a yellowish surface perhaps, like a sheet of paper yellowed with age, and on it a slightly lighter patch, but nothing else. He wanted somehow to continue with the picture he had possessed earlier when he'd been standing in front of her, wanted at the same time not to see the signs of devastation, the ravages on her face, wanted to see the picture he'd had of her before, the picture he saw when he thought of her—he wanted this on the pretext of really seeing her now, of having her in front of him like a photo in an album. But the picture wasn't there any more—all that could be seen was a slightly lighter patch on the yellowed surface of his retina which showed: the picture had once been here.

Leo no longer understood anything, didn't understand either why Judith suddenly pulled him towards her, didn't even realise immediately that she was doing it—she pulled with no strength, only with the barely perceptible pressure of her hand on his shoulder—its weight became a little heavier, began to seep into his body, but was resisted by his tenseness which then gave way, however, under the gentle pressure of her hand. He couldn't feel anything any more, just something drawing to an end—where was this going to lead? Suddenly his head was lying in her lap—Judith began to stroke him—her fingers dipped erratically into his hair and stroked it back. Leo was seized with a rapt and mournful feeling of happiness—he didn't have the courage to relax and enjoy this, he feared that even the smallest movement on his part would result in her stopping. So he lay there with his body braced and with bated breath, waiting fearfully to see whether her hand, when it reached the back of his head, would meander back to his forehead and the stroking movement would begin again. And again she started, ran her fingers through his hair, and again, and—yes, again, she had only moved back a bit to get more comfortable and so had paused a moment. She stroked him in such a monotonous rhythm, so mechanically and mindlessly, so detached and without any real sympathy that it irritated Leo in the extreme. They were blindly robotic movements, the last dying reflex reactions, perhaps, to the poison still working in her and which she was working out of herself. Leo lay in a strangely angular position on her lap and tried to be happy that she was stroking him. In this position the waistband of his trousers pinched him—besides he felt a painful pulling sensation in his back and along the leg lying under his bent haunches— he also didn't dare to breathe for fear that he wouldn't any longer be able to control the air penned up inside his stomach. He remembered suddenly that he ought to be taking his medicine. He didn't have it with him. At any moment he expected the onset of severe colic pains. Leo grew aggressive towards Judith because she didn't notice that her fingers were continually getting snared in his hair, that she was pulling hairs out—she wasn't stroking his hair so much as rubbing it, matting it, tearing at it, and this put him in a panic. He doubted suddenly if she knew it was him she was stroking, for you had to stroke *his* particular head gently and carefully and, most important of all, with the grain. She'll stroke out my last few hairs, he thought, and in self-defence his scalp became electrically charged. Between her lap and her hand his face glowed—he felt an enormous pain and at the same time a complete numbing, a suppression of the pain. Both were subsumed in an image—what image? It was the Man of Sorrows on the lap of this clumsily executed figure of a woman.

Judith's stroking grew more and more sluggish, her hand became heavier until it eventually came to rest. Judith was sleeping. She was saved.

Leo stood up. What should he do now? Drive home? He couldn't drive home. Next to the door he could see the window of the *sala* which, because of the darkness outside, had become a mirror in which the *sala* was reproduced. If Leo were to leave this room though the door next to the window, he would simply be re-entering this room. And in the reflected duplication of this room there was again a window, behind which this room was reflected which he'd have to go out of and so on, ad infinitum. One step outside and it would become his lot to haunt without rest an endless corridor consisting of an infinite succession of Judith's rooms. Hesitantly he walked through the house, went into Judith's study and sat down at her desk with his hands in his pockets. It was true that the danger of Judith dying seemed removed now, but he remained nevertheless on his guard against touching anything and leaving any fingerprints behind. It was like an inner command that had become independent of him and which from now on he unquestioningly and blindly obeyed. He leant over the top of the desk which he had polished to a sheen a short while before, over the sheets of paper and folders lying there, and began to read. He skim-read at first, his eyes darting about, too impatient to decipher words or sentences that were sloppily written and unclear.

Then he stood up, went into the kitchen, put on the rubber gloves that he'd seen there earlier and sat down again at the desk. He wanted to be able to turn over the pages, put them back straight, open the folders.

The hands in the gloves didn't seem to belong to Leo any longer—they looked like the instruments of some impersonal force. Leo was just an unfeeling clod: all that remained of the body, between these hands and his eyes, that which was needed for breathing and for the functioning of the inner organs, so that objective understanding could establish itself in his head. He felt nothing in particular, everything in general as he looked through these papers and folders.

In one of the folders was Leo's essay about morality and culture. Judith had never said anything about it. But she'd kept it and had obviously read it, too. When Leo opened it at a certain place, he found a sentence highlighted in luminous yellow: 'Obligation kills life'. Three other folders were stuffed full with sheets which were a mixture of records of conversations, diary sketches and essays on Judith's favourite book, *Tristram Shandy* by Laurence Sterne. During the course of countless sleepless nights Judith must have manically written down from memory everything she'd experienced, everything she'd heard, in records as exact as possible or at least in detailed summaries. The records went back about nine months, that is they began at the time when Judith had started to take cocaine. Everything that Leo had said to her at this time, everything he held forth about in the bar, in front of her and Roman, here it was again. His step-by-step attempts in the bar to school Roman in his Hegelian thesis were all documented here, in some cases expanded with quotations from the literature that Leo had referred to and Judith had looked up. 'Today Leo talked about . . . Roman asked . . . to which Leo replied: . . .' These records were brilliant. The odd gaps could easily be filled out, the mistakes put right. Hadn't Leo been desperately looking for the first sentence of his book today? It seemed like for years. Basically what he had here was the completed rough draft of his book. Hadn't Judith always jeered that he talked only and did nothing? This here is what he had done. This was his book. Leo was an objective authority looking at the objectivisation of his own thinking. There were no longer any difficulties preventing him from completing his oeuvre. All he had to do was polish, smooth, supplement—and edit out the nonsense. Judith's excursus on *Tristram Shandy*. It was completely beyond him how Judith was able to get from Leo's theory to Tristram all the time, to how Tristram backs out of his self-imposed task. Clearly had to be deleted. Also the conversations with Roman about *Tristram Shandy*. But Judith hadn't just discussed things with Roman. She'd had a relationship with him, too. Not much comfort to be had from the fact that it soon ended. 'Roman always looks at you like a gramophone horn—he is the little dog that listens to His Master's Voice.' Minute descriptions of this affair. Moments of bliss that Judith had had with another. The cocaine as the sound funnel for these moments, their amplifier. Every word a goad, in a succession so stinging that the phrases began to vibrate, to whirr—they produced a sound, a succession of sounds—Judith's voice. Leo heard Judith's voice while he was reading, as if she were excitedly recounting this, and when Leo noticed that he had Judith's voice in his ear as he read, it was as if the voice became aware that he was listening, for suddenly Leo heard a sentence that wasn't there on the page, a sentence addressed to him: You turn up and I feel sick.

This voice must be silenced. These passages must be deleted—most definitely. Then just one thing would remain: his book. The hands in the rubber gloves shuffled the sheets of paper together, chucked them back in the folder, put the folders in a pile on top of each other. The instruments of impersonal force assumed rightful ownership.

Leo took the pistol out of Judith's bag and went into the *sala*.He leant over Judith who was still lying on the sofa, put the pistol in her open hand, closing her fingers carefully round the butt. She didn't wake. He had no pity and didn't hesitate for one second. He was completely beside himself and yet never before so at one with himself as now. She had to die. She had to die, if his life were to make any sense, if the senselessness of his life till now were to be extinguished and atoned for. And after all Judith wanted to die. Rather than live with him she wanted to destroy herself. And to mock him in written records that documented his failure. But he could restore sense to his life. Success. It was contained within the failure—needed only to be released. He lifted her hand with the weapon up to her temple and looked into her face. He couldn't imagine destroying more in this face than was already destroyed. He hated her without emotion, coldly and quietly. What's so bad about destroying the statue over a grave? It's merely anticipating

262

its allotted disintegration and decay. Creating a correspondence with the process of decay, over which it lifelessly keeps guard. Leo's soul was now devoid of all psychological content, a pure white sheet of paper on which fate writes its absurd command, and this command is blindly, recklessly and cruelly carried out. Leo felt his blindness to be clear-sightedness, his cruelty, kindness, and his readiness to act, mercy. He fired. He straightened up and listened. Nothing could be heard—it hadn't even set some neighbouring dog off barking. Using Judith's typewriter and still with the rubber gloves on, he wrote a farewell letter in her name. Then he took the typewriter over to the dead woman and pressed her lifeless hand onto the keys a few times so that her finger-prints would be found, should the police want to examine the type-writer. He picked up her folders, left the house, threw the folders into the boot of his car and drove home. He took a shower and changed his clothes. Then he drove to the police to make a report. He had driven to Judith's and had found her dead—obviously suicide. Why had he driven to her place at such an unusually late hour? She had always worked at night—just like he did, incidentally. They had often called on each other in the wee small hours. Hadn't Leo been here before a while ago as a witness after the hold-up at that bar near here? Yes. Wasn't the dead woman the *Senhora* who, on that occasion, used a bottle to . . . Must have been a crazy lady. Yes, very unpredictable. Had he altered any-thing after he'd found her? No, said Leo, he hadn't altered anything.

The police harboured no suspicions. No further investigations were conducted. Leo was now a widower in deep mourning. In the bar he shifted once more to the centre, but was, for reasons of discretion and delicacy, kept on its outermost periphery. People admired the way he would stand there stonily at the end of the bar—'strong' was one word mentioned, or 'incredibly composed'—silently drinking his beer and his pinga. He spoke not a word and no-one spoke to him. But people would always be standing him glasses of pinga and giving him pats of solidarity on his back and nods of condolence. Leo didn't have to dissemble. The feeling of being a tragic and profound character suited him perfectly and now it could express itself genuinely, as it were, in its purest form. All the tragedies of his life were a thing of the past—they had scored the face which, stolidly silent, he bent over his glass. He no longer had any reason to hold forth—he had his 'opus'. And the fact that he could now quickly complete what he had never started did not make him suspiciously euphoric and talkative either, but only served to deepen the feeling he had, and which he coldly and silently displayed, that something of profound significance was at work.

He made an exception just once in a conversation with Roman. He announced to him that he would soon be completing the study he'd been working on for many years. He owed it to Judith to do this, said Leo and nearly gave himself away when he recounted how he'd found some debate about his theory in Judith's papers on her desk. The result of our long discussions, he said quickly, which had flowed into her work on *Tristram Shandy*, a very interesting literary study—a tragedy that she hadn't been able to finish it and get it published. Apart from that, he treated Roman coolly. When Roman asked him whether he had loved Judith very much, Leo replied by asking whether Roman hadn't perhaps loved Judith. Showing no expression, he gloated to see Roman turn away. Significant, thought Leo, the way Roman behaved at the burial: he started to weep and ran off.

Roman even turned up once some time later at Leo's home. He wanted to speak to him urgently. Leo threw him out without further ado. He had nothing more to say to Roman. He wanted to be alone and to work.

Leo devoted the next weeks exclusively to completing his book. He cut out the *Tristram Shandy* passages, deleted everything private from Judith's writings, destroying the relevant pages in a characteristically cool manner—he was now entirely the impersonal force for whom the particular means nothing. What remained was a summary of his own theory as he had delivered it to Judith and Roman over a period—he arranged this sheaf of papers into chapters, which he then revised. In doing this he couldn't resist very privately crowing in triumph over Judith and Roman. The work quickly took shape. It didn't take much to complete. The sentences missing emerged out of those that were already there. He almost felt he could lean back and watch the book write itself. Passages Judith had overly condensed he was immediately able to rewrite completely. One after the other the sentences in the text darted of their own accord like lightning from one approved block of text to the next. Had he thought he couldn't write any more? Rubbish. Here was his book. It would change the world. By making the world conscious of itself. The world couldn't stay as it was if it was well-informed about itself. That was obvious. Excited by this thought, Leo immediately wrote three more pages. At the end, when the work was, by and large, finished, he wrote a preface. Then he went through the whole book once more from the first to the last pages, making final finishing touches and improvements. The book was completed. It wasn't that bulky but, thought Leo, that would only make it all the more effective.

Leo spent one more day at his desk. This book embodied what had been important during his time with Judith. Everything else had sunk without trace, as if it had never existed. Leo now wanted to dedicate this book to Judith, to return it to her, so to speak, to do something which, while containing a good measure of mockery, arose also from Leo's passion for putting full-stops to things. He wrote countless drafts of all kinds of dedication, detailed, ambiguous, kitsch, icily heroic—late in the evening an exhausted Leo finally decided on the formula: 'In grateful memory of Judith Katz.'

Leo didn't have the patience to send his manuscript off to countless publishers and wait around forever for an answer. He approached a small but well-established scientific publishing house who were prepared to publish the book, if Leo bore the costs of the printing. Leo paid seven hundred and twenty thousand cruzeiros for a first print-run of two thousand copies. He was surprised how cheap it was to conquer the world.

Löwinger fell ill. Leo spent days by the side of the bedridden Uncle Zé, eagerly telling him that the first volume of his philosophical system was about to come out. It was, however, barely possible to communicate any more with Löwinger, who was sinking fast and who died before he was able to see Leo's book appear. Leo inherited Löwinger's property along with capital investments, the income from which more than sufficed to cover the running and maintenance costs of the house and the staff's wages. The collection of paintings was transferred to a public foundation to which Löwinger had also bequeathed extremely generous financial endowments.

Leo moved up into the big house. For the staff there nothing had changed. They waited on an elderly gentleman who walked bent and shuffling through the corridors of a house that was far too large and whose fame had long since faded, or else through the park. After some weeks he walked down again for the first time to the gatehouse and visited his former study.

There was too much silk there, wine-red, purple silk: the curtains were made of it as well as the upholstery of the suite of chairs, which were arranged along the narrower side of the room opposite the second door and in front of a Gobelin tapestry that spanned almost the entire wall. There were baroque armchairs with small upholstered armrests grouped about a round metalclad table, and behind this stood a sofa in the same style sporting plush silk cushions. The bookcases took up the whole length of the wall between the two doors. These were made of mahogany, like the writing desk—or rather like the bureau, equipped with a curving roll-top, which had been placed between the windows— and these bookcases had glass doors with green silk behind. In the corner to the left of the sofa you could see a work of art, a large wooden sculpture, painted and raised on a red-covered pedestal, a deeply shocking piece, a pietà, unsophisticated but powerful, verging on the grotesque: the Mother of God in a cowl with eyebrows drawn up to a point and a howling, twisted open mouth—the Man of Sorrows on her lap, its hanging head bristling with thorns, the face and limbs spattered and running with blood, thick gouts of blood oozing out of the wound in the side and from the holes made by the nails in the hands and feet. The horizontal stripes of the wallpaper were the same green as the soft carpet which was spread over the red floor-covering. The ceiling was bare and cracked. From it there hung a small venetian chandelier.

Leo pushed his glasses back into his hair. This room, too, must be committed to oblivion. He turned on his heels and walked slowly back up to the big house. He had someone bring him a telephone book, looked up the number of a demolition firm, rang them up and con- tracted them to pull down the gatehouse.

The little house had gone—there where it had stood the gardener set to work—and Leo's book came out. *The Phenomenology of Despiritualisation. The history of vanishing knowledge.* He was on tenterhooks for weeks, during which not a single review appeared. Finally he composed a self-advert- isement, in which he described the contents and significance of the book and this he had published in the specialist magazine *Leia Livros*, in the editorial section, although he paid for it. He left several copies of this edition of the magazine lying around in the bar.

At the end of the year Leo received the first royalty statement from the publishers. Five copies had been sold. Two had been ordered by the libraries of the universities of São Paulo and Porto Alegre, the book- shops only being able to sell three.

Four months later he heard that his publishers had gone into bank- ruptcy.

Leo wondered why he wasn't dying. Since that night at Judith's he hadn't taken his medicine any more. He had a check-up. He was told he was in good health. Leo no longer understood the world: when he read the papers, watched TV, went to the cinema, listened to other people talking in bars, it was continually brought home to him that the world was exactly as he had described it. But this the world failed to recognise.

So, pleasure, then. He drove to the *Boca*. The *Locomotiva* no longer existed. In fact, just the name had changed. The nightclub was now called *Wagão*. He didn't know the young girl who came to his table, after he had asked for Regina. No-one could remember the Regina he meant. So off he went to a hotel with this Regina, who didn't stop laughing happily all the time. The name had stayed the same, just the woman, in fact, was different. But Leo got no pleasure from it. No sooner did he feel Regina's arms around him than he remembered the reviews of his sexual performance that he'd found in Judith's journal reports and which he had destroyed. He became so aggressive that he almost gave the girl a beating. He didn't. Get lost! he screamed. Go on, scram!

No, no way could she leave like this—the memories she'd now leave behind would be all the more impossible to deal with.

Stay! he said, and now he was a limp rag.

To amuse himself Leo took a trip to Europe. Perhaps, he thought, he could use the opportunity to forge some links with European universities, with the philosophy departments of the Sorbonne in Paris, of the University of Berlin, the University of Vienna. He couldn't, of course. After he arrived in Vienna, he drove straight to the seventh district, to his former flat. When he went into the courtyard and got to the second staircase, he stopped, astonished. The angels weren't there any more.

Leo found out from the caretaker that Zahradnik had died. He had owed so much money, apparently, that the angels had been taken into receivership. It seemed to Leo that the caretaker looked mournfully around the courtyard as she told him this. They could have left us one of the angels at least, she said. One of them she particularly liked, the one with the wings spread out. That one had an expression as if he were able to look directly into the future. Now he, too, was probably standing by a grave, she said, watching over some dead person.

Leo left. A strong wind got up. As long as people need angels for their graves, thought Leo, history is not at an end. Not at an end.